# SENECA FALLS INHERITANCE

## Miriam Grace Monfredo

BERKLEY PRIME CRIME, NEW YORK

Visit Miriam Grace Monfredo's Web site at
www.miriamgracemonfredo.com

This Berkley Prime Crime Book contains the complete text of the original hardcover edition. It has been completely reset in a typeface designed for easy reading and was printed from new film.

SENECA FALLS INHERITANCE

A Berkely Prime Crime Book / published by arrangement with St. Martin's Press, Inc.

PRINTING HISTORY
St. Martin's Press ediiton published 1992
Berkley Prime Crime edition / October 1994

ISBN: 0-425-14465-8

Berkley Prime Crime Books are published by The Berkley Publishing Group, a division of Penguin Putnam Inc., 375 Hudson Street, New York, New York 10014. The name BERKLEY PRIME CRIME and the BERKLEY PRIME CRIME design are trademarks belonging to Penguin Putnam Inc.

PRINTED IN THE UNITED STATES OF AMERICA

10   9   8

*Berkley Prime Crime Books by Miriam Grace Monfredo*

SENECA FALLS INHERITANCE
NORTH STAR CONSPIRACY
BLACKWATER SPIRITS
THROUGH A GOLD EAGLE
THE STALKING-HORSE
MUST THE MAIDEN DIE
SISTERS OF CAIN

CRIME THROUGH TIME
CRIME THROUGH TIME II
edited by Miriam Grace Monfredo and Sharan Newman

*For Frank,*
*who listened, read, and solved problems*
*With love*

# ACKNOWLEDGMENTS

I wish to express my thanks to those who have contributed in different ways to this book.

I owe a debt to the outstanding libraries that supplied research materials: the Rare Book Division of the Rush Rhees Library, University of Rochester, Rochester, New York; the Printed Book and Periodical Collection, Henry Francis du Pont Winterthur Museum, Winterthur, Delaware; the Strong Museum Library, Rochester, New York; the Seneca Falls Historical Society, Seneca Falls, New York.

Also, special thanks are due Wayne Arnold, division head, Local History Division of the Rundell Library, Rochester, New York; Sara Clarke, special collections librarian, New York State Historical Association, Cooperstown, New York; and Bill Leonard, administrative assistant, the Seneca Falls Historical Society. A very special thank you to Betty Auten, Seneca County Historian and a gold mine of information.

For consultation on various matters, I am especially grateful to Dr. William H. Siles, executive director of the Slater Mill Historic Site, Pawtucket, Rhode Island, formerly historian of the Strong Museum, Rochester, New York. His remarkable series of lecture courses on the history of western New York were a rich source of material.

For their unique contributions I am grateful to my family, especially my husband, Frank Monfredo, who gave me the benefit of his legal expertise, trial experience, and his problem-solving skills. My daughter, Rachel Monfredo, Boston Museum of Fine Arts, provided answers to questions on American Material Culture with professional dispatch; my sons Scott and Shawn Monfredo and daughter-in-law Lizabeth gave their support and humor. My father, Horst J. Heinicke, M.D., donated medical knowledge and flowers.

For their sustained enthusiasm, my gratitude to members of the Hollow Hills Writers Group, especially Nicholas DiChario. I would like to express particular thanks to writer, teacher, and friend Nancy Kress.

# Author's Note

In 1848 in New York State, two historic events started the wheels of justice creaking ever so slowly toward legal equality for American women. The New York legislature, in April of that year, enacted the Married Women's Property Act, the first of its kind in the country. In July, the first Woman's Rights Convention was held in Seneca Falls, New York. Although the singular possessive "Woman's" seems cumbersome today, I have preserved this form when referring to the Convention.

All other events and major characters in *Seneca Falls Inheritance* are fictitious. However, actual historic figures do appear from time to time; the interested reader may find them listed with annotation at the novel's end. The characterization of Elizabeth Cady Stanton, and the material directly pertaining to the historic Convention itself, are based on the author's interpretation of Stanton's autobiography, *Eighty Years or More: Reminiscences 1815-1897* (1898), and volume I of the *History of Woman Suffrage* (1889), edited by Stanton, Susan B. Anthony, and Matilda Gage.

I have taken some liberty with the topography of Seneca Falls and have described the Seneca River/Canal more as it appears today than in 1848. This was done to simplify for the reader what was then a complicated system of river, canal, islands, and an industrial and residential area known as "The Flats," which no longer exists, having been flooded in 1915 by New York State Engineers to upgrade water transportation into the Barge Canal System. However, the location of the river and streets described in the novel is essentially the same as in 1848.

"Heir follows heir as wave succeeds on wave."
—HORACE, *Epistles*

"The next heir is always suspected and hated."
—TACITUS, *History*

# PROLOGUE

◦∿◦

## MAY 1848

IT DID NOT occur to Friedrich Steicher that he would die. He had everything he thought assured life: good health, wealth, love from some, respect from many, and a God who did not greatly confuse him. When the sky lowered and the first blasts of wind flattened him against the boat rail, he saw the storm as challenge, not agent of death.

The wind increased. The flat-bottomed packet boat slammed against roiling surface water of the canal, while powerful currents tugged from beneath. Ahead on the mud-slick towpath, mules strained for footing, their eyes rolling white as they slipped sideways toward the canal bed. Towlines from their harnesses to the boat groaned, drawing sharply taut, then sagging. Under their driver's whip, the mules struggled forward against the rain. The wind rose to a shriek.

"Hold 'em steady!" yelled the steersman from the boat.

"Lightning's spooked 'em," the mule driver shouted back.

"Keep 'em *steady*!" yelled the steersman again. "The lock's right ahead."

In the packet boat's stern, Friedrich Steicher turned to his wife. Caroline was pressed against the railing beside him; rainwater streamed from her hair, and her face contorted with rage. The thought crossed Steicher's mind that his wife must believe he had caused the storm. And having caused it, he should be able to stop it.

Gripping the rail with one hand, he stretched his other

hand toward her. She recoiled, backing away along the railing. As he reached for her, his foot caught in the deck rigging of the overhead canvas awning. He tripped and staggered. The awning collapsed, its wooden frame striking his forehead just as the wind filled the canvas and sent it sailing out across the water.

Steicher fell to his knees. He grabbed the lower rail, shaking his head to clear it. Flashes in his mind, like blinks of an eye: Glynis standing in her library, lifting the leather-bound Shakespeare from a shelf, opening it; the old king, mad and dying, tormented by his children, their avarice, the storm.

Steicher knelt with his forehead against the rail. Why do I think of Lear? I am not old. I have not divided my kingdom. Steicher raised his head against the wind, for suddenly he felt the threat. But I did not think I would die—not yet. Then, at the last, Steicher saw the danger.

The boat pitched, the bow plunging into the water as it rose and fell. Steicher gasped for breath each time spray foamed over the deck. He gripped the rail and crawled toward his wife.

The wooden gates of the canal lock loomed ahead like a fortress. Streaks of lightning outlined the steersman's desperate attempts to direct the boat through the lock's approach walls.

"Hold the mules!" he screamed. "Hold the mules! The goddamn gates are closed!"

The wind gusted. Frayed towlines snapped.

The boat listed to port, then surged forward, crashing through the gates.

Ten days later, in the city of Boston, an old woman gripped her cane with both hands, wincing as she shifted her weight, and stood staring through the window at light boats sculling over the Charles River. She then turned and made her way to a high-backed chair. Since she had, years ago, lived longer than her own or anyone else's expectations, each step forward was grimly satisfying. She settled herself in the chair and lifted the letter once again from the table beside her.

32 Washington Street
Seneca Falls, New York
May 8, 1848

My dear Mary,

I fear I must begin this letter with some dreadful news. Three days ago, Friedrich and Caroline Steicher died in a terrible accident on the Erie Canal. A mule driver said that Friedrich, who could barely swim, made a desperate effort to pull his wife's body out of the water, but was dragged under by the current and himself drowned in the attempt.

It is a tragedy for all here who knew them. And Friedrich's death will most certainly affect the entire Seneca Falls area, for, as you know, his was one of the largest wheat farms in the state. Whether Karl Steicher can run the farm as successfully as his father is uncertain.

I feel strongly that now you *must* reveal to your dear daughter her true and complete family history. As you may have read in the Boston newspapers, the New York legislature finally passed the Married Women's Property Act; it became law on April 8th. Because of this, I pray that you will give my sentiments concerning Rose your sincerest consideration.

I sadly miss Boston, and you, and my other friends there. It is difficult for me to believe we left just a year ago. Winters are long and hard here in western New York, and my life comparatively solitary. The children are over the Genesee Fever (a fearsome sickness), and my nursing chores are done, but I am afraid the novelty of housekeeping has passed away and much that was once attractive in domestic life is now irksome.

Again, dear Mary, you must consider telling Rose. We cannot know what will come of it, but your daughter should have the truth, and the secret can surely no longer be worth the keeping.

I send my love to you, and my fondest hope that your condition will improve with the warmer weather.

Devotedly yours,
Elizabeth Cady Stanton

The woman's swollen limbs throbbed as she replaced the letter on the table and leaned back against the chair. Her eyes searched the ornate molded ceiling; her fingers clenched and unclenched, nails scratching against the horsehair upholstery of the seat cushion.

# ONE

***

THE ROOM WAS SO still she could hear the books whispering. Her eyelids flew open, gray eyes narrowing as she glared at the crated volumes on the floor beside her library chair. The whispering ceased. Her eyelids fluttered closed.

Glynis Tryon leaned forward, arms resting on the desk, her head nodding as if the thick red-brown hair piled on top was too heavy for her neck. Now and then she blinked like a drowsing cat against the sun streaming through tall windows.

It was a violent jerk of neck muscles that brought her upright, recalling her to the remaining crates of Friedrich Steicher's books. They had not unpacked and catalogued themselves, had not arrived on the shelves by way of wishful thinking. They just lay there accusingly. She let out a long sigh.

Steeple bells in the church down the road tolled. . . . Eleven. Glynis glanced around the quiet room. She was alone: at this time of year, library patrons were scarce until afternoon. She frowned, catching her lower lip between her teeth, and picked up Elizabeth Stanton's survey sheet.

For two days the survey had lain on her desktop; in that time, there were just six signatures under the question "If a Discussion of Woman's Rights Was Held in Seneca Falls . . . ?" There were four signatures under Would Not Attend, one under Not Certain, and one Would Attend, the last signature being that of a young, unmarried woman who lived next door to Glynis's boardinghouse. But if comments from male patrons—and some females—who had glimpsed the survey were any indication, a fourth response was implicit: "This is a most ill-conceived idea."

Suddenly the library entrance door swung open, crashing against the wall. Glynis jumped, wrenching around in her chair. The Reverend Magnus Justine was already striding across the room, white linen band straining against his throat, black frock-coat slapping thighs like tree trunks. When he reached her desk, he stood with eyes fixed on the survey sheet. His large jaw aimed downward like a weapon; beneath it, Glynis clasped her hands under the desk.

"Miss Tryon!" The reverend's voice swelled. "Miss Tryon, may I remind you that you hold your position in this library at the pleasure of the board of directors."

Well, yes, she could hardly forget that, having been hired six years before by then chairman of the board, Friedrich Steicher. She tried responding to Justine's threat but couldn't; she coughed, and had a vision of vocal cords thrumming in her throat like stressed cello strings. Swallowing hard, Glynis stared dumbly at Justine's mottled, wine-colored cheeks.

"As a member of the board," the reverend went on, "I find it not in keeping with your librarian's role to be promoting discord in the very town that you are supposed to be assisting."

Glynis wondered what, if anything, would placate him. Nothing short of her resignation, apparently, since this was not the first time the two of them had had this type of one-sided conversation.

"May I also point out"—Justine's finger jabbed the desk—"that you no longer have a wealthy protector to assure your continued employment. I should be worried if I were you, Miss Tryon—certainly your moral flexibility has been a source of much concern to *me*."

He turned and stalked back out the door, pulling it shut with a thump.

Glynis watched the door for a time, biting on her lower lip until she tasted blood. Then she slid the offending sheet of paper into her desk drawer. Forced into subterfuge. But a hidden survey would be even more useless than the visible had been. How had she gotten into this? It now seemed that the next step Elizabeth Stanton had proposed would have to be undertaken: the personal approach. And Glynis dreaded it.

She could hardly bear thinking about it. She propped her elbows on the desk, chin in her hands, and stared at a tall vase of peonies, plucked in their prime from her landlady's garden. The peonies now were wilting, dropping their petals like snow—like the ones that sat every June on her mother's rosewood piano. Each time Mama would play a chord with force, ivory petals fluttered down. At the end of a Liszt rhapsody, the piano top would be covered with little creamy drifts. But the peony bed had been overgrown and choked with weeds the June her mother died— "acute melancholia," the doctors had said—long after the time Liszt had ceased to be heard in that house. Sprays of trumpet lilies, smelling of mold, splayed across the coffin as it was lowered into the ground next to three tiny marble headstones. . . .

Glynis shifted sideways in her chair, gripping the edge of her desk. From the corner of her eye she became aware of movement, and she heard the unmistakable rustle of taffeta. Turning, she saw a slender woman walking toward her, reminding her of the solemn, cream-skinned beauties of Italian baroque paintings. Grave dark eyes held her own. The woman's step faltered, and she looked around, as if questioning whether she would leave or stay. Glynis closed the drawer in which she had put the survey and rose from her chair.

"Can I help you?"

"A Constable Stuart directed me here." The voice was as grave as the eyes. "I'm trying to locate Mrs. Henry Stanton. I've recently come in by train, and I'm unfamiliar with the town." As she spoke, she pulled off lambskin gloves and stood twisting them in her hands.

Glynis wondered if her own uneasiness was caused by

Justine's tirade or was a response to the woman's nervousness. "I'm Glynis Tryon. And you're . . .?" she said.

The woman gave her a startled look, then smiled thinly. "I'm sorry. It's Mrs. Walker. Mrs. Gordon Walker."

"Elizabeth Stanton's in Waterloo," Glynis said. "She's visiting friends. I'm afraid she won't be back until Wednesday—tomorrow."

The woman frowned. "How far is this Waterloo? I need—that is, I want to meet Mrs. Stanton, and I don't have much time."

"Waterloo's six miles to the west," Glynis answered. "You can rent a carriage at the livery up the road."

The woman's shoulders drooped, and she swayed slightly, brushing against the desk.

"Please, Mrs. Walker, please sit down," Glynis said, gesturing toward her chair.

The woman came unsteadily around the desk and sank into the chair. She seemed to struggle with herself for a moment, then finally said, "I'm interested in the Married Women's Property Act passed here in New York—that's why I want to see Mrs. Stanton. But"—she waved her hand toward the shelves of books lining the room—"perhaps you know something of that, too?"

Glynis nodded. "Elizabeth Stanton worked on passage of that law; as it happens, I did some research for her." She unlocked the doors of a tall cabinet and, moving a brown leather-bound Bible out of the way, began taking folders from its inner shelves.

"You might want to look at these articles from western New York newspapers. The Buffalo paper, Rochester's, and our own *Seneca County Courier*."

"That's a magnificent Bible," Mrs. Walker said. She had gotten up to stand directly behind Glynis.

"It belongs to a local family," Glynis told her. "Brought here by accident—I only just discovered it yesterday. Apparently no one's missed it yet."

"May I see it?" The woman reached out her hand.

Glynis shook her head. "I'm sorry, no. It's a family Bible, and rather private, I would think."

Mrs. Walker abruptly turned and walked to the bookshelves. Glynis stared after her. The woman seemed offended.

"I am sorry, Mrs. Walker. If you're going to be in town a few days, the Steicher family will likely let you see the Bible. I just don't think I have the right to do so without their knowledge."

Her back to Glynis, the woman shook her head. "It's quite all right. Please think nothing of it. I just happen to like old books, as I'm sure you do."

She turned, smiling, and passed her hands over the dark wings of hair covering her ears; she reminded Glynis of a cat smoothing ruffled fur.

"Perhaps, Miss Tryon, you'd tell me about the law just passed?"

"The Married Women's Property Act?" Glynis said. That she could do. But still vaguely uneasy, she began cautiously, feeling her way. "It deals mainly with inheritance, simply allowing a married woman to own property and gifts that have been willed or given her, free from her husband and her husband's debts."

Mrs. Walker nodded, and appeared to be interested.

Glynis went on, "But that's hollow. Women can't dispose of the property themselves unless it's outright cash, which is usually not the case, because we still don't have the right to sign contracts. A woman can't sell what she's inherited, or even give it away, without her husband's signature of approval. And of course the law doesn't touch the problem of a working woman's wages. They still belong to her husband."

Mrs. Walker's eyes were wandering over Glynis's desk, coming to rest upon the tall cabinet. Glynis wasn't sure she was even listening. The woman probably wouldn't find interesting an account of the difficulty of getting the law enacted by a reluctant legislature. After several years' debate, it had finally passed, only, Glynis believed, because fathers didn't want their money handed over to spendthrift sons-in-law after they died. And because businessmen going through bankruptcy wanted their property in their wives' names—to keep it away from their creditors.

Mrs. Walker's gaze returned to Glynis. "Apparently, you don't think the law much of a reform, Miss Tryon."

Glynis shook her head. "But the fact that it passed at all is encouraging to women who are struggling for some of the same legal rights men have. So this law may be more important over the long haul than it now appears."

"And are you involved in the struggle, Miss Tryon?" The question was asked with a faint smile; the woman seemed a little less tense.

"In my way," Glynis said.

She did not say that there was a feeling among some in Seneca Falls that it was not a librarian's place to be involved in politics; or that several days before she had learned that two of the five-man library board were questioning the wisdom of renewing her contract in September. One of those must be the Reverend Magnus Justine, but who was the other?

"Mrs. Walker, would you care to look at some of these newspapers now?"

The woman had suddenly gone to stand again in front of the cabinet. Her face was in profile, and Glynis could see her jaw working, as though she was clenching her teeth against some private pain.

"Mrs. Walker . . . ?"

"I don't think I have time to see the papers after all, Miss Tryon. Could you just direct me to the livery stable instead?" The woman snatched her gloves and pink beaded purse from the desk.

Glynis hesitated, but Mrs. Walker was staring at her, the grave eyes seeming to send a frantic appeal for haste. The woman's former aloofness had vanished, replaced by something resembling fear.

"Well, yes, of course," Glynis said quickly. "Just let me put these things away and I'll take you there." She replaced the papers on the shelves and locked the cabinet.

Mrs. Walker stood twisting the gloves in her hands.

# TWO

❧

STANDING ON FALL Street, Glynis watched the horse trot
west from the livery stable toward Waterloo; Mrs. Walker
was driving the carriage. The woman seemed to know
what she was doing, and she was determined to go alone.
Although it was peculiar that she couldn't wait one day
until Elizabeth Stanton came back. But at least she
wouldn't get lost; there was only the one road.

Glynis turned to walk back to the library; she needed to
get the last of Friedrich Steicher's books uncrated. Perhaps
then she could rid herself of the feeling that he was going
to reappear at any minute. Glancing across the road, she
saw Lydia Abernathy—and suddenly remembered that she
had promised Elizabeth Stanton responses from the survey
by tomorrow.

Several weeks before, Elizabeth had rushed into the library sparking like a Roman candle. Glynis had loaned her
the 1840s state regulations on suffrage. Like most states,
New York limited voting privilege to classes of citizens
thought capable of its wise exercise. To this end, the state
had excluded children, idiots, lunatics—and women, the
grounds for exclusion being a presumed lack of capacity
for reason and sound judgment. However, Glynis had told
the smoldering Elizabeth, aliens, indigents, Negroes, and
criminals were also excluded, on the grounds that they
weren't citizens.

"Imagine being lumped together with idiots and lunatics!" Elizabeth had snapped. "It's time to do something!"

The something she had come up with was the discussion meeting that was the subject of the survey. The first

step, she told Glynis, was to ask women if they would support such a meeting.

Glynis did not want to do the asking. She voiced her objection, protesting that she was by nature shy. It was embarrassing, the shyness, but there it was.

Elizabeth Stanton had dismissed this with a flick of her wrist. "Glynis, you know more of the women in this town; you've lived here five years longer than I."

Unassailable logic.

Lydia Abernathy was now retying the ribbons of her lace morning cap as she stood on the steps of the Red Mills Bank, of which her husband was vice president. Lydia was Ambrose Abernathy's third wife. She had a delicate, porcelain quality; from the tips of her silk slippers to the pink rosettes on each rib-end of her parasol, Lydia gave the impression of a doll too fragile for anything more vigorous than being displayed on a shelf.

Glynis went toward her reluctantly, smoothing her brown cotton skirt and trying to keep in mind Elizabeth Stanton's arguments and enthusiasm.

Lydia listened, her blue eyes wide with what had to be incredulity. "Oh, heavens ... No, Glynis," she said. "I don't think I could possibly go to a women's meeting—not something like that! Ambrose wouldn't approve. Besides, I have all the rights I want."

"But what about other women?" Glynis said. "Don't you feel, for instance, that women who work in factories should be entitled to keep their wages, instead of having to give them to their husbands or fathers?"

"I don't work in a factory, Glynis. And Ambrose gives me anything I ask for. Why would I want rights I couldn't use?"

Why, indeed? Lydia Abernathy Would Not Attend. Glynis left the young woman staring after her in bewilderment—Glynis could feel it. This personal-approach business was going to be even worse than she'd imagined.

She walked down Fall Street toward the library, maneuvering around wagons and carriages standing in the wide dirt road that passed through the center of Seneca Falls. Most of the villagers had finished their noon meal; farmers and tradespeople, gathered under tall vase-shaped elms at the road's edge, nodded the day to her. The smell of horses and their warm dung rose from the dust.

To Glynis's right and parallel to Fall Street was the Cayuga and Seneca Canal section of the Seneca River, dividing the town north and south; northeast of the village the smaller canal joined the Erie Canal system. On both sides of the Seneca Falls waterway were the smokestacks of two dozen mills and factories, which produced leather, flour, paper, axes, cotton and wool cloth, boots and boats, window sashes and water pumps. And enough liquor to float a barge.

Waiting for a carriage to clatter by, Glynis saw a young woman—really just a girl, she thought—walking toward her across the river bridge. Wisps of straight blond hair swung across the girl's kohl-lined eyes. Her lips and cheeks were red-rouged. The women who worked the tavern on the south side of the river were not usually seen in this part of town, certainly not in the middle of the day. Glynis stepped quickly into the road to remove herself from the girl's path, frowning as her cheeks grew hot. The revulsion she felt for the girl's profession was one thing, but she was ashamed of her reaction to the girl herself—surely no woman sold herself by choice. Glynis considered the survey sheet in her purse. But her cheeks throbbed and she rejected the impulse; she just couldn't approach the girl with townspeople watching.

She hurried down a few steps to the small fieldstone library set between Fall Street and the canal-river below, stopping to shoo a feisty little rooster and his hens from the bottom step. Brushing off the ivory linen and lace of her blouse and shaking clean the hems of her long skirt and petticoats, she started to unlock the library door. Suddenly, behind her, she heard shouting, and pounding horses' hooves. Whirling around, she saw the street scene freeze, then explode into motion.

"Runaways! Out of the road!" men yelled, grabbing the

harnesses of their own horses. Women's high alarmed voices called to their children, and they ran to scoop them up into their arms. People and animals scattered.

A team of heavy draft horses appeared, thundering down the center of Fall Street, a wildly careening wagon behind them. A young boy was fighting to keep from being thrown off. He was jolting back and forth, bouncing up and slamming down. His thin arms yanked at the whipping reins. He looked like a twig tossing in a hurricane.

The team galloped past the library, the horses' ears back, nostrils flaring red, saliva frothing over their bridle bits. The wagon jounced furiously. The boy's face was ashen. Men ran shouting after them in the wake of swirling dust.

They will go right into the water, thought Glynis, running behind with the others.

The canal-river's retaining walls ended where the river changed course and curved north around the bottom of Fall Street. Above the river the dirt road narrowed, but the frenzied horses showed no sign of slowing.

Reaching the end of the road, the team at last attempted to pull up—too late: their own momentum and that of the wagon behind plunged them down the bank and into the river. Airborne, the wagon soared before it crashed. As it hit, water spouted around it like geysers; then it settled slowly into reeds and cattails. The young driver had been thrown into the shallows along the bank. He lay motionless, face to the sky.

Cullen Stuart brushed past Glynis; the stunned crowd parted as the police constable pushed his way through. Wading into the water, he lifted the boy's limp body and carried him to the grassy bank. Cullen bent over the youngster a moment and then quickly knelt beside him. The crowd shuffled nervously.

Silence.

There were scattered chuckles of relief when Cullen stood and hauled the youngster to his feet, searching him for injuries. Flushed with shame, the boy shook his head and pulled away from Cullen. He stood biting his knuckles, staring at the horses standing quietly in the water. The ruined wagon was wedged behind them against the bank.

"Some of you men help him get the team out," Cullen called into the crowd.

Glynis watched him climb up to the road. As Cullen walked toward her, his eyes seemed almost black in a face gone pale despite its dark sunburn.

"No real harm done to the boy. Just his pride," he said to her.

"That's quite a lot of harm, at his age," Glynis said.

"Right. And his father's going to be plenty mad when . . . Well, let's not think about that." Cullen turned back to help the men pulling the team up the bank.

Glynis watched as he braced himself against a horse, his sand-colored hair pressed against a wet flank. Moisture sheened his face, beaded his thick mustache; his coarse-woven, blue cotton shirt was dark with sweat by the time the animals were pushed and pulled reluctantly onto the road.

He wiped the back of a hand across his forehead, then glanced around and met Glynis's look. She saw the lines beside his eyes tighten, and she stepped closer to him.

"Are you all right?" she said quietly.

Cullen shrugged his shoulders, let out a deep breath, and nodded. He picked up the horses' reins, slung an arm over the boy's shoulders, and together they started up Fall Street toward town. The crowd began to break up, ambling back the way they had come.

Glynis saw several women she should question for Elizabeth Stanton's survey, but she just couldn't face them, not right then. She walked alone down the steps to the library. The stone building was quiet and cool, and she stood just inside with her back to the door, her head resting against the wood. Cullen had looked so shaken, she thought. The wagon crash must have brought back terrible memories. How long ago was it—seven years?—that his wife and baby had died beneath an overturned wagon. But there was nothing she could say to him, not with half the town listening in.

She stood a moment longer, then moved toward her desk.

Several hours later, Glynis wiped her hands on a cotton cloth, stepped back, and looked at her library desk, which was stacked with the last uncrated books. They included all of Jane Austen between brown leather covers crafted by Friedrich Steicher. He had tooled his name on the bottom of each spine.

Glynis picked up one of the volumes and ran her fingers across the leather. Friedrich's own taste in fiction had run more to Edgar Allan Poe. Glynis recalled when the author had passed through town several years before and had been prevailed upon by Friedrich to read some of his work. A carafe of sherry at Poe's elbow had prevented his delivering all but a very few paragraphs. This was said to be not uncommon for Poe. Friedrich believed the writer's bouts of drinking were necessary to produce his horror fantasies; Glynis believed that was perhaps putting the cart before the horse. Although she loved Poe's Auguste Dupin detective stories, she thought his alcoholic binges might well be attempts to drown his more macabre visions.

On the shelves beside her desk were previously uncrated donations, among them the new English novels. Earlier in the year newspapers had reported that the author of *Jane Eyre* was the daughter of a Yorkshire clergyman. Thus the book had created a sensation. "Offends the sensibilities, the standards," Glynis remembered a Boston reviewer writing. Imagine, a story of love and passion, written by a *woman*.

She couldn't keep it in the library, people were handing it back and forth fast. But some few in town, the Reverend Magnus Justine for one, questioned her judgment in allowing such a book on the library shelves to begin with.

Just a few months ago, Friedrich had ordered another copy.

"You don't think passion an unseemly subject for a woman?" he smiled. "An unmarried woman?"

He had seemed unconcerned with the furor surrounding

*Jane Eyre*, and so she had ignored it herself at the time. Now she realized that that had been a mistake.

Who was the other board member rumored to be siding with Justine, who wanted her dismissed? Could it be Karl Steicher, who was filling his father's position? That was certainly possible. She had to see Karl in the next day or two, but she knew she wouldn't have the courage to ask him.

She had gotten more in Friedrich Steicher's last library donation than he had intended. That morning she had come across his Bible, hidden at the bottom of a crate, the one about which the unsettling Mrs. Walker had been so curious. Someone, probably a farmhand, had just taken it off the study shelves with the rest of the books without noticing what it was. She had to return it to Karl Steicher, of course. But she wouldn't be getting any more donations, now that Friedrich was gone: Karl Steicher was not as generous as his father, she was certain of that.

Glynis glanced around at the library shelves, filled with Friedrich's brown leather-bound volumes. She reached into her sleeve for a handkerchief and walked quietly to her small back office, where she closed the door behind her.

# THREE

IN A SECOND-FLOOR office of the Waterloo Court House, Jeremiah Merrycoyf, Esquire, shifted his weight in the small chair. The lawyer was listening to J. K. Richardson, Seneca County Surrogate; he glanced at Richardson over square wire-rimmed spectacles that rested not so much on Merrycoyf's nose, which was small, as on plump flushed cheeks.

A hot breeze through the window ruffled the stack of legal papers on the desk between the two men. Merrycoyf wiped a handkerchief over his forehead. He sighed, leaned forward, and shook his head.

"There *is* no will," he said. "Never was one. Friedrich Steicher died intestate. I tried for years to convince him to make one, but he ignored me. Stubborn, for a man so careful about other matters. But not uncommon."

Surrogate Richardson got up from behind his desk and went to the office door to summon his clerk. "No," he said, "that's not uncommon. A man makes a will, he concedes the possibility of mortality. Men like Steicher don't care to think like that."

Merrycoyf nodded. "And Friedrich had remarkably good health. He certainly didn't expect to die when he did."

Mr. Finch entered quietly and stood just inside the door; Richardson handed his clerk a file of papers. "Mr. Merrycoyf here is petitioning on behalf of his client, Karl Steicher, for letters of administration of his deceased father's estate. The son, Karl, is the sole issue of Friedrich Steicher and his wife Caroline, also deceased. Please get the documents ready for me to sign as quickly as possible, so Mr. Merrycoyf doesn't have to travel here again. It appears to be a perfectly straightforward matter. You have all the necessary information in that file."

Mr. Finch put the file under his arm and started through the door.

"One minute," Merrycoyf said. "We also need a certificate of the letters of administration, noting Karl Steicher's authority to administer his father's estate. For the bank and so on."

The Surrogate nodded to his clerk, and Mr. Finch slipped out of the office. "Shouldn't take too long," Richardson said to Merrycoyf. "Although there's obviously a great deal of money involved here. And the son's going to keep the farm, I assume?"

"Yes, certainly. Karl's worked on it as hard as his father—though they argued constantly about the direction it should take. Nearly brought the two of them to daggers drawn, on several occasions."

"Well, as sole survivor, the son owns all of it now," said Richardson. "He can do with it what he likes."

Merrycoyf struggled out of the chair. "Tragic thing, that canal accident. Folks really ought to learn to swim, they're going to travel by water. Tragic. I'll miss Friedrich." He stood fingering the skull-and-bones charm on the gold chain threaded through his waistcoat buttonhole. Finally he pulled out his watch.

Richardson stood up and passed a handkerchief over his face.

"Warm day. While we're waiting on my clerk, I'll buy you a whiskey, Mr. Merrycoyf."

Merrycoyf returned by carriage to Seneca Falls along the road following an Indian footpath. On either side stood fruit trees, stretching their swollen, ripening boughs across the Finger Lakes valleys. While apple seeds had been brought in packets in apron pockets from Massachusetts, the peaches, cherries, and plums were offspring from orchards of Iroquois tribes, who farmed the land centuries before the arrival of fur traders, missionaries, pioneer families, guns, and rum.

During the time of colonial revolt, the men of General Sullivan's expedition had dispersed or killed the Iroquois and burned their fields and orchards. After the war the soldiers went home to New England, packed their families into ox-drawn wagons, and returned to New York to burn the forests. Forests so dense and dark the settlers said they had to look up to look out. So dense they could not see the noonday sun.

That was just a half century ago, Merrycoyf thought. Seneca Falls was now a village of four thousand people: Yankee, Scot, German, Irish, French, Canadian, Dutch. There were freed and runaway slaves, and indentured servants, and a few remaining Indians. Mills and factories had been built, and five churches, four hotels, four schools, and countless taverns.

Merrycoyf slowed the Black Hawk trotter. He was passing the southern boundary of the Steicher farm on his left.

Took Friedrich twenty-eight years to acquire this land, Merrycoyf reflected; he bought the last north parcel just a year ago. Gave him over eight hundred acres of the most productive land ever worked by man, purchased for less than thirty dollars an acre. He made his fortune after the canal was completed in 'twenty-five, giving him access to the eastern markets.

But what a fight last spring between Friedrich and Karl. Friedrich wanted more land, his son wanted livestock. And Karl could have been right when he claimed the future in Seneca Falls would be in dairy cows and fruit orchards, not wheat; with the railroads completed to carry it east, competition for the grain market from the new western states was fiercer every year.

Merrycoyf's carriage rolled by winter-wheat fields of the White Flint variety, which yielded a superfine flour demanded by the eastern markets. The slender spikes rippled silvery-green under the hot sun. Planted the previous autumn, the grain heads were beginning to swell, ripening for July harvest.

Merrycoyf winced as the carriage jounced over the uneven corduroy road. Karl was already spending his father's fortune on milk cows and the new horse-drawn seeders and harvesters. Well, now it was his to spend.

Some distance on he passed a fieldstone wall and slowed the horse again. A gold-and-white collie stood on a hillock, watching a flock of Merino sheep grazing to the north.

Merrycoyf grinned. Those sheep were keeping Cullen Stuart's three golf links trimmed. Thought someday he was going to have six holes, like his grandaddy played in Scotland. The man was daft.

Still grinning, Merrycoyf drove on, thinking of his new golf club. Its iron head was being forged that day by the town's blacksmith.

# FOUR

HER LANDLADY WANTED mackerel for Tuesday supper. As Glynis stepped inside the market, Zeke Clapper appeared from behind a row of wooden barrels that glistened with melting ice and stiff curled fish tails. The man himself was shaped like a barrel and had small, almost white eyes. Glynis barely nodded to him.

"Well, well. Miss Tryon. And how's our fine-looking librarian today?" His smile oiled the space between them. He moved into the aisle, blocking her way, his eyes darting over her like minnows in the bait jars.

Glynis almost stepped back. The man was her age and not much taller than she; why did she always let him make her feel like a bird fluttering between the claws of a cat, a grotesque plaything? She hated coming in here, but it was the only fish market this side of the river.

"The *Courier* advertisement said you have a shipment of mackerel, Mr. Clapper. How much is it today?"

"Not much at all—to you." The man grinned, his eyes flicking over her as she moved around him past the barrels. Her shoulders hunched forward to conceal what he wanted to see.

"Lot of excitement down by the river this afternoon, Miss Tryon. Exciting, that's what it was." He moved to stand in front of her again.

Not raising her head, Glynis pointed to the fish she wanted and counted coins from her purse. Clapper continued to grin. He wrapped the mackerel in a newspaper and handed it to her, his wet fingers slithering over hers. She snatched her hand away and whirled toward the door, catching her petticoats on a splintered barrel stave. For a moment she couldn't see where she was snared. Then she heard Clapper's boots behind her and yanked the fabric free.

She left the market with a shaky, prickling feeling of shame. If she had to go without fish for the rest of her life, she wasn't going in there again.

Nell Steicher, Karl's wife, was just coming out of the drugstore next door. Nell gripped the railing and stepped down carefully onto the plank sidewalk. Her abdomen swelled under a cotton pinafore.

She moved like an old woman, Glynis thought. Nell's skin used to look as though it had been dipped in cream; now it looked like parchment. And another baby on the way. Four children in six years, was it?

Glynis bit her lower lip. Should she approach Nell with the survey question? Bother her? But Nell could be a good weather vane; she was a farmer's wife, even if her husband was now one of the wealthiest farmers in western New York. Glynis took a deep breath—why had she ever agreed to do this?—and put out her hand to steady Nell as the woman sagged against the railing.

"The heat is tiring, isn't it?" Nell said, her breath coming in little gasps. It reminded Glynis of her mother in labor with the last, stillborn child. She concealed an involuntary shudder with a nod of her head. How could she approach this exhausted woman and trouble her about something like women's rights? But wasn't that the point?

"Nell, may I ask you something?" she began, her fingers smoothing the folds of her skirt.

Nell shook her head while she listened to Glynis. "No, Miss Tryon. I couldn't attend a discussion of that sort. It would be disloyal to Karl. And the Bible, First Corinthians, says, 'The women should keep silence in the churches. For they are not permitted to speak, but should be subordinate—' "

"Nell," Glynis interrupted. "Nell, we don't know where this discussion is going to be held. It won't necessarily be in a church."

" '—If there is anything women desire to know,' " Nell continued, " 'let them ask their husbands at home.' "

"Well, yes, Nell, I can see where a public discussion would be out of the question for you." Would Not Attend.

A carriage pulled up alongside and the driver jumped down to assist Nell. One of the Steicher farmhands. Nell gave Glynis a tired smile before climbing into the carriage.

Suddenly shouts cracking like rifle shots came from Hornsby & Levy's Hardware.

"Goddamn machines, putting good men out of work." The voice was thick. Bobby Ross fell out the doorway, shoved by the store owner behind him.

"You got no right," yelled Bobby, stumbling into the road. His eyes were bloodshot; he staggered on short, heavy legs, struggling for balance.

"I got every right, Ross, you coming into my place all liquored up." Young Abraham Levy stood on the step, arms folded across his chest. Glaring at Bobby, Levy remained stock still, only his curly beard quivering slightly.

Nell Steicher's carriage wheeled around the man weaving in the street and took off in the direction of the Steicher farm. People began emerging from nearby shops and offices, craning their necks to see. They edged cautiously toward the hardware store.

"Heard Bobby Ross just lost his job," said a woman, whose thin body curved around the child she was carrying in her arms. "Karl Steicher fired him yesterday. Caught him in the fields drunk again." She looked after the departing carriage.

"Nothing unusual for Bobby Ross," said another, winking at Glynis.

The women walked a little closer to the store. Glynis followed them at a distance.

"You oughta be ashamed, Abe Levy, selling those bloody machines," Bobby yelled. "We'll all lose our jobs, you greedy bastard!"

Abraham Levy's face went pale. His arms dropped to his sides; with his hands clenched, he stepped into the road.

"C'mon, take a swing," roared Bobby. His fists were raised in front of the other man's chest. He feigned a punch, swayed to one side, and staggered backward, dancing to keep his balance.

Cullen Stuart came around the corner from the lockup at the rear of the firehouse. Women clustered along the road straightened when they saw him. They smiled, their hands going up to smooth their hair. Cullen strode directly toward the hardware store; the crowd shifted its feet in anticipation and went silent.

Bobby suddenly regained his balance and rushed forward. His punch, aimed at Levy's jaw, glanced off the man's shoulder. Levy swung and connected, knocking Bobby to the road. Bobby sat in the dirt, cursing loudly, then struggled to get to his feet.

Jeremiah Merrycoyf rumbled out the door of his law office. He lowered his head and surveyed the scene over his spectacles, then he hooked his fingers in his belt and heaved his trousers up to his broad waist. Finally, he sighed.

"This sort of thing is not supposed to happen on a hot afternoon." He waited for a response from Cullen.

Cullen watched the men.

"Constable!" Merrycoyf tried again. "Constable, we're supposed to be building a civilized town here. There's a law against disturbing the peace, such as it is."

"Jeremiah, if I arrested every man who swung a punch around here, we'd have to build ourselves a real jail. Nobody's been hurt yet. Bobby's drunk as a lord—he'll go down for good any minute. And I don't think Abe Levy's out to kill him."

The lawyer shrugged and turned back toward his office, catching sight of Glynis.

"Miss Tryon. I trust you don't find this entertaining?"

Having managed to gather himself into a crouch. Bobby Ross again started toward Levy. He took four steps, tripped, stumbled, and collapsed in the road like an unstrung puppet. His legs jerked several times. Then he lay still.

"Passed out cold, most likely," muttered Cullen, moving toward the two men.

Abraham Levy brushed himself off and faced Cullen.

"You'd better lock up that drunk, Constable. The man's lost his job, he's got a right to be upset. But not in *my* shop."

Levy turned and walked back toward his hardware store, past the seed spreaders and Cox & Robertson threshers set to the side of the shop. Glynis wondered what the young Jew could be thinking; he had left England to escape a charged atmosphere where his rabbi father had been harried to his death.

"Dan!" Cullen called to a boy who stood looking disappointed. "Saddle my horse at the livery, and bring him here."

The onlookers, some relieved, some also disappointed, gradually thinned. Glynis walked over to Bobby, who breathed shallowly, his face in the dirt. Six years ago, he had been a popular young man, good-natured, usually roaring with laughter. The change in him was the fabric of nightmare.

Cullen had come to stand beside Glynis. He bent down, rolled Bobby over, and felt his pulse.

"I'll take him home to Daisy. The woman's not going to be happy, her husband drunk again and acting like a damn fool."

"Cullen, do you think Bobby's drinking is the reason Karl Steicher fired him? Or the new machines, as Bobby said?"

"Some of both, probably. Karl's buying a lot of equipment. But he won't be the only one around here buying— just the first. This town's going to see some hard times if men are let go on the farms."

The boy emerged from the livery leading a compact black Morgan horse. Cullen hoisted Bobby Ross over the horse like a sack of grain, then mounted. "You look all done in," he said to Glynis, looking down at her.

"I'm fine," she said. "It's just been a long day. For you, too."

"You don't look like you're fine, Glynis. But by the way, were you able to take care of that Mrs. Walker?"

"Not very well, I'm afraid. The woman didn't seem to want taking care of. Cullen, did you think there was anything, ah, peculiar about her? She seemed so high-strung. As if she were afraid of something."

Cullen nodded. "She was high-strung, all right. But what would she be afraid of?" He looked down at Bobby Ross. "After all, we've got such a nice peaceful town here."

Glynis walked alongside him until he turned the horse toward the river bridge. She went on toward the library.

Some nice peaceful town! Zeke Clapper could leer like a satyr, and she couldn't do anything about it, short of making a stupid scene. Cullen thought it was all right for men to brawl in the streets, as long as they didn't kill each other.

And young Daisy Ross worked herself to death taking in laundry—so Bobby could take the money for whiskey. But what was Daisy supposed to do? She couldn't leave him; she had five children. The law said Bobby could keep her money *and* the children, even though he was drunk half the time.

If women would only pull together long enough, the laws could be changed. They knew that now. But would women even come to a meeting to discuss change?

As she walked down the library steps, Glynis wondered if Mrs. Walker had found Elizabeth Stanton in Waterloo.

# FIVE

❧

SOUTH OF THE Seneca River, the tavern had opened for Tuesday's trade. Its wooden sign, swinging by chains from a black iron beam jutting over the towpath, creaked softly in the breeze off the water. Another sign hung over the dirt road that ran in front of the tavern. The signs read SEREN-ITY, in gilt scrollwork letters as shiny as though they were painted daily. The entrance door was open.

On the second floor of the tavern, late afternoon sun struggled through a grimy window, silhouetting the young woman bent over a checked wool jacket draped on a chair. Dust motes settled on the wisps of straight blond hair hanging over the girl's eyes like a tattered curtain. With one hand she tugged at the bottom of her tight black lace corset. With the other hand she removed the contents of the jacket pockets, inspecting them one by one. She held up a gold money clip and ran her red-nailed fingers over the engraved monogram. Then she riffled the bills under her thumb.

The man coming through the doorway of the room froze. The girl seemed unaware of his presence behind her. He stood watching while she finished her search, replaced most of the items, and dropped the jacket on the chair.

"What do you think you're doing?" he said in a low voice, pulling the door shut. His fingers silently slid the bolt.

The girl had spun around. She recovered quickly to move behind the chair and untie the laces of her corset. Bending down for the jacket, she slowly pulled it up over her breasts. She ran her tongue over red-rouged lips.

"You got some fancy duds, mister," she said. She grinned at the man. One upper front tooth was gone.

She fingered the label sewn inside the collar. "Pretty well fixed, I would say you are."

The last words she would say.

Minutes later, the man slapped shut the door of the wardrobe cabinet that stood against the wall and stepped back, wiping his hands on his trousers. He moved to the window and peered down at the alley below. Still too light.

He picked up the jacket from the floor where it had fallen during the girl's struggles. Removing the items from the pockets, he put them in his trouser pockets. But he seemed preoccupied during this transfer and kept glancing toward the window. Suddenly the sound of raucous laughter reached his second-floor room. The man appeared to panic. Dropping the jacket, he moved again to the window and anxiously looked down. Three men in the alley were fumbling with the latch on the tavern door. While shouting drunkenly, they managed to pull the door open and began, one by one, to stagger inside.

The man heard footsteps thump on the stairs. He raced to the door, grappling clumsily with the bolt in his haste before he yanked the door open. Keeping his head down, he hurried out of the room. The door swung closed behind him.

# SIX

AFTER TUESDAY NIGHT supper, Glynis stood leaning against the open kitchen door of her boardinghouse, absently winding strands of red-brown hair around her fingers. A small shaggy white terrier appeared and crossed the flagstone path. He trailed a frayed piece of hemp rope, one end held between his teeth. Ears and short tail erect, he trotted behind a lilac bush and disappeared. Glynis's eyes narrowed.

Behind her there was a sudden clatter of iron skillet on cast iron stove. "Shh, Harriet. Not a sound," she whispered to her landlady. "I think we've found Duncan's hiding place."

Glynis stepped down onto the flagstone and tiptoed after the dog. A breeze caught the kitchen door, swinging it shut with a bang. Barking furiously, the terrier reappeared from behind the bush.

"It's no good, Duncan, you little thief—the game's over! Stop barking and get out of the way." Glynis pushed the lilac's branches aside and looked down into a treasure trove.

A sliver of metal shone through roots and dirt; she bent over, then straightened and walked back to the house. Pulling open the door, she stumbled over Duncan, who was intent on getting into the kitchen ahead of her. Glynis scowled at the dog and held up a dirt-caked silver teaspoon.

"Found it, Harriet. He's got a real cache back of that bush. Afraid he's exposed a lot of the lilac's roots, and they'll need to be covered. I'll ask Mr. Fyfe to do it—or did he leave after supper?"

"Yes; he's gone visiting his old canal cronies. I'll have him take care of it tomorrow morning. But you found the spoon. Anything else?"

"Bones, pieces of rope, what looks like a child's chewed slipper, a couple of pipe stems—which means that Mr. Fyfe wasn't losing his mind after all. Duncan, what are we going to do with you?"

The dog danced around Harriet's feet, eyes fixed on his food dish at the sink drainboard above. Harriet set the dish on the floor in front of him. Duncan's head plunged into the food.

Pouring herself coffee from a pot on the stove, Glynis sat down at the table in front of the open window. The sun had just disappeared behind bushy pine trees, and the smell of roses drifted across the warm kitchen. She looked out over the garden at spires of delphinium, roses just beginning to open, clumps of low-growing purple and white rock cress.

With a glance at the savaged lilac bush, she turned back to the kitchen to watch the terrier gulp his supper. His small body was rigid with concentration.

"Wonder why Duncan's turned to thievery, all of a sudden," she said. "He's not a puppy anymore."

Harriet replaced the cleaned treasure in the spoon drawer. "It's spring. He's probably collecting presents to court a lady."

Silver spoons? No, Glynis thought; it was more likely something darker, some degenerate flaw passed down from his ancestors.

"Harriet, what do we know about Duncan's bloodlines? After all, his sire's in Scotland—doing who knows what."

Harriet Peartree turned from the wood-fired stove with a pan of rhubarb slump. She was tall, her body ample and firm; her cheeks were ruddy with heat and white-streaked gold hair swirled around her face. She reminded Glynis of a handsome, ageless Athena. Stepping over Duncan, who was rubbing his whiskers clean on the hooked rug, Harriet set the hot pan on a trivet and leaned forward with her hands flat on the table.

"Glynis. What's the use of accusing Duncan's ancestors? They're not here—he is, and somehow we've got to break him of stealing. That's that."

Glynis watched her landlady settle herself at the table and reach for a pitcher of cream. *That's that.* That was Harriet, ever practical. While courting, marrying, and burying three men, what did she do with all the silver spoons she must have collected—melt them down?

Three husbands, and Harriet had survived them all. Glynis hadn't thought herself able to survive even one when the decision had to be made ten years ago. The choices were limited: marriage and dependence, or Oberlin College and freedom. There were no confusing alternatives. Women did one or the other. They usually got married. Simple.

She knew now there was more to it. She had made the decision not to marry, but if she lost her library position, just how independent would she be?

Elbows propped on the table, Glynis laced her fingers under her chin. Her choice had never felt irrevocable until a month ago, when the quilt arrived from Rochester two days before her birthday—her thirtieth birthday. A signature quilt: signed blocks of cotton fabric sewn together like a soft puffed page of autographs, recording the names of girls, now women, she had grown up with. Above the pen-and-inked name in each cream-colored block was a short verse. Each verse was different; some mocked, some applauded. But all were composed to commemorate her spinsterhood.

It didn't usually work out this way; they usually gave one another the quilts as wedding presents. Glynis had sewn and penned blocks herself for betrothed former members of the Young Ladies Sewing Society. Of the original group, only she and one other had remained unmarried, though all had taken the single-forever vow.

How old were they that afternoon—twelve, thirteen?—sprawled in the sun, their textbooks unopened, when they swore never to hand their lives over to a husband. And promised quilts to one another on their thirtieth birthdays.

Harriet leaned across the table to offer her the last of the rhubarb. "You've got that look again, Glynis. You going to live out the rest of your days with that woeful expression? What are you worrying now?"

"Quilts. Other things."

Harriet frowned. "You go through this business every so often. Glynis, you *could* have married if you'd wanted. Men asked you. Still do, if I'm not mistaken about—"

"You know being asked isn't the point," Glynis interrupted. "Never was." She shook her head and looked out at the garden.

"I think it was the right choice for me, Harriet. It's just that every once in a while . . ." She stared at the lilac bush, its spent blossom heads brown and dry beside the unfolding pink roses.

# SEVEN

THREE OF THE five churches in Seneca Falls had bells in their steeples. The cast of the bells, the weight and size, varied, so the sound they produced when they tolled the hour together approached a scale of ungodly cacophony.

The morning air trembled, vibrating with seven clapper strokes from each and every bell echoing back and forth high above the village. Those below with any thoughts of sleeping one or two minutes longer mostly gave up and climbed out of their beds.

Glynis lay face down at the edge of her four-poster. Holding a pillow over her head with both hands, she clutched it around her ears. "Five . . . six . . . seven!" she groaned, and released the pillow. Eyes still closed, she slid one leg over the side of the bed, inching it downward until her foot touched the hooked rug on the floor.

Village shops and offices were not yet open. Though mill wheels along the canal-river creaked slowly, factories had just begun to exhale puffs of smoke.

But farmers, who had their own inner, earlier bells, were already driving fringe-footed draft horses over dirt roads toward the town. Atop their wagons were the last of the season's dark green asparagus and newly ripened radishes and strawberries; underneath were rhubarb and the white stakes of freshly·dug parsnips. Scattered over all lay bunches of mint and parsley, and twine-tied bundles of fragrant lavender.

Glynis stood in front of her bedroom window. The curtains hung limp. A warm haze lying over the village filtered sunlight like layers of cheesecloth. Yawning, she lifted the thick nighttime braid from her neck, and turned to a water pitcher sitting beside a porcelain basin on the commode.

The screech of a train steaming into the rail station announced crates of dry goods from eastern New York merchants. At the canal's edge, brawny men unloaded barrels from flatboats, the containers smelling of brine and filled with iridescent ice-flecked fish. The men heaving the barrels grunted and sweated.

Outside village houses, mansions, cottages, and log cabins, dogs barked and cats yowled and spit. Inside, the aroma of coffee, and slabbed bacon and grilled cakes hissing on fire-bellied stoves was accompanied by the complaining voices of children, reluctant to waste time eating breakfast—or going to school.

Despite the symphonic dimensions of the June morning, the white Gothic house on Cayuga Street was relatively quiet. Mist rose like smoke from the grass, shrouding the back-yard trees and shrubs and flower garden. Glynis was sitting in the kitchen drinking coffee when Harriet appeared from her first-floor bedroom.

"Morning. I'm late."

"Too warm to sleep last night?" Glynis said.

"Oh, I slept all right. But your little Duncan must have had himself a time. Didn't come home until the wee hours," said Harriet, moving to the stove.

"How do you know?"

"Moon was so bright coming through the curtains it woke me. I got up to pull the shade, and there he was, big as life, trotting across the yard with a scrap of cloth or some such hanging out of his mouth. Sure enough, he went behind the lilac bush. That's the last time he'll do that—a fence goes up this morning."

Harriet turned as her other boarder, white-haired Dictras Fyfe, came into the kitchen. "Ah, Dictras!" she said. "Just the man for the job of preventing Duncan's dirty work."

Mr. Fyfe's thread-thin eyebrows lifted as he edged his slight frame into a chair.

Glynis got to her feet. "I may be late to supper. I'm go-

ing to stop now at the library and open up. If Professor
and Mrs. von Lentz come in, they can watch things while
I go out to the Steicher farm to return their Bible. It somehow got in with the books Friedrich sent. No telling when
I'll be back."

"Cold supper, anyway," said Harriet. "Last of Sunday's
ham."

Glynis went into the hall beyond the kitchen and
glanced in a tall oval mirror. To soften her sharp cheekbones, she pulled a few wisps of hair around her face from
her thick topknot, while murmuring to herself, "Vain
woman. Vain!" with the inflections of a revivalist preacher.
Loosing a few more strands, she jabbed a hairpin back in
place.

When Glynis crossed Fall Street some minutes later, the
last empty farm wagons were rolling out of town. Their
huge wheels creaked and rumbled, and horses' hooves
sounded *thwock-thwock-thwock* as they churned the gritty
yellow dust of the road. It was still too early for most
shops and offices to open.

Glynis unlocked the front door of the library, looking
around for Duncan, who had been beside her moments before. His shaggy rear end was vanishing around a corner
of the stone building. She called and started after him,
slipping on the dew-soaked grass. She glanced down at her
high-laced white shoes; retrieving him wasn't worth green
stains. Glynis turned and went into the library.

The terrier had seen a flash of brown fur in the grass,
and instantly generations of breeding took over. He
crouched and inched toward his moving prey. Gathering
his back legs under him, he pounced, sliding on the wet-
ness underfoot. The mouse scurried into some secret hole
below a broken window in the library's foundation wall.

The dog trotted down the shallow incline behind the library, which ended at a towpath edging the canal's narrow
retaining wall. The water level was high, rippling six
inches below the wall. The dog leaned over and lapped at

it, then traveled a few yards farther down the path. And stopped.

A breeze fluttered something ahead of him in the water. The dog knew his territory well; something was there that should not have been. Barking, he jumped back and forth on the towpath.

Glynis, opening the library windows above, heard the high-pitched, agitated sound. What was the matter with the dog, she wondered, looking out the window.

"Duncan, be quiet. You'll wake the dead. Quiet!" she called.

Duncan kept barking.

Glynis stood at the window. That wasn't like him, to go on and on like that. He sounded almost frightened. What was wrong with him?

She saw Duncan run partway up the slope, then turn and run back to the edge of the canal. The sound of his short, explosive barks sent Glynis to the door.

She had had enough of him—stealing silver, destroying bushes, and now this. She was taking him home and closing him in the basement; he could bark his fool head off down there for as long as he liked.

She started down the slope, slipping in her haste. She slowed to keep her balance and looked ahead at Duncan running toward her. Her gaze went beyond him, to something bobbing in the water next to the canal wall. She squinted. What was that? A bundle of clothes?

"Duncan, get down. Don't jump on me. And be quiet!"

Glynis bent and picked him up. He finally stopped barking, but he whined and quivered in her arms. She moved down the slope a little farther, and stopped.

No. It wasn't a bundle of clothes. Her thoughts slowed, confused. Fear replaced confusion. She sucked in her breath and turned to run up the slope.

But she couldn't—just leave without looking. With the dog still in her arms, she walked closer to the water, putting one foot carefully in front of the other until she was on the towpath, a few feet from the canal.

The breeze again, and an odd flapping noise. Glynis

stood as though rooted, looking into the canal. It could not be.

The body was face down in the water, gently rocking against the wall. Crinoline petticoats had caught on something just below the surface, and the ruffled taffeta skirt slapped the water above Mrs. Walker's floating form.

Glynis stepped back, letting Duncan jump to the ground. He inched forward, sniffing.

"Duncan, get away," Glynis whispered. She stared at the body of the woman for a moment longer. Then she turned and began to run up the slope toward Fall Street.

When she reached the lockup at the rear of the firehouse, Cullen's office door was open. He looked up from behind his desk as she stepped inside and closed the door behind her.

He stared at her face, then quickly stood up. "Glynis, what is it?"

"That Mrs. Walker. You talked to her yesterday? She's dead. Drowned. In the canal, behind the library—"

He was past her and opening the door before she finished.

"Cullen, wait. Shouldn't we get Dr. Ives?"

"Yes. Bring him."

He went out the door and walked swiftly toward Fall Street. In confusion, Glynis followed him a few feet; she stopped, looked around, and crossed to the office of Dr. Quentin Ives.

Cullen was on the towpath, kneeling beside the body, when Glynis and Dr. Ives came down the slope. He straightened and stood as they approached. Glynis hung back some steps behind the doctor.

Cullen gestured toward the canal. "I pulled her out of the water. Skirts were tangled in a boat tie-up hook."

"This canal's getting to be a mighty dangerous place," Ives said. He leaned down and opened his leather grip, a slender, even-featured man with clean-shaven pink cheeks beneath blue, worried eyes.

"She's been dead some time, Quentin."

"That seems obvious," said the physician, rolling the dead woman's head with difficulty to one side.

Glynis moved back toward the slope. "I'm going up to the library now, Cullen."

He went to her. "You came to my office right after finding her?"

Glynis nodded. "Duncan found her. He was barking, and I just came down to find out . . . I really want to leave now, Cullen. If you need to talk to me, I'll be in the library, for a while at least."

She started up the incline, then turned around. "What could she have been doing down here? How could she have drowned?"

Cullen looked back at Dr. Ives kneeling over the body. "I'm not so sure she drowned, Glynis. I'll have to call for an inquest to decide that."

Glynis stared at him. "What?"

Cullen shook his head. "Are you going to be all right?"

"I don't know. Just go on with—your job."

He started back to Dr. Ives, but she felt him looking after her as she hurried up the slope. She reached the library and went inside; only Professor and Mrs. von Lentz were there, seated at their usual table.

Glynis hurried past them to her office and closed the door. Slumping into a chair beside the window, she poured a glass of sun tea from a covered pitcher on the sill, sloshing the amber liquid over the edge of the glass when she tried to lift it to her mouth.

# EIGHT

❧

BY MONDAY THE 19th of June, the steady rain of the past weekend had dwindled to a fine gray mist. Fingers of vapor curled around Cullen Stuart and Quentin Ives as they rounded the town green on horseback and reined in their mounts in front of the Waterloo Court House of Seneca County.

In the open carriage behind, Glynis sat beside hotel manager Simon Sheridan, who had been determined not to muddy himself riding a horse. However, livery owner John Coons had guided his trotter through every rain-filled hole in the road—deliberately, Glynis decided; Sheridan's pearl gray trousers were muddied long before they arrived in Waterloo. Her own brown and white striped bustled dress, chosen with mud in mind, had fared better, but not much.

Well, she thought, at least the rain had broken the hot spell, and now they could fret about whether the river would flood.

Elm trees stretched over the three-story courthouse. The five people climbed wide steps framed by pillars, and the men stomped clumps of mud from their boots before entering the building. Once inside the lobby, they went up curving stairs, walked down a short hall past the surrogate's office, then entered a large, high-ceilinged courtroom.

The rain had kept many of the curious back in Seneca Falls, but Glynis recognized a number of her neighbors sitting on slatted wooden chairs. Waterlooers as well, probably farmers and their wives; the rain had kept them from their fields, and an inquest was sometimes interesting. This one unfortunately should be. She knew Rose Walker's husband wouldn't be there. The funeral was to have been yesterday. Too far away. But surely, at some point, he would want to know how his wife had died.

She lifted her bustle, leaned forward, and sat down between Cullen and Quentin Ives.

"You'll probably be called first, since you discovered the body," Cullen said to her.

"You didn't tell me that before!"

"What good would it have done? You'd just have been more upset than you already are." Cullen's voice softened. "I wouldn't put you through this if I didn't have to."

Quentin Ives was silent, reaching under his damp frock coat for several sheets of paper in his waistcoat pocket. He ruffled the papers and fiddled with the buttons of his coat.

"This shouldn't take long, Quentin," Cullen said. "Here's the coroner now."

A large man in black morning coat, his bald head glazed with perspiration, entered from a side door at the front of the room and stepped up onto a platform behind a waist-high wooden railing. His clerk followed him, going to a small table. The coroner looked around the room. When he saw Cullen, he nodded and seated himself behind a broad oak desk, rapping a gavel for silence. The buzzing quieted.

"This inquest is now open," the coroner said.

The clerk began to write.

"We are here today," the coroner continued, "to determine the cause of death, in the village of Seneca Falls, of a female person known as Mrs. Gordon Walker. Although this is an informal proceeding, all who give statements are bound by oath, as in a court of law.

"Will Miss Glynis Tryon please come forward?"

Cullen stood in the aisle while she edged past his chair. In a low voice he said, "You'll be all right. It won't take long."

As she walked to the front of the room, her hands felt icy and her teeth began to chatter; she clenched her jaw. She didn't think she would be all right, but she didn't want everyone in the room to know that. She lifted her chin and took a deep breath. When she reached the platform, the coroner motioned her forward, so she stepped up through the rail opening to stand between his desk and the clerk's.

"Would you please state your name to the clerk for the record?"

"Glynis Tryon."

"And you are a librarian in Seneca Falls?"

"Yes."

The coroner smiled. "I have just a few questions, Miss Tryon. Everyone is always a little nervous in court the first time. Just try to relax."

Glynis concentrated on watching the clerk's rapid hand movements, making the circles, loops, and hooks of the Pitman shorthand method developed a decade before.

"I understand you discovered the body of Mrs. Gordon Walker, Miss Tryon. Please explain for the record how this came about."

"My dog was barking and I went to see what was wrong with him. Mrs. Walker . . . Mrs. Walker's body was floating in the canal behind my library. Apparently her skirts had snagged on a boat hook, which is why she hadn't drifted downriver."

"What did you do then, Miss Tryon?"

"I went directly to Constable Stuart's office. I told him what I had found, and we agreed I should get Dr. Ives."

"And when was this?"

"Wednesday morning—last Wednesday. I think it was around eight o'clock."

"June fourteenth?"

"Yes."

"Had you seen this woman before the morning of the fourteenth?"

"Yes. She came into the library the previous day, just before noon, I believe. . . ."

She looked at the coroner. Was that what he wanted?

He nodded. "Please go on. How long was Mrs. Walker with you on the previous day, the thirteenth?"

"Not long at all. Perhaps twenty or thirty minutes. We

talked a bit, and then she suddenly announced she must go to Waterloo."

"Did you mark any change in her manner?"

"Yes. She seemed disturbed. I thought at the time that she was very—well, uneasy."

"What happened then?"

"I walked with her to the livery stable. When we got there, she thanked me and said she would be fine. I offered to help her hire the carriage, but she refused. I had the impression she wanted me to leave—"

"Excuse me, Miss Tryon, but did you think that was odd?"

"Well, yes, I did. But I thought perhaps I had offended her. I waited outside, and a short time later she drove off toward Waterloo."

"Did you see her again that day?"

"No. The next time I saw her she was . . . she wasn't alive."

"Is there anything else you wish to add?"

"No, I don't think so."

"Thank you, Miss Tryon. You may step down."

As Glynis moved past his desk, the coroner leaned toward her. "Now that wasn't so bad, was it?" he said, smiling.

"Yes, it was," she said, and walked back to her chair.

Behind her the coroner said, "Will the owner of the livery please come forward?"

John Coons walked briskly to the front platform, loudly announced his name to the clerk, and stared at the coroner.

"Mr. Coons, I understand you rented a carriage to Mrs. Walker on the day of June thirteenth?"

"Yes, sir, I did that! Tried to rent her a driver too, I did, but she weren't havin' none."

"What time of day was that?"

"Oh, someways past noon, if I was to guess. Can't be sure."

"Did she state where she was going in the carriage?"

"No, sir. Not exactly she didn't. All's she did was ask directions." Coons paused with emphasis and looked out at the crowd. "That is, she wanted to know how she could find the Steicher farm."

Glynis heard Cullen swear under his breath. "Damn grandstander, he didn't tell *me* that!"

The courtroom hummed. The coroner rapped his gavel sharply. "We must have quiet in here. Continue, Mr. Coons."

"Well, I gives her directions—that big farm ain't hard to find. Same road out as to Waterloo here. Then she left."

"Did she return that day?"

"Yes, sir. Come back before sundown, but late it was. Past supper, I can tell you that. I'd already et and was fixin' to close down for the night."

"Did she say where she had been?"

"Nope. Didn't say nothin'. Just gets out of the carriage, pays me, and leaves. Seen her walk toward the hotel across the street."

"Did you notice anything in particular about her? How she looked, for instance."

"Well . . . she was a good-lookin' woman, sir. That's about all I noticed."

"Thank you, Mr. Coons. If that is all the information you can give us, you may step down."

Glynis thought John Coons looked disappointed at the dismissal. He walked slowly back to his seat, grinning at his audience.

Quentin Ives frowned as he edged past Glynis and Cullen when the coroner called him forward. He unfolded his papers as he walked to the front of the room.

"Dr. Ives, did you examine the body of the deceased, Mrs. Walker?"

"Yes. I did a cursory examination of the body at the edge of the canal. Mrs. Walker's body was then removed to my office."

"Please state your findings, Doctor."

"I found no water in the deceased's lungs. Therefore she did not, in my opinion, die of drowning. I examined her throat, where external contusions—bruises—were apparent. In fact, Constable Stuart said he had seen them when he pulled her body out of the canal. The contusions were in a pattern consistent with thumb and finger marks, indicating evidence of death by strangulation."

"Dr. Ives," said the coroner, "Please define the term 'strangulation' for the record."

"Inability to breathe because the air passage is blocked. In addition to the external bruising, I found the deceased's larynx was fractured." Ives pointed to a place on his own neck.

"So, Dr. Ives, is it your opinion that Mrs. Walker was dead before her body was placed in the canal?"

"Yes, it is."

"Is it possible to determine the time of death?"

"Not precisely." Ives consulted his papers. "From an examination of the internal organs, it appeared that death took place some three or four hours after she last ate."

Glynis had noticed the coroner making notes of his own during the witnesses' testimony. Now he wrote something and looked up at Ives.

"Thank you, Doctor. That will be all."

Quentin Ives stepped down and walked back to his seat beside Glynis.

"Will the Seneca Falls police constable please come forward and give his name to the clerk."

"Cullen Stuart, constable, Seneca Falls."

The coroner nodded. "Please proceed, Constable Stuart."

Cullen removed several papers from the pocket of his brown frock coat. "I have a written statement from Mrs. Henry Stanton, of Thirty-two Washington Street, given to me before she left Seneca Falls to accompany the body of Mrs. Walker to Boston."

"Please read the statement into the record, Constable."

Glynis sat with her hands clutched in her lap. She knew what was coming: Cullen had given her Elizabeth Stanton's statement to read several days ago. He hadn't wanted her to learn its contents for the first time here in court. But she still wished she could leave the room.

" 'I, Elizabeth Cady Stanton,' " Cullen began, " 'swear

under oath, on this day of June fifteenth, in the year of
Our Lord 1848, that the following statements are true and
accurate.

" 'On Wednesday, June fourteenth, at the request of
Constable Stuart, I identified the body in the office of Dr.
Quentin Ives as that of Rose Walker, late of Boston, Massachusetts. Before my family's move to Seneca Falls a
year ago, I resided in Boston, and there I knew the family
of Mary Clarke and her daughter Rose, and Rose's husband Gordon Walker.' "

Cullen paused, shifted his weight, and continued to read
from Mrs. Stanton's statement: " 'I was informed by Mary
Clarke, and I believe it to be true, that Rose Walker was
born of the union between Mary Clarke and Friedrich
Steicher. They were married in the year 1816. The marriage was annulled the following year.' "

Cullen had to stop reading. The spectators, having first
listened in stunned silence, now interrupted with loud
voices.

Of course, Glynis thought miserably. What else could
we have expected?

The coroner rapped his gavel; finally he stood and ham-
mered it on the desk. The noise quieted to an uneasy murmuring.

"We will not continue until there is silence in this
room," said the coroner. "Any more outbursts of this kind
and I will order the room cleared. Go on, Constable."

"There's not much more," Cullen said. "The statement
ends with Mrs. Stanton saying, 'In a letter sent by me to
Boston three days after the canal boat accident in May of
this year, I told Mary Clarke of Friedrich Steicher's death.
I advised Mary to tell her daughter about her history, as
Rose did not know the facts concerning her mother's marriage, or even who her father was. Therefore, I can only
assume Rose Walker came to Seneca Falls to gather more
information about her father.

" 'I have been advised by Constable Stuart that on Tuesday, June thirteenth, Rose Walker inquired as to my
whereabouts. I state that we did not meet in Waterloo, or

elsewhere, that day.' The statement is signed," Cullen said, " 'Elizabeth Cady Stanton.' "

The room had begun to hum again. The coroner sat forward to watch the clerk, who was still writing. When finished, the clerk looked up and nodded.

"Quiet," said the coroner, punctuating with the gavel. "Now tell us, Constable Stuart, of your own knowledge of the events of Tuesday, June thirteenth, concerning the deceased."

"Mrs. Walker came into my office that morning, asking where she might find Mrs. Stanton. She said she had come into town the day before.

"Earlier that morning I had been at Coons's Livery, which stables my horse, and had seen Mrs. Stanton leave for Waterloo. When I told Mrs. Walker this, she seemed upset to find Mrs. Stanton out of town. She wanted to rent a carriage and start for Waterloo immediately. I suggested she first talk with Miss Tryon, who is friendly with Mrs. Stanton and might know when she would be back in town. I directed the woman to the library. That was the last I saw Rose Walker alive."

"Very well, Constable. If you have nothing further to add, you may step down."

The coroner followed Cullen to the edge of the platform. He waited for Cullen to regain his seat and then addressed the crowd.

"I understand that you are all interested in the proceedings. But I want no more outbursts such as we've had. And someone open those windows; it's getting too close to breathe in here. The rain must have stopped by now." He went back to his desk and sat down. "Will the hotel manager come forward."

Simon Sheridan stood up. The pearl gray trousers of his morning suit were still mud-streaked, but his jacket hung perfectly from his shoulders. He ran a hand over his carefully barbered hair, straightened his soft neckcloth, and walked slowly to the front of the room.

"Seems a tad reluctant, doesn't he?" Quentin Ives said. Glynis recalled Cullen telling her that Sheridan had not wanted to come and had resisted the day before. "The hotel doesn't need that kind of publicity, Constable," he had argued. "The Bristol is a respectable establishment. Notoriety is not good for business."

"C'mon, Sheridan," Cullen had said. "Notoriety is great for business, and you know it. Besides, Mrs. Walker just stayed at your hotel—she didn't die there, did she?"

Cullen said Sheridan had looked startled. "What do you mean, did she? Of course not. She drowned in the canal. What are you talking about, Constable?"

"Forget it," Cullen had said. "But you plan on attending that inquest tomorrow, Sheridan."

Now Simon Sheridan stood ramrod straight beside the coroner's desk. His fists were clenched at his sides, and his eyes shifted between the coroner and the clerk.

"You are manager of what hotel, Mr. Sheridan?"

"The Bristol, sir. One of the finest hotels in this part of the country."

"Very good, Mr. Sheridan. And the deceased had been registered at your fine establishment?"

"Yes. Mrs. Walker came in last Monday—the twelfth, it was. Said she had arrived here by train from the east."

"You were able to give her accommodations, I take it?"

"Oh, yes. Monday is not a busy day for us. And she was obviously a woman of refinement and breeding . . ."

Sheridan stopped, as laughter punctured the thick air of the hearing room. The coroner scowled.

Beside Glynis, Cullen slouched down in his chair, loosened his neckcloth, and stared straight ahead at Sheridan. Out of the corner of his mouth, he said, "Damn fool fop!"

"Are you saying, Mr. Sheridan," said the Coroner, "that she looked like she could pay her bill?"

Sheridan flushed and nodded. "Yes," he mumbled.

"All right," the coroner said. "When did Mrs. Walker leave the hotel on the following morning, Tuesday?"

"I'm not sure. I wasn't on duty yet. The morning desk clerk thinks he remembers her leaving before noon."

"And were you on duty later that day? The livery owner

has stated that Mrs. Walker left his establishment after his suppertime and walked toward the hotel."

"Well, I don't know when Coons eats his supper, but our hotel dining room was serving when she came in. And yes, I was on duty at that time."

"Did you notice anything in particular about Mrs. Walker's appearance? Did she seem distressed, upset in any way?"

"I did notice that she looked fatigued. And rather pale. In fact, I suggested that she might want something to eat before the dining room stopped serving at nine. She went up to her room—at least, I assume that's where she went—but came down a short time later and went into the dining room."

"Do you remember what time that was?"

"Yes. When she came downstairs I looked at the clock to see if she was in time to be served. It was eight fifteen."

"And did you remain on duty that night, Mr. Sheridan?"

The hotel manager shifted his weight, pulling a handkerchief from his trouser pocket. He patted his forehead and neck, then carefully replaced the handkerchief.

"Ah, I'm sorry. What was the question?"

The coroner raised his voice. "I said, were you on duty the night of the thirteenth?"

"Well, yes. Yes, I was, the whole evening. Monday is the front desk clerk's night off, so I covered that. It's usually a slow time, as I said before."

"Did you see Mrs. Walker leave the hotel later that night?"

"No. But then, I wasn't at the desk constantly. I had numerous other things to attend to."

"On a slow night?" the coroner said.

Sheridan hesitated. "Well . . . I had to check the kitchen and the tavern room. I'm just saying she could have left without my seeing her—well, she must have, mustn't she? The last time I saw her was when she went upstairs from the dining room."

"What time was that?"

"I think it was somewhat after nine. That's really all I

can tell you. I'm sorry I can't be more helpful about the poor woman, but I don't know when she went out."

"Mr. Sheridan, if Mrs. Walker finished eating around nine P.M., then, according to the testimony of Dr. Ives, she must have died . . ." The coroner looked down at his notes. "She must have died sometime between eleven P.M. and two A.M. It is Dr. Ives's opinion that she was dead before her body was placed in the canal. So please consider my question carefully, Mr. Sheridan: Did you hear or see anything at your hotel that evening which might be pertinent to the woman's death?"

Beside Glynis, Cullen leaned forward to stare at the hotel manager, who stood fidgeting next to the coroner's desk.

Sheridan whipped the handkerchief out of his pocket and again patted his forehead. "No. No, sir. I didn't hear anything—well, wait. There was one thing I remember. When she came out of the dining room, she had a piece of paper in her hand, a folded piece of paper. She asked me if I'd seen anyone leave it at the front desk. I told her no."

"Are you saying that a person could have left her a communication of some kind without your seeing that person?"

"Yes. Yes, it must have been left while I was—"

"Attending to other things. Yes." The coroner's voice was unsympathetic. "Mr. Sheridan, could someone walk into your hotel, leave something at the front desk, and walk out again without being observed by anyone?"

"Certainly, it's possible."

"That's right," said the coroner. "You did say it was a slow night—several times if I'm not mistaken."

Cullen stretched out his legs in front of him and leaned back in his chair.

"I don't believe I have any more questions, Mr. Sheridan. That will be all," said the coroner. "Unless you can add something *else* that might be pertinent."

"No, sir. I'm sorry, I can't tell you any more."

"I'll just bet you can't," Cullen muttered as Sheridan left the platform.

Ives leaned behind Glynis and said to the constable, "What do you think, Cullen?"

"I think it's damn peculiar. Here's this woman, a stranger in town, dressed up like a picture in one of Glynis's ladies' magazines, and nobody notices her leaving the hotel that night?"

"It is possible, Cullen. Things get pretty quiet after dark, Fall Street side of the river."

Cullen shrugged. "The real question is, why did she leave the hotel at all that night? And what the devil was Sheridan babbling about, some paper being left? Sounds peculiar to me."

"Why, Cullen?" Glynis asked. "Do you think he was lying about the paper?"

"Took the heat off him, didn't it? Mysteriously appearing while he was conveniently away from the front desk?"

"But what if it was some kind of note, asking Rose Walker to meet someone somewhere? That could explain why she went out. That is, if she did. . . ." Glynis flushed, realizing that Cullen and Quentin Ives were staring at her.

"Never mind," she said. "You must be right."

The coroner rapped his gavel. The hearing room quietly vibrated with anticipation.

"On the basis of testimony given here today, my finding is that on the night of the thirteenth or early morning of the fourteenth of June of this year, Mrs. Rose Walker died of unnatural cause, at the hands, literally, of a person or persons unknown. I therefore direct the office of the police constable of Seneca Falls to conduct a full and complete investigation, and to report the results to the county district attorney.

"This inquest is now closed."

The courtroom's occupants jumped to their feet; chattering and clomping their boots, they began to exit the courtroom. Glynis remained seated. Cullen and Dr. Ives stood and watched as the townspeople filed past, poking one another and whispering comments. The group from Seneca Falls went by them accompanied by their new celebrity, John Coons.

"This should feed the rumor mills for the entire summer," remarked Ives. "You're going to have your hands full, Cullen; this is a very nasty business. Let me know if I can help further. But I'm going to start back now. Good day, Miss Tryon."

She nodded as Ives went past her and walked out of the room. Simon Sheridan started to follow him. He was stopped by Cullen's hand gripping his shoulder.

"I wouldn't discuss this with your hotel staff until I've had a chance to question them," Cullen said. "I'll be by tomorrow. Make sure I can locate all of them. In the meantime, continue to keep Mrs. Walker's room closed off. I assume her valuables are in your safe."

"Yes, they—I can have them brought to your office if you want, Constable."

"No," said Cullen. "I'll be by. And tell Coons that Miss Tryon will be outside shortly."

Sheridan nodded and hurried out.

Glynis stood at the back of the room while Cullen exchanged a few comments with the coroner. When they got outside the courthouse the sun was shining.

Cullen looked up at the bright sky. "Glynis, when we get back to Seneca Falls, it'll be too late to open the library. Why don't we see if Jeremiah Merrycoyf wants to play some golf. He's going to hear soon enough about the coroner's finding, and I'd like to get to him first, talk to him before he's had time to think about how this affects his client, Karl Steicher. Will you come with me?"

Glynis nodded. "Yes. Thank you, Cullen."

The sun's warmth had already begun to dry the road as they started the ride back to Seneca Falls. Cullen rode on ahead. Glynis was alone in the back seat. Simon Sheridan, Coons had said, was going back in another carriage.

Glynis wondered if Jeremiah Merrycoyf knew about Friedrich Steicher's daughter. But would he tell them if he did know?

# NINE

LATE AFTERNOON SUN skimmed over the pasture, over the backs of grazing sheep. A collie stood watching the flock, the fringe of his tail sweeping the tall grass beside the cropped fairway.

Glynis squinted in the sunlight that glinted off the new golf club's iron head. Leaning on the club's shaft, Jeremiah Merrycoyf stared at them.

"It's hard to believe," he said, "*Very* hard to believe. Friedrich Steicher had a daughter? A daughter in Boston, that no one knew anything about?"

Glynis glanced at Cullen. "Mrs. Stanton knew about her," she said.

"Or says she did," said Cullen.

Merrycoyf sighed and looked ahead up the fairway. Sheep were munching grass between them and the last hole.

"I've known Elizabeth since she was a little girl, rooting around her father's law office in Johnstown," he said. "Judge Cady lost all five of his sons before Elizabeth was eleven years old. I've always thought she tried to make it up to him for being a girl—and having lived. She asked more questions than any child I've ever heard of, but she's not a storyteller as far as I know, Constable."

Glynis nodded. Elizabeth Stanton had first appeared in the library several days after she and her family arrived in Seneca Falls from Boston. Glynis had come to admire her dedication to abolition, admired her still more when Elizabeth began to involve herself with rights for women despite her husband's disapproval. Elizabeth and Henry had met and married while working against slavery; Henry felt his wife was now abandoning their cause for something he considered irrelevant and frivolous. But there was nothing frivolous about Elizabeth Stanton, and she certainly was *not* a storyteller.

Glynis and Merrycoyf watched as Cullen swung his club, lofting the little leather-covered ball filled with goose feathers high over the sheep and beyond. She saw the collie's eyes follow the flight before he began to lope down the fairway with an easy, reaching stride.

Glynis walked to stand behind her feather ball where it lay in scrub grass just outside the sheep-cropped fairway. She positioned herself to swing the long, hickory-shafted club, drawing her right foot back as best she could under her full skirt and petticoats. The heel of her boot sank slightly in the still-damp ground, and she pivoted. Her skirt swung out, snagging on a shrub; there was a ripping sound. Thrown off balance, she tumbled into the low weeds.

She struggled to sit up, but a torn strip of lace from her petticoat was still ensnared in the shrub. She could feel her face flushing as she tore the lace free from the bottom of her petticoat.

Mr. Merrycoyf peered at her over his spectacles. Cullen came to her, grinning, and reached down to pull her to her feet.

"Glynis, those skirts don't make sense. Why don't you wear trousers? Nobody's going to see you out here. We're a long way from the road."

Merrycoyf hooked his fingers in his belt and rocked back on his heels. "Takes a fair amount of mettle to ignore a centuries-old dress code, Constable."

"Jeremiah, she's already ignored more than one code, just being out here. What's another?"

"True—uncommon for a woman to be golfing."

"Not so uncommon," Glynis said, brushing herself off. "I might not want to make a public spectacle of myself, but if Mary Queen of Scots could play golf in the sixteenth century, I don't see why I shouldn't."

"If I recall my history, Queen Mary came to no good end," Merrycoyf said.

Glynis smiled. "As a matter of fact, one of the charges brought against her was that she was seen playing golf a few days after her husband Darnley's murder. But Darnley was a treacherous scoundrel, so I say, good for her!"

Glynis put the strip of lace in the ball pouch slung over her shoulder. Positioning herself again, she tucked her skirts carefully around her legs—and hit the ball straight down the pasture. It thumped the ground, bounced once, and stopped a short distance from the hole.

The two men looked at each other. "Wasn't it just last week you agreed to increase her handicap those four strokes, Jeremiah?"

Merrycoyf grunted. He leaned down and picked up a sodden lump at his feet. "This feathery's wet. It's coming apart at the seams."

"They get that way when they're hit into streams, Counselor." Cullen pulled another ball from his shoulder pouch and dropped it in front of Merrycoyf. The lawyer started to position himself but then hesitated, leaning forward on his club.

"How did you happen to have Elizabeth Stanton identify the body?" he said.

"She drove back into town right after we took Mrs. Walker's body to Quentin Ives's office," Cullen said. "I assumed the two women had met in Waterloo, so I thought Mrs. Stanton might know more about Rose Walker than I did. She was shocked, I can tell you, when she walked into Ives's office and saw the dead body of a woman she'd known in Boston."

"She didn't know Rose Walker was coming to Seneca Falls?"

"She says she didn't."

Merrycoyf shook his head. "And Elizabeth Stanton never said a word to anyone about Friedrich Steicher's past in the year she's lived here?"

"We thought she might have said something to you, Mr. Merrycoyf," Glynis said.

"No. No, she didn't. Probably gave her word not to, to her friend in Boston."

Cullen nodded. "That's what she told me. Jeremiah, I know Karl Steicher is your client. Do you object to answering a few questions about him?"

"Probably depends on what you're going to ask."

Merrycoyf stepped behind his ball, positioned himself, and swung. The ball lifted, flying far to the left. It landed with a thud.

Cullen smiled. "Nasty hook."

They walked toward Merrycoyf's ball. The collie ambled to meet them. Cullen reached down to rub the dog's head, saying casually, "Do you think Karl Steicher knew he had a sister? Half sister, that is."

"No, I can't imagine that Karl knew," Merrycoyf said quickly. "Last week I filed with the county surrogate for his inheritance. When Karl signed the affidavit, he had to swear under oath that he was the sole heir. I have no reason to think he would lie. Karl's headstrong, we know that, headstrong and stubborn. But I hope not a liar."

"Yet Karl needs money to run that farm, Mr. Merrycoyf," Glynis said.

"Yes, and Karl's not the type to share anything. But still . . ."

"I guess now he won't have to share, will he?" said Cullen.

"Oh, I'm not so sure about that, Constable."

"His sister's dead!"

"But her husband isn't," said Merrycoyf. "And unless that man's a total fool, I'd expect him to show up here any time to try and collect his wife's half of the estate. If she *was* Friedrich Steicher's daughter. Now see here, Cullen— those sheep are grazing around my ball. Can't you get your dog to move them?" Merrycoyf gestured toward the collie and snapped his fingers.

The dog's tail swirled over the grass several times. Then he sat back on his haunches and looked up at Cullen.

"Guess you'll just have to play through them, Jeremiah."

Merrycoyf dropped his new iron. Glynis and Cullen watched him walk reluctantly into the flock, pushing sheep aside. With his own backside brushing against a fleeced rump, Merrycoyf swung his baffling spoon, lofting the ball over the sheep and skying it straight down the pasture link toward the hole.

"Interesting hazards you provide around here," he said as he pushed his way out of the flock. When they started down the fairway, Merrycoyf said, "Let's hear Elizabeth Stanton's account."

Cullen nodded. "She said that a year after Friedrich Steicher arrived in Boston from Germany, he met Mary Clarke and became infatuated with her—a beautiful woman, fourteen years older than he was. Unusual, but not unheard of. Certainly not impossible."

"Anything is possible between the sexes, Cullen, my lad," Merrycoyf said. "Especially when it *is* sex." He glanced at Glynis, who stared straight ahead down the fairway. "Begging your pardon, Miss Tryon."

Cullen went on, "You're about right, Jeremiah. Mary Clarke told Mrs. Stanton she had wanted a child, and she was thirty."

"Sounds reasonable enough to me," said Merrycoyf. "But then, I am not a believer in spontaneous seduction; women have generally known what they're about in these things since the beginning of time."

"Mr. Merrycoyf . . ." Glynis frowned, then shook her head. It was not the time.

"I meant no disrespect to the fairer sex, Miss Tryon. In fact," Merrycoyf said, "I was giving them credit for something more intelligent than merely random coupling."

Glynis pressed her lips together. Was she being too defensive about women, or just about the age thirty?

Cullen scowled at them both. "So Mary Clarke and Friedrich Steicher married," he continued. "In April of 'sixteen. But Friedrich's older brother, who had been living in Boston for some time before Friedrich's arrival, immediately filed for an annulment, on the grounds that Friedrich was underage. Mary Clarke didn't contest it, but

before the annulment went through, she was pregnant—
with Rose."

"Did Friedrich know about the pregnancy?" Glynis said.

"No. She didn't tell him, according to Mrs. Stanton, until after Rose was born. Then Mary Clarke left Boston for
several years. And three years later, Friedrich married Caroline Hess. They started for western New York immediately after their wedding."

"Well, that's quite a story," said Merrycoyf. "And I
don't suppose there's any reason to disbelieve it. Though
all but Mary Clarke are dead now, so there aren't many
ways to prove it."

"Are there *any*?" asked Glynis.

Merrycoyf shrugged and shook his head.

They walked on to the cropped green; Cullen must tie
the sheep here for days, Glynis thought. She managed to
get her ball into the hole in three strokes; Cullen in one.
When Merrycoyf chipped his ball onto the green, it rolled
erratically, then stopped four inches from the hole. He
sighed.

"Jeremiah, you owe us a whiskey," Cullen said, smiling.
He picked his and Glynis's balls out of the clay flowerpot
sunk in the ground. The collie ran ahead, disappearing behind Cullen's cobblestone house a short distance beyond.

"You haven't answered Glynis, Counselor. Is there a
way to find out if Rose Walker was really Friedrich
Steicher's daughter?"

Merrycoyf leaned on his club once again and stared up
at the sky. "Bible!" he said suddenly. "Friedrich's family
Bible."

"Dear Lord," Glynis whispered. "The Bible—of
course."

She turned away from them, walking ahead to the porch
steps of Cullen's house. Behind her, she heard Cullen say
to Merrycoyf, "Would Friedrich have recorded the birth in
the Bible? Or the marriage?"

"If it all actually happened, I think he would have entered the dates, yes," Merrycoyf said firmly. "Never met a
man as meticulous as Friedrich about keeping records.

Yes, he'd have recorded them, all right. They were part of the Steicher family history—Friedrich would have respected that."

Glynis seated herself on the bottom step. When they approached, she turned her face away from them. What would they think of her when they knew?

"Glynis?" said Cullen.

"That day in the library," she said. "Rose Walker wanted to see the Bible. Well, of course she did! I'd opened my cabinet—it was in there, on its side." She saw the confusion on their faces.

"That Bible was in your library?" Merrycoyf asked.

"Yes. It had been in a crate with other books Friedrich had donated, just before he died. I didn't unpack that crate until last week. Don't you see? Friedrich's name was on the spine of the cover he'd made. Rose Walker must have seen it." Glynis drew a shaky breath. "It was her father's Bible—and I wouldn't let her touch it. Told her it was private. A family possession!"

She gripped her hands together in her lap.

Cullen leaned down. "You didn't know. How could you have known? But Glynis, when you found the Bible, did *you* look at it? Inside it?"

"No. I wouldn't do that. It was private."

He nodded. "No, I guess you wouldn't. But is that Bible still in your cabinet?"

"Yes. I was going to return it to Karl Steicher, the morning I found Rose Walker dead. But then I forgot about it, with all that happened. Cullen, the Bible was a part of her father, something of him she could have touched. Held in her hands."

For a moment Cullen looked away. Then he sat down on the step beside her.

Merrycoyf cleared his throat. "Perhaps, Miss Tryon— Glynis—it might be useful to remember that this tragedy was quite probably a premeditated event. I say probably, because no one wants to consider a senseless, random killing. Such things do occur, but not often. In any case, you have no reason to feel you wrongly denied Rose Walker a part of her past. That was done by others long before her visit to your library."

Glynis nodded slowly. "Yes, and you're right, Mr. Merrycoyf. But that doesn't mean I can't feel terrible about it."

"The thing that really gets me," said Cullen, "is that Friedrich never told anyone, not even you, his lawyer. And why didn't he ever try to contact his daughter?"

"Don't know," said Merrycoyf. "But he'd built a fine life for himself here; he was a respected, wealthy man. Perhaps the past was just too painful to rake up. Or maybe he thought"—Merrycoyf glanced at Glynis—"that he was making up for it the best way he could. Or that he still had plenty of time. I don't envy you, Cullen, having to get answers that might not exist anymore."

"I'm going out to the farm and talk to Karl tomorrow," Cullen said.

"I'd expect you would, Constable. You have a murder to unravel. But whether Karl Steicher is the murderer . . ." He shrugged.

"He had a strong motive, Jeremiah," said Cullen, getting to his feet. "But right now we should get into Glynis's library and take a look at that Bible."

Cullen walked toward his horse tethered at the rear of the house. "I'll meet you there," he said.

# TEN

❦

GLYNIS WINCED AND grabbed the edge of the leather seat as the carriage bounced out of a rut. Beside her, Jeremiah Merrycoyf didn't appear to notice. He held the reins loosely in his hands, concentrating on the horse's muscled rump and hindquarters. Or so it might seem to a casual observer, Glynis thought. But Merrycoyf's forehead was creased, and he seemed to have withdrawn inside himself, oblivious to anything but his own thoughts. She rearranged herself and watched the passing roadside, where daisies and saucy yellow mustard clumps flecked the sunny spaces between the trees. And thought about last Thursday, when Cullen had arrived at Harriet's boardinghouse just before sundown.

She had thought the strain in his voice was fatigue. There had been another death to investigate, he said; a girl who worked in a tavern down by the canal.

"Cullen, what is *happening* to this town?"

"Afraid this kind of thing isn't all that unusual," he said. "The tavern's a gambling spot, and the crowd down there—mostly men heading west, drifters, canal boat gypsies—gets rough sometimes. Tavern owner was pretty vague about what happened; said the girl's body was found in an upstairs room, and it looked like it had been there awhile. Hard to tell what she died of, or even when she died. I left Jacques Sundown to ask more questions."

Cullen's young French-Indian deputy had acquired that name through the white man's transformation of his Seneca name, Man Who Walks the Forest at Sundown. It offended Glynis, this arbitrary changing of another's name. It seemed imperious. It was common practice.

Cullen wanted to know if anyone was in the back garden.

"No, no one's here," she said. "Harriet's next door at the Ushers' house, and Mr. Fyfe is out for the evening."

"All right, good," he said as he tethered the black Morgan to the porch rail. Gripping her elbow, he steered her around the side of the house. It had rained all that day, Thursday; the sky had cleared to the west a few hours before, but the air still smelled of wet leaves, and the ground was spongy under their feet. Cullen was so quiet—what *was* it?

Duncan was stretched out asleep on the flagstone walk. He jumped to his feet when they came around the corner of the house, but the growl in his throat died when he recognized Cullen. He waved his tail several times, then sprawled back on the stone. Glynis sat down on a settee; the cast iron felt clammy, but she was too intent on watching Cullen to get up and wipe it off.

"Glynis, I wanted to wait until we could be alone to talk to you about this."

She had been afraid then; Cullen was never melodramatic, not ever. What was wrong?

He sat down next to her. "It's something I found out yesterday, and it's better you should hear it from me now, before the inquest. It's about Friedrich Steicher."

His voice was steady, almost flat, as he told her about Rose Walker—Friedrich's *daughter* Rose Walker.

"Cullen, no. That can't be." She tried to stand, but he clamped his hands around her wrists and pulled her back down beside him. His hands felt unfamiliar, like a stranger's, hard and rough as pumice stones. He held her so close she could see the pulse throbbing in his neck. She concentrated on watching the vein move in and out.

At last Cullen shook her a little. "I don't believe any of this," she said. "You can't believe it either. Friedrich had a daughter? He was married to someone before Caroline? He was with this woman, this Mary Clarke, before Caroline, before . . ."

She couldn't think, couldn't even remember what it was

she'd started to say. She pressed her face against his neck, feeling the heartbeat against her cheek. Cullen took the papers with Mrs. Stanton's written statement out of his shirt pocket and put them in her hand.

"Read this, Glynis."

She shook her head and tried again to stand. Cullen drew her back down onto the settee.

"Read it."

She read Elizabeth Cady Stanton's statement, her eyes stopping, going back to reread as the words first grew small, then swelled on the pages. Her mind felt jammed, going round and round in the same groove: it couldn't be true—how could Friedrich have kept that hidden? She thought she knew him. It couldn't be true. . . .

She lay the pages down on her lap with her fingers curled around them, thumbs rubbing the paper. Cullen opened her hands, took the pages from her fingers, folded them and put them back in his shirt pocket. She stared at their white edges protruding from the blue cotton over his breast, until the white began to blur.

With the air warm against her skin, it seemed strange that she felt so cold, as though she were frozen over, encased in ice, like a fish trapped at the bottom of the winter-drained canal. Cullen's breath ruffled her hair. "Glynis, say something. Don't sit there so quiet. This has to hurt you."

"How could you know?" she whispered.

"I know you had strong feelings for Friedrich Steicher." He shifted away from her then, hunching forward to study the grass.

Glynis stood up and walked to the edge of the flower bed, where the roses were studded with raindrops that winked like silver ornaments in the last sunlight filtering through the pine trees. She stared at the roses, thinking about those that climbed on her library's stone wall—the library built six years before with Friedrich Steicher's money.

Funds from New York's Library Assistance Act were available only to school libraries, and as Friedrich had predicted, those proved inadequate for adult use. He thought

Seneca Falls needed another, social library, so he had built one himself. And although most librarians were men, he had promised Glynis the librarian's position—if she graduated from college.

With a loan from Friedrich, she had gone to Oberlin, the first four-year institution to admit women students. Before Glynis left Rochester that fall, there had been long, painful scenes.

College was unnatural for a woman, her aunts had said, an affront to God's plan, and why on earth would she want to do something that females clearly were not created to do? It was obvious: men went to college, women did not. What would people say? And just how, pray tell, did she expect to get married? Men, her aunts said, voices shaking with conviction, did not like women who learned too much for their own good. Everyone knew that.

Her younger sister, betrothed at eighteen, had assumed Glynis would keep house for her anticipated family—"If you really insist on not marrying, Glynis. After all, it's what old maids *do*." Her sixteen-year-old brother sulked: just who, he wanted to know, was going to cook if she left? Her father, on the rare occasions he came home from his flour mill before dark, kept his typical silence and closed himself in his study.

It was not so much the scenes themselves that had distressed Glynis. It was the feeling of being isolated, of being different from the people she had known all her life—as though she were insane. Dangerous. She thought now, though it had not been clear then and she couldn't have put it into words at the time, that the worst of it was the shame of having her madness exposed, so that she felt uncovered, soft, like a crayfish without its external skeleton. She craved some gesture of approval from her family: a word, a hug, a sign that she was still one of them, even though she struggled between a longing to be loved and a need to be free. How much she was like other women in this, she had no idea. She had felt alone.

For days she wavered. Finally, it was something inner, something private, that allowed her to leave for Ohio: the memory of her mother's unplayed piano. But a troubled conscience and lack of confidence had made her miserable most of her time at Oberlin.

Four years later, when she was leaving for Seneca Falls, the aunts had been just as shocked: "What is *wrong* with you, Glynis? It's just not done! An unmarried woman going alone to live in a strange place with strange people?" Glynis had had a sudden vision of those people the aunts considered strange, all living together in Seneca Falls, New York—and she left almost immediately.

That last night in Rochester, her father extended his cool hand and said good-bye. It was all he said. His face held the emotion of the marble bust of Alexander Hamilton sitting on his desk.

She had traveled the forty miles east to Seneca Falls on the two-year-old railroad. Friedrich Steicher met her with his carriage at the rail station and drove her to Harriet Peartree's boardinghouse.

She thought Cullen had understood when she told him that conditions changed between Friedrich and herself with her arrival in Seneca Falls—when she learned he was married. It was one thing to be a girl who fell in love with an older man, her father's business acquaintance who lived in another town, and who hadn't indicated that he had a wife. . . .

Now Glynis drew in her breath sharply as a long-ago rage began piercing the coldness, breaking it into jagged shards like a pickax splintering ice. The anger surfaced from wherever it had been submerged, disguised for years as something else: sadness, remorse, a nagging feeling of shame.

No, Friedrich hadn't mentioned his wife. Glynis had only learned her first week in Seneca Falls; she tried not to remember how much she had wanted Caroline to die then. But that had been years ago. Surely she had detested herself for it long enough.

She suddenly realized her feet were wet: how long had she been standing motionless in front of the flower bed? She let out the breath she had been holding and turned to look at Cullen. He was leaning back against the settee, hands clasped behind his head, staring at the sky. She went to sit beside him.

"Cullen, I told you my infatuation with Friedrich was over long before you and I met."

He straightened on the settee. "Yes, and I believed that. But I never thought Friedrich did. He used every reason he could find to be around you. If he hadn't been so powerful in this town there would have been a lot more speculation about the two of you. As it was, people wanted to accept what seemed the most obvious explanation: that you were like a daughter to him."

Cullen stopped, staring at her. Glynis thought about what he had just said. "Who knows," she sighed. "Maybe he *was* partly trying to make up for ignoring the daughter no one knew he had ... Cullen, do you think Caroline knew about Rose, and about Mary Clarke? She must have, don't you think?"

Cullen shrugged. "If she did know, she had reason to be plenty bitter. First Mary Clarke, then you. Caroline Steicher wasn't a pleasant woman; maybe now we can see why." His voice had an edge. "Friedrich wasn't quite the man he made himself out to be, was he?"

Glynis started to shake her head but she hesitated. "Or the man we made him up to be. He did seem larger than life. That was his attraction. But I don't remember Friedrich himself ever saying he was more than human. Though you're right, Cullen, about Caroline."

They watched the sky. The sun was going down and a flush had appeared over the pines; the trees' outlines cut sharply against the glow of sky, their thick, needled branches turned to amber. Duncan stretched and yawned. He slowly got to his feet and trotted off around the house.

Glynis felt her arm tingle; pressed against Cullen, she hadn't moved for some time. He stirred, stood, and gazed down at her.

"You all right?" he said.

"Yes, I think I am. Or I will be. You?"

He nodded. Thrusting his hands into his pockets, he leaned back to look up at the sky. High thin clouds curled like plumes over the expanse of dark blue, thickening toward the western horizon.

"Mares' tails," he said. "Going to rain again. Better get moving."

He waited for her to walk beside him over the wet grass to the front yard. The horse nickered softly as Cullen untied him.

"Cullen, who could have wanted Rose Walker dead?"

"She'd just arrived here in town," he said. "Karl Steicher was the only person who could have known anything about her—if she was his sister."

"No. No, he wasn't the only one. Remember that Elizabeth Stanton knew her too."

"Mrs. Stanton had no reason—"

"Oh, I know, Cullen. Of course not. At least I hope not. I'm just saying that you didn't even know there was a connection between her and Rose Walker until yesterday, so perhaps there is someone else as well."

"I think you're straining," Cullen said, "for someone other than Friedrich's son to be responsible for this murder. Glynis, Karl could have lost the farm."

"Maybe so. But I just can't believe that Karl would do something like killing that woman—and no matter what I feel about Friedrich right now, I still owe him a great deal. Enough to hope whoever murdered Rose Walker was someone other than his son."

Wind suddenly gusted, whistling through the pines. Cullen mounted and turned the horse toward the road. He reached down for Glynis's hand and held it a moment.

She was still listening to his horse's hoofbeats when the first drops of rain touched her face.

Glynis suddenly realized the carriage had stopped. Jeremiah Merrycoyf was looking at her with a puzzled expression. She glanced past him and saw they were in front of John Coons's livery stable on Fall Street.

Now they would have an answer. If Rose Walker was really Friedrich Steicher's daughter, the Bible in Friedrich's library should confirm it.

# ELEVEN

AS SHE WALKED toward the library, Glynis saw Cullen ahead on the steps. She had left the carriage and Jeremiah Merrycoyf at Coons's Livery.

The sky behind her was fiery with sunset; shops and offices and street were washed with orange. Below, the canal-river shimmered gold in the oblique light from the west.

While unlocking the library door, she said to Cullen, "Mr. Merrycoyf wanted to stop at his office and look up something or other on inheritance law."

Cullen laughed. "I'll bet he did!"

"He said to come by with the Bible."

"We'll see," he said slowly. "Jeremiah's a friend, but he's also Karl Steicher's lawyer. I'm not going to hand over that Bible to him just yet."

Glynis pushed open the door and paused with her hand on the jamb. "Cullen, you're *not* suspicious of Mr. Merrycoyf, are you? Surely you don't think he—"

"No," Cullen said, shaking his head. "No, of course not. I just want to be cautious, that's all."

They went through the doorway, and the dry odor of books instantly overwhelmed the brief puff of outside air. The library interior was darkening, despite the tall windows framing the glow to the west.

Glynis took white phosphorus matches from a wall-mounted tin safe, scratched the safe's sandpaper strip, and lit the tapers in a floor candlestand next to the door. Candlelight stretched far enough for her to reach the glass-globed whale oil lamps that sat on her desk.

Pulling out the desk drawer, she groped for the brass key on its ribbon at the back. Cullen stood behind her as she opened the cabinet door.

Glynis stared at the shelf.

"It's not there," she breathed, moving aside the folders of newspaper clippings and small books. "Cullen, it's gone!"

"Keep looking." He took the folders and books she handed him as she emptied the cabinet. When the shelves were bare, their contents stacked on her desk, she stepped back and stared at him.

"It's gone. It was right on that middle shelf—and it's not there."

Cullen fingered the files, shifted the books around, then sat back on the edge of the desk.

"When was the last time you saw the Bible? The *last* time, Glynis."

She leaned against the cabinet and looked up, eyes searching the dimly lit ceiling. "The morning Mrs. Walker was here," she said finally. "I'm sure of it. That was last Tuesday."

"Six days ago? How can you be sure?"

"Those are very select items," she said, pointing to the things on the desk. "No one has asked to see any of them in the past week; I would remember if they had. So I haven't opened the cabinet.

"Rose Walker said she wanted to see The Married Women's Property Act material. Obviously, that was a ruse, Cullen, so no one would know why she was really here in Seneca Falls. Although I can't imagine why . . . of course—she wanted to see Karl before anyone else got to him with news of her arrival."

Cullen nodded. "That makes sense, if she assumed Karl Steicher didn't know he had a sister. She certainly would want to get to him first. But are you sure no one else saw the Bible in there?"

Glynis moved from the cabinet and sank into her desk chair. "As sure as I can be. Look, the only people who come in here and want items from that cabinet are Elizabeth Stanton and her husband Henry, and a few others working in the abolition cause. And remember, I discovered the Bible in that crate only a week ago—the day before Mrs. Walker died."

"Think, Glynis. Who knows about that locked cabinet?"

"Anyone who comes into the library might know about it. It isn't a secret hiding place, just out of the reach of youngsters, really. I kept the key at the back of my desk drawer—anyone could have seen me get it out at some time."

"But who's been in here since last Monday?"

"I'm trying to remember. Not very many; it's a busy time of year for farm families. There's the von Lentz couple, of course. They're here every day now."

"Who are they, Glynis? I know them by sight, nothing more."

"Professor von Lentz teaches German and literature at Geneva College. He and his wife are spending their summer here, translating some popular fiction for the German communities in Rochester and Buffalo. But the von Lentzes wouldn't have taken the Bible, Cullen."

He shook his head. "Probably not. But in the past six days, someone did. Where are the von Lentzes staying?"

"They're renting a room at the Hotel Bristol."

"The Hotel Bristol!" Cullen got to his feet. "I think we better have a talk with them tomorrow."

"Cullen, about the Steicher Bible. It was here in my library because of Friedrich's generosity. I'm the one who should tell Karl Steicher what's happened."

"If he doesn't already know! Glynis, who stands to gain the most if that Bible can't be found?"

Glynis nodded. "Karl, of course—but only if it recorded the birth of a sister."

Cullen began returning the cabinet's contents to its shelves. "I'll walk you back to Mrs. Peartree's when we finish this."

Glynis felt a shiver crawl up her spine. She was sure that someone had broken into her library, the place where she felt most at home; it seemed in some way a personal violation. "It doesn't feel quite as safe in this town anymore, does it?"

Cullen continued what he was doing. "I'd walk you back anyway, Glynis. Always have. I hope . . ."

"You hope what, Cullen?"

"The murder and that missing Bible—there's too much coincidence to think they're not related. I just hope no one's in danger from knowing, even accidentally, something that someone doesn't want known.

"Anyway, you'd better not open up here in the morning," he said. "First thing, we'll take a ride out to the farm, and you can tell Karl Steicher about his missing family Bible."

# TWELVE

BY THE NEXT morning a high unbroken cloud cover had formed, with the smell of distant rain hovering in the air. Glynis gritted her teeth as the carriage jounced over a narrow dirt horse path, and she braced herself against the seat. Beside her, Cullen tried to steer the trotter around the deepest ruts. A large red farmhouse and barns finally came into view under the tin-gray sky.

"Karl's pouring money out for machinery and livestock. You'd think he could spare a few dollars for road repair," he muttered.

"The rumor is that he might not have many dollars left to spare," Glynis said, gripping the side of the carriage with both hands.

The dirt path to the house abruptly evened out. Cullen sat back and let the horse choose its way. "What rumor?" he said. "Who's the source of intelligence about Karl Steicher's financial situation?"

"You know Ambrose Abernathy?" asked Glynis.

"He's vice president of Red Mills Bank."

"Yes," Glynis said. "I heard it from someone who is very friendly with Abernathy's wife Lydia."

"Lydia Abernathy—is she the one who looks like a baby doll, has big, empty blue eyes? A lot younger than Abernathy, talks like a little girl?"

"I guess that does describe Lydia. She's Ambrose's third wife."

"Remind me not to put my money in Red Mills Bank," Cullen said. "Confidentiality doesn't sound like Ambrose Abernathy's strong suit. What's he doing talking about his

clients' business to a wife who doesn't have sense enough
to keep her mouth shut?"

He steered the trotter toward the side of the Steicher
farmhouse and pulled in the reins. "This might not be too
easy, Glynis."

"I'll just be quiet and listen."

"No, if you've got something to say, say it." He helped
her down from the carriage.

Cullen tethered the horse to the porch railing, and they
walked toward voices at the rear of the house. Although
the sky was overcast, several women were pinning wet
laundry to lines strung between poplar trees.

Nell Steicher appeared at the top of basement steps,
holding a filled laundry basket against her hip, beside her
swelling abdomen. Three towheaded boys followed her up
the steps. They shrieked with laughter as they ran past her,
weaving under and through the laundry hanging on the
lines. The smallest boy, a toddler, clutched at the wet
clothes to keep his balance. The women spoke sharply and
swiped at the boys with wet towels. Nell sighed, seeming
to sag. When she saw Glynis and Cullen, she walked toward them slowly, still clutching the basket. Her steps
were careful, heavy and shuffling.

Karl Steicher suddenly rounded the back of the house,
went quickly to Nell, and lifted the basket from his wife's
arms.

"Nellie, you don't have to do that. It's why we've got
help—expensive help! I don't want you carrying anything
this heavy." He hoisted the basket easily up onto his shoulder, taking it to a spot under a vacant line. He walked back
to Nell, put an arm around her waist, and pressed his
mouth to her straw-straight hair. Nell leaned against him
and gestured toward Glynis and Cullen.

Karl let go of her and approached them, his hand extended to Cullen. He gave Glynis a short nod.

"Figured you'd be by, Stuart. Guess you want to talk.
Hold on a minute." Karl turned back to his wife. "Nellie,
why don't you go inside and rest a while." He glanced
down at her swollen ankles. "And put your feet up. We've

got help for you," he said again. "You don't have to work this hard."

Nell opened her mouth, closed it, and shook her head.

It must be lonely for her way out here, Glynis thought. Nell probably wanted the company even though she needed the rest. Glynis wondered what Nell thought about Rose Walker.

"It's good to see you, Nell," she said. "The children are beautiful. They've shot up so fast. Your youngest was barely walking the last time I saw him."

Nell's mouth smiled; her pale blue eyes remained somber and tired. "Thank you. They *do* grow fast. All of them." She glanced down at her bulging belly, then stared at Glynis's slim waist. "I'll just go in and make you all some iced tea."

Glynis's offer to help with the tea was cut off by Karl Steicher.

"No, Nellie. We don't need tea—this isn't a social call. Just go in and rest."

Nell finally nodded, called to the children, and went slowly up the back steps. When she got to the kitchen door, she turned for a moment to look back at Glynis. Then she stepped inside the house.

Two of the youngsters followed her. The youngest boy hung back, peeking around a wet sheet and slapping it with his dirty palms. Karl stepped forward, grabbed the child and swung him squealing high in the air, then carried him on his shoulder up the steps. He tousled the boy's hair and pushed him into the kitchen.

Karl's manner changed the instant the boy went inside; his shoulders stiffened and the dark blue eyes, lively just moments before with his wife and children, had become expressionless. Glynis studied him and thought, not for the first time, how much he looked like his father. The short beard and hair were the same white-blonde as Friedrich's had been; he had the same solid frame, same ruddy, alpine coloring.

But Karl's eyes, the same blue his father's had been, were different. It was impossible to guess what Karl was seeing, or how he was responding. Friedrich's eyes were like reflections of the man. At least that's what Glynis had always thought—now she wasn't so sure. Perhaps the father was simply a better actor than the son.

Karl motioned them toward the house. "We'll talk out front." He led them to the porch, which ran the width of the house, and gestured toward rattan chairs. The wicker creaked when he and Glynis sat down. Cullen leaned against the porch railing.

In the distance there was a soft rumble. Karl was instantly on his feet again, staring at the northwest sky. Columns of black clouds swelled above the horizon.

"Not a good time for a thunderstorm," Cullen said, looking toward the fields of ripening wheat.

"No," Karl agreed. He watched the clouds. "It's always touch and go this time of year. Not enough rain, and the grain heads won't fill. Too much rain at the last minute and the wheat's flattened to the ground, practically impossible to harvest. It's a great life, farming. Like an endless, high-stakes poker game—sky high!" He returned to the chair, but his eyes flicked constantly toward the horizon.

"Hear about the inquest yesterday?" Cullen's voice was casual.

"Oh, I heard, Constable. Been expecting you to appear."

"I didn't think it was necessary to call you to testify, Steicher, because Mrs. Walker died in town. I only called the people I thought had seen her while she was there. I didn't know, then, that she'd been out here to see you."

Karl's face was impassive.

"And from Mrs. Stanton's statement," Cullen went on, "I assumed you wouldn't know much about Rose Walker. Still, I thought you might show up yesterday in Waterloo."

"As a matter of fact, I intended to go," Karl said. "Didn't think the inquest had anything to do with me, but I was curious. Then there was some mix-up about a shipment of apple trees for the new north parcel, so I didn't make it after all." He frowned. "Afraid the orchard will have to wait another year."

Cullen hoisted himself up onto the wide railing, bracing

his back against one of the round columns that supported the porch roof. He looked down at Karl Steicher. "But Rose Walker did come out here last Tuesday, didn't she?" he said.

"Last Tuesday?" Karl hesitated a second. "Must have been. Yes, she was here."

Glynis sat not moving in the creaky chair, studying the porch ceiling. Was he going to tell Cullen the truth about that?

She realized Karl's eyes were on her. "Is Miss Tryon involved in this?" he asked.

Otherwise, why is she here? Glynis silently finished for him.

"Yes, she is, indirectly," said Cullen. "We'll get to that later. Meantime, I'd like to hear more about Rose Walker's visit."

He smiled easily at Karl, who did not noticeably relax; who, instead, got up to look at the sky again. Although there was an occasional far-off rumbling, the thunderheads seemed to remain fixed on the horizon. But in the air was the uncomfortable prickly feeling of impending storm.

Karl returned to lean against the railing not far from where Cullen sat.

"So Rose Walker drove out here by carriage, last Tuesday afternoon," Cullen prompted.

"She walked in the front door," said Karl. "Announced she was my long-lost sister."

"Did you believe her?" Cullen said.

"Believe her! She might as well have said she was the queen of England for all I believed her."

"You thought she was mistaken? Or lying?"

"Thought she was lying—you bet I did! Knew she was. What do you take me for, Stuart, a complete fool?" Karl moved away from the railing to stand directly in front of Cullen. "Listen to me, Constable. My father dies in May, leaving a sizable estate. And then this woman, this stranger, shows up on my doorstep and claims he was *her* father. Come on, Stuart, would you have believed her?"

Cullen shrugged. "Have you ever looked at your family Bible?"

"Bible? Certainly I've looked at it."

"Did it record a previous marriage of your father's? The birth of a daughter?"

"No," said Karl. "No, of course it didn't."

Watching him, Glynis thought, Those level eyes—they betray nothing, neither truth nor lie. But he kept rubbing the flat of his palms against his trouser legs. Or was it the storm that worried him?

She said, "Did Rose Walker mention the Bible to you? Ask you if it might contain records, a family tree?"

Karl turned, moving toward her until he was standing over her chair. "I'll tell you what she mentioned. Both of you, now hear me good and clear. She said she'd like an immediate cash settlement, would even be willing to take less than her share of the estate. You like that? *Less than her share!*"

He glared down at Glynis, then turned to Cullen. "Well, *I* didn't like that. Thought it was damn revealing. Cash settlement! If she thought she could make a legitimate claim—which she couldn't—then why the rush? And why take less? You want to try answering that, Constable?"

Cullen shifted on the railing. "But even if you'd been inclined to believe her, you couldn't have made a cash settlement. Could you, Steicher?"

Karl's gaze moved from Cullen to Glynis, then back to Cullen. His shoulders dipped slightly.

"No. No, I couldn't. All my cash is tied up in capital investments, machinery and so on. I've fully extended my credit. But you can find that out at the bank easily enough. Anyway," he said, "the whole thing was nonsense. A confidence game."

Cullen said, "After she left here that afternoon, did you see Rose Walker again?"

"No!" Karl stared at Cullen, then the corners of his mouth twitched with what might have been wryness. "But if what you're really asking is did I go into town that night and kill her, the answer is still no. No, of course I didn't. Why should I? She was nothing to me."

"You were here, then, Tuesday night?" Cullen said. "All of Tuesday night?"

Glynis was watching Karl. Did he hesitate, just for the flick of an eye? Or was it her imagination?

"Yes," Karl said. "Of course I was here."

He paced away again to scan the clouds. "Look, I've got work to do," he said over his shoulder. "If that's all you want to know . . ."

"No, not quite," Cullen said. He nodded to Glynis and eased himself off the railing to look out at the sky himself.

Glynis rose as well. "I asked about the Bible because I'm afraid it's missing," she said to Karl.

"What d'you mean it's missing?" Karl snorted, turning to her. "It's right in there, in my—in my father's study."

"Is that a fact?" Cullen said. "Well, in that case, I'd like to look at it."

Karl's eyebrows went up only a little. He started for the door, with Cullen right behind him.

Glynis remained on the porch; it reminded her of being made to stay after school for something she'd done wrong. But what was she so uneasy about? If the Bible was there, Friedrich's son was in the clear. He would never show them something that proved a sister existed. But then, why secretly take the Bible from the library? And if he did take it, when had he done it?

The clouds had shifted east above the skyline and looked to be farther away. From inside the house, she heard Karl suddenly growl, his words unintelligible. Glynis waited, gripping the porch railing.

He came striding out through the door, and stood so close to her she could feel his breath on her face.

"All right, Miss Tryon. What the devil's going on?"

Cullen appeared in the door, his eyes on Glynis. She said nothing. She wasn't sure she could.

"The Bible's not there, obviously," Karl said. "Stuart says *you* had it. So where is it?"

"You hadn't noticed it was gone, then?" Glynis said.

She knew it was simple minded the moment she said it, but she was distracted; there was a persistent thudding in her chest. She wondered if it sounded as loud as it felt.

"Of course I didn't notice," Karl said tightly. "I don't look at that Bible every day. Last I remember, it was right there on the shelf behind the desk. Though God knows, I should have seen it was gone, along with most of his other books. In your library, aren't they, Miss Tryon?"

Cullen came out onto the porch. "Why does that sound so damn unpleasant, Steicher? If you knew—"

"You were aware your father donated much of his collection to the library," Glynis broke in.

"Oh, yes, I know. My father was very fond of you, Miss Tryon, wasn't he? Those books he gave to your library, they cost a small fortune, over the years you and he—"

"That's enough, Steicher," Cullen interrupted. "The books stay right where they are, in case you're thinking otherwise." He had moved between Glynis and Karl. Karl stepped back.

Glynis began, "The Bible was delivered—"

"Yes, yes," Karl dismissed her. "So Stuart tells me. And now it's disappeared?"

Glynis nodded. "I'm afraid so."

"And Stuart thinks it was taken right out from under your watchful eyes, correct? The other members of the library board will probably find that interesting, Miss Tryon, when we discuss your contract."

Glynis felt Cullen tense beside her; she said quickly, "I am sorry. I'll do everything I can to find the Bible and return it to you."

Karl's eyes shifted away. He shook his head and turned his face again to the sky. The thunderheads were disappearing along the horizon.

"You don't have any idea who else might want that Bible, do you?" Cullen asked, his voice sounding casual once again.

"Who else would want it? It's of no value to anyone else." Karl's face was still turned toward the sky.

Cullen went to the porch stairs and started down. He

said to Karl, "Thanks for your time—know you don't have much of it, right now. We'll try to get this cleared up. Let you know."

Glynis started down the steps after Cullen, but Cullen stopped and turned back to Karl again.

"Steicher, did it occur to you that Rose Walker's husband may have a claim to half the estate? Or has Jeremiah Merrycoyf already mentioned that?"

Karl said tightly, "Rose Walker's husband has to prove his wife was my sister. Let him try."

He came down the steps and brushed past them, heading in the direction of the wheat fields.

As Glynis climbed into the carriage and Cullen untied the trotter, he said to her, "Steicher doesn't make it any too easy to sympathize with him. I wonder if he grasps how much trouble he's in. If I hadn't been so mad, I might have told him that you're possibly the only person in Seneca Falls who thinks he's innocent of murder. You and his lawyer—and I'm not so sure about Jeremiah," he added, climbing up beside Glynis.

He was steering the horse and carriage toward the path when Nell Steicher came down the front steps, gesturing to them. Cullen reined the trotter in as Nell approached the carriage.

"I heard part of your talk with Karl," she said. She lifted the hem of her apron and dabbed at her eyes. "He sounded angry, and he was kind of short with you, I know. But you have to understand . . ." Nell hesitated.

Glynis felt Cullen shift in the seat beside her. He cleared his throat, about to say something; her fingers gripped his arm. Let Nell talk; she seemed worried about what went on here. What did she know?

Nell's voice had a pleading quality. "You have to understand that losing his father and mother, so sudden like that, was a terrible shock. Karl hasn't got used to it. He's had to take over running the whole farm. Working such long hours, he's been a little short-tempered lately. Not that he ever *loses* his temper—I didn't mean that," she added quickly.

Glynis leaned over the side of the carriage. "We do understand, Nell," she said. "And please don't trouble yourself about it."

Nell's eyes filled; she wiped at them hastily with her apron. "I'm sorry. I seem to weep for no reason these days."

When she looked up at Cullen, her pale eyes seemed to spill anxiety. "Dr. Preston says it's natural, in my condition and all. He said I should stop feeling sorry for myself. He's right, of course. Karl is so good to me and the children. I have nothing to weep about."

Oh, fine, Glynis thought. Nell was all worn out, and frightened about something, and her doctor made it sound as though it were her fault. She wanted to tell Nell to find another doctor. Instead she pressed her lips together. Cullen would say it wasn't any of her business. It probably wasn't.

Cullen leaned forward beside Glynis. "Sorry to have upset you, Mrs. Steicher."

Nell's eyes filled again. She stepped back, waved, and turned to climb the steps. Cullen snapped the reins and the trotter started back toward the road.

Nell watched them go. Her stomach felt queasy; gripping the railing, she eased herself down to sit on the top porch step.

She had heard Karl tell Constable Stuart that he'd been there at the farm the night Rose Walker was killed. But Nell didn't think he had been—at least, not all night. It was just a feeling she had, and she told herself she couldn't be sure.

During that night, her bladder aching, she had gotten out of bed to use the closet commode chair. Karl had not been in the bedroom. Hot and uncomfortable, she had wandered into the sleeping children's room. Their faces were flushed, their nightclothes damp with perspiration, but they breathed evenly, untroubled.

Nell went downstairs to the study, where her husband occasionally worked late. He was not there, and in the quiet house she had heard the clock in the hall strike twelve.

She thought he might be outside, smoking on the porch. He wasn't. She then decided he was down at the barns assisting a calving. That wouldn't have been unusual, and she hadn't thought much of it at the time, just that she missed his hard back braced against hers in the bed. She hadn't remembered until today that she had gone back upstairs to bed and drifted into a restless sleep, waking only when she felt Karl move beside her.

But before that, she thought she remembered hearing a horse's hooves below the window—or had she dreamed it? The sound was so out of place at that late hour; it made her wonder if Karl had left the farm that night. But she hadn't asked him about it the next morning. It hadn't seemed important at the time, or perhaps she didn't want to know.

Nell felt a soft poking in her womb. She put her hands over her belly and closed her eyes. She knew she was no longer pretty—pregnant all the time, swollen, awkward, always tired; how could she be? Karl was a good-looking, healthy man. It wasn't the first time she wondered if he visited the tavern women on the south side of the canal. Men would do that, her mother-in-law had told her, if they weren't satisfied at home. The way Caroline had said it, it sounded like a threat.

Since almost everything her mother-in-law said to her sounded like a threat to Nell, she had given this no more weight than Caroline's other cruelties. And now, today, the tavern seemed no worse than the thought that Karl might have gone into town to see Rose Walker. Offered her money to get rid of her, her and her story about being Friedrich's daughter.

After Rose Walker had left the farm last Tuesday afternoon, Nell had gone into the study. The Bible was not on the shelf. She wondered if Karl had hidden it. If so, the woman's story must be true. Nell had felt relieved; Rose Walker couldn't pursue her claim without some kind of proof.

But now she was afraid. If Karl hadn't had the Bible to hide, if it had been in the Seneca Falls Library, and if Rose Walker's story *was* true, what might he have done to protect his inheritance? His family? If he *had* left the farm that night?

They would be punished. Nell knew. The Lord would raise up evil against them if Karl had sinned so profanely as to kill his sister. None of them would be safe from His wrath. The child in her womb would die, as King David's son had, because of the father's transgressions. David's wife had been punished even though she was blameless; Nell did not understand why this was so, but she understood there was no escape, no place to hide.

She struggled to her feet. Nausea gripped her, and she clasped her arm around the porch column. She laid her cheek against the smooth wood until the sickness passed. Breathing heavily, she went unsteadily to a wicker rocking chair and lowered herself into it, staring out at the fields beyond the house.

The earlier thunderheads had blown by, but the sharp tingling remained in the air. It would storm again.

# THIRTEEN

❦

THE HOTEL BRISTOL had risen from the ashes of a crude log tavern built by one of Seneca Falls's first settlers in 1800. The tavern had burned in 1840. On the corner of Fall and State streets, the present owner had constructed the hotel three stories high, with a Greek-temple front entrance on Fall Street.

Glynis and Cullen walked toward the hotel's tavern room door on State Street; before dark it was usually the busiest place on the north side of the river.

"Glynis, did you know Simon Sheridan lives at the hotel? Has a suite on the second floor."

"I don't think that's surprising, is it? He is the manager, and he's not married. Where else would he live?"

Cullen shrugged. "I don't know the man, never had any dealings with him. He's been in town about six months now; seems odd nobody knows anything about him."

"You don't think Simon Sheridan's somehow involved in Rose Walker's death?"

"I think he knows more than he's saying. Remember how uncomfortable he was at the inquest?"

"Cullen, did you or Jacques Sundown find out anything more about the girl killed at the tavern?"

"No," Cullen said. "Didn't expect to. Women like that lead a dangerous life. You wouldn't know, Glynis."

Perhaps not, but she could assume they didn't want to be murdered any more than anyone else. No one seemed to care very much, though; she hadn't heard a word in town about the girl's death.

They passed the stone walls of the Episcopal church;

just ahead was the white brick hotel. Cullen squinted down a narrow alley between the two buildings.

"Wait a minute, Glynis. I think there's another outside door back there somewhere."

He started down the alley, maneuvering around barrels of trash and through a flock of chickens scratching in the dirt, and disappeared behind a pile of firewood stacked against the back wall of the hotel. Glynis stood waiting, smoothing her dress's skirt and petticoats; the pale-yellow Merino wool was sheer, frothy as egg white, and its soft folds just cleared the ground. It was woven from the fleece of Cullen's sheep, but still it had cost her two day's wages to have made. She shook dust from the hems.

Behind her in the alley there was a loud crash, followed by a bloodcurdling yowl. As Glynis spun around, an orange cat hurtled toward her as though shot from a cannon. It streaked past and vanished. Chicken feathers eddied in the air like pale leaves.

Glynis peered down the alley. A trash barrel was rolling toward her. Smashing against a corner of the building, it catapulted beyond her into the street and finally rumbled to a stop.

Cullen reappeared, rubbing his knee. He scowled and shook his head at her. She hadn't been *going* to say anything!

As they stepped into the hotel lobby, Cullen said at last, "There is another door. It was locked. It's probably smarter to see where it's located from inside the hotel."

Glynis resisted commenting on the genius of that idea.

Candles threw shadows over the high ceiling of the lobby; tall brass candelabras grouped along the walls stood like many-armed ceremonial torchbearers. Professor Walfred von Lentz and his wife were seated on twin sofas that flanked the fireplace, little Gerta von Lentz all but cocooned in the plump cushions. Her husband sat erect. He rose immediately upon seeing Glynis.

Glynis introduced the couple to Cullen, as Simon Sheridan strutted out of the dining room. The coattails of his green evening suit fluttered like a peacock's train. His hand ran lightly over his hair.

He bowed. "Good evening, Constable Stuart, Professor, Mrs. von Lentz. And Miss Tryon."

Glynis nodded as Sheridan's eyes skimmed over her. He appeared a great deal more self-possessed than he had at the inquest.

"I thought when we met before that this town was fortunate in having such a lovely librarian." He smiled, his eyes holding hers.

"Thank you," Glynis murmured, dropping her eyes.

What role was he playing? she thought. The convivial Don Juan? Making certain they noted the contrast between this, his confident perona, and his curious selfsame other at the inquest? But where, behind the masks, was Simon Sheridan?

Sheridan turned to Cullen. "I heard you talked to my staff this afternoon. Sorry I was called away on business."

"Well, you're here now," Cullen said. "We'll talk after dinner. Since you live on the premises, that won't be a problem, right?"

Sheridan frowned but nodded his head. He turned to the others and gestured them into the dining room, seating them at a window overlooking Fall Street, and lit the silver candelabra on the table with a flourish.

"Please enjoy your meal," he said. He started to walk away.

"Just a minute," said Cullen. "The waiter that served Mrs. Walker last Tuesday—is he here tonight?"

Sheridan paused. "Yes . . . but he's assigned to tables on the other side of the room."

"I imagine you can reassign him to this table," Cullen said.

Sheridan sucked in his breath as if to say something, but just nodded and left.

Professor von Lentz stroked his gray-speckled black sideburns and said to Cullen, "The waiter served us also that night—the night that poor lady was killed." His German accent was light.

Gerta von Lentz reminded Glynis of a delicate pink and white Dresden figurine. Her movements were dainty, and her voice was high and sweet. "What a dreadful thing that was," she said. "One might expect such a thing in a large city, but in a small town?"

"It does happen, though," Cullen said. "Glynis will have told you that I want to ask you both a few questions. I thought you'd be more comfortable here than at the lockup." He smiled warmly at Gerta. Glynis saw her relax.

Professor von Lentz arched long fingers together under his beard. "Seneca Falls is our summer home, Constable Stuart. We will, of course, tell you anything we can."

The waiter quietly appeared at the table. "Mr. Sheridan says I'm to serve you this evening. It will be my pleasure."

Simon Sheridan trains his staff well, Glynis thought. She looked around the dining room; this was the first time she had eaten here since Sheridan had become manager. Each table held sprays of roses and delphinium on white damask tablecloths. The high ceiling absorbed the sounds of individual voices, sending them back down to the room as a blended hum. She recognized some of the diners at the widely spaced tables: mostly mercantilists and mill owners. Jeremiah Merrycoyf sat by himself, gazing downward first at the food before him and then at the newspaper at the side of his plate.

Around a large table in the middle of the room were seated, among others, the Reverend Magnus Justine and his pallid wife, Verity; Aurora Usher, who lived next door to Glynis's boardinghouse; and Ambrose Abernathy, vice president of Red Mills Bank and his wife Lydia. The lovely Lydia appeared to be holding court. All were turned toward the banker's young wife, as she gestured with motions that tossed pale yellow hair over her bare shoulders. Her husband watched her as though she were a favored pet, a toy poodle perhaps, Glynis thought.

Ambrose Abernathy was probably twenty-five or more years older than his wife. A beefy, florid man, there was a satyrlike sensuality about hm. Glynis found some of the same quality in Justine. However, the reverend wore his high white collar like a noose, whereas Ambrose had his clothes tailor-made in Rochester, Aurora Usher had reported, and ordered French wines for his cellar from New Orleans.

While Glynis watched, Simon Sheridan approached the large table and bent to kiss each of the women's extended hands. Glynis stifled a laugh: Sheridan really was a bit much for Seneca Falls. She glanced at Cullen, who was also watching the hotel manager. She caught his eye and smiled at his frown: Cullen was making the same assessment of Sheridan that she was, but he didn't think it was funny.

With some reluctance she brought her attention back to their table as the food began to appear. The waiter first came with kickshaws: oysters in half shells, glasses of celery, transparent jellies, and plates of sweet pickles. Spicy mock turtle soup was followed by boiled salmon with fresh green peas and radishes. The roast course arrived: an immense silver platter of carved spring chicken, ham, crisp golden-brown canvasback duck, green goose, and sirloin of beef trimmed with parsley. This was accompanied by mashed potatoes, asparagus, green beans, and parsnips. The next course was French salad, fragrant sage cheese, pastries, and soft puddings. Lest someone should feel unfulfilled, the waiter brought a tray of fruit just arrived from New Orleans: prunes, figs, dates, oranges, and pomegranates.

There was a pause—to prepare for dessert. Glynis felt the seams of her corset straining. She could barely concentrate on the conversation. When a crystal bowl of strawberries appeared, she swallowed a groan and refused her portion. Even Cullen shook his head.

Professor von Lentz, swirling his strawberries through thick clotted cream, said, "You knew, did you not, Miss Tryon, that the Geneva Medical College admitted a female student last November?"

Glynis nodded, accepting coffee from the waiter at her elbow. "Elizabeth Blackwell. She's having a difficult time there; not with the academic work, but the male students are treating her admission as a joke. She's been barred from the laboratories and classroom demonstrations, and the townspeople think she's a freak—or immoral."

"Perhaps she should have expected that," said the professor, wiping cream from his beard. "Indeed, if she does become a doctor, would it be proper for her to be examining *men*?"

Out of the corner of her eye, Glynis saw Cullen stiffen and glance at her with—could it be alarm? She smiled. "Surely you'd agree, Professor von Lentz," she said, "that that would be no more improper than male physicians examining *women*, as they have been doing for centuries.

"However," Glynis said quickly, as Professor von Lentz seemed about to interrupt, and Cullen was frowning, "don't you think it's interesting that the first woman physician in America should come out of western New York? One would hope that more could follow, but Geneva Medical College is changing its admission rules, and no more women will be accepted."

Gerta von Lentz pursed her lips. She seemed about to say something, but at a glance from her husband she was silent.

Cullen stopped staring at Glynis and appeared to relax when the waiter arrived to pour more coffee. "What time do you finish working tonight?" Cullen said to him.

"Nine o'clock, sir."

"I want to talk to you. Please make sure you see me before you leave."

The waiter raised his eyebrows but nodded.

"One thing now, though," Cullen said. "There's a door at the rear of the hotel that opens on an alley. Where is that door located in the hotel? The kitchen?"

"No sir. It's in the back hall beyond the tavern room, between the kitchen and a rear stairway leading to the upstairs rooms."

Glynis straightened and looked up at him. "So you don't have to go through the lobby to get to the guest rooms on the second and third floors?"

Professor von Lentz cleared his throat and said to Cullen, "But that door is not used by guests, leading as it does to the alley. Also, the stairs are narrow and would be dark at night—very unsafe for a woman in long skirts."

Cullen's eyebrows went up, and he stared at the professor, who smiled and looked faintly embarrassed. "Perhaps, Constable Stuart, I assumed too much from your questions."

"But you're right, sir," the waiter said. "That door and stairway are only used by the kitchen and cleaning staff."

"Thank you," Cullen said to him. "And I'll talk with you later."

The waiter bowed and left the table. Glynis avoided looking at Cullen, knowing he didn't want to say any more in front of the von Lentzes—the professor certainly caught on very fast. Perhaps he and his wife did know something.

Cullen pushed his chair away from the table, leaned back, and stretched out his legs. He looked casually at the von Lentzes, as though he were about to discuss the weather. Glynis had seen Cullen do this before.

"So tell me," he began. "Do you happen to remember about what time you got to the library last Wednesday morning—the morning Rose Walker's body was found?"

"Not the time, exactly," Professor von Lentz said. "But we did see Miss Tryon come out of the library and start down the slope behind. We were just crossing Fall Street. We heard her little dog barking and thought she was going after him. The library door was open, so we went to our usual table and began working. It was some time after that when Miss Tryon returned and went straight into her office. We thought that unusual, as she always speaks with us; later we understood why she seemed distracted."

Distracted! thought Glynis.

"Were you the only ones in the library?" Cullen went on. "I mean from the time Glynis left until she got back?"

Both von Lentzes nodded. "Oh yes," Gerta said. "No one else came in until much later that morning; not until long after the poor woman's body was taken away."

"Are you sure about that, Mrs. von Lentz?" Cullen

asked. "What I mean is, while you were watching the goings-on down at the canal, could someone else have come into the library?"

"No," said Professor von Lentz. "Constable Stuart, we were working on a difficult translation and had no idea what was happening down at the canal that morning—that is, until a wagon arrived to take away the body. And then we watched from the open door. We never left the library."

"Did either of you happen to see Rose Walker while she was staying here at the hotel? The night she was killed?"

They nodded. "We saw her that night," Professor von Lentz said. "We had gone to Geneva by carriage that day—I had an appointment with colleagues—and had just come back into the hotel as she was leaving the dining room. About nine o'clock, Gerta?"

Mrs. von Lentz agreed. "That was the only time we saw her. She went from the dining room to the front desk and talked for a moment to Mr. Sheridan. Then she went upstairs. She looked rather confused, but perhaps that was her way."

No, thought Glynis, *confused* was the wrong word. Rose Walker did not strike her as a woman who was easily confused. Nervous, yes, but not confused.

"Did you happen to overhear what she said to Sheridan?" Cullen asked.

The von Lentzes said no, they weren't close enough and were not paying attention, as they were tired from the trip to Geneva.

Gerta von Lentz leaned toward Cullen. "There is something, though, Constable Stuart. Perhaps it is not important, but . . ." She glanced at her husband. He nodded to her, and she continued. "We had retired as soon as we got to our suite. I was just falling asleep when I heard voices in the room next to ours. Walfred woke a few minutes later."

"The voices, a man's and a woman's, became rather loud, but the words themselves were not clear," said Professor von Lentz.

"Constable Stuart," Gerta said. "Simon Sheridan's suite is next to ours."

Glynis glanced at Cullen. His face was expressionless. He said, "And was Sheridan's one of the voices you heard?"

Gerta nodded. "Yes, it was his voice. That much we could tell. The conversation was unclear through the wall, but it sounded angry."

"Angry, yes," said the professor. "The only words we could make out sounded, perhaps, like 'bank' and 'money.' But we could be mistaken."

"Sheridan isn't married," Cullen said. "Do you have any idea who the woman was? Could it possibly have been Rose Walker?"

Both von Lentzes shook their heads. Gerta said, "We don't know. We had never before heard her voice. All we can say is that the other voice was not familiar, but certainly a woman's."

Glynis wondered how many women were staying at the hotel that Monday night. Not many, she guessed. They could probably check the register to find out.

She asked, "Aren't there women on the hotel staff?"

"But they wouldn't ordinarily be here at night," Cullen said.

"No," said Gerta. "Only the upstairs night maid, Clara. I think I would have recognized her voice, if it had been she we heard with Mr. Sheridan."

Cullen started to say something but stopped. Loud voices were coming from the tavern.

A group of men burst through the dining room entrance. They glanced over the diners; one of them spotted Cullen, and they started toward him. The man walking unsteadily in front of the others wore a trainman's uniform. He held a bloody kerchief to his forehead.

"Constable Stuart!" he said as he approached their table. "Constable, there's been a robbery—on my train!"

Cullen shoved back his chair and stood up. "Go on."

The engineer staggered forward and grabbed the back of Cullen's chair, then leaned on it, holding his stomach. "My train got stopped . . . two miles down the line east of here. . . . They was on horseback in the middle of the track."

The dining room was hushed as people strained forward to listen. "How many?" Cullen said.

"Four. Three of 'em went through the passenger car, wavin' their guns at the passengers. The other stayed in the cab. Roughed me up some."

The man took the kerchief from his forehead. Blood had congealed over a gash above his eye. "He shot Jim O'Brien—he's my fireman—when Jim grabbed for his gun. Jim's hurt bad."

"The passengers?" Cullen said.

"None of 'em's hurt, I don't think," said the engineer. "They just handed over their money. But I can tell you, they was goddamn scared. . . ." He stopped, looking around, and then swayed forward.

Cullen caught him under the arms and eased him into a chair. "What kind of guns did they pack?" he said. "C'mon, man, get a hold of yourself. I need to know." He had to shout over the noise that had broken out in the dining room.

"Six-shooters." The engineer spat out the words. "The new ones, the repeaters."

Cullen nodded. "Colts. I was afraid of that." His face was grim. "Which way did they head?"

"Rode due east, toward the wetlands," said the man, slumping in his seat.

Cullen turned toward the diners. "Everybody quiet down!" He waited until the noise diminished. "Someone get this man to Dr. Ives, and see to O'Brien. I need a couple of you younger men to ride with me. Get your horses and rifles. Meet me at the lockup."

Cullen turned to Glynis, who had stood up to hear better. He took her arm and brought her over to the window. With his back to the room, he said, "This sounds like the same bunch that hit a train outside Auburn last week—packing Colts. I'll likely be gone awhile."

Glynis desperately tried to focus on something other

than the danger. "Cullen, should I—do you want me to talk to Simon Sheridan?"

He nodded. "I'll see him on the way out and tell him." He smiled. "I'll tell him I've deputized you. You like that?"

"How can you joke about this?" Glynis whispered. "I don't like anything about it."

"Have Sheridan show you Rose Walker's room. I've got to go, Glynis. Let's find someone to see you home." His eyes searched the noisy room.

Glynis was saying, "Cullen, don't worry about me," when Jeremiah Merrycoyf appeared beside them.

"I'll see Miss Tryon home," he said to Cullen. Cullen nodded, already moving toward the door.

Glynis saw their waiter intercept him and say something. Cullen shook his head. He turned, looked back at Glynis, and gestured toward her. The waiter nodded. She watched Cullen push through the crowd at the door and disappear. "Be careful," she murmured after him.

The waiter walked up to her and said quietly, "Miss Tryon, I've remembered something about that Mrs. Walker. Constable Stuart said I should tell you."

## FOURTEEN

GLYNIS SWALLOWED A yawn as she stepped down off the
boardinghouse porch the next morning. Her head throbbed.
The sky was overcast, the air so heavy and humid it felt as
though she were breathing soggy fleece. Her ivory linen
shirt was damp enough to wring by the time she reached
the tavern entrance of the Hotel Bristol ahead.

After Cullen had left the night before, she and the
waiter had stood just inside the door of an empty cloakroom. Glynis had asked him what it was he remembered
about Mrs. Walker.

The waiter had looked uncomfortable. "I don't guess it's
very important now, the lady being dead and all, but I
thought the constable might want to know about it."

Glynis nodded. "I'll relay what you tell me to him.
Only to him," she added.

The man looked a little more at ease. "It was the night
I served her in the dining room, late, the night she . . .
well, it's just that I brought a note to her as she finished
eating," he said.

"A note?" Glynis asked. "You mean a posted letter?"

"No, it was hand-delivered. A sheet of paper folded
over with her name written on the outside."

"Who delivered it to you?"

He shook his head. "Not to me. I went into the lobby to
find Mr. Sheridan for one of the guests in the dining room.
He wasn't behind the main desk, but the registration book
was open, and I saw the note lying on it. I took it to her
table and gave it to her." He looked troubled. "Ma'am, after she looked at the note she seemed, well, upset. I was

clearing her table: she had knocked over a wineglass, and she sat there twisting her napkin like she didn't even see the wine spreading all over the tablecloth. Then she stood up, sudden like, and said she had to leave. Couldn't wait for coffee, even."

"Did she take the note with her?"

"Yes, crumpled in her hand. I watched her leave the dining room—I thought it was strange she seemed so worried. Mr. Sheridan was back behind the front desk. I saw her stop and talk to him, for a minute maybe."

"Did you hear what they said?"

"No, ma'am. I was too far away." He paused. "Maybe she was asking him who left the note. She didn't ask me that, though."

Because she already knew, Glynis thought. The signature or content of the note had told her. "Do you have any idea who left it?"

The waiter shook his head. "Anyone could have come in the front entrance and left it on the desk."

"Or someone in the hotel could have," Glynis said.

"Then why wouldn't they just go into the dining room and hand it to her themselves?" the waiter said.

"Because they didn't know she was in the dining room." Or because they didn't want to be seen. "What time did she leave the lobby? Did you see where she went?"

"It must have been about nine. The kitchen was just closing. I don't know where she went, but she didn't go out the front entrance or I would have seen her."

Glynis said, "One more thing; do you know about how long Mr. Sheridan was away from the desk?"

The waiter shook his head. He had nothing more to add, so Glynis had thanked him and then gone to look for Simon Sheridan. She found him with Jeremiah Merrycoyf, standing in the lobby entrance to the tavern room. Pleading fatigue, she asked Sheridan if she might see him the next morning. She hadn't wanted to go through Rose Walker's room right then.

Mr. Merrycoyf had driven her home in his carriage.

Neither of them said anything about the murder: she supposed he was concerned about his client relationship with Karl Steicher, and she couldn't tell him what she had just learned without Cullen's consent.

She had spent a miserable night, churning the bedsheets, anxious about Cullen. And the note delivered to Mrs. Walker—it was obviously important, since it had upset the woman. Had it been written by her killer, to lure her out of the hotel? Or could she have been murdered in her room and her body then carried to the canal? That had seemed unlikely at first—it would still seem unlikely, but for the argument the von Lentzes had overheard between Simon Sheridan and a woman in Sheridan's suite.

Glynis had thrashed about in the bed trying to find a comfortable position, trying not to think. Failing both, she had curled up in her chair by the window and stared out at the moonlit garden. When she dozed off it was just before sunrise. And now she had to cope with Simon Sheridan, and with whatever Rose Walker had left behind.

Edgar Allan Poe's detective, Monsieur C. Auguste Dupin, had simply sat in an armchair and reasoned out the mystery's solution; he didn't do anything much bodily except observe. Glynis didn't have much confidence in her ability to solve mysteries. And she didn't want to do something of which Cullen might disapprove.

Glynis knelt beside the open steamer trunk, its top tray on the floor beside her full of bonnets and parasols already examined. She felt ghoulish pawing through the dead woman's belongings, but Cullen had thought they might reveal some clue to Rose Walker's murder. What exactly he had expected to find, Glynis couldn't imagine.

Simon Sheridan was standing outside in the corridor talking to the cleaning staff. He had been pleasant enough when taking her to the room Rose Walker had occupied; in fact, he had been cloyingly polite. But Glynis found herself waiting for the mask to slip. While he was out of the room, she concentrated on working quickly to get through the layers of clothes in the trunk.

Why on earth would Rose Walker have packed all these things for a trip to western New York in the summer? Glynis lifted up a fur-trimmed cape and muff folded around walking boots lined with lamb's wool. Had Rose expected to stay in Seneca Falls for the winter?

Raising the layers of clothes with one hand, Glynis groped around beneath them on the bottom of the trunk. Her fingers encountered a heavy flat object wrapped inside a flannel dressing gown. She slipped the gown out of the trunk, rocking back on her heels to unfold it. Inside was a gold frame enclosing a silvery daguerreotype. A beautiful dark-eyed woman stared at her; Glynis gripped the frame and sat back on the floor.

The woman reminded her of Rose Walker—the same heart-shaped face, the same widow's peak of dark hair. This woman was older than Rose, but the likeness between the two was striking. Glynis drew in her breath. Of course: this must be Rose's mother.

Glynis vaguely recalled the excitement following the announcement of the daguerreotype technique. It was during the time she was at Oberlin, seven, eight years ago. The woman in the picture *could* be sixty-some years old, although she looked younger. It must be Mary Clarke.

Friedrich Steicher's first wife.

Glynis's fingers relaxed around the frame. It was like looking into Friedrich's past. Had he managed to put this woman out of his mind over the years? And a daughter— the daughter he couldn't know so much resembled her mother?

Glynis heard Simon Sheridan's voice in the hall just outside the door. She quickly rewrapped the daguerreotype in the dressing gown and tucked it back under the other garments in the trunk. It was instinctive: for some reason she couldn't quite explain to herself, she didn't think Sheridan should see it.

He came through the doorway. "Have you found anything of interest, Miss Tryon?" Sheridan came to stand over her. His grin made Glynis think of a cat sitting in a window with its tail switching, looking down at a bird on the ground.

She shook her head. "I'm not quite finished yet," she said, "but I'm quite all right here, if you have other matters to attend to."

"No, you just continue. No hurry." Simon Sheridan positioned himself in the doorway and leaned against the jamb. Glynis glanced sideways at him, relieved to see his arms folded over his chest. She pushed away a mental picture of him twirling his moustache over her like some ladies' magazine villain.

Her fingers fumbled with the buttons fastening a pocket sewn along the back of the trunk. She managed to get the pocket open and pulled out a small leather folder. Inside were railroad ticket stubs: Boston to Albany and Albany to Seneca Falls. She shook the folder upside down; there was nothing else.

"Mr. Sheridan, what besides Rose Walker's jewelry is in the hotel safe?" she asked, turning to look up at him.

Sheridan's eyes narrowed for an instant, and he seemed to deliberate. "Jewelry is all she handed me when she registered," he said. "I'm quite certain of it. There were two jewel cases. At her insistence, we went through them and checked the list she had made of the contents. A very careful lady," he said.

A very smart lady, Glynis thought. "Apparently, Mr. Sheridan, there was quite a quantity of jewelry then?"

Sheridan nodded. "Unusual," he said.

"Unusual?" Glynis asked. "You mean the jewelry itself was unusual, or the amount of it?"

"I mean it's unusual for a woman, especially one traveling alone, to carry that much with her. I was surprised."

"I haven't come across her list," Glynis said.

"One is in the safe with my signature," he said smiling. "She kept the duplicate."

"I don't suppose," Glynis said, "that she had you put a pink beaded purse in the safe that Tuesday night, did she? The night she was killed, I mean."

He looked at her a long moment, then said, "No. No,

the only time I deposited anything for her was when she registered. That was the jewelry."

So where was the woman's purse Glynis had seen that day in the library? Probably at the bottom of the canal, if the current hadn't carried it to who knew where.

Glynis sat back on her heels again and closed the trunk cover with a soft clunk. Lavender scent whooshed into the air.

Sheridan came into the room. "Done, Miss Tryon?"

"Yes, I think so." Glynis stood up and looked around a last time. She had not found the note the waiter said he had brought Rose Walker, although she'd searched as soon as Sheridan had left. Sheridan, of course, had always had access to this room: if he had sent the note, wouldn't he have destroyed it by now? The tall wardrobe cabinet standing beside the bed was empty. Rose Walker had not unpacked anything from the trunk, as far as Glynis could tell; perhaps she had thought she wouldn't be at the hotel for long. Had she thought Karl Steicher would invite her to stay at the farm?

"Constable Stuart must have great confidence in you, Miss Tryon." Sheridan looked amused. "I'm not certain it's legal to deputize a woman, but then, who am I to question the constable's procedures?"

Had Cullen actually told him that? The night before she had thought Cullen was joking about the deputy business. Sheridan couldn't believe such nonsense! No, he was making fun of her—or Cullen. She couldn't decide which was more offensive.

"On the other hand," Sheridan said as they left the room and went toward the stairs, "I suppose Constable Stuart felt a woman might see something in Mrs. Walker's things that a man would overlook. Did you? Find anything unusual?"

"Nothing at all, Mr. Sheridan. I think perhaps, though, I should see the jewelry cases," she said when they reached the bottom of the stairs.

Sheridan led her into his office, closed the door behind them, and went to a large metal safe. With his back to her, he opened the lock and reached in, turning around to hand her two oblong carved wooden boxes.

Glynis set them on his desk and lifted the hinged lids; the boxes were lined with pale green silk. She was no expert on jewelry quality, but the quantity in front of her was startling. Rose Walker had brought with her to Seneca Falls a collection that would have satisfied most women for their entire lives.

"Quite a few things, aren't there?" said Sheridan. "I told you I thought it was unusual."

"Some women are very attached to their jewelry," Glynis said. "Perhaps Mrs. Walker couldn't bear to be parted from it." She wondered if that sounded plausible to him. It didn't to her, but she felt she should say something—she couldn't very well just stand there staring.

"Mr. Sheridan, I wonder if you might help me. I'm not experienced at this kind of thing. I recognize a few items of probable value, like those jet earrings, the jet and silver necklace, and the silver brooch; would you say there is much here that is valuable? Other than for its possible sentimental worth, of course."

Sheridan reached into the boxes and fingered some of the items. He held up a few, then shook his head. "I don't think so. Those aren't expensive things. The necklace perhaps, and the brooch. But most of it is what I would call paste, or costume jewelry.

"Very nice," he added, "but nothing that could have cost a great deal, I would say."

Glynis looked over the collection again and studied the list in Sheridan's sprawling handwriting, which had been tucked into a side pocket of one of the boxes. "I guess that's all I need to see," she said.

While Sheridan returned the boxes to the safe, Glynis went to the door. "By the way," she said, "would you happen to remember how many women were staying here at the hotel that Tuesday night? I imagine your register would show that, though, wouldn't it?

"No need to look," Sheridan said. "Although you certainly may if you wish. But the only female guests registered here that night were Mrs. Walker and your friend Mrs. von Lentz."

"How many women staff members would have been here after the dining room closed?"

"None," Sheridan said. "Our night staff is all male, for obvious reasons of propriety."

"Clara, the upstairs night maid, wasn't on duty?"

"No. She leaves here at nine. Why do you ask?"

"Oh, I just wondered. I assume that none of the women diners who were not staying at the hotel would have had any reason to go up to the second floor?"

Sheridan's face seemed to undergo a minuscule transformation. Glynis could not tell herself exactly what she saw, but it was as if her little Duncan had secretly grown fangs, then suddenly curled back his lip to expose them.

Sheridan took a step toward her. His lips were pulled over his teeth in what she told herself must be a grin. "Miss Tryon, just what is it you want to know?"

Glynis hoped she looked like she was smiling. "Oh, nothing, really, Mr. Sheridan. Just trying to account for everyone's whereabouts that night," she heard herself chirping.

She couldn't very well ask him where he had been during his absence from the front desk, or who the woman was in his room with whom he had been arguing. She would just report to Cullen; he should ask the questions.

"Miss Tryon, why did you ask—"

But she had opened the office door and was stepping into the lobby. "Thank you so much for your time," she called over her shoulder. "And your cooperation. Good day, Mr. Sheridan."

It wasn't until she reached the street that she realized how clumsily she had taken leave of him. Or how rapidly her heart was beating.

# FIFTEEN

MR. FINCH HUNCHED over his desk as he listened to J. K. Richardson's boots clacking down the courthouse stairs. The surrogate's clerk secured his steel pen in its holder, then straightened and braced himself against the chair back. He cautiously flexed his right hand. Wincing, he examined each extended finger; the joints were badly swollen. Again he wondered how long it would be until his hands were permanently deformed, like the gnarled claws of his aunt and mother. If that time came, and Mr. Finch had little doubt that it would, how could he work to support the three of them? When he had left the house that morning, the two old women were in the garden gathering the large, hairy comfrey leaves they boiled for their poultices.

Mr. Finch pursed his lips in distaste and sighed. The small inner office was warm, and his thick spectacles slipped down his nose as his head nodded forward.

He heard footsteps on the staircase from the first floor. Not the deliberate tread of the surrogate; these were uneven steps, as though stairs were being skipped. Mr. Finch opened his eyes. Outside the office door the silhouette of a man appeared backlit by a hall window. The man stood for a moment as though scrutinizing the room. Mr. Finch started to rise from his chair but hesitated, arrested by his initial glimpse of the figure coming through the doorway.

Like a magazine illustration of the romantic hero, Mr. Finch thought. The man's thick hair curled over his collar; the curls were not a common yellow but reminded Mr. Finch of gold coins strewn in a shining heap. The fine-boned face, the smooth, clean-shaven skin was almost too perfect. The man was like a marble statue come to life.

Mr. Finch cleared his throat. "Can I help you?"

The man smiled, stepping forward and extending his hand, shattering the illusion of cold marble.

Mr. Finch pushed his chair back and rose to his feet. "Can I be of help?" He stretched out his own hand without thinking.

The man reached across the desk. Mr. Finch suddenly remembered and started to pull his hand back, then held it still with an embarrassed grimace.

The man looked down. He clasped Mr. Finch's hand gently, in what felt almost like a caress. "My mother had arthritis, too," he said. Then, "I'm looking for the Seneca County surrogate. Is that you?"

"No! Oh, goodness, no," said Mr. Finch. "Mr. Richardson is out. I'm just his clerk, Enoch Finch."

"In that case, Mr. Finch, perhaps you *can* help me. My name is Gordon Walker."

Walker? The name sounded familiar to Mr. Finch. "Do you live here in Waterloo?" he asked.

"No," Gordon Walker said. "I've just arrived today. Came by train from Boston."

Boston? Mr. Finch stiffened. Oh, yes—oh, dear!

Walker continued. "I've come because my wife died here recently, in the town of Seneca Falls. That's nearby, isn't it? In this county?"

Mr. Finch nodded. He had heard about the inquest earlier that week. Who hadn't? "I'm sorry, Mr. Walker. Your wife's death—a tragic affair. I *am* sorry. But how can I help you?"

"My wife had discovered that her father, a Friedrich Steicher of Seneca Falls, died a few months ago. She traveled here to discover whether she was provided for in his will."

Mr. Finch hesitated before he spoke. "Well . . . I guess there's no harm in telling you that Friedrich Steicher died without a will. It's a matter of public record that the son has been appointed administrator of his father's estate."

"The son—is that so?" Walker said slowly. Lines appeared on his smooth forehead. "Who appointed him? A judge?"

"Karl Steicher signed an affidavit swearing he was his father's sole heir," said Mr. Finch. "At the time, it seemed to be perfectly straightforward so, yes, the surrogate, who is the county judge, appointed him."

"Is the affidavit also a matter of public record?"

Mr. Finch nodded.

"What I mean is," Walker said, "I'd just like to find out whether this son has a right to claim the whole estate." He shrugged and lifted his hands palms up, as though appealing to Mr. Finch. "I don't know anything about the law. I just think I should find out. After all, my wife was apparently . . ." Walker looked away, blinking several times. "Rose was murdered, Mr. Finch. And I think it might have something to do with the estate money. There can be no other reason someone would want to harm her."

Mr. Finch thought it must be terrible for him, having to come here where his wife had been murdered. Surely there was nothing prejudicial in trying to help him.

"Mr. Walker," he said. "If you would accept a suggestion? You really should hire an attorney to assist you in this."

"An attorney? You think so?"

"Oh, yes," said Mr. Finch. "I would think that is definitely the best course for you to follow."

"Are there any lawyers in Seneca Falls, do you know?" Gordon Walker asked. "Although perhaps I should hire someone here in Waterloo, someone you might recommend."

"There are several lawyers in Seneca Falls," said Mr. Finch. "The best is Jeremiah Merrycoyf, but he's Karl Steicher's attorney."

"Then if you would be so kind . . ."

Mr. Finch nodded. "Some say the best attorney in western New York is right here in Waterloo. Orrin Makepeace Polk."

"Polk? Like the president?"

"He's a distant cousin of the president."

"Would he take my case, do you think?"

"Of course, I can't say for certain," Mr. Finch said. "But truth to tell, Orrin Polk didn't have much use for Friedrich Steicher. His mother was a Quaker, Polk's was, and he represented the Friends in a land claim he thought they had against Steicher. He lost the case. To Steicher and Jeremiah Merrycoyf. So it might be worth talking to him."

Mr. Finch wondered if he should have said so much. But Gordon Walker seemed like a decent man. And why should Karl Steicher get away with . . . well, whatever he was trying to get away with. The whole Steicher family just rode roughshod over everyone. Because they had money.

Gordon Walker went to the door. "I'm obliged to you, Mr. Finch. Can you tell me where to find this Polk?"

"His office is across the square. The gray house. His shingle is out in front."

Mr. Finch listened to Walker's quick, light steps on the stairs. He walked to an outer office window and watched the man cross the square. He was suddenly aware that his hand had stopped aching. The swelling even seemed to have gone down some.

# SIXTEEN

❧

"MR. WALKER, I must interrupt you! Apparently you didn't hear me the first time. I will repeat what I said earlier."

The sharp black eyes snapped. Orrin Makepeace Polk once had been described by an adversary as having the look of a ferret calculating the weakness of its prey. The lawyer's sparse frame was rigid as he leaned forward over his desk.

"Please listen this time, Mr. Walker. The fact that your wife was killed, unfortunate as that was, has no bearing whatsoever on your claim that you are entitled to half of Friedrich Steicher's estate. And your suggestion that Karl Steicher might be responsible for the act of murder, unless proven, is also no grounds against his perfectly legitimate right to inherit his father's money. Proof, Mr. Walker. You need *proof* that your wife was Friedrich Steicher's daughter."

Polk sat back in his chair to watch Walker's reaction. Was the man really as naive as he sounded? He said he had graduated from Harvard College, so it wasn't stupidity that allowed him to think Karl Steicher would hand over half a fortune without a whimper. Especially a Karl Steicher this Walker fellow thought capable of murder.

Gordon Walker sat in a straight chair facing the lawyer's desk. He shrugged, crossed one leg over the other, and smiled at Polk.

"I heard you the first time, Mr. Polk. And I certainly don't want to argue the law with a man I've been told is the best attorney in western New York. But with all re-

spect, sir, you seem to suggest that you think Mary Clarke
was lying when she said she and Friedrich Steicher were
married, and that Rose was conceived during that marriage. I am sure she was *not* lying. I am sure that Friedrich
Steicher was my wife Rose's father."

Walker uncrossed his legs and sat forward to grip the
edge of Polk's desk. "And lest there be some misunder-
standing here, let me tell you that it's not for myself that
I'm seeking Rose's inheritance. It's for her mother. Mary
Clarke is a lame old woman. She is in almost constant
pain. Mr. Polk, can you imagine what it was like for her
to learn of her daughter's death? The least I can do is try
to recover something for her out of this tragedy. Something to make what's left of her life more comfortable."

Polk drew his finger along the side of his bony nose.
"All right, Mr. Walker. I am fairly convinced you believe
what you're saying. But convincing *me* isn't the point. We
have nothing with which to build a case. Are you willing
to do some work? Because you are not my only client, you
know. I simply don't have the time to spend rooting
around Boston or Seneca Falls for evidence."

"If you'll take the case, of course I'll do whatever needs
to be done," Walker said. "But what can I find out in Seneca Falls?"

Polk reached for a pen and tablet. "The first thing we
have to do," he said, scribbling as he spoke, "is find some
way of establishing Friedrich Steicher's paternity. Do you
know if Mary Clarke had a midwife to attend the birth of
her daughter? Or, given this newfangled notion of doctors,
I don't suppose that your wife was born in a Boston hos-
pital?"

Walker shook his head. "No. That was thirty-two years
ago. But I asked my mother-in-law about some record of
the birth; she says Rose was born at home, but the midwife has since died."

Polk sat studying the man opposite. Indeed he was not
so naive after all. Perhaps we can give the Steicher family
a deserved comeuppance, thought Polk. This Walker was a

nice enough looking fellow, and a jury sometimes relied on such things.

"Mr. Polk, wouldn't a written statement from Mary Clarke be good enough, if in it she swears that Steicher was Rose's father?"

"It would certainly go a long way. Is the woman able to travel? Karl Steicher's attorney, and I assume that that is Jeremiah Merrycoyf, has to have the opportunity to cross-examine her—we can be sure that Merrycoyf will not waive that right, no matter what your mother-in-law's circumstances."

"There are times when she barely can stand," Walker said. "I don't know that she could make it here."

"Then a written statement from her is all but useless." Polk scratched out *Clarke statement* on his tablet.

Walker fidgeted in his chair; his hands toyed with the inkwell on the desk. "Then what else is there?"

"Young man, in law there is usually more than one way to skin a cat. In Seneca Falls, you should find out who Friedrich Steicher's acquaintances were, whom he might have confided in about his past. A banker, perhaps; his physician or minister, who might not feel they were violating the confidence, now that Steicher is dead. Even a mistress, though I never heard anything in that vein about Steicher."

He paused, staring at the ceiling. "Wait ... There was something, a long while back, about a young woman in whom he had an interest. A librarian, I think. And this Mrs. Stanton, she seems to have been in Mary Clarke's confidence. Could she also have spoken to Steicher himself?"

Walker frowned. "Isn't it unlikely these people will talk to me?"

"Not necessarily. Steicher must have had enemies—every successful man does. And I didn't say this was going to be easy, Mr. Walker. Do you still want to proceed?"

"Yes, of course. There's a principle involved here."

Polk made more notations on his tablet. "Naturally, the

most convincing evidence would be some written admission by Steicher of paternity."

"Like what, for instance?"

"Letters, other documents."

"Mr. Polk, my wife and I were just told in May that Friedrich Steicher was her father. Up to that time Rose believed that her father had died before her birth. I don't know of any letters. I guess I assumed Mrs. Stanton's statement would be all that was needed."

"Her deposition that was presented at the inquest?" Polk said.

"Yes. Last Sunday I heard her telling my mother-in-law about it, at Rose's funeral in Boston."

"Mr. Walker, the inquest was held to determine cause of death. The deposition was simply to establish Elizabeth Stanton's ability to identify your wife's body. Whereas anything she said that she learned from Mary Clarke was hearsay, not admissible in a jury trial."

Walker got to his feet and began pacing in front of the window. "Then what else is there? Steicher was Rose's father! Why would anyone make that up?"

"That seems rather obvious, I would think." Polk turned in his chair to look past Walker out the window. To the left of the courthouse across the square, the white clapboard Presbyterian church's spire vanished into the branches of elm trees.

Polk turned his gaze back to Walker. "It is not uncommon for births to be recorded," he said, "in a family Bible. If the Steichers kept such a Bible, and they may well have, your proof could be there, Mr. Walker."

Walker stopped pacing and stood in front of Polk's desk. "I'll go to Seneca Falls tomorrow," he said. "I'm going to find something!"

"Then I will expect to hear from you," said Polk. "In the meantime, we'll proceed as though we already have the proof of your wife's parentage. I'll file a petition with the Seneca County surrogate to make your claim, as the administrator of an heir—your wife, Rose—to Friedrich Steicher's estate. My assumption is that Karl Steicher will most surely challenge your claim. Which will result in a public hearing to determine heirship."

Polk stood up and walked with the man to his office door. "Mr. Walker, before you leave. Keep in mind that your task is to obtain information. I want you to avoid Karl Steicher; leave the job of finding your wife's killer to the Seneca Falls police constable. I've had some dealings with him, and you may be certain that Cullen Stuart is no fool. I assume I have made myself clear?"

Walker nodded, and went out the door, closing it behind him. Polk walked back to his desk, restraining himself from rubbing his hands together. So, Jeremiah Merrycoyf. You thought this was a simple, straightforward inheritance matter, did you?

# SEVENTEEN

❦

GLYNIS HELD THE footstool steady while Morwenna Cleary's sturdy legs stretched under her gingham dress. The girl had to stand on tiptoe. Morwenna's chapped red fingers gripped the top bookshelf and finally managed to wriggle out *Jane Eyre*. With the book clutched in her hand, Morwenna hopped off the stool.

"Sure an' I'm grateful to you, Miss Tryon," she grinned, stuffing *Jane* into her canvas sack and pushing it to the bottom. She pulled the sack's drawstring tight. "Glad the mill shut down early today—happens just once in a blue moon."

"Will your father be angry if he sees you reading that?" Glynis asked. A little late to ask now!

Morwenna gave Glynis an appraising look, then shook her head. "Dad won't know I'm reading it, not unless you tell him, Miss Tryon."

Glynis sighed. Morwenna Cleary was seventeen, and Glynis wasn't her priest or her conscience. She was glad the girl read anything at all: Morwenna had had to leave school four years ago when her mother died, to take care of her eight younger siblings. But it was for just such as Morwenna that the Reverend Justine had stormed the library several weeks ago, demanding that if Glynis refused to remove the book altogether—heart in her throat, she did refuse—then the depravity should be shelved up out of sight. Glynis wondered if the reverend believed the only people incorruptible enough to read *Jane Eyre* were those with a seven-foot reach. Which of course eliminated children—certainly reasonable—but also eliminated all of Seneca Falls's women.

"I'd want to come to the women's discussion," Morwenna said, "but the mill doesn't shut down until six in summer. Would you be having it in the evening?"

That was a thought. Young women like Morwenna, who worked in the woolen mills all day, six days a week, wouldn't be able to attend otherwise.

"Then would you come, in the evening?" Glynis asked.

"With others, I'd come. Sure an' a lot of us would, if we were invited." Morwenna grinned. "I'd like to find out if there's some way to keep Dad's paws off me wages!"

Sometime later, while reading at her library desk, Glynis heard a sound like wind sweeping across a wheat field. She glanced up to learn the owner of the whispering skirts, then rose to grasp Elizabeth Stanton's outstretched hand.

"Morning, Glynis. I had laundry to drop off with Daisy Ross and thought I would stop by."

As Glynis pulled a chair to the side of her desk, she thought how thoroughly the woman's cherubic face disguised the tough mind beneath. Elizabeth was thirty-two; small and pretty, she usually looked younger. This day her vivacity was muted.

"My, these western New York summers are warm," she said. "Much warmer than those I remember in the Mohawk Valley when I was growing up. And the air here is almost as humid as Boston's was last week."

"You still miss living in Boston, don't you?" Glynis said.

"I miss the excitement of a big city, the lectures and concerts, the luxury of servants and my beautiful furniture. I didn't realize until we moved here how pampered I'd been. And I miss my friends in Boston, of course."

Glynis nodded. "I am so sorry about your friend's daughter. It must have been a terrible shock for you, that day in Dr. Ives's office."

"It wasn't as terrible as telling Marry Clarke of her

daughter's death. And I felt a certain responsibility, having urged Mary to reveal to Rose that Friedrich Steicher was her father."

"Surely you are not at fault," Glynis said.

"The truth is, I should have anticipated that Rose would come here. She was always headstrong. She never took advice gracefully."

"That was my impression of her," Glynis agreed. "In that respect, I shouldn't have been surprised to be told she was Freidrich's daughter."

"And she *was* his daughter! Despite what Karl Steicher has been saying," Elizabeth said. "Mary Clarke is not a woman who would make up something like that."

"Elizabeth," Glynis asked, "do you have any idea who might have killed Rose Walker?"

When Elizabeth shook her head, the dark curls framing her face bounced like silken corkscrews. "None whatsoever! But then, I can't imagine one person killing another, not even Karl Steicher. But he would seem to be the one to benefit from Rose's death."

Glynis leaned back in her chair. "You're not alone in thinking that," she said.

"He impresses me as a very unsympathetic man. It's difficult to believe he is Friedrich Steicher's son." Elizabeth's voice dropped as she added, "But Karl is also Caroline's son, and that poor woman never seemed to find much joy in life, did she?"

Glynis didn't answer. "Did you know Rose's husband in Boston?" she said. "Jeremiah Merrycoyf thinks he may arrive here."

"I met Gordon Walker on several occasions," Elizabeth said, "but only briefly. At the funeral last Sunday, I spoke to him for just a minute or two, so I don't know his plans. I can't say much about him, except that he is a very handsome, very charming man. I remember Mary complaining that he had rather expensive tastes, but then so did Rose. Mary Clarke came from a fairly well-to-do family, and I never quite understood why she fussed so about their money. But Glynis, I'm afraid it distresses me to talk about Rose."

"Yes, I'm sure it does. I shouldn't have brought it up."

Elizabeth Stanton sat forward and rested her clasped hands on the desk. "Did you have a chance last week to work on our survey about a women's meeting? With all that's happened ... Well, I haven't seen you since you volunteered to undertake it."

Glynis smiled. Volunteered? That was not quite the way she remembered it. She glanced around; they were alone in the library. She pulled the survey sheet from her drawer and handed it to Elizabeth, along with the results from her 'personal approach' questions, watching Elizabeth as she studied them.

Glynis recalled vividly the morning Elizabeth had been so furious about the state's suffrage regulations. After she had finished a tirade about women being lumped together with children, idiots, and lunatics, she had sat back and quietly stared at Glynis. Then, in the most ingenuous fashion imaginable, she had begun.

"Glynis," she had said, "didn't you write some articles that ran in the *Seneca County Courier*? About the abolition movement, weren't they, for Dexter Bloomer?"

"Yes," Glynis said. "Dexter asked me for some research on the history of slavery in the American Colonies. I wrote up what I found, and he printed it. He asked me to do several more articles."

"Did you know," Elizabeth said, "that Amelia Bloomer intends to publish a journal devoted to temperance? She hopes to have the first issue of *The Lily* ready by year's end."

Glynis nodded. "She spoke to me about writing for it. I told her I would consider doing so if I could concentrate on women's activities in the movement, as I did in the abolition articles."

"Yes, so Amelia told me."

"Elizabeth, not one history book at Oberlin had anything about women except bare mention of a few queens.

You'd really believe, after reading them, that one half the human race didn't exist before this very day. How can we know what we're entitled to do if we don't know what we've done?"

Elizabeth smiled. "Glynis, what would you think about a meeting, a public meeting to discuss women's lack of rights?"

Glynis felt something skitter down her spine. Could they actually do something like that?

"It sounds daring," she answered carefully.

"I've no doubt it would be," Elizabeth said.

Glynis thought it would be more than daring for herself—it would probably mean the end of her library job. Elizabeth must not know of the board members' discussion of her contract renewal.

"But you hold a public position in Seneca Falls," Elizabeth was saying, "so I wouldn't ask you to be directly involved, or to compromise your vocation. But I'd like to know your feelings about the idea."

"I think it's a remarkable idea. Why not a public meeting?"

Then Elizabeth had proposed the survey.

Now she finished looking at the sheets and laid them on Glynis's desk. "How representative do you think these numbers are?" she asked.

"Not very," Glynis said. "Six women, out of nineteen, said they would come. And some of those are friends of mine, so their responses might be suspect; they might not have wanted to hurt my feelings. But, Elizabeth, Morwenna Cleary said something that might be important. She said she would come, *with others*. I think if women believe their friends and neighbors will attend, then they will, too. But a survey wouldn't indicate that. Which means a meeting would have to be promoted, openly." Glynis was about to add, "And not by me," when Elizabeth interrupted.

"Exactly," she said. "We should write a newspaper notice announcing a public meeting. But closed to men; only women could attend."

Glynis shook her head. "I'm not certain men should be excluded," she said slowly. "After all, there are some who are supporters—should you risk offending them? Or deny them the opportunity of voicing their support?"

Elizabeth Stanton frowned. "You weren't at the World Anti-Slavery Convention in London, where woman delegates were kept out of the meeting and not allowed to speak. After all the work we had done, we were forced to sit in a railed-off area to one side of the floor. I was, and still am, *outraged* at the injustice of it! And I was stunned by the hypocrisy of the abolitionists. It was that experience that set off my concern for the rights of women. So I believe you have a higher opinion of male beneficence than I do, Glynis."

"It's true I don't have your experience," Glynis said, "but I don't think much can be accomplished without men's goodwill. They hold the votes to change the laws, as well as the purse strings."

Elizabeth Stanton sat back against the chair and sighed. "We've talked of this before," she said, "and I know you feel women's suffrage is the ultimate goal, as I do. But most women I've talked with are afraid asking for the vote is an extreme position."

"I know that without the vote we will forever *be* asking!" Glynis said. She got to her feet and went to the window. The abolitionists were justifiably questioning why human beings should be enslaved, denied legal rights, because of their color. Why couldn't it also be asked: should human beings be denied legal rights because of their gender? Weren't women without those rights also in a sense enslaved? Her opinion of male beneficence was not so high she couldn't see that.

"In my mind," Glynis said, returning to her desk, "the vote should be the first and only goal now, otherwise it will take years of pleading and petitioning to achieve the others. If we spread proposals, no matter how worthy, all over the landscape, there will surely be some things that

someone, somewhere, including some women, can object
to. Put all those somethings together and we can't possibly
succeed against them. At least if we consolidate opposition
to one issue, we can also consolidate support."

"But you are one of the few who feel that way," Elizabeth said, "at least at this time. Which is why it is so important to bring women together. For discussion and
planning. And education. Next month," she went on,
"Lucretia Mott—she's a Quaker minister, you know, an
abolitionist and advocate of women's rights—will be with
mutual friends in Waterloo. I hope to see her and suggest
the idea of a meeting. With her help, I think we can do it."

"Where would you hold it?" Glynis asked. "In Waterloo?"

"Wherever we can find a hall willing to accommodate
us, I suppose." Elizabeth stood up, shaking out her skirts.
"I must be on my way. I left my boys with a neighbor—
they'll have driven her mad by this time."

They walked together to the door. "You know, Glynis,
when I first met you I was surprised that you hadn't married; an attractive woman doesn't ordinarily get past eighteen unbetrothed. And I think you quite like men. But after
I read the book by de Tocqueville you loaned me, I
guessed it might be his comments that convinced you to
remain single. Am I correct? Or is that too personal a
question?"

"The things de Tocqueville spoke of are among the
main reasons," Glynis said.

Elizabeth Stanton nodded and took Glynis's hand. She
pressed it firmly, then drew in her wide skirts and swept
through the door. "I shall see you at the Usher ladies' musicale on Saturday," she called as she climbed the steps to
Fall Street.

Glynis went back to her desk and reached for a volume
on the shelf beside it: *Democracy in America*, by Alexis
de Tocqueville, written after the French nobleman's visit in
1830. When she laid the book on her desk, it fell open to
a section of worn pages:

In America the independence of woman is irrecoverably lost in the bonds of matrimony; if an unmarried woman is less constrained there than elsewhere, a wife is subjected to stricter obligations. The former makes her father's house an abode of freedom and of pleasure; the latter lives in the home of her husband as if it were a cloister. . . . The Americans are at the same time a puritanical people and a commercial nation; their religious opinions, as well as their trading habits, consequently lead them to require much abnegation on the part of woman, and a constant sacrifice of her pleasure to her duties. . . . Thus in the United States the inexorable opinion of the public carefully circumscribes woman within the narrow circle of domestic interests and duties, and forbids her to step beyond it.

# EIGHTEEN

DAISY ROSS PULLED the last shirts off the line. She tossed them into the laundry basket unfolded as the first drops of rain splattered on the hard ground. What grass had once grown in the small yard had long since disappeared under her children's feet.

Rain clouds had threatened all afternoon, but the clothes had finally dried enough to press. The thought of firing the stove to heat the irons made her pause, and she ran the back of a hand over her forehead, pushing a strand of damp brown hair under her kerchief. The drops of rain increased. Grabbing the basket, she lugged it up the steps of the porch and set it down by the open kitchen door.

She stood for a minute catching her breath. Inside the house, the youngest children yowled. Daisy sighed, leaned over the loose railing, and put out her hand to cup a tight red bud on the rosebush growing next to the porch.

At least the rain was soft. The opened roses would survive, as had the bush itself somehow; the wonder of that still astonished her. The glossy, pointed leaves, thin dagger thorns, and fragrant blooms—all from a cutting rooted in a clay pot given her by Mrs. Peartree three years before.

Daisy had carefully cracked the pot, set the plant in the hard ground and put a corral of stones around it. During dry spells the first summer, she had carried pails of water to it from the canal; to feed it, she had scooped chicken droppings from neighboring yards. The stones had kept the children away, although, she thought, they too seemed to recognize the rosebush as something unusual.

The bush had grown. Now almost as high as the porch

railing, it was covered with blooms that splashed blood red against the peeling gray paint of the house.

Behind her she heard the sound of a sharp slap. The yowling stopped. A moment of silence was followed by a child's whimper of pain, and the voice of her husband coming through the door.

He scowled when he saw her on the porch, his watery eyes sliding back and forth as if struggling to focus.

"You think supper's gonna cook itself?" Bobby's voice was thick.

Daisy picked up the laundry basket and tried to inch past him through the doorway. Bobby leaned against the jamb and thrust out an arm to bar her way.

"What's yer hurry? You weren't in no hurry before."

There was no point in answering him. Daisy knew from countless times before that he always began the torment like this. She felt Bobby's drinking was somehow her fault. It wasn't clear to her why this should be so, but it must be. If she could just figure out what she was doing wrong, he would stop. Then things would be all right.

She stood waiting for Bobby to get out of the way. He finally moved aside onto the porch. As she stepped past him through the doorway, the laundry basket brushed against him. He swayed and grabbed at the railing to steady himself; already split in several places, the railing gave way under his weight. Arms flailing, he lurched forward and stumbled off the porch into the rosebush.

Daisy heard branches snap as Bobby fell; she dropped the basket and looked down. Caught by thorns, he struggled to pull away from the bush, but he was entangled in its broken whippy branches. For what seemed a long time, he looked at his hands and arms with an expression of surprise. Beads of blood began to ooze from his scratched skin.

He probably didn't even feel anything, thought Daisy, hoping against hope that that was true.

"Goddamn stupid bush!" With a roar, he leaned over and began tugging at the bush's thick stems. He cursed steadily. Red petals flew through the air like clots from a wound.

Daisy ran down the steps. She hurled herself at him, her hands clawing at his back. Bobby shoved her away and returned to the bush. With a grunt, he wrenched hard on the main stem. There was a crackling noise as he yanked the bush out of the ground.

Bobby glared at it. Then, covered with petals and leaves and with branches still gripping him, he walked to the trash heap at the rear of the yard and threw the bush down. He tore the remaining branches from his ripped shirt and trousers and started back to Daisy.

Lying where she had fallen when he shoved her, she stared at the gaping hole by the porch. Bobby walked to stand over her. When she finally glanced up at him, he was looking toward the hole. His fury of a few moments before was gone, and something resembling remorse was beginning to form on his face.

She looked away. Bobby reached down to touch her shoulder. She swatted at his hand and began crawling toward the porch. Bobby straightened, spat at the hole, and walked to the front of the house. Rocking on his feet, he stood looking toward the end of the road and the Red Mills Tavern.

Daisy raised her head to look above her; frightened eyes in the small faces at the window had watched their father shuffle away. The children made no sound, and the faces disappeared one by one. They would stay in the house until they were sure he was gone.

Daisy slowly got to her feet and walked to the trash heap, where she searched for the roots of the bush. She found them still partly covered with dirt, dangling from the main stem. She carried the roots and stem behind the trash pile and, on her knees, began to scratch at the ground with her fingernails. Finally she managed to scrape a small depression. She laid the roots in, carefully spread them, and covered them with dirt. Then she sat back on her heels.

I hope he dies. I hope he dies and goes to hell.

There was no feeling, just the thought; she wasn't even crying. She was thinking how strange that was when, from the corner of her eye, she caught a glimpse of pale pink under the trash.

She leaned forward, pushing away shards of broken crocks and splintered pieces of wood. The thing was soiled and torn but tiny pink beads, still shimmering, fell from the silk as she lifted it into her lap.

What had he done? A slow grinding fear began to displace the numbness. Had he taken to stealing? Was that where the money had been coming from since Karl Steicher fired him?

She had wondered about the money but had had enough sense not to ask about its source. Now with fear growing, she opened the pink purse. Inside she found a tortoiseshell comb, a lace-edged handkerchief, a powder puff, hairpins, and some folded sheets of paper. When she pulled out the papers and unfolded them, a fragrant dust of powder fell from their creases. One sheet was a list of what seemed to be jewelry; the others were pages of a letter.

As she scanned the letter, the fear became panic. Dear God, what had he done? She refolded the papers and stuffed them back in the purse. What was she going to do? What *could* she do?

She heard a sound behind her; she whirled around to see her youngest son toddling across the yard, his pudgy arms stretched toward her. His face was tear-streaked, and a red welt was rising on one cheek.

Quickly, she pushed the purse far back under the trash and ran to pick up her child. Clutching his small body tight against her own, she began to cry.

# NINETEEN

GLYNIS REACHED THE end of Trinity Lane and turned to walk along the riverbank. Her white lawn dress drooped in the heat like a limp handkerchief; she shook loose the folds of skirt that clung to her cotton stockings and unfastened the top buttons of her bodice. In the trees overhead, locusts whirred with a hot metallic buzz. She wondered why their sound always made the air feel even more sweltering than it was.

She hadn't slept well the night before, unable to ease her concern about Cullen. Where *was* he?

Harriet had said, "He's only been gone two days, Glynis. Even after the posse catches up with those thieves, they'll still most likely have to take them on to Auburn Prison. That alone's a day's ride from here. You can't start fretting yet."

She was assuming a lot, Glynis had thought. Who knew what had happened? Those men wouldn't let themselves be taken easily. And that was aside from the dangerous miles of swamp the posse would have to pass through, with its snakes, and its quicksand . . .

She tried to shake off the image, bending down to pick white daisies spread across the riverbank like a dotted-swiss shawl. Why couldn't Cullen have been a sheep farmer, like his father? Or safer yet, have gone on with the law school. But no, he'd quit after three terms because everything about law bored him except criminal law—and he didn't want to defend criminals! Well, fine! So now he was out there chasing them instead, making himself their target.

She had come to the bend in the river where the canal walls and towpath began. Ahead was the place where she had found Rose Walker's body. Glynis stared into the canal for a moment, her flesh beginning to prickle. She turned away from the water and started up the slope.

Something white flashed in the grass fronting the library foundation wall, and she heard Duncan's short frustrated bark. Missed a mouse again. Where were all those mice in the library coming from? She walked around the foundation to try and spot their entry point. Pausing, she frowned: nearly hidden by tall weeds was a broken basement window. Duncan was sniffing in front of it. She picked him up, although there didn't seem to be any trace of shattered glass.

Now what, or who, had done that? The children she had just heard playing along Fall Street? Then why wasn't there glass all over, and the weeds trampled? It was odd: those windows had been checked just a few weeks ago. . . .

When? She thought suddenly. *When?* Of course, it was the Saturday she and Cullen came down looking for broken windows, when a shipment of glass came in on the canal packet—it must have been the Saturday before Rose Walker's death! She could check the shipment date at Hornsby & Levy's Hardware, but she was sure it had been that day. And they had found nothing that needed replacing, so the window had been broken afterward.

She dropped Duncan and walked quickly around to the front of the library. Inside, she grabbed matches and lit an oil lamp before going down the basement steps. Even with the lamp the basement was dim. She went toward the opposite stone foundation wall. There was glass on the floor below the window frame.

So it had been broken from the outside, she thought. She swung the lamp close to the floor, bending down to examine the reflecting broken shards. Some of the fragments seemed almost powdered, as though they had been ground into the floor by heavy boots. The children couldn't have done that. There was a trail of ground glass leading toward the stairs; stuck to the bottom of the boots, she decided.

She held the lamp up and examined the window opening. A few pieces of jagged glass remained on one side of the frame, and a shred of fabric dangled from a sharp edge. She reached up and picked it off. Light blue cotton. Someone had knocked out enough glass to crawl through the opening. Glynis stood staring at the scrap in her hand. Her initial excitement was giving way to the shock of incredulity. Why would anyone break into the library . . . ?

The Bible!

She started for the stairs, hearing glass crunch under her shoes. She scraped it off against the bottom step and climbed the stairs, trying to ignore the obvious implications. But they were impossible to ignore. How could she reason that anyone other than Karl Steicher would have had motive enough to break into the library to take the Bible? The Bible that he now claimed he didn't have?

Rose Walker was the only other possibility. Glynis tried unsuccessfully to imagine Rose Walker breaking the window, crawling through the hole, and finding her way around in the dark. Karl, however, knew the library layout, and he could easily have found his way using only a candle.

She sank into her desk chair. Had Karl lied about not leaving his farm that night? What if, after Rose Walker left him in the afternoon, he had gone into Friedrich's study and discovered the Bible missing? He could certainly figure out where it might be, since he knew other books had been delivered to the library. Did he know the Bible recorded the birth of a sister?

Karl had been in the library any number of times, so he probably knew about her cabinet. Rose might even have told him where she had seen Friedrich's Bible that day, suspecting herself that it might contain a record of her birth. Would Karl have been desperate enough to break in there in the middle of the night? To save his farm, he might have.

And then what? Glynis hunched over her desk, twisting

the scrap of blue cotton between her fingers. Did Karl take the Bible and then send a note to the hotel telling Rose to meet him? To kill her?

She didn't want to believe that, not of Freidrich's son, a man who was so obviously devoted to his family.

The library door swung open. Professor and Gerta von Lentz came in complaining of the heat. Glynis reluctantly stood up, found the books they needed, and asked them to watch things for the next hour. She left the library and walked toward Hornsby & Levy's Hardware. The heat was so intense, her head throbbed.

Glynis emerged from the hardware store, uncomfortable that she had not been candid with Abraham Levy about why she wanted to see his records on the glass shipment. But she realized she couldn't tell anyone about the library window. If she had pieced together an explanation implicating Karl Steicher, then someone else could. So she had mumbled something to Abe about wanting to check the going price of window glass for future purchase. It was not clever, but it was the best she could do on the spur of the moment. Abraham Levy, occupied with his ledgers, didn't question it.

His invoices showed that the last glass shipment had arrived Saturday, June tenth—three days before Rose Walker's murder. That narrowed down the time the library window could have been broken to the past twelve days. Of course, it might have happened anytime during that period, even yesterday. But nothing was missing from the library that she could determine, other than the Bible. And why break into the library other than to steal something?

It was clear that she had to keep quiet until Cullen got back. She certainly couldn't imagine going out to the farm and confronting Karl—with what? A scrap of blue cloth? And the irony was that the Bible was Karl's to begin with! If he now had it, the implications of his concealing it were Cullen's province. Besides, to her knowledge librarians weren't required to be brave. Resourceful, yes. Not brave.

Glynis sighed. She lifted off her straw bonnet and

fanned herself as she walked. The heat had driven almost everyone indoors, and Fall Street was empty. Even the village cats, who customarily sunned themselves on front stoops of shops and offices, had abandoned their stations.

She opened the door of the library, grateful that it was still relatively cool inside. The von Lentzes were talking to a man standing beside their table, his back to Glynis. He turned as she walked toward them, and she was surprised when their eyes made contact. Although she was sure she had never seen him before, he looked vaguely familiar.

He extended his hand. "You must be Miss Tryon. My name is Gordon Walker."

He held her hand in a firm grip. Glynis started to speak, found herself without words, and stood silent, smiling. She knew she must look like a simpleton, but what did one say to a man whose wife one had found murdered?

"We told Mr. Walker you would be back soon," said Gerta von Lentz. "I was just saying . . ."

She continued talking. Glynis was glad of the opportunity to pull herself together. She still hadn't found anything to say when the von Lentzes announced they were leaving. Glynis nodded and helped them gather together their materials.

The von Lentzes seemed oblivious to her discomfort and talked their way out the door. As it closed behind them, there was an awkward silence. Glynis took a deep breath. "Mr. Walker, please forgive my rudeness. I haven't said anything because I just don't know what to say— except that I am terribly sorry about your wife."

Walker waved his hand to dismiss her embarrassment. "Of course," he said. "The coroner told me you were the one to find Rose. It must have been difficult for you."

"Yes. Yes, it was."

"Miss Tryon, I certainly don't want to cause you any more discomfort, but I'd like to ask you a few questions, just for my own peace of mind. Would you permit me to do so?"

Glynis nodded, motioning him toward her office, as several people were just entering the library. She assumed he wanted privacy, but she left the office door ajar so she could watch the library area. Glynis seated herself at her worktable. Gordon Walker moved to the open window. The fragrance of wisteria clusters, their woody vine creeping around an old tree just outside, drifted into the room. Walker breathed deeply.

"There's nothing in Boston that smells like that!" He stared down toward the canal.

Glynis shifted uneasily in her chair. She supposed the coroner had told him where his wife's body had been found. But he said nothing, just stood quietly looking down the slope.

Glynis watched him; his face was in profile. Elizabeth Stanton was right, she thought: he was a handsome man. Almost pretty, in fact, like a romantic poet . . . and that was why he looked familiar!

She glanced into the library at the Harlowe steel engraving of George Gordon Byron hanging next to the poetry shelves. Not the same—this man's hair was dark blond—but a similar look, nonetheless. He seemed out of place in Seneca Falls, with his wide scarf-cravat covering most of his shirtfront. While Cullen would call it dandified, Glynis had seen the same sort of cravat on Harriet's son, Niles, whenever he left New York City long enough to visit his mother. But then, Niles *was* a bit of a dandy.

Gordon Walker seated himself in her wing chair; he appeared to be studying her.

"Forgive me, Miss Tryon, but may I say that you do not look at all like my idea of a librarian. Not in the least." His smile indicated this was fortunate.

"Dare I ask, Mr. Walker, what that idea might be?" Glynis's smile was internal: she had not played this game for a long time.

"My experience in Boston," he said, "has been that there the few female librarians are dry old ladies with steel-framed spectacles, and hair pulled back so tightly their lips scarcely move when they talk. And they wear black, black dresses which button up over their chins."

Glynis restrained a smile and resisted the impulse to

check her dress's top buttons. "I believe, Mr. Walker, you wanted to ask me some questions."

Walker leaned forward, his fingers gripping the arms of the wing chair. "I read the transcript of the coroner's inquest. I know you talked to Rose the day before . . ." He hesitated, clearing his throat. "The day before she died."

Glynis nodded. And wished she were somewhere else.

"I wondered," he went on, "if she said anything to you about why she was here?"

"I knew nothing other than the reason she gave me," Glynis said, "which was that she'd come to see Elizabeth Stanton. Now, of course, I understand why she was so anxious to meet with Mrs. Stanton."

"Then you weren't aware that she was Friedrich Steicher's daughter?" he said.

"I wasn't even aware that Friedrich had a daughter until . . . well, until the time of the inquest." She did not intend to give him further details. Her relationship with Friedrich, after all, was not Gordon Walker's business.

But his next words were, "I've been told that you and Mr. Steicher were close friends. Please don't misunderstand, Miss Tryon. I'm just trying to determine whether he might have talked to you, or anyone for that matter, about Rose."

"I'm sorry, Mr. Walker, I can't help you. He didn't talk to me about your wife, but then there's no reason why he should have. Friedrich Steicher funded this library and took a continued interest in it. That was the basis of our acquaintance."

Gordon Walker's eyes were on her hands, and she realized she was plucking apart a daisy she had lifted from the vase on her table. She dropped the petals in the trash basket. Whatever Gordon Walker was searching for in Seneca Falls was nothing she could give him.

She stood up. "Mr. Walker, I'm truly sorry about your wife's death. But there's nothing I can tell you that would shed any light on whether she was Friedrich's daughter."

"She *was* his daughter! That's why she came here, to try and receive some small part of what her father had denied her all those years. How would you feel, Miss Tryon, if you were suddenly told about a father you didn't know existed, a father who had ignored you all your life? How would any daughter feel when she understood that her father didn't love her?" His voice scaled upward.

Glynis thought of her own father, who had seemed unable to love anyone. Her eyes began to fill, and she walked quickly to the office door. Poor Rose. Poor Gordon Walker.

He rose, saying quickly, "I'm sorry, Miss Tryon. I let my emotions run away with me, and I apologize. It's just very difficult—"

"Mr. Walker, you surely don't have to apologize. I feel so bad about what happened. It must be a terrible strain for you, being here."

"Thank you. You're very kind."

The library now was empty. As Glynis was seeing Gordon Walker to the door, he stopped in front of the bookshelves next to her desk. "Friedrich Steicher must have been very fond of books to fund this library," he remarked.

"Books were his great enthusiasm," Glynis agreed. "He was a collector, as well as a reader, and this library benefitted greatly from that."

"Did he donate books then, as well as funds? That is, I can't help but notice his name on the binding of many of these."

"Those were his," Glynis said. "He bound them himself, before he brought them here."

"Then you were familiar with his collection? I mean, had you ever seen any of those he didn't donate?"

Glynis suddenly was afraid she knew where he was going with this. "Those he didn't donate?" she said. "I'm not sure what you mean." She moved toward the door.

"Without beating around the bush, Miss Tryon, what I mean to ask is, did you ever see a Bible of Steicher's? The kind that might contain a family chronicle, of marriages, deaths—"

"And births?" Glynis interrupted. There was no point in pretending ignorance—he would know soon enough anyway. "Yes, Mr. Walker. The Steicher family has—had such a Bible, though whether it chronicled those things, I don't know. I never opened it."

"What do you mean, the family *had* a Bible?"

"Through an error, the Bible was here for a time. It isn't anymore."

Walker stared at her as though he didn't believe her. "What are you saying? Do you know where it is now?"

"No." Glynis could see that he wasn't going to give up until he had it all. "It was taken from the library."

"Taken? Do you mean to say it was stolen?"

"I mean stolen. And since you are no doubt going to ask me, yes, it was after your wife died. I don't know exactly when—no one does. And I don't know by whom."

"I think by whom is obvious, Miss Tryon. Who gains if that Bible vanishes, if indeed the birth of a daughter is recorded in it? I know about Karl Steicher. I know he has claimed his father had no other children, that Friedrich Steicher's estate belongs to him alone. It would seem apparent who has that Bible."

"Well no, Mr. Walker, it is not apparent because, you see, Karl Steicher says he doesn't have it. And, in any event, he says the Bible does not record the name of any child born to Friedrich other than himself."

Glynis thought Gordon Walker was going to laugh. But he was too polite. Instead he just smiled and nodded. "What I see, Miss Tryon, is that you're going to defend Friedrich Steicher's son."

"Mr. Walker—"

"No. No, don't apologize. I admire loyalty. And I've put you in an uncomfortable position, for which I'm sorry. I don't blame you. In fact, I envy Karl Steicher. I wish you were on my side in this."

"You're right about making me uncomfortable," Glynis said. "Believe me, I wish I could help you."

She opened the door. Oppressive heat surged into the library, and the steps beyond seemed to rise and fall as if on waves.

Gordon Walker stood in the doorway. "Good day, Miss

Tryon. I am most glad to have met you. I only hope we can talk again about more pleasant things." He smiled and took her hand before he walked out the door. Slipping off his suit jacket, he slung it over his shoulder, turned to smile at her again, and ran up the steps to Fall Street.

Glynis's neighbor, Aurora Usher, was standing at the top of the steps. Glynis saw Aurora quickly adjust her bonnet over her bedraggled blond curls. Before Glynis turned to go back inside, she saw Gordon Walker hesitate on the top step. Aurora Usher smiled at him and extended her hand.

# TWENTY

❧

SEVERAL HOURS LATER when Glynis stepped out of the library, she felt a shift in the air. It was still hot. But wind was swirling dust in the road, layering a fine coat of grit over everything in its path. Glynis looked to the west, where immense pink-and-gold-lined thunderheads were rapidly building like fairy-tale castles. A storm would clear the air, but she'd better get home fast.

As Glynis neared her boardinghouse, she passed the young Usher sisters' brown brick house, looming against the sky with its dark-gabled pitched roof and black shutters. Poe would have approved, she thought, smiling at the happenstance. How many families named Usher were there?

Just ahead was Harriet Peartree's white Gothic cottage, inherited from her favorite husband. The Usher sisters were standing with Harriet's other boarder, Dictras Fyfe, who was leaning on his scythe handle at the edge of short grass. He appeared to be listening attentively to them. Mr. Fyfe's neat white head was bowed; his slight frame inclined forward from his waist in a courtly stance.

Duncan's shaggy white coat and whiskers were veiled with dust from the road. He ran to plant his front paws on Glynis's skirt. Glynis lifted him and held him at arm's length, shook him like a mop, and released him on the sweet-smelling grass. A far-off rumble made her glance up; the thunderheads looked closer, towering above the treetops.

Vanessa Usher gave a soft moan and shook her head on its long neck. Glynis had often wondered if Vanessa pulled her black hair back so tightly into its chignon to keep facial lines at bay. But that would be a trifle premature, since Vanessa was younger than she.

"We've had so much rain this summer," Vanessa complained. "I declare, it's just like the Great Flood of Genesis—perhaps because Seneca Falls is becoming such a wanton place."

Glynis bit her lip to keep from smiling.

"We might just as well be living down in . . . oh, you know, Glynis, dear." Vanessa waved her arm toward the thunderheads. "Down there where that war is?"

"Mexico," Glynis said. "The war was over in February, Vanessa."

Aurora Usher, pretty as Vanessa but corn-tassel blond and smelling of jasmine, laughed nervously and then turned to Mr. Fyfe. "Do you think we're in for a bad storm?" she said, her voice anxious.

Mr. Fyfe stood a bit straighter, studied the sky, cleared his throat, and said, "Could be."

"I just knew it," Vanessa groaned. "All of you better get down on your knees and pray. Pray the storm doesn't ruin our musicale tomorrow."

"A musicale?" Glynis had asked six years ago, when she had been in Seneca Falls only a few months and it was learned that she played flute. "A musicale here? In Seneca Falls?"

Vanessa had taken a step or two backward, tilted up her chin, and sent down her elegant nose a look that Glynis could only describe as withering. .

"My dear Miss Tryon." The chin had gone up another notch. "We are not all primitives here. *Some* of us make every effort to expose our fellow man to the finer things."

As would always be the case, Aurora had rushed in to deflect Vanessa's cudgel. "Our mother started the musicales long ago; they've become rather a tradition for celebrating the summer solstice. Of course, you couldn't be expected to know that." And Aurora had smiled her conciliatory, please-don't-mind-Vanessa smile.

But, as Glynis had discovered, for all that it often

seemed Vanessa had been trained in generosity and tact by the Prince of Darkness, she played harpsichord like an archangel. Glynis had not been able to figure this out, unless it was one of nature's more spectacular acts of compensation.

A sudden streak of lightning was followed by a long roll of thunder. Mr. Fyfe swung the scythe over his shoulder, and they all moved quickly toward the Peartree porch. Duncan was already there, waiting by the front door.

Glynis went directly upstairs to her room to change her damp shirt. When she came down she started for the kitchen, where she heard the Usher sisters talking. Harriet stepped out into the hall to meet her.

"Glynis. You look exhausted."

"It's the heat, Harriet. But we're in for a storm any minute."

"I hope it cools things off. I can't remember a June so hot."

"How are the musicale preparations coming?" Glynis said to Aurora as she went into the kitchen. "Everything ready?"

"Heavens, no! We've got a houseful of cooks and cleaning help, and the gardener is cursing the heat—all the flowers are wilting. I just hope this storm doesn't ruin his hard work."

Vanessa had draped herself over a kitchen chair. "Glynis, I didn't want to gossip in front of dear Mr. Fyfe," she said sweetly, "but we heard you had the most fascinating visitor this afternoon at the library."

Here we go, Glynis thought. Vanessa would try to wring information out of her, drop by drop. "I'm sure Aurora's told you all about him, Vanessa." She collapsed in a chair in front of the window. The curtains had been fluttering, but now they began to billow into the room.

"We should get home, Van, before this storm hits," Aurora said, moving toward the back door. A deep roll of thunder sounded. It instantly became darker in the kitchen, as though a cloak had been thrown over the house.

"Better stay put now, until it's over," Harriet said.

"Do you suppose our housekeeper has enough sense to close the windows?" Vanessa said to her sister. "I think that woman's getting senile lately; she seems to ignore me most of the time."

Aurora shot Glynis a long-suffering look, and said, "So what did you think of Gordon Walker?"

"I thought he was very pleasant, especially under the circumstances. Didn't you?"

"I was just on my way to you when he came out of the library. I didn't realize you'd seen me."

"Apparently once you saw Gordon Walker, you didn't realize anything," Vanessa said. She turned to Glynis. "Aurora said he was the most handsome man she'd ever laid eyes on. What a shame he's so recently widowed."

Glynis heard Vanessa's voice vibrating with insincerity. She had never figured out exactly how old the Usher sisters were, and they had certainly never volunteered the information. Harriet guessed, from something she had heard them say, that Vanessa was the older of the two by a few years, and probably just a year or two younger than Glynis. Glynis found this hard to believe—she thought of Vanessa as perpetually hovering somewhere around the brat stage of early childhood.

Lightning flashed through the darkness. Glynis counted three before the thunder rolled. The curtains were streaming around her; she turned and shut the window. Cool air began to flow through the open door.

"My, that feels good," Harriet said. She closed the door with a reluctant sigh as rain began to pelt through, followed by a loud clap of thunder. "Getting close." She lit an oil lamp and set it on the table.

Western New York was known for its violent summer thunderstorms. Where was Cullen? Was he somewhere in the middle of this?

A tremendous crack of thunder rattled the windowpane. The ground beneath the house shook. The women all jumped, then grinned nervously at one other.

"Sounded like lightning hit somewhere close by," Aurora said, trying to peer through the rain-blurred window.

Vanessa moaned. "The garden—everything will be an absolute shambles."

Glynis got up, lit another lamp, and went down the hall to look for Duncan. He was stretched out asleep at the bottom of the basement stairs. Thunderstorms never seemed to bother him; she supposed they wouldn't bother her either if she hadn't seen the damage they could do. She hated them.

She thought it would calm her to move about, but the sound of tree branches striking the house and thunderclaps booming overhead drove her back to the kitchen. The three other women were sitting silently, staring out the window—at what, Glynis couldn't imagine, since the rain obscured everything.

She knew they were listening. They all worried about lightning-set fires, although it was doubtful whether they would hear the fire bells over the wind and thunder. But they listened; fire was the single most dangerous event in a town where most structures were wood.

In one sense, Glynis knew it was irrational of her to fret so about lightning, when far more fires were ignited by the volatile burning fluids used to create light. Nearly all, except the expensive whale oil, consisted of turpentine and alcohol combinations, which were unstable and explosive. But she felt she could control that danger to some extent. Against the storms, she felt powerless.

Another thunderclap split the sky directly overhead; she hunched her shoulders and screwed her eyes shut. The window chattered. Lightning and thunder resounded like huge sheets of paper crackling over drums in a cave.

She opened the door an inch to see the pine trees thrashing in the wind. Birches bent almost to the ground, their slender branches lashing like long strands of hair. The muscles in her neck felt knotted. She reached back and kneaded them with her fingers.

Harriet came to stand beside her, putting an arm around her shoulders. She said softly, "Cullen's all right, Glynis. Never knew a man who could take better care of himself. Don't worry."

Suddenly the wind began to die, as quickly as it had risen. The storm moved off, and the rain diminished. Harriet opened the window and door; the air streamed in, cool and smelling fresher than it had for days.

"I guess we'd better go and survey the damage to the garden," Aurora said.

Vanessa stood up and said to Glynis, "Do you think we should rehearse the music one last time, tonight?"

"No, I don't!" Glynis said. "We've rehearsed those pieces almost to death—there'll be no spark left tomorrow night."

Vanessa looked doubtful. But she said, "Very well. I trust you're right. And your flute, as usual, sounds good. By the way, have you heard anything from Cullen Stuart? Will he be back in time?"

"Yes, that's right, Glynis," Aurora said. "Gordon Walker wanted to talk to Cullen. I walked with him to the lockup, but that young man Cullen left in charge said he didn't know anything about the posse yet. What have you heard?"

"Nothing. And I have no idea when they'll be back, though I doubt it will be before tomorrow night."

"Aurora invited Gordon Walker to the musicale," Vanessa said.

Harriet frowned. "Isn't it a little soon after his wife's death for him to be attending a party?"

Aurora shook her head. "I told him it was an annual affair, and not exactly a party. More a concert, really."

Harriet rolled her eyes at Glynis.

"Anyway," Vanessa said, "he told Aurora he would be honored to attend."

"Aurora," Glynis asked, "are Karl and Nell Steicher going to be there?"

"I assume so. They were invited, and they always have come."

That could be unpleasant, Glynis thought. But she couldn't say anything to the Ushers about the conversation she'd had with Gordon Walker.

"I think it's delightful that Mr. Walker will be coming,"

Vanessa said with a smile. "The poor man, all alone here. And he can't be intending to stay a widower forever."

"Van, that's tasteless!" Aurora said. "How can you say that kind of thing?"

"Well, heaven knows we can certainly use another handsome man in this town. *I* haven't taken any vow not to get married." Vanessa pouted, looking at Glynis. "And I must say, I think it's rather unfair for someone who *has* to monopolize the most attractive men around."

Aurora and Harriet both interrupted her, but Glynis was already through the kitchen doorway. Out in the hall, she heard their voices scolding.

Aurora caught up with her just as she was about to climb the stairs. "Glynis, I apologize for my tactless sister—I seem to spend half my life doing that! You know how she is. Please think nothing of it. I'm sure she doesn't even realize what she said. She never thinks! Maybe she *can't*, for all I know."

"Never mind, Aurora. I'm just tired. And I should be used to Vanessa by this time."

Aurora sighed. "Before we go, there was something I wanted to tell you. You might find it interesting."

Glynis stopped with her hand on the bannister. Aurora moved closer to her, as though she didn't want her voice to carry into the kitchen. "I was having dinner at the Hotel Bristol the other night with Lydia and Ambrose Abernathy. As a matter of fact, you were there with Cullen and that German couple."

Glynis nodded.

"Well," Aurora continued, "when Lydia and I were in the ladies' parlor after dinner, she told me that Ambrose said it didn't surprise him at all to hear that Friedrich Steicher had relatives in Boston."

Glynis had to think—didn't Friedrich's brother live in Boston?—before she said, "Aurora, wasn't Ambrose Abernathy Friedrich's banker?"

"Yes, of course. Glynis, Ambrose is *everyone's* banker."

"But did she say what he meant by that?" Glynis asked. "*Why* wasn't Ambrose surprised?"

"She didn't tell me. She just said she thought it was an odd thing for him to say. She didn't say more."

Vanessa appeared in the hall. "Glynis dear, I'm sure I don't know why you're upset. I would never say anything to offend you. I simply meant it was unfortunate that for some odd reason men seem to like you, even though you so obviously care nothing about—"

"Enough, Vanessa. Good night!"

Glynis climbed the stairs to her room. She was sitting on the bed when Duncan padded through the doorway and jumped up beside her. She put her face down and buried it in his fur. What a day it had been. She knew she should think about what Aurora had just told her, but she couldn't. She felt shaky, as though she was going to cry.

She awakened to the sound of rifle shots. She struggled upright, opening her eyes to see Harriet standing outside the half-open door of her bedroom, her knuckles poised to rap again.

"Glynis, are you asleep?"

"Not anymore. Come in, Harriet."

"I knocked several times. You must have been dead to the world."

"What time is it?"

"About eight. I called you for supper an hour ago. I thought you might be sleeping—didn't think it was worth waking you then. But I have something here I think you'll want to see."

Harriet came toward the bed holding out a brown envelope. "Pete Morrow stopped by a few minutes ago with this for you. It's from Cullen, Glynis. Pete and the others of the posse are back. Jacques Sundown stayed with Cullen."

Glynis lunged toward the edge of her bed, gripping the bedpost. "Harriet, what's happened to Cullen?"

"Nothing's happened to him. Pete said they were all fine. The letter will probably explain everything."

She handed the envelope to Glynis. "Come down and eat when you've finished reading it. You look like you could use some food."

When Harriet left, Glynis ripped open the envelope and anxiously read the contents:

Thursday, June 22

Glynis—

Am staying at an inn across the road from Auburn Prison with Jacques Sundown. We're waiting on the circuit judge to get here from Syracuse, to hold trial for the men we captured. These trials are usually dispatched quickly—I'll leave here as soon as it's over, so will probably be back in S.F. by next week's end.

Have picked up some interesting information, here in Auburn, about our friend the hotel manager. Sheridan apparently has a long history with women—women and money—none of it good.

Seems on one occasion he was caught, how do they say? in 'a compromising situation' with another man's wife. The husband tried to shoot Sheridan but missed him. (Unfortunately!) Couple of weeks later Sheridan supposedly ran off with the wife and the husband's money. Sheridan was arrested, but the woman's husband for some reason refused to press charges, so Sheridan wasn't brought to trial. There are quite a few of these stories floating around involving S.S. and women.

And rumor has it that he worked in at least two other hotels in western N.Y., in Elmira and then Ithaca, and left both of them under some kind of cloud concerning money—the hotels' money. Am trying to run those stories to ground. In the meantime, you be careful with Mr. Sheridan!

Other than being hot and bone tired, am all right. So don't worry. I can't get home fast enough. I will not be sorry to miss the Usher ladies' party, but I do sorely miss their flute player.

Yours,
Cullen

# TWENTY-ONE

⚓

GLYNIS HAD LONG ago recognized that it was the closest she would come to flying: the sensation of her and the flute and the notes airborne. A swoop under the harpsichord's light tinkling to hover just above the cello, a steep climb over the violin to soar in the rarified octave above high C. The silvery bright tones of a lark, then the glide down to flutter-tongued pigeon tones, breathy and dense.

Now she could hear the applause but thought if a railroad train had rumbled across the Usher lawn in the midst of the last piece, she never would have known.

She looked at Vanessa standing beside the harpsichord bench, and shook her head slightly: no more encores. Apparently of the same mind was Martin Seward, who lifted his cello by the neck with one hand, embraced its body with the other arm, and danced off the low platform. But Brendan Fitzwater waved his violin at the audience. Glynis gave him a slight nudge from behind to get him off; he would play all night given half a chance.

She stepped down from the platform and went to the terrace, where she had left her flute case. Aurora approached, handing her a glass of lemonade. "It went splendidly, Glynis. Did you hear that applause?"

Glynis nodded. "I thought Vanessa was going to keep us up there forever—it seemed as though we'd been playing for hours."

"Miss Tryon, I enjoyed your playing enormously." Gordon Walker had appeared behind Aurora. "I was surprised to hear something so professional-sounding outside of

Boston," he said. "You and your group are fine musicians."

Aurora moved closer to him. "Mr. Walker, you mustn't think we're completely without the finer things of life here. And you probably couldn't know that Glynis's mother was a distinguished pianist."

Gordon Walker stood watching as Glynis took a thin metal rod out of her case and wrapped a soft cloth around it. She ran it up and down inside the black flute tubes.

"Your flute seems to be wood; what kind?" he asked.

"Cocuswood," she told him. "It has a mellower sound than ivory." She finished swabbing the tubes and placed them in the case, giving the silver keys and mouth-hole band a cursory swipe with the cloth. Aurora was called by someone on the other side of the terrace and drifted away.

"Your mother was a musician?" Walker asked. "Mine was too. A singer. In fact, my father met her when she was performing with a troupe in Milan. Of course, after she and Father married, she didn't perform anymore.

"You can imagine," he added, smiling, "what my father's upper-class English family said when he arrived back in Boston with a bride who was not only a performer, but Italian as well. That she was also very beautiful didn't help much."

"Not easy for your mother," Glynis said.

"Or for Father either. But he married for love. As I did."

Ah, Glynis thought, so Rose was not of the same social class as the Walkers. How hard it must have been for Mary Clarke, a woman alone, with a daughter to support.

"My mother died when I was nine," Walker said. He frowned slightly. "I ran away from home a number of times after that. It added to Father's distress, which delighted me; I always thought he must be to blame for her death."

Glynis could understand that. When her own mother had died, she blamed everyone. The most terrible realization, which came much later, was to find that she blamed most of all her mother. The shame of that discovery had never quite gone away.

"Miss Tryon, I think I should say good night now. But before I go, could you point out Karl Steicher to me? And his wife." Walker gestured toward the throng of people on the Usher lawn.

Glynis remembered seeing Karl just before she started playing. She looked toward the crowd, hoping she wouldn't see him now.

Walker apparently read her mind. "I'm not going to speak to him, Miss Tryon, and risk a nasty scene here. This is hardly the place for a confrontation, if for no other reason than that he's among friends, and I'm not. I just want to know what he looks like."

That sounded reasonable enough. Glynis looked over the people who could be seen from where she stood. The light was dusky and she found herself squinting, still hoping that Karl was there, but hidden from her in the deepening shadows.

Candles in the ornamental tin lanterns were being lit and hung on trees by the Ushers' domestic servants. "I'm sorry, Mr. Walker, I can't seem to find him. It *is* getting rather dark."

Vanessa came swirling across the lawn toward them, fringed shawl and ribbons floating around her. "My dear Mr. Walker, you've been hiding back here too long. You must come and meet all our neighbors. I'm sure they're just dying to talk to you."

One simply never knew what ghastly thing Vanessa would come out with. The man's wife had been murdered here, just days ago; Glynis could hardly look at Gordon Walker for embarrassment. But he didn't seem to hear, or chose to ignore.

"Miss Usher, I was just about to take my leave." He smiled at Vanessa's protestations and patted her hand, which rested on his arm. "No, I'm sorry. I think I really must go. So kind of you to ask me for the music. I enjoyed it thoroughly."

He turned to Glynis, bowed slightly and, with Vanessa still clinging to his arm, began walking toward the street. Inclining his head toward Vanessa, he said something to her, and she turned back toward the lawn and scanned the crowd for a moment. Then she gestured toward a clump of birches, where Glynis now saw Karl Steicher talking with Jeremiah Merrycoyf. Glynis turned back to look at Gordon Walker; his expression was inscrutable. He abruptly extricated himself from Vanessa's grasp, bowed to her, and walked away.

Vanessa returned to Glynis. "What an engaging man. I do wish he hadn't thought he should go so soon. But I suppose he still feels he should grieve. How long does that sort of thing usually take, do you know, Glynis?"

Glynis felt herself more than usually stupefied by Vanessa. She walked briskly toward the relative solitude of the back porch steps, where she sat looking out across the lawn. In the flickering light of what must have been hundreds of candles hung from trees in tin lanterns, women in soft summer dresses moved from shadow to shadow. The men's swallow-tailed evening suits and high-collared white shirts made them look like tall birds, bobbing and bending toward their companions. Glynis smiled to herself at the varied birdlife of Seneca Falls. And a lot of it was there that night. She guessed there might have been as many as a hundred or more people grouped across the lawn.

She picked out Ambrose Abernathy, who rocked back and forth on his heels while listening to Seabury Gould and the Reverend Magnus Justine discuss something that made them all frown. From a shadowed corner Lydia Abernathy emerged into the candlelight. Her blonde hair was swept back from her face into a coil interwoven with ribbon and flowers; her gown was rose-colored silk that seemed to be reflected in her cheeks.

Simon Sheridan appeared under black-barked locust trees in full bloom, clumped strategically in the northwest corner of the Usher property; every breeze that crossed the lawn carried the heavy, honey-orange fragrance from their long pendants of white flowers.

Directly below Glynis, Harriet and Aurora stepped toward the terrace and began directing the placement of long rectangular tables spread with white damask tablecloths, looped up at the corners with bunches of daisies and buttercups. The domestic help began the parade of desserts.

Glynis recognized Daisy Ross among the women Aurora had hired for the evening and thought how tired the young woman looked. Daisy stood for a moment, listlessly smoothing a tablecloth, then she turned toward the steps where Glynis sat. Her forehead creased. Glynis was about to identify herself, thinking Daisy couldn't see in the candlelight, when the young woman started toward her. Someone called her name from inside the house. Daisy hesitated, then turned and went inside; but before that, Glynis thought she saw the glitter of tears.

In the center of each table stood a tower of molded Charlotte Russe: sponge cake filled with rich custard and ornamented with whipped-cream frosting and sugar-candy flowers. Each tower was surrounded by baskets filled with alternate layers of Silver and Gold cakes—one made with egg whites, the other with the yolks. Strawberry and rhubarb tarts and pies and strawberry shortcake were dolloped with thick cream. Cut-glass compotes held Shrewsbury, lemon, and nut tea cakes; others displayed sweet or savory puddings, turned out from earthenware molds, or creamy custards laced with brandy.

Another table held Country Syllabub: sugar, cider, milk, and brandy whipped together, so frothy it had to be eaten with spoons. There were peach, raspberry, and strawberry cordials. Black tea sent up a flowery fragrance; orange sassafras tea was sweetened with honey. A crystal bowl foamed with Roman punch: lemon juice, sugar, beaten egg whites, and rum. There were whiskies and wine and brandy, and coffee in silver pots.

Aurora walked over to the foot of the porch steps, wringing her hands. "Do you think there will be enough?"

"Enough for what, Aurora?" Glynis said. "The entire population of New York State?" She stood and came down the steps.

People on the lawn began to drift toward the tables. Glynis stepped off the terrace and walked down a stone path through a small cottage garden. She was sure the Ushers had had it planted with the evening party in mind; its pale flowers gleamed in the light of the lanterns hung from tree branches overhead. She heard someone on the path behind her and turned to look up at Karl Steicher.

They were some distance from the crowd now gathered on the terrace. Glynis believed that this was not a chance meeting, that Karl had seen her and come after her; it was not that dark, and her gown was ivory silk that gleamed like the flowers. She waited for him to speak.

Karl always seemed very large to her, yet he was probably not much above average height, about the same as Gordon Walker, and some shorter than Cullen. Karl was broad-chested, with wide shoulders, but he didn't look heavy. Perhaps it was his energy, a kind of coiled-tight tension, that made him seem bigger.

He stared down at her. "I wanted to talk to you before I leave. Nell said to thank you for the books you sent out to the farm for her and the children."

"Isn't Nell here?" Glynis looked behind him toward the terrace.

"No. She didn't come. She feels uncomfortable with crowds right now."

Glynis nodded. There was an attitude among many that expectant mothers should avoid social events and confine themselves to their homes, as though pregnancy were a somehow shameful condition that shouldn't be paraded in public—as though it made evident an activity in which people pretended they themselves never engaged.

"I don't feel all that comfortable myself," he added. "Wouldn't have come tonight if I hadn't thought I had to."

Glynis waited, wondering what had really prompted him to seek her out. Surely it was more than Nell's message.

"The rumors," he said. "The talk that I had something to do with that woman's death. I know what everybody's saying. Figured if I didn't show up, people would believe I was hiding something. Afraid."

"I don't think everyone would believe that," she said.

"Maybe not." He stood as if both his feet were planted

in the path. "Anyway, I don't give a tinker's damn what people think. I didn't kill that woman. And nobody's got any right to say I did."

Why was he saying this to her?

"Nell thinks I was uncivil to you the other day at the farm. I don't much care for you, Miss Tryon. I think you're out of place in this town, and that my father was the only reason you came to Seneca Falls."

Glynis averted her eyes from his. What could she say?

"Look, I don't mean to talk about that now," he said quickly. "What I wanted to do was apologize for the other day. I shouldn't have been rude. That's all."

"That's not all!" Glynis said. She startled herself, but she didn't want the conversation to end this way; there was some reason for his apology, other than an attack of conscience or Nell's comment. "Karl, why are you apologizing? I do think you were rude, but why bother yourself? What do you care what I think?"

He looked away, as if trying to decide whether to answer. Finally, his tone a bit less brusque, he said, "Jeremiah Merrycoyf told me that you don't believe I killed Rose Walker. I'm obliged to you for that. Maybe you can convince the constable to stop concentrating on me and look elsewhere for a killer."

Glynis decided to take a chance. "I want to believe you're innocent of Rose Walker's murder, Karl," she said. "But you make it difficult. I don't think you're telling the truth about the evening she died. Not that I think you killed her, but—"

He shot her a fierce look that she couldn't read, turned abruptly, and strode back toward the terrace. She watched him speak briefly to Aurora, then cross the lawn toward the horses and carriages.

Glynis frowned, wishing she had been less outspoken, and went unwilling back to the terrace and the groaning tables.

# TWENTY-TWO

SEVERAL HOURS LATER, Brendan Fitzwater bent over and laid his violin carefully in its case. He then very slowly collapsed at the edge of the platform. At first there was no alarm among those around him. Brendan was a prankster; everyone assumed he was clowning. But when he did not respond to offers of yet another glass of whiskey, friends then had reason for concern. Quentin Ives was frantically summoned to the platform, and the party held its breath.

"Too much fiddling, too much whiskey," was Dr. Ives's diagnosis. Brendan was hoisted with a cheer and carried into the house to sleep off his excesses.

Glynis watched the proceedings without much worry. She knew Brendan. Ives returned to the little group on the lawn and dropped back into his chair. Jeremiah Merrycoyf said to Katherine Ives, "A demanding profession, medicine."

Katherine sighed and nodded. "It goes in fits and starts. There are stretches where he's home every night, like a normal husband, and then others when I won't see him for days at a time."

Glynis thought of Cullen—and resolved not to. From where she sat, she could see that a few people had already left. Simon Sheridan had gone before the desserts were served, pleading a busy night at the hotel and making Vanessa lament the curious lack of eligible men that year. She did this every year, Glynis recalled.

She hadn't realized until Karl left that all five members of the library board had been present at the Ushers' that night; it was fairly obvious who was disputing her contract renewal. The rumor had come to her from Aurora by way of Lydia Abernathy. Glynis assumed it was accurate; Ambrose Abernathy was a member of the board. The other members were Karl Steicher, Jeremiah Merrycoyf, Seabury S. Gould, and, of course, the Reverend Magnus Justine.

She had eliminated Merrycoyf, if for no other reason than her certainty that he would have told her if he had reservations about her library contract.

At the moment, Seabury Gould was seated opposite her, describing the erratic performance of windmills with regard to pumping water for railroad trains. Often trains were delayed for days, like ships becalmed on a windless sea, Glynis imagined. The problem could be solved, Gould explained, by steam-powered pumps. A handsome, intelligent man, Gould was clean-shaven but for his long-whiskered sideburns that quivered with enthusiasm. He had just become president of a newly formed pump manufacturing company, and though Glynis was not wildly interested in pumps, Seabury S. Gould could make them sound like the saviours of humankind. She hoped he was satisfied with her work. Not just because he was persuasive. Because she liked him.

Friedrich Steicher had stacked the board with associates, and Glynis had wondered if her present problems with Justine were due to some concealed rancor toward his deceased sponsor. But no—she had probably rancored him sufficiently all by herself.

Earlier, the reverend had approached her. In the warm weather his prominent jaw lay pillowed on sweaty jowls; she had to stop herself from envisioning a neighbor's bulldog.

"You looked quite fetching, playing this evening, Miss Tryon," he had said. "How very appropriate that you are a flutist. Tell me, do you know the story of the Pied Piper?"

Glynis had stared at him. Of course she knew. She had a sudden image of herself tootling her flute down Fall Street, while followed behind by all the . . . Surely the

Reverend Justine didn't really think of Seneca Falls's library patrons as rats or as children.

She had walked away from him without reply. What could she do but hope that Karl and Justine wouldn't convince another board member of her inadequacy?

Suddenly she saw Daisy Ross come out the side door with her apron bundled under her arm. Glynis got to her feet, excused herself from the group on the lawn, and walked quickly toward the house, calling to Daisy. The young woman paused by the front porch, where Glynis caught up with her. In the light of the three-quarter moon just emerging from clouds, Daisy's face looked haggard, and her whole body slumped.

"Are you on your way home?" Glynis asked.

Daisy nodded. "The Usher ladies wanted me to stay, but I can't. I have to get home to the children. I left my oldest to look after the others—she's only ten."

Ten! thought Glynis. How old was Daisy? Perhaps twenty-five. Perhaps.

"Daisy, I understand your need to get home, but should you be walking alone? Could Bobby . . ." She stopped as Daisy shook her head, and Glynis saw again the shine of tears.

"It's all right, Miss Tryon. I really have to go." She started walking toward the street. Glynis heard a soft whinny and looked ahead at the carriages lined up at the hitching rail. She remembered Bobby's performance in front of the hardware store; Daisy had no other family to turn to. She was alone.

Glynis hurried after Daisy. She caught the young woman's arm and led her toward what she thought she recognized as Brendan Fitzwater's buggy. "Come on, Daisy. I'll drive you home."

Daisy stopped and stared at Glynis. "Miss Tryon, you can't—"

"Yes, I can. Brendan's passed out cold as a mackerel. He won't be using this for hours. Get in."

"Are you sure this one is his?" Daisy's voice sounded shaky.

"If it's not, I'll probably hear about it when I get back."

Glynis unlooped the trotter's reins from the rail and gathered her skirts to climb in beside Daisy. The young woman was still staring at her. Glynis couldn't read her expression and thought it was probably just as well.

What was she doing?

What needs to be done, she told herself. Stealing a carriage. She slapped the reins lightly across the trotter's back, and they started down Cayuga Street.

I didn't steal this carriage, I just borrowed it, Glynis explained to herself some time later, as she retied the trotter to the hitching rail. And with such rationale each life of crime begins. She walked toward the glow of the Usher back lawn.

She hadn't been gone long; Daisy lived barely half a mile away, across the bridge on the south side of the canal. She had been silent during the ride, although several times she had turned toward Glynis and seemed about to say something. Each time she had turned her face away again. When Glynis pulled the trotter to a stop in front of the small gray house, she took a deep breath and asked Daisy where Bobby was.

Daisy flushed and started to climb from the carriage. Then she sat back and stared down at her hands. "I don't know where he is. He sometimes disappears for a day or two. He never tells me where he's been. I don't ask anymore."

Glynis pressed her lips together; she wanted to yell, tell Daisy that she should lock the door and not let him in, that she would be far better off if he never came back. As if that would help! Daisy hadn't asked for advice. She hadn't asked for anything. For all Glynis knew, she probably still loved the wretched man.

"Daisy, I'm sorry," was what she had said. "I'm sorry."

Now as she reached the terrace, she realized she had no idea what time it was. She saw that many had left the party. But the Iveses and Jeremiah Merrycoyf were sitting where she had left them. Probably Quentin and Katherine were glad for a night out together. And Merrycoyf had no one to go home to. His wife had died some years ago; he had not remarried. They had had no children. Glynis didn't know much else about his personal life; he rarely talked about himself.

As she started to walk toward them, she heard Aurora's voice behind her.

"Glynis, where have you been? We've been looking all over for you."

"Why?"

"Just come in the house, will you? I'll tell you in there."

Glynis followed her through the porch into the kitchen. The room was a shambles, the help up to their elbows in tubs of soapy water, stacked dishes and remnants of food everywhere. She noticed that most of the platters and servers were empty. Could all that food have been eaten?

Aurora was motioning her toward the front parlor, and she virtually pulled Glynis through the doorway. In a large stuffed chair at the far end of the room, Lydia Abernathy was dabbing at her eyes with a handkerchief. Vanessa, tragic-faced, was sitting on a cushion at her feet. She reached up and patted Lydia's hand.

"What's happened?" Glynis whispered.

Aurora pushed Glynis back out of the room. "It was dreadful," she said. "Vanessa was talking to Lydia and Ambrose—so I'm told. I didn't hear the beginning of it. Van asked Ambrose how it was that he knew Friedrich Steicher had some connection with Boston. You know, Glynis, I told you about that last night. Unfortunately, I told Van, too. Really, she is such a ninny—"

"Go on," Glynis interrupted. Of course Vanessa was a ninny. That went without saying.

"Well," Aurora said, "Ambrose just exploded. I mean he was furious! He turned on poor Lydia and absolutely snarled at her: 'How dare you trumpet my confidential comments to the world?' he roared—he really did roar, Glynis. It was appalling."

"He did have a point, though," Glynis said. She would have been more amused if Vanessa's question had been less important. "So what happened then? Did everybody on the lawn overhear this?"

"No, thank goodness, I don't think so. The three of them were in a far corner of the terrace, and everyone else was too far away to hear the actual conversation. But they could hardly have missed Ambrose's bellowing. Then he just turned on his heel and left."

"He left the party? Without his wife? Sorry; of course he did—she's in the parlor. Well, it must have been exciting, Aurora."

Aurora raised her eyebrows. "You have odd ideas about what's exciting," she said. "Poor Lydia."

Glynis didn't know how sorry she should be for Lydia: she did know she wanted an answer to Vanessa's question of Ambrose.

"Aurora, I need to talk to Lydia alone. Please help me out."

She started through the doorway before Aurora could refuse. When Lydia saw her, she looked up at Glynis with reddened eyes, dabbing at them again.

"I really must try to get home," she said, rising from the chair. "Perhaps," she said, turning to Vanessa, "you could find someone to drive me?"

Glynis said quickly, "I'm sure there are people left who can do that, Lydia. While Vanessa and Aurora ask them, I'd be happy to stay here with you." She gave Aurora what she hoped was a significant stare.

Aurora's forehead wrinkled, but then she rallied. "Yes, yes, we'll be glad to help."

She took Vanessa's arm and tugged. Vanessa frowned. "I don't see why we *both* have to go." But Aurora dragged her across the parlor and out the door, still protesting. Lydia stared after them.

"I need to talk to you, Lydia," Glynis said. "It's about the business of Friedrich Steicher having had some connection with Boston. How did your husband know that? Before it came out at the inquest?"

Lydia stood very still. "Please, Glynis, I'm sure Aurora

told you what happened earlier. I really can't say any more about it."

Glynis thought a moment. It was important to know, and Lydia was not very bright. It would be crude, but . . .

"Well, I'm sorry, Lydia," she said, "but I'm afraid you're going to have to say more. You can either talk to me now or to Cullen Stuart when he gets back. I don't know how your husband would feel about you being questioned by the police. . . ."

"Oh, my God," Lydia gasped. "Oh, no. I don't want that."

Her face was pale, and Glynis thought she looked frightened. Could the woman be that afraid of her husband?

Lydia cleared her throat several times. "I think it was the day after the inquest, when Ambrose said he wasn't surprised to learn that Friedrich Steicher had a relative in Boston. I didn't know exactly what he meant at first. Then I realized that he was talking about Friedrich's brother. I'd never heard about this brother before the inquest, had you?"

Glynis nodded. "Yes, I remember Friedrich mentioning an older brother who emigrated from Germany before he did. But Lydia, what was it your husband said that made you think he was talking about a brother?"

"Because Ambrose said something about how he had transferred money of Friedrich's to a bank in Boston, for years."

"Was that *all* he said? Please think, Lydia."

Lydia nodded. "Yes. That's all. I'm sure."

Glynis sank into a chair and stared at Lydia. The existence of Friedrich's brother had become common knowledge after the inquest, she thought. So why had Ambrose gotten so angry with Lydia for repeating his comment?

A shout abruptly interrupted her thoughts, followed by loud voices on the terrace outside the parlor window. One of the voices belonged to Karl Steicher.

# TWENTY-THREE

⌒⌒⌒

GLYNIS LEANED OUT the parlor window. The only words she could distinguish were Karl's: "Nell's been hurt." And someone calling for Dr. Ives.

Lydia stood beside her with hands clasped at her breast. "Glynis, what's wrong out there?"

"I don't know. Something about Nell Steicher. Lydia, thank you for telling me what you did. If you can think of anything else your husband said about Boston, please let me know."

Lydia shook her head. "There's nothing else I can remember." She settled back into the stuffed chair. Unaccountably, she began to weep again.

Why was the woman so distraught? Her husband? Glynis had been under the impression that Ambrose Abernathy adored his beautiful young wife. She stood over Lydia, torn between the woman's distress, which she herself had intensified, and the commotion on the terrace.

More concerned voices came from outside the window. Glynis dashed out of the parlor and, after weaving quickly through the kitchen clutter, stepped onto the terrace. Karl Steicher and Quentin Ives were striding across the lawn. Jeremiah Merrycoyf and Katherine Ives were right behind them. Glynis saw Aurora standing nearby. "What's happened to Nell?"

"I don't really know," Aurora said anxiously. "Karl just ran to Dr. Ives, yelling that Nell had fallen, or something like that."

Glynis heard Ives saying, "I'm willing to go out to the farm, Karl, but I'm not Nell's physician."

They reached the terrace and stopped. Karl's face was drained of color. "Listen," he said, "I stopped by Dr. Preston's, but he wasn't home. His wife said he was out delivering a baby and she didn't know when he'd be back. Doctor, let's go! It's Saturday night—except for one old farmhand, Nell's alone with the children."

"You ride ahead then, Karl. I have to stop at the house for my bag first." Ives looked around at the small group on the terrace and spotted Glynis.

"Miss Tryon, would you come and help out? The children will need attending, and I may need your assistance myself. Karl doesn't believe his wife was badly hurt by her fall, but he thinks her labor has begun."

Karl, who had taken several steps toward the street, turned around scowling. He glanced toward Ives's wife. Katherine Ives said, "Karl, I'd come, but I don't know your wife at all, and Glynis does. And while our children aren't small, I still don't want to leave them alone all night."

Glynis looked at Karl. "Of course I'll come."

He began, "I don't think—"

"Karl, Miss Tryon can think straight in an emergency," Ives interrupted him. "Let's not argue about it."

Karl shrugged. "What difference does it make? Let's just get going!" Still scowling, he sprinted for his horse.

Glynis glanced at Quentin Ives as he reined the trotter into the dirt path leading to the farmhouse. Despite the moon, it hadn't been easy covering the distance to the Steicher place as fast as they had. But here there were lanterns lit on posts along the path.

Glynis thought about how quickly Dr. Ives had cut off Karl's protests about her coming. She wondered if he knew why Karl disliked her. He hadn't said much on the drive, just asked if she had ever helped with a birth. She had.

"I hope there won't be complications," he said. "Karl tells me his wife has had one stillbirth and a miscarriage." He sighed. "She shouldn't be having another child so soon." Glynis hadn't know about Nell's difficulties, but she wasn't surprised. The surprise was that Nell had survived. Many woman didn't; nor could they stop having children if their lives were endangered. There was no reliable method to avoid pregnancy, no safe way to abort one. Glynis knew many women died from self-induced abortions, more in fact than died in childbirth.

She remembered her mother saying, her voice shaking with desperation after the euphemistic 'missed headache,' that the only way to stop having babies was to die. Women chose this means of birth control more often than was generally admitted.

Glynis frowned and dug her nails into the carriage's leather seat. Too often excessive pain accompanied a dangerous childbirth. Earlier in the year anesthesia had been used for the first time during labor. The newspapers had reported strong opposition to the procedure, mostly from clergymen who accused doctors as well as women of disregarding God's decree that "in sorrow shalt thou bring forth children."

And sorrow there was. When Annie Monroe had been about to deliver her first child in April, the young woman's screams could be heard five houses away. Quentin Ives was among those doctors willing to use anesthesia, but a minister, a priest, and Annie's husband blocked the door of the house, refusing to let Ives enter. Of course the men couldn't have known, their supporters later said, that Annie Monroe's baby had been breech. It was simply the Lord's will that the baby had died that night, and she a week later from infection and exhaustion.

For some time afterward, it had been all that women in town had talked of. Harriet's opinion was that most clergymen disliked women—from Eve on down—so naturally they would oppose anything that made childbirth easier. Aurora said the clergy was just making women obey what they believed was God's word. Glynis thought it didn't matter one bit what the clergymen disliked or believed— they weren't the ones having the babies.

Dr. Ives stopped the carriage in front of the Steicher

farmhouse, and Karl came running down from the porch to
grab the trotter's harness. Carrying a lantern behind him
was a tall Negro farmhand. Karl handed him the trotter's
reins and gestured to Ives.

"Nell's in the front parlor. I didn't know if I should
move her upstairs."

He rocked with impatience while he waited for the doctor to climb down from the carriage, finally grabbing
Ives's bag and running ahead up the steps. Ives motioned
for Glynis to follow. Gathering up her skirts, she stumbled
over the carriage step. The farmhand caught her and lifted
her free of the carriage.

"Thank you." Glynis looked up into his face. "I'm
Glynis Tryon—I think we've met before?"

The man nodded. "Charles Douglass, ma'am. Brought
my grandchildren into your library, a few years back, to
show them around."

"Yes," Glynis said. "I remember now. You've been with
the Steichers for a long time."

"A long time." He smiled faintly, lifted the lantern, and
waited for her to climb the porch steps. There only were
a few black families in Seneca Falls. Most of those who
arrived as slaves with the early settlers had been emanci-
pated in 1827, when New York State abolished slavery;
then they had left.

Inside, the house glowed with lamplight. Glynis heard
Karl's voice and followed it into the front parlor. Nell lay
on a sofa on her side, her knees drawn up under her belly.
Her face was sheened with perspiration. Quentin Ives held
her wrist and silently counted, while Karl stood watching
him, drumming his fingers on a nearby table.

On a love seat at the far end of the room, the three towheaded little boys sat quietly. Their eyes were as round as
blue marbles. The youngest had his thumb in his mouth
and leaned against his oldest brother. Glynis thought they
didn't look like the same children she had seen previously.
There was a stillness about them now, as though they were
too frightened to move. They probably were.

"Miss Tryon." Nell struggled to sit up, and Glynis went

quickly to the sofa. Dr. Ives motioned Karl to follow him out into the hall. When the children started to slide off the love seat, they scrambled back up at a look from their father.

Glynis knelt down beside the sofa. Blood had dried in scabs over an angry red gash on Nell's cheekbone. "Nell, what happened? Karl said you fell."

Nell's eyes flicked away for an instant. Glynis thought she started to shake her head, but instead she winced and said, "Stupid of me. I shouldn't have been roaming around in the dark."

"Why were you?"

Nell stared up at the ceiling. "I—I thought I heard Karl come home from the party, so I started down the stairs. The moon seemed bright enough to see by, and I didn't bother lighting a lamp. I guess I tripped over something about halfway down."

"Did you fall the rest of the way? Nell, that must have been terrifying."

Nell shook her head. "No, I didn't really fall. I grabbed the bannister and just—well, I sort of staggered the rest of the way."

"And hit your face on the bannister?" Glynis said.

Nell put a hand against her cheek and cringed. "Yes, that's what happened. It's not that bad. And now the pains seem to have stopped. I'm afraid Karl got you and Dr. Ives out here for nothing."

Glynis sat back on her heels. Nell's explanation of what happened didn't sound very plausible. Would a pregnant woman really wander around in the dark? Glynis knew where the stairway was. She had been in the house before, when Friedrich was alive, and she had seen it again tonight. It was opposite and to the right of the front door, against a wall with no windows. And there were no windows in the entry hall. How could Nell have depended on moonlight?

Karl and Dr. Ives came back into the room. "Nellie, we're going to get you upstairs and into bed," Karl said.

"Dr. Ives thinks he should stay for a while and see if the pains are going to start again."

From the far end of the room came a soft cry. The children had been forgotten. The smallest boy rolled off the love seat and toddled over to the sofa; with tears dribbling from his eyes, he tried to climb up beside his mother. When Karl plucked him off the sofa, the child began to wail.

Karl held him against his chest and kissed the top of his head. "It's all right, Erich. Mama's going to be fine." Erich wailed louder and Glynis stepped toward him, her arms outstretched. Karl turned away from her and handed Erich to Dr. Ives.

"Quentin, if you'll bring him upstairs, I'll carry Nell."

Glynis pressed her lips together, walked to the love seat, and squatted down in front of the two remaining youngsters.

"I'm Miss Tryon. Will you tell me who you are?"

"Fritz." The older. Probably six.

"Julius." Four?

"Fritz and Julius . . . Fritz. Is that your real name? Or is it short for Friedrich?" Glynis asked him.

"It's Fritz *and* Friedrich."

"Yes. Of course. Well, don't you think we should go upstairs? It's very late, and you were probably in bed before—before your mother fell. Were you?"

They both stared at her. Glynis looked at the older boy. "Were you in bed, Fritz *and* Friedrich?"

Fritz's eyes widened. He scrutinized Glynis carefully. "It's not Fritz and Friedrich at the same time," he said at last.

"Oh. Of course not. How silly of me. Well then, Fritz, were you in bed when your mother fell on the stairs?"

"No!" Julius leaned forward to contribute this, then sat back. He resumed staring at Glynis.

"We were sort of in bed," said Fritz.

Glynis wondered why she had started this. Then Fritz surprised her.

"We were over by the window, because we thought we

heard Papa come home . . . I mean his horse come home."
He frowned. "We heard his horse, I think."

"Yes," said Glynis. "I understand." She wasn't sure she
did, but she wanted him to keep talking.

"Then there was funny noises downstairs," Fritz continued. "We were . . ."

"Scared," said Julius.

"*I* wasn't scared." Fritz turned to his brother. "*You*
were!"

"So what did you do then?" Glynis asked.

"We got in bed," said Fritz.

"Fast," said Julius.

Naturally, what else? Glynis thought. Exactly what any
sensible child did: jumped into bed and prayed the trolls
underneath didn't grab him.

"Do you remember what the noises downstairs sounded
like?"

"Thumping kind of noises."

Glynis's legs ached; she stood up. Her knees almost
buckled under her. It served her right: interrogating inno-
cents.

"Then the front door slammed," said Julius, and hopped
off the love seat. "I want to go to bed."

He started for the stairs. Fritz looked up at Glynis and
shrugged—exactly like Karl, she thought—then followed
his brother. Climbing the stairs behind the boys, Glynis
could hardly see the steps in front of her, even with a lamp
at the top.

In the children's room, she found the library books she
had sent to them; she picked one out and sat down on the
end of Julius's bed. Muffled voices filtered down the hall.
She couldn't hear Nell's.

The boys sat in their beds, looking at her with solemn
expressions.

"Your mother is going to be all right," she said. "You
should try not to worry about her. Will you try?"

Neither of them moved. They still looked solemn. Or
scared, Glynis thought. She felt a pressure against her side
and looked down. Erich had quietly come into the room.

His thumb was in his mouth, and he leaned against her. She pulled him up into her lap.

All three of them were scared. What if something did happen to Nell? She remembered how, when she was young, she had been terrified at the idea of her mother . . . leaving her all alone? She had to guess at that, because she couldn't have known what dying meant then. The memory was indistinct, beyond reach. But it upset her, even now.

She said to the boys, "Your father always will be here to take care of you. Always. You know that, don't you?"

Her voice faltered. She had forgotten she was talking about Karl, a man who might hang for murder; she had been thinking of him only as these little boys' father. She laid her face against Erich's blond hair.

Three heads swiveled toward the doorway. When Glynis looked around, Karl was standing just outside the room; it was too dark to see his expression. He stood looking in for what seemed a long time. Then he moved away. The light from his lantern dimmed. She heard his footsteps on the stairs.

Some time later, Dr. Ives walked past the children's room. All three of them were finally asleep. Glynis picked up the lamp and tiptoed out of the room. She saw a light down the hall and followed it, hesitating in the doorway of Nell and Karl's bedroom. Nell was lying in a high four-poster. No one else was in the room.

"Nell," she whispered. "Nell, are you all right?"

Nell raised up slightly from the pillow. "Miss Tryon? Are the children asleep?"

Glynis went to stand beside the bed. "Yes, they're sleeping. And they're fine, Nell. How are you?"

"The pains haven't started again. Dr. Ives thinks it will still be two or three weeks before the baby comes. Tonight was probably just a false alarm."

She struggled to sit up in the bed. "I think he and Karl are downstairs in the parlor. You and Dr. Ives should go back to town, Miss Tryon. I'm fine."

Glynis thought "fine" was optimistic, though Nell did

look better than when they'd arrived. Her color was good,
and her eyes didn't seem as frantic. Glynis bent forward to
see the laceration on her face, but it was covered with a
bandage, and Nell's cheek was toward the wall. Glynis
suddenly grasped what had bothered her earlier.

"Nell," she said. "I don't want to upset you again, but
you said you hit your face on the bannister. At the bottom
of the stairs?"

Nell nodded.

"But the gash is on your left cheek."

Nell's hand started toward her face, then dropped and
smoothed the sheet. She sank back against the pillows.
Glynis wanted to stop harrassing her, but she couldn't.
Nell was lying.

"Nell, what really happened here tonight? I don't believe you fell on the stairs. Coming down, the bannister
would have been on your right side, and—"

"Please, Miss Tryon. Please. You've been kind to us,
but please don't ask me anything more. I fell on the
stairs!"

She looked up at Glynis. With a jolt, Glynis recalled
seeing the same look earlier that evening, on Lydia
Abernathy's face, and on Daisy Ross's. Why were these
women so afraid?

"I'm sorry, Nell. I shouldn't have pressed you. But if
there's some way I can help you, well, just please let me
know."

Glynis walked out of the room. She looked in on the
sleeping children, then went to the head of the stairs. She
could hear voices coming from the front parlor. She crept
down the steps, hoping they wouldn't creak. At the bottom, she lifted her lamp over the newel post; there were no
marks on the post, no blood. Stepping down off the bottom
stair, she could hear Karl's voice in the parlor to her left,
so she turned right and started down the hall toward the
back of the house.

Her foot slipped on the floor. She teetered, certain she
would fall. Swaying toward the wall, she put out her free

hand to steady herself and regained her balance. She held her breath and listened. Karl was still talking.

She had slid on something. Bending over with the lamp, she saw what looked like a grease spatter. She reached down to touch it, rubbed her fingers together, then smelled them. Whale oil. As she straightened, out of the corner of her eye she saw something on the wall at the level of her shoulder. Holding the lamp close to it, she could see a faint dark red smear.

Glynis listened again, then looked down the hall toward Friedrich's old study—Karl's now, she assumed. She told herself not to be foolhardy, that she had no business skulking around someone else's house. She cocked an ear toward the parlor. Confident she heard Ives's voice, she crept down the hall.

Once in the study, she went immediately to the far end of the room. The Bible, she remembered, had stood on a shelf directly above Friedrich's desk, alongside volumes of Shakespeare and Dickens. Now the shelf was empty but for farm journals and what looked to be ledgers. To see better, she bent forward over the desk. Her knee banged hard into the edge of something, and her breath came out with a gasp.

She stood still, listening, not wanting to hear that someone was coming down the hall.

Lowering the lamp, she looked for whatever she had banged against. One of the desk side drawers was open a crack. She set the lamp down and pulled the drawer out partway. The Bible was lying on its side.

She let go of the drawer as if it were scalding. She should close the drawer and get out of there. Let someone else do whatever had to be done.

But the Bible was right there! She had to see what she now was certain must be a family tree. Evidence that Rose Walker was Friedrich's daughter, Karl's sister. The question shot through her mind that if she hadn't felt she should open the Bible when it was in the library, why should she do it now?

This was different. No, it wasn't, unless she believed

murder overruled privacy. She reached into the drawer. She was lifting the Bible when she heard voices in the hall.

Glynis seized the lamp, lifted the glass, and turned down the wick. Stealing toward the half-open door, she moved her hands before her like a blind person, praying she wouldn't trip. Moonlight coming through the window was muted, but she found the door and crouched down behind it. It was surely futile, because the sound of her heartbeat must be audible from there to the village.

The footsteps came toward the study and paused, as though someone was standing in the hall on the other side of the door. She desperately tried to think of any legitimate reason why she should be in Karl's study.

Dr. Ives's voice called, "I think I've taken the wrong turn. Where's the outside door?"

Karl's voice, then the footsteps continued on. A door opened, and closed. Dr. Ives was making for the privy. Glynis peered past the hinges into the hall. She saw Karl at the bottom of the stairs. It seemed as though he was looking right at her, that they were playing a horrible kind of hide-and-seek. If he went upstairs he would see that she wasn't in the children's room.

He started up the stairs. She waited until she couldn't hear his steps, then rushed to the window. It was closed, but she hoisted it up and climbed onto the sill. She had just swung her legs and skirts outside when she heard someone walking toward the house. Dr. Ives?

The only thing she could think of was to get out of the room. She looked down—the ground wasn't too far. She wriggled to the edge of the sill and jumped, landing just below the window in some tall weeds. Ducking into them, she pressed herself against the side of the house. The footsteps slowed. Then she heard the outside door open and close again.

She crept toward the front of the house, brushing her dress as she went. Reaching the front porch steps, she sneaked up them as quietly as she could and collapsed into a chair.

Her breathing slowed somewhat. She obviously couldn't do anything more until Cullen got back. It wasn't as though Nell and the children were in danger—Karl would never hurt them. Whatever had happened earlier that night, whatever Nell was afraid of, Glynis felt certain it wasn't Karl.

Some time later, she heard Karl and Dr. Ives calling her. She waited until their footsteps sounded in the entry hall, then she opened the front door.

"I stepped outside for a breath of air," she said. "I guess I fell asleep. How is Nell?"

"She's resting quietly," Ives said. "I think we can go back to town now. It's practically morning."

Karl came through the door and stood in front of Glynis, staring down at her. Her pulse quickened. Did he know?

"Thank you, Miss Tryon," he said, and turned and walked back into the house.

# TWENTY-FOUR

SEVERAL DAYS LATER, Jeremiah Merrycoyf stood in front of his office window. He scanned the letter in his hand, then turned and tossed it onto his desk. Karl Steicher leaned forward and picked it up.

Karl read the letter silently, now and then scowling across at Merrycoyf, who had settled himself in a capacious chair behind the desk and appeared to be snoozing. The lawyer's chin rested on his chest, his hands overlapped on his stomach. But his eyes behind the square, wire-framed spectacles studied Karl.

Finally Karl flung the letter back onto the desk. "You said this letter from Orrin Polk is a notice of claim? What does that mean, exactly?"

Merrycoyf sighed and rubbed his palms on the arms of his chair. "In simple terms, what it means is that Gordon Walker applied for and subsequently received from the surrogate limited letters of administration for the estate of his wife. It was necessary for him to go through that procedure because Rose Walker was a resident of Massachusetts. The letter from Polk is giving you notice of the fact that Walker has filed a claim of inheritance. In other words, Walker is challenging your claim of sole heirship. He's demanding half your father's estate."

Karl threw himself back in his chair and gazed at the ceiling. "What are the chances of Walker succeeding in getting half?"

Merrycoyf sat forward. "There's no way for me to assess that, because I had no idea that Friedrich was married before. If he was, he never took me into his confidence.

And *you* knew nothing of it—you made a sworn statement that you were the sole heir. You told me everything when you did that, I assume." He stared at Karl.

Karl stood up and went to the window facing Fall Street.

"There's Mrs. Stanton's inquest statement. How much damage could that do?" he said.

Merrycoyf grunted. "Neither you nor I could know the basis of her assertion that your father was previously married. At this point, her statement is just hearsay, which would be inadmissible in court. And the case is Walker's to prove; *we* don't have to *disprove* his claim of heirship."

Karl turned from the window to face Merrycoyf. "Jeremiah, I thought the woman who came to my farm was an imposter. But even she wasn't demanding half the estate! She wanted ten thousand dollars, cash."

"That's less than ten percent of the estate," said Merrycoyf. "That *would* make you doubt her authenticity. Of course, how could she have known what the estate was worth?"

Karl returned to the chair. "Actually, Jeremiah, I've been thinking. In a few weeks we'll be harvesting the wheat. It looks good—a bumper crop, I'd say. And then I'll have some ready cash. Do you think this Walker would take ten thousand to get out of our lives? Should we offer that to him?"

Merrycoyf had risen and was bending over his desk straightening an inkwell. His head shot up at Karl's question. "Why would you want to offer him anything? Offering Walker money is tantamount to admitting that you think he can prove his wife was Friedrich's—your father's—daughter. I told you Karl, *they're* the ones that have to prove that."

Karl nodded. "I heard you. But listen, Jeremiah. I've got a big farm to run, acres of wheat to harvest in the next few weeks. I sure as hell can't afford any more time spent on this nonsense. Besides that, Nell's expecting any time now, and she isn't strong. This thing's upsetting her. You know there are rumors all over town that I was somehow involved with the death of Walker's wife. I figure the longer Walker stays in town, the worse it's going to get. If ten thousand dollars will get rid of him, I say let him have it!"

Merrycoyf shook his head. "I don't like it, Karl. It might be pragmatic, but it won't look good. As your lawyer, I can't advise you to offer Walker money."

"Who cares how it looks! I just want to get this thing over with. Make the offer."

Karl rose and went to the office door, where he turned to look at Merrycoyf. "I mean it, Jeremiah," he said, and walked out.

Merrycoyf stared after him. Shaking his head, he at last plucked his pen from its stand beside the inkwell and sank back into his chair.

# TWENTY-FIVE

◈

STANDING IN THE door of the library, Glynis smiled at the strident blast of the stagecoach horn and waved her thanks to the driver who had just dropped off Cullen's letter. The circuit judge had been delayed, the letter said, consequently the trial in Auburn had had to wait. Cullen now thought he wouldn't be home until Monday night. At least he would be back for the Fourth of July celebrations, Tuesday.

Glynis went to her back office and leaned out the window with her elbows on the sill. The slope to the canal was covered with drifts of Queen Anne's lace, daisies, and black-eyed Susans. Clumps of orange tiger lilies bordered the towpath; wild roses climbed under her window. They were sturdy, tenacious flowers, blooming without supervision, without approval, without constraint. They must have been named in another time: Anne, Daisy, Susan, Lily, Rose.

She heard a tentative knock on the half-open door and turned. Daisy Ross stood outside.

"Daisy . . ." Glynis stopped. Daisy's eyes were swollen half shut, the lids an angry pink. In her hand she clutched what looked like a folded pillowcase. She stepped hesitantly into the office and stood just inside the door.

"Are you very busy, Miss Tryon? I can come back another time."

"No, it's all right, Daisy. Really. It's almost six; hardly anyone comes in this late, especially this time of year. Please sit down." Glynis settled in her wing chair and motioned Daisy toward the other.

Daisy sat and stared at the floor, shifting her feet back and forth.

"Would you like some tea, Daisy?"

Daisy shook her head. She seemed even more distressed than she had the night of the party, and Glynis couldn't tell whether it was pride or fear that kept her silent. Maybe both.

"Daisy, how can I help? I know there's something wrong—I knew it the other night."

Daisy's lower lip trembled; she caught it between her teeth. Finally, "I just don't know," she stammered. "I have to do *something*. But I don't know how to tell you this."

Glynis nodded. She was afraid if she said anything Daisy would stop talking. She kept nodding.

Daisy stared at her, then she straightened in the chair and sucked in her breath. "I've thought and thought about this, and I decided you're the right one to tell. And to help me figure out what I should do. I'm so scared I can't think straight myself."

Glynis leaned toward her. "In that case, you'd better tell me, so you don't have to struggle with whatever this is alone."

Daisy held out the folded pillowcase. "Maybe you'd better open this first."

Glynis took the case, placed it on her lap, and unfolded it. As she did, she heard a faint pinging sound.

"It's the beads," Daisy said. "They're falling off."

At first, Glynis just stared at them rolling onto the floor, not grasping what it was she was seeing. Then she quickly gathered the pillowcase up around the torn pink silk purse.

"Daisy, where did you get this?"

"It was in the trash heap, in our yard. It belonged to that dead woman, didn't it?"

"I don't know—Rose Walker had one like it. Why do you think it's hers? Daisy, how did it get in your trash heap?"

Glynis could hear her own voice rising. She didn't want to frighten Daisy into silence, but she couldn't imagine

how the purse had found its way onto the Ross's trash
heap.

"I knew it was hers," Daisy answered, "because of the
letter inside. Open it up."

Glynis opened the purse, placing its contents, one by
one, on her worktable. Three wrinkled sheets of paper fluttered in her hands. One was a list of jewelry. Her eyes
brushed over the precise handwriting; it was the duplicate
of the one in Simon Sheridan's safe. The other two sheets
of paper looked to be a letter, which began *My dear Rose.*

Glynis studied the items on the table. "Is this all? Everything?"

Daisy nodded, her lip trembling. "That's all there was
when I found it."

Glynis looked inside the purse again. "There wasn't any
money?" she asked. She hadn't found any in Rose Walker's things at the hotel; she assumed it had disappeared in
the canal with the purse. But the woman certainly
wouldn't have traveled without any cash.

"Daisy, you think Bobby hid the purse in your yard,
don't you?"

Tears coursed down Daisy's face. She tried to answer,
and choking, finally got to her feet. "Bobby was spending
money . . . after Karl Steicher fired him. It was a lot more
than what I make, so I didn't know where it was coming
from." She pointed at the purse. "*That's* where it was coming from."

"When did you find this?" Glynis said. "In the past few
days? No—it was before the party, wasn't it?"

"Yes. Three days before. I wanted to tell you that night,
but I couldn't because I know you're—well, you're friends
with the constable. Miss Tryon, I don't know exactly how
Bobby got that purse, but . . ." She started to choke again.
Pulling a cloth from her sleeve, she wiped her eyes and
nose.

"But what, Daisy? What were you going to say? How
do you think Bobby got the purse?"

Glynis reached up for Daisy's arm and pulled her down
into the chair again; she said as calmly as she could man-

age, "Are you afraid Bobby killed Rose Walker? For her money?"

To her surprise, Daisy stopped weeping, as though having her worst fear spoken aloud had reduced her torment. Now what Glynis saw on her face was resignation.

"Miss Tryon, a few years ago I couldn't have believed Bobby would hurt anybody. That's not true anymore. He's changed so much. He hurts our children; he hurts me. It's the drinking. That's what it does to him. And he knows— sometimes he promises he'll stop. But it's like he can't stop, as if he *has* to drink, even though he doesn't want to. Nothing I do seems to help. And he's getting worse.

"I think he killed that woman. I don't think he knew what he was doing, but I think he killed her just the same." She stared at Glynis.

She really believes it, Glynis thought. But there was something wrong.

"Daisy, I'm trying to remember what happened the day Rose Walker died. That afternoon, Tuesday, it was, Bobby was involved in an incident—"

"He was in a fight with Abraham Levy," Daisy interrupted. "I know."

"Yes. And he passed out. Cullen took him home. Were you there?"

Daisy nodded. "Constable Stuart brought Bobby in the house. He had him slung over his shoulder, and he dropped Bobby on the daybed."

"Well then, Daisy, how could Bobby have killed anyone later that night? If he was passed out?"

"He wasn't. Passed out the whole night, I mean. He woke up sometime after dark, and he was sick. He was shaking all over. Said he needed whiskey. I was scared, he was so sick.

"We didn't have whiskey in the house. I—I got rid of it all, months ago. He knew that, but he still looked for some. When he couldn't find something to drink, he wanted money, but I didn't have any to give him. He was crazy, throwing the furniture around, yelling at me. I didn't know what he might do, so I took the children to the cellar. We waited down there until we heard him go out. He didn't come back for two days. And I know he didn't have any money when he left."

Glynis reached forward to grip Daisy's hands. How had she ever survived—a small, young woman with five children, and all that going on? And the worst of it was that Daisy had to be the one to come forward, to accuse her own husband of murder. After all she had been through with him.

But Glynis couldn't help but feel a sense of relief. It was over. Rose Walker had been killed for nothing more complicated than money for whiskey. It was almost too horrible to think about, but it wouldn't be the first time. She thought Daisy would eventually be all right; she'd been supporting her family by herself anyway.

But what should they do now?

"Daisy, I've just heard from Cullen. He won't be back here until day after tomorrow. I don't know how you feel, but I think you should wait and talk to him. He can handle Bobby. But there's a young man Cullen left in charge, so you could talk to him if you—"

"No," Daisy protested. "I can't. I just can't. I hoped you would." Her eyes were pleading; she was like someone looking down a rifle barrel.

"Do you know where Bobby is right now?"

Daisy shook her head. "I haven't seen him since yesterday. I locked the doors—I'm not letting him in the house. I'm afraid of him, and so are the children."

Glynis nodded. "All right, then, let's wait. In the meantime, I'll ask Cullen's man to locate Bobby and keep an eye on him until Cullen gets back, to make sure he doesn't harm you or the children."

Daisy rose, gesturing at the purse on Glynis's table. "You'll keep that? I don't want to touch it again."

Glynis nodded. She got up and pulled Daisy close. The young woman clung to her, then turned and walked slowly out of the office. Her head was down. Her shoulders drooped like an old woman's. Like a trampled flower.

*        *        *

Glynis walked to the firehouse, wondering what kind of compelling, misleading reason she could give to keep track of Bobby Ross. To her relief, she found Jacques Sundown behind Cullen's desk.

"Circuit judge got to Auburn yesterday," Jacques said, getting to his feet. "Started the trial right off. I gave my testimony. Constable said I should ride back." He went to a wall rack to replace the gun he'd been cleaning.

Glynis didn't know Jacques's age; she didn't think *he* knew exactly how old he was. Cullen figured he was about ten years younger than himself, so Jacques would be in his mid-twenties, the son of a French trapper and his Seneca Indian wife. Looking like neither the French nor the Senecas Glynis had seen, with his sharp features and high cheekbones, Jacques's copper skin and black hair were the only things that identified him as Indian. He was a striking-looking man—a half-breed, neither one thing nor the other, claimed as their own by no one. Not an easy thing to be, Glynis had thought more than once.

A year before, Cullen had been caught in a bar brawl, surrounded by armed, drunk canal drifters with a grudge against lawmen. Jacques had materialized out of nowhere, and within seconds the drifters were either shot, knife-slashed, or cowering behind the bar—Cullen said he had never seen a man move so effectively so fast. That marked Jacques a Seneca more than his appearance; of all the Iroquois the most feared had been the Senecas, Keepers of the Western Door of the six-nation Iroquois Long House.

Cullen had hired Jacques Sundown that night.

Glynis looked around the office, then checked outside the door again. "I don't think I want anyone else to hear this." She sat down opposite the desk. "Jacques, something has happened."

Jacques's flat brown eyes stared at her; his smooth, coppery face was, as usual, expressionless. He might have been sitting by the river fishing. And Glynis knew he would continue to look that way no matter what she said. His lack of reaction usually bothered her; now it was reassuring. She was upset enough for both of them.

"Something happened." Jacques's tone indicated total uninterest.

"Yes. Daisy Ross just came to see me. She doesn't know where her husband is. Without going into a lot of details, I think it would be a good idea for you to find Bobby. And watch him. . . ." Her voice trailed off; that must sound absurd to Jacques. She half turned toward the door. Had she heard something out there? No. She was just jumpy.

Jacques was staring at her. "You want me to watch him. Ross."

"Yes," Glynis said. "What I mean is, I don't think Bobby should be allowed to . . . well, for instance, leave town."

"Why would he want to do that?"

"I don't know that he *does* want to do that. Jacques, his drinking is really dangerous, for Daisy and the children."

"Man's been drinking hard a long while now. This the first time his wife thinks it's dangerous? Anyhow, you can't swear out a complaint against him. She has to do that."

"That's not exactly what I'm talking about, Jacques."

She was handling this badly. And he wasn't helping any. She deliberated. Cullen trusted Jacques; should she tell him the whole thing? She felt uneasy about that. What if Bobby found out he was wanted for murder and went after Daisy? She thought Cullen might handle him better than Jacques. And something else had begun to disturb her. She couldn't put her finger on exactly what it was, but the uneasiness was strong enough to make her cautious.

Cullen would be back day after tomorrow. She decided to go halfway. She hesitated, cocking her head toward the door. No; she was hearing things.

"Daisy gave me some information for Cullen," she said. "About something important. I want to be certain Cullen gets it, before Bobby finds out what Daisy's done. I know this probably doesn't make any sense to you, but you must believe me when I tell you it's serious."

She watched his face with small hope; it didn't change. She didn't know if he believed her or not. Probably not.

"Jacques, this has to do with Rose Walker's murder."

Just as she was feeling heartened, having caught a glimpse of something resembling surprise cross his face, Jacques sprang to his feet, vaulted over the desk and charged out the door. When Glynis herself looked out, Jacques had disappeared. There was no one.

A few minutes later he returned, not even breathing fast. "Maybe somebody out there overheard. Maybe not. If they did, maybe they'll keep their mouth shut." He looked at Glynis with his level eyes. "Or maybe the Seneca River will freeze over tonight."

"Yes." Glynis clutched the folds of her skirt. "What I just told you will be all over town. And then what?"

"Then we'll know somebody overheard." He sat down behind the desk.

Glynis thought that Cullen, who enjoyed Jacques immensely, must see some quality in the man that eluded her. But she said, trying to keep exasperation out of her voice, "Will you try to locate Bobby Ross? Watch him for the next couple of days?"

Jacques looked at her. "Watch him. Sure. All you had to do was ask."

# TWENTY-SIX

GLYNIS CROSSED THE river bridge and walked up the quarter-mile grade of Washington Street to reach the Stanton house. That morning after church she had told Elizabeth she needed to see her and had been invited for supper.

After the meal, she and Elizabeth left the house to escape the clamor of children and dogs, and the dominant personality of Henry Stanton. They walked to the northern boundary of the two-acre Stanton property. The house and land had been given to Elizabeth by her father, Judge Daniel Cady; the house was in Elizabeth's name, and with the April passage of the Married Women's Property Act her property was no longer legally Henry's, but her own.

The two women sat down on the short goat-cropped grass overlooking the Seneca River. Elizabeth straightened her skirts and leaned back against the broad trunk of a hundred-foot white oak.

"If I hadn't seen you in church this morning, Glynis, I would have come by the library tomorrow. I received a letter from Mary Clarke."

Glynis could feel old, knotty, above-ground roots digging into her thighs; she shifted her body, tucking legs and skirts under her.

"Mary wanted to know whether Rose's killer had been found," Elizabeth said. "I was surprised, because while I was in Boston, she expressed no interest in the details of her daughter's death. I was relieved, truthfully, not to have to tell her how dreadful it had been."

"Perhaps she's more angry now than she was then,"

Glynis ventured. She wanted to stay away from that subject; she wasn't going to say anything yet about Bobby Ross.

"Do you know if any progress has been made, Glynis? I suppose not, what with Constable Stuart away. I really don't know what to write Mary."

"You could tell her that the investigation of Rose's death is proceeding," Glynis suggested. "I wouldn't want her to think nothing is being done. And Cullen will be back tomorrow."

"Mary said her own condition had somewhat improved. Although she doesn't know if she is well enough to travel here, she told me that it might be possible, if it was absolutely necessary."

"Why would she say that?" Glynis asked.

"I'm not sure. Frankly, I thought it was odd. I shouldn't think she would want anything to do with this town."

"Nor I," Glynis said. "And just think of the distance involved: Boston's over three hundred fifty miles from here!"

"You said this morning you wanted to show me something?" Elizabeth said. "Something that had to do with Rose?"

Glynis got to her knees, twisted her skirt around, and pulled the letter from her pocket.

"This letter was—that is, just before he left, Cullen asked me to look through Rose's things at the hotel. This letter was apparently sent to her in Boston. I can't read the signature. I thought you might know who the writer could be."

Elizabeth took the letter and smoothed the pages on her lap.

"I wonder if you'd mind reading it aloud," Glynis asked. "It might give me a different perspective, because I'm rather mystified by it."

Elizabeth nodded and began to read:

c/o Oliver Winchester
57 Court Street
New Haven, Connecticut
June 5, 1848

My dear Rose,

I was overjoyed yesterday to receive your letter. When I did not hear from you for so long a time, I thought perhaps your mind had been changed and I could no longer look forward to seeing you. Now I understand your silence.

At the outset, I must declare myself concerned regarding the strategy you intend. It appears complicated and taxing, even for your indomitable spirit. I beg of you, my dear Rose, to give the undertaking a goodly amount of thought before you embark on such a perilous mission.

Furthermore, western New York is said to be fraught with the most primitive dangers. I am told that wolves roam the forests and few roads are passable except in finest weather. Diseases of the most debilitating nature abound; the newspapers carry stories of Genesee fever epidemics and other pestilence.

"Heavens, Glynis," said Elizabeth, lowering the letter. "Did you know we lived in such a place? Although, I must say, I am all too familiar with Genesee fever."

"I know." Glynis smiled. "It does sound formidable here, doesn't it?"

"Like Hades, is what it sounds!" Elizabeth laughed, and resumed reading:

I am settled quite comfortably here in New Haven. I have rented rooms from another new resident, one Oliver Winchester. He is a collector of firearms and has the most extraordinary assortment of guns. Although he presently owns the shirt factory next door, he anticipates soon manufacturing superior rifles of his own design.

You may find his house on the map at the bottom. It will be a simple matter for you to take a carriage from the rail station. As for me, the house is only a few minutes' walk to the college.

I shall await your arrival with the greatest eagerness. Again, please take great care, as you may very likely encounter resistance, as well as a fair amount of skepticism.

As I write this, I find my heart is quite filled with trepidation for you, my dear, brave Rose. Do be most cautious and prudent.

Yours with love,

Elizabeth looked puzzled. "You're quite right about the signature—I can't make it out either. It's just a scrawl. I have no idea who this might have been from. But whoever it was had good reason to be worried for Rose!"

Glynis inched on her knees to Elizabeth's side and looked over her shoulder. "Does that first letter look like an *E* to you? Perhaps an *E* and then a *V*?"

Elizabeth half closed her eyes, tilted the sheet of paper, and finally shook her head. "It might be. Glynis, I can't imagine what this letter means. And the map is no help."

She handed the pages back to Glynis.

The map wasn't helpful. It was just a few lines, drawn from a square labeled *Railroad Station*, with *Court Street* and *Church Street* written alongside. Glynis would willingly wager that most towns in the nation had Church and Court streets, so their existence in New Haven meant nothing.

"Elizabeth, look at the date of the letter. Rose Walker must have received it immediately before she left Boston to come here. Had she any Boston relatives who recently moved to Connecticut?"

"None that I know of. But I could ask Mary Clarke when I write."

Glynis nodded. "I thought perhaps I might write this E person. I have the address, if not the name, and it occurred to me that whoever this is might not know what happened to Rose and is still waiting for her to arrive."

"What a dreadful thought. Yes, Glynis, do write. I think you are the best one to do it, since I didn't even talk with Rose when she was here."

Glynis rubbed her knees and stood up. "The sun's getting low. I should be starting back."

They walked slowly toward the house. "I'm glad you took my cue at supper," Elizabeth said, "and didn't ask about our conversations of the past weeks. Henry is quite distressed by my interest in women's rights. He thinks I'm abandoning the abolition cause.

"I've worked hard on behalf of abolishing slavery; so have other women. But all of a sudden that work is seen by the men as political, and unsuitable for women. And this is after we wrote the petitions, spent heaven knows how much time circulating them for signatures, and talked until we were hoarse. Now the men have decided we aren't competent enough to participate in public debate."

Elizabeth's face was flushed. She stopped by the well to draw up the bucket.

Glynis leaned back against the stone well wall. "But you're still considering a public meeting about women's rights?"

"More than ever! The survey showed interest among at least some women." Elizabeth smiled. "If your mysterious letter writer should hear of it, 'E' might consider this an even *more* dangerous place."

She took a swallow of water from the wooden dipper, then handed it to Glynis. "But why shouldn't we do it here in western New York? We have to begin somewhere. And this is where women have learned writing and speaking skills in the cause of abolition—we've never been allowed that experience before."

Won't it be interesting, Glynis thought, when the men who believe women fit only for the drudge work of male campaigns learn those same women have been honing their skills for a battle of their own.

Crossing back to the north side of Seneca Falls, Glynis thought she saw Jacques Sundown riding along the tow-path. The twilight was fading fast, but she paused on the bridge to look at the dark river below. *Sha-se-once*, swift or rolling water, the Seneca Indians had called the mile-long rapids existing there until the completion of the canal twenty years before.

Jacques had reined in his piebald horse at the end of the bridge and appeared to be waiting for her. Had he located Bobby Ross? She hurried toward him.

"Man's disappeared," he said, looking down at her. "Can't watch him if I can't find him."

Glynis pushed his horse's muzzle away from her straw bonnet. The horse snorted softly and swung his head back; she could hear his lips nibbling at the straw. Glynis took three steps backward. The horse took one forward, and nuzzled her hair. Glynis shoved his head away again. The reins hung slack in Jacques' hands.

"Jacques, are you going to just sit there and let your animal eat my hat? I think I'd rather talk to you when you feel like being more considerate."

Despite the flat eyes, the expressionless face, she knew Jacques was laughing. She turned on her heel and began striding toward Fall Street, walking so fast her petticoats caught between her legs; she stumbled and almost fell. Her cheeks were hot as she stopped to untangle herself. The man was no doubt watching her, thinking she couldn't even manage a dignified huff! Thinking she was a half-wit. Just a half-witted woman who didn't have brains enough to know he was laughing at her.

She suddenly hated them all—Jacques, Bobby, Karl Steicher, Henry Stanton, Cullen . . . Cullen. And where was *he*? Oh, yes. He was sitting in some cosy inn, across from some stupid prison—full of stupid, dangerous men! While she was here, doing the job *he* was supposed to do! Well, she didn't care for the job, didn't care whether insufferable Jacques Sundown found Bobby Ross or not. Go ahead, Jacques, let Bobby murder half the population of Seneca Falls!

It was almost dark, the trees obscuring the remaining twilight. She realized she had been talking to herself since she crossed Fall Street, stamping her feet for emphasis. She slowed to catch her breath.

And thought she heard someone behind her. Jacques? Had he followed her to apologize? Unlikely! She wouldn't turn around—she wouldn't give him the satisfaction of turning around. Then the idea flashed across her mind that it might be Bobby Ross, creeping up behind her, and she found herself thinking it would serve Cullen right if he came back and found her strangled. . . .

She whirled around. The road was empty. But she was sure she had heard the sound of footfalls.

She turned, walked a few steps, then looked back over her shoulder. There was no one behind her. It must have been blood pounding in her ears that she'd heard. Served her right. Working herself up into such a fury. She was exhausted, hearing things.

She saw the Usher house ahead and walked a little faster—and heard the footfalls again. She was absolutely certain this time: someone was walking a short distance behind her and stopping when she did, probably ducking into the shadows of the trees. She was too frightened to turn around again, and it was too dark to see anyway. If she could get to the Usher house—but what if no one was home? She couldn't run; her petticoats would trip her. She hiked them up and walked as fast as she dared; the Usher house was still a few hundred feet ahead.

Then, thudding behind her, she heard horse's hooves. The breath caught in her throat, and she turned, barely able to see the horse and rider coming toward her. At the same moment, from the corner of her eye, she thought she saw something move at the side of the road. When she narrowed her eyes to peer through the darkness, it was gone.

Jacques Sundown reined in his horse beside her. "Getting dark."

How could she have been angry with this man? He was heroic. So was the horse.

She let out her breath. "Jacques, did you see anyone else in the road? Behind me, I mean?"

He leaned over his saddle horn and stared down at her. "You think somebody was following you?"

Now he thought she was a lunatic. "Not exactly following me, Jacques. I just thought I heard . . . never mind."

"Saw somebody start up this street a bit after you did,"

he said. "Couldn't figure where they came from. Popped right out of nowhere. Couldn't see who it was—too dark. Thought I'd better take a look, see you got home all right."

Glynis felt her skin prickling. There *had* been someone. "Maybe it was just a child, trying to get home before dark," she said.

"No. Too tall for a child."

She started walking again. "I appreciate your coming after me, Jacques. Although I'm sure there was nothing to worry about."

She kept telling herself that, one shaky footstep after the other. Jacques walked the horse beside her. When they reached Peartree's, he said, "Funny about Ross. Nobody's seen him since yesterday. Expect he'll turn up, though. Then I can watch him."

In the darkness, she thought she saw the trace of a grin, a flash of teeth, gone in an instant, like a candle snuffed in a jack-o'-lantern. She could have imagined it.

He wheeled the horse around and seemed to vanish. Like the headless horseman, Glynis thought, and darted into the house.

# TWENTY-SEVEN

⌾⌾⌾

THE EXPLOSIONS BROUGHT her bolt upright in the four-poster. Rumbling Stygian booms overlaid the peals of church bells tolling the arrival of Judgment Day. She struggled awake. No—the Fourth of July.

Glynis patted her perspiring face with a corner of the sheet and glanced at the clock beside the bed. Groaning, she flopped back against the pillows. It was a holiday, for heaven's sake. Surely those who made these weighty decisions could have elected to start the day later than seven o'clock in the morning. But the cannons on the town green were blasting away: the whole town must be awake.

She climbed out of bed to look out the window. The sky had a harsh metallic glaze. The locusts were buzzing. Since the storm the night before the Ushers' party, the weather had been of the sort that western New Yorkers comforted themselves by recalling while enduring the long winters: sunny, warm, breezy days, air sparkling like clear glass. But gradually, it had been getting hotter.

Glynis pulled her damp nightgown away from her skin, blessing Mr. Fyfe for the shower stall he had built behind the kitchen. A cloudy day would not warm the water in its tank attached to the roof's cistern, and Glynis had found standing naked under the sky took some getting used to, but in the warmer months it meant not having to lug water from the back-yard well to fill the indoor tub.

She opened her bedroom door and sniffed. The fragrance of baking ham was already drifting up the stairs; Harriet must have met the dawn. When Glynis reached the kitchen her landlady was up to her elbows in flour, rolling pastry. Under the table, Duncan sat waiting for something to drop.

"Ham smells wonderful, Harriet. What time is the picnic?"

"Noon, same as every year," Harriet sighed. "Gets the women up early."

"What would happen if they took the holiday off too?"

"Nobody would eat, that's what would happen." Harriet drew the back of her hand across her forehead, leaving a snowy streak from temple to temple. "Going to be a hot day."

"I'll help as soon as I get a shower," Glynis said.

"Cullen ever come last night?"

"No." Glynis headed for the outside door. Where *was* he?

The acrid odor of exploded firecrackers mingled with the fragrance of fresh-baked berry pies and velvety hams. Glynis didn't usually enjoy crowds, but the Fourth of July picnic on the town green was different, an event that brought out most of Seneca Falls in good humor. People who barely nodded to one another the rest of the year stood elbow to elbow along the road as the Men's Bugle Band marched into the green. Above the din of horns and drums and cymbals, a piccolo could be heard like the sharp whistle of wind through fir trees.

While women loaded the tables with food, herded their children, and hushed barking dogs, interminable orations poured forth as speakers addressed the crowd from a wooden platform. The speakers cited the February victory in Mexico, the defeat of Santa Anna's immense army, and the acquisition of vast western territory. The year 1848, so speaker after speaker thundered, would go down in the annals of history as the year the Mexican War created a great and glorious country that now stretched from ocean to ocean.

Gold had been found at Sutter's sawmill and California was ours! Anything was possible!

Glynis, standing below the platform, wondered how

many ways there were of saying the same thing. Hearing her name called, she turned and saw Cullen coming toward her across the grass. Just then the last speaker wound down, the crowd sprinted for the food, and Glynis lost sight of Cullen in the surge. She tried to push her way through and found herself staring at him across a table, surrounded by people. Cullen was trying to answer the questions of those around him and watch her at the same time.

He must have stopped at his house: his shirt was fresh, and he'd shaved. Even the thick sand-colored hair and mustache were trimmed. But his face looked drawn, and his eyes were sunk like black depressions in his face. He piled food on his plate, looking over at her and jerking his head in the direction of the deserted speaker's platform. She nodded and tried to back out through the throng of people behind her.

It took some time before she could extricate herself; Cullen was leaning against the platform when she finally reached him. They walked to the far edge of the green and sat down on the grass. Cullen put his plate beside him, took her hand briefly, and smiled.

"So what have you been up to?"

Close up, he looked haggard. His tanned skin had the dry, yellowish cast of very old paper.

"Cullen, you look exhausted."

He nodded. "Trial didn't finish until yesterday afternoon; I rode all night to get back. Now, what's been going on here? I saw Jacques Sundown on the way into town. He said you've got him tracking Bobby Ross."

"Has he found him yet?"

"No. C'mon, Glynis, what do you want with Ross?"

She told him. Cullen listened, picking halfheartedly at the food on his plate. "That's hard to believe," he said when she'd finished, shaking his head. "I've known Ross to do some dumb things since he's been drinking heavy, but I never figured him for a killer. Has to be a fair amount of evil in a man to kill a woman for the money in her purse."

"I know," Glynis said. Those had been her thoughts too. "But Daisy believes he was capable of it. She knows him better than we do."

Cullen sighed. "Well, I better get moving. Help out Jacques, although if he hasn't been able to find Ross in the past couple of days, I'd say the man probably can't be found."

He didn't move. Glynis saw perspiration glisten on his forehead.

"Cullen, you don't look well. And you've hardly eaten a thing. Why don't you just sit for a while, try and get some food inside you."

He looked relieved. Which wasn't like him.

"I rode down to Ithaca while we were waiting on the circuit judge," he said. "Seems like our friend Simon Sheridan is a real shifty character. I would have thought he was a good candidate for Rose Walker's killer, until you told me about Bobby Ross."

"Were those train robbers convicted?"

Cullen nodded. "They'll be in prison for a good stretch. I just hope we don't start seeing a lot of these train robberies. Not around here, at least—I don't want to go through that again any time soon." Cullen smiled at her, looking more like himself. "I was gone a long time, Glynis. You did notice that, didn't you?"

They sat and talked quietly; Glynis realized they were examining their words, and each other, to make sure things were as they had been, as those who have been disconnected by time and distance seem to do. They glanced up now and then at the picnic games. When the call went out for tug-of-war teams, Cullen started to get up, then grinned ruefully and lay back on the grass. He clasped his hands behind his head; immediately she heard his breathing slow in sleep. She hadn't yet told him about the Bible's reappearance in Karl Steicher's study. There would be time later.

The crowd around the food tables ebbed and flowed. Glynis could see almost everyone from where she sat, and she idly began to note who wasn't there. Karl and Nell

Steicher were not. Nor was Gordon Walker, whom Cullen
had yet to meet, but she hadn't really expected to see
Walker at a celebration. It seemed strange she hadn't seen
the Abernathys—Ambrose liked his brew, and barrels of
ale had rolled from flatbed wagons even before the
speeches began. Maybe Ambrose was behind the platform
with the barrels. Glynis hadn't seen Lydia Abernathy since
the night of the party. Jeremiah Merrycoyf had disappeared
soon after several helpings of food. At the moment she
couldn't locate Quentin or Katherine Ives, although she
had seen them earlier, and Simon Sheridan had also disappeared.

Cullen had said that Sheridan had been charged with
embezzling money from the Ithaca Inn when he'd been
manager there, but he hadn't been convicted. There was a
rumor about Sheridan and the hotel owner's wife; the
owner had suddenly declined to testify, and the charges
were withdrawn.

Glynis shifted her position and saw Jacques Sundown
appear at a far corner of the platform. He never mingled
with townspeople and always stayed on the fringes of activity. She rose beside the sleeping Cullen as Jacques approached.

"Constable around?" he said, and then looked beyond
her to where Cullen was stretched out. "Didn't see him
down there."

"He said he rode all night. Did you really need to talk
to him, Jacques?"

"No."

"Good. Let's let him sleep. You haven't found Bobby
Ross, have you?"

"No. Man's invisible. Or he left town. His wife hasn't
seen him either."

"Where could he be? He doesn't know why you're
looking for him—does he?"

Jacques stared at her. "*I* don't know why I'm looking
for him."

"He's a suspect in the Walker murder," said Cullen, getting to his feet behind them. Glynis saw him run his hands up and down his arms. "Damp on the ground," he said.

The ground was dry as a bone, Glynis thought. And was he shivering? "Cullen," she began.

"C'mon Jacques, let's get moving," Cullen said. "You said you asked at the railroad ticket office and the canal toll booth. If Ross hasn't left town, then he's got to be around somewhere." He turned to Glynis. "I'll be back later. If I don't find you here, I'll stop by Peartree's."

Glynis nodded. There was no way to stop him, and he did look better than earlier. He and Jacques walked toward the livery on Fall Street.

The sun had long since disappeared behind gray clouds rolling in from the northwest. Rain had threatened for several hours, but those on the grass singing "Wayfaring Stranger" seemed unconcerned. Glynis sat on a blanket with Harriet and Aurora in front of the platform, where Vanessa was playing guitar as accompaniment to Brendan Fitzwater's fiddle, a tune Brendan called "Open Thy Lattice, Love" by a young songwriter from Pittsburgh named Stephen Foster.

The crowd had begun to thin as people with children headed for home. The food had finally run out, but there were still pitchers of ale and cider. Glynis asked Aurora, "Have you seen Ambrose and Lydia Abernathy today?"

"Lydia was here for a while early on, before you arrived," Aurora said. "I haven't seen her recently."

They both looked up as several creaking hay carts loaded with young people rolled by the green and headed toward the fields beyond. Glynis supposed they didn't care whether it rained or not. She suddenly felt very old.

Getting to her feet, she wandered toward the south edge of the green until she reached a place that overlooked the town. While she stared into the distance, something caught her eye on the far side of the canal. Warehouses and factories stood outlined against the rain clouds, but it was a holiday; everything was shut down. So why did she see something moving in the dark sky behind one of the factories? She looked again, squinting. It must have been the clouds. She started to turn back to the singing, and across the canal again thought she saw upward movement, like a white snake rising.

Dictras Fyfe and Pete Morrow were standing some distance behind her on the grass.

"Would you two please come here a minute?" she called.

She pointed, and the men's gaze followed her finger. Pete started to shake his head, then craned his neck forward. He stood with his hands cupped like a horse's blinders around his eyes.

Suddenly he began to run toward the canal, yelling back over his shoulder, "Fire! There's fire down by the pump factory!"

And the bell in the firehouse began to clang.

# TWENTY-EIGHT

~∽~

AS SHE STEPPED from the bridge, Glynis was jostled by people running from all directions. Every able-bodied person in the village was needed for the bucket brigade, and the firehouse bell was still clamoring furiously, but it seemed as though half of Seneca Falls was already at the burning pump factory.

Downs & Co. had recently relocated; their original two-story factory, fronting the canal, had been empty for several months. Even so, there was more than enough to burn. The structural components of the building were hewn fir; the outside walls were pine board and the roof was cedar-shingled. Inside was assorted trash, wood scraps, broken workbenches. The lazy white smoke that Glynis had spotted earlier now was black and rolled in billows up through the factory's deteriorated roof.

She could feel the heat from where she stood on a slope well back from the alley that ran along behind the factories and warehouses. The scene was lit by scores of lanterns and by tongues of flame, licking around blown-out window openings; the flickering orangish light was demonic. A witches' Sabbath. The smoke smelled bitter, and Glynis's eyes smarted. She squeezed them closed, forcing tears. Then she looked for Cullen.

Finally she saw him, helping to position a red hand-pulled pumper. The men who had run with it from the firehouse panted as they drew the stiff leather hose from two-wheeled carts. Glynis could hear them cursing when the riveted seams of the hose slashed their hands. An eight-man team worked the pumper, using a seesawing

motion at the long handles at either side of the water tank.
Bucket brigades had formed from the canal to the pumper
to keep the water tank filled. Glynis was surprised to see
Gordon Walker, his face grim, roll up his sleeves and step
into line. It was a backbreaking job. But even Ambrose
Abernathy grabbed a bucket, pulling off his waistcoat as
he lumbered toward the canal.

At last a thin stream of water began to spout from the
tank. Sweat ran down the men's faces; the inflexible hose
and short range of the water stream made it necessary to
keep the pumping apparatus close to the burning building.

Another line of people was throwing tubs of water on
the building to the west of the burning factory; so far the
blaze seemed to be concentrated on that side. Glynis cal-
culated the distance separating the two buildings as about
seventy feet—not enough to keep flying sparks from landing and setting a new blaze. Coming across the bridge, she
thought she had felt scattered raindrops, but only a downpour at this point could stop the catastrophe of fire leaping
from one structure to the next.

To the east of the burning factory was the Phoenix
Mills, a four-story building of limestone blocks. Since it
was in less danger of igniting, most of the older people
and children had gathered in front of it. From there, Glynis
saw a child suddenly dart forward to the front door of the
burning factory. A woman screamed and several people
rushed toward the child, as a crash accompanied the col-
lapse of an outer wall on the far side.

The heads of those grabbing at the child went up. A
young girl peered through a window on the factory's
ground floor. "In there!" she shrieked over the fire's roar.
"Somebody's in there!"

She was pulled away from the window, but kept
shrieking, and Glynis heard her words being relayed
among the crowd. Through an eerie pall of suspended
soot, Cullen and Jacques Sundown appeared like masked
phantoms, tying dripping cloths over their faces. Stunned,
Glynis watched them approach the factory door. Heads

low, they crept through it. A thin veil of smoke curled around them before they disappeared.

Cullen was exhausted; it was the only thought in Glynis's head—that, and how stupid he was being. She ran toward the building, pushed aside those in her way. When she reached the door, she could hear coughing inside. She felt hands grab at her and Harriet's voice in her ear.

"Glynis, keep away! There's nothing you can do. Wait for them to come out. Keep away!"

She hesitated, staring at Harriet, watching her lips move but barely hearing her. As she stepped over the doorsill her shoulder was seized and she was pulled backward. With the strength of one possessed, she twisted her shoulder free; the force of it made her fall forward. She was caught from behind in a powerful grip and half carried, half dragged back from the building. She tried to struggle, felt herself being shaken, and looked up into the face of Karl Steicher.

The shock was like being thrown into a snowdrift. She gasped for breath and he released her, as people around them began to yell. She looked toward the doorway. Jacques emerged first, carrying a man's legs, followed by Cullen with his hands under the man's arms. Both were bent over and choking.

For a moment the crowd went still. Then a scorching surge of flames howling through the window openings drove them backward. Glynis ran beside Cullen up the slope. He and Jacques laid the man down on the grass and Cullen squatted beside the inert body. There was just enough light from the flames for Glynis to recognize the man on the ground: Bobby Ross.

Cullen reached out and pulled her toward him. He was still coughing. "Don't get too close, Glynis. He's been dead a while."

A sweetish odor rose from the grass. Glynis knelt beside Cullen, burying her face against his shoulder. He was shivering, and his shirt was wet. For a moment, Glynis thought he was being sprayed with a hose. Then she realized they were both drenched: it was raining.

She kept her face against Cullen's shoulder; she

couldn't look at Bobby Ross. Behind her she could hear sharp intakes of breath as people saw the body. She looked around finally and saw Daisy Ross coming toward them.

Daisy just stood, staring down at Bobby. Her hands were in fists pressed against her mouth.

"Daisy." Glynis stood up and put her arm around the silent figure; she felt Cullen struggle to his feet beside her and turned to see him stumble and sway. Jacques Sundown caught him and lowered him to the ground.

Suddenly the rain was streaming down as if a curtain of water had dropped. There was a tremendous hissing as smoke rolled upward in great clouds, accompanied by thunderous shouting. The factory was still a burning mountain of rubble, but the flames were no longer leaping into the sky. The surrounding buildings were secure.

Through rain like a translucent wall, Glynis could just see Daisy's blank face, her eyes still on Bobby's body. Quentin Ives pushed through the crowd. He knelt down and looked at the body for a long moment, then reached forward and pressed the skin on Bobby's arm. Ives stood up without feeling for a pulse.

"I'm sorry, Mrs. Ross."

Harriet was beside her, putting her arm around Daisy's waist. She pulled the young woman away across the slope and called over her shoulder to Glynis, "I'll take her home." She and Daisy walked through the downpour and were gone.

Some of the crowd continued to mill around the small group on the slope, despite the rain pelting them. Cullen was on his feet; he, Jacques, and Quentin Ives stood between the curious and Bobby Ross.

"The man's dead," Ives said to them. "Nothing you can do for him now. Go along home."

"Did he die in the fire, Doc?" someone asked. "He don't look so burned."

Ives shrugged. "Could be the smoke killed him. We'll know more later. Why don't you all go on home, now."

In an undertone, Cullen said, "Thanks, Quentin."

Ives nodded, then stared at him as though he had just

seen him. "Cullen, you shaking? Get too much smoke in there?"

Glynis waited for him to answer, but Cullen didn't say anything except, "Guess we'd better get him"—he nodded toward Bobby—"to your office."

He turned to Jacques. "You want to get the horses?"

They trooped in: Jacques and Abraham Levy carrying Bobby's body, Cullen and Quentin Ives behind them. Glynis tethered the horses and followed them. She brushed back the wet hair plastered to her face and reached for the lantern Cullen handed her; his hand was trembling so hard the glass rattled.

She held the lantern up and looked at him. He scowled, then rubbed the back of his neck. Glynis pointed to a chair behind him, grabbing his arm when he started to stagger and helping him into it.

Dr. Ives lit more lanterns, and the white walls of the room took on a yellow cast. Katherine Ives came through the door from the living quarters beyond the front office in a dressing gown. She saw Bobby Ross lying on the table and gasped.

The room smelled fetid; Glynis opened the window and tied the curtains back away from the rain.

"Jacques, you and Abe might as well head on home, now," Cullen said through chattering teeth. "Nothing more you can do here."

Jacques stood in front of him. "Somebody should see you get home."

Cullen shook his head. "I'm fine now. If I need help, Glynis and Quentin are here. Thanks, Jacques, but go on. I'll see you tomorrow."

Jacques and Abe went out, and Glynis turned to Ives. "I didn't want to say anything in front of the others, but I think Cullen is really sick. I thought so earlier today."

"I think so too," said Ives, moving around the table toward a washstand against the wall. He poured water into a basin and soaped his hands. Katherine handed him a towel.

Cullen was leaning forward in the chair, his head in his

hands. Glynis crouched down beside him. "Cullen." She spoke quietly. "How long ago were you in the swamp?"

Ives turned sharply from the basin. "How long ago, Cullen?" he asked. "And how long did you stay? Did you just ride through?"

Cullen started to shake his head, and Glynis heard his teeth grind. "Hell, I don't know how long. Had to camp there a couple of nights."

Ives reached down, put his fingers under Cullen's chin, and tilted his head back. Cullen's teeth were clenched, and his whole body shook.

"You been shaking very long?" Ives pulled his eyelid up, holding the lantern close to his face.

"Since this afternoon," Glynis said. "It's Genesee fever, isn't it?" She knew, had known earlier, but still prayed Ives wouldn't confirm it.

"I'm afraid so," he said, his hands pressing Cullen's stomach. "You feel queasy, like you're going to vomit?"

"All day," Cullen said hoarsely. "Thought I was just tired."

"This isn't fatigue. We'll know for sure if you start to fever. Think you better stay right here tonight."

Cullen jerked his head away from Ives's hand. He looked at the body on the table.

Glynis stood up. "Dr. Ives . . ."

"He doesn't mean in *here*," said Katherine. She almost smiled. "There are beds in the next room."

Glynis realized this sort of thing was not new to Katherine Ives. Had she known when she married Quentin that she was taking on not only him but his patients too?

"I'm going to stay," Glynis said. "I've seen fever before." A younger sister had died from it. She had told Cullen long ago; she hoped he wouldn't remember.

"Well, yes, of course," Quentin agreed. "Right now, I want to get this examination of Ross over with, so we can get him into the ground."

He reached down to help Cullen. Glynis moved to take his arm. Cullen shook his head, rose, took two steps forward, and passed out.

# TWENTY-NINE

ᘒᕉᕊ

GLYNIS WRUNG OUT the soft cloths in the bucket, then hung them over a chair. Hauling fresh water from the back-yard well could wait a few minutes. She sat down on the end of the bed.

Cullen's breathing was rapid; the fever had begun almost as soon as they got him into the bed. In the time it took to get his clothing off, she saw his face and chest turn from a ghostly gray to the color of fresh meat. He threw off the blankets and pillows she tucked around him and lay flat, panting like an exhausted runner. She had sponged him down several times in the past hour. It could still be some time before the fever broke—if it did.

Glynis had seen others gripped by Genesee fever writhe and yell as though pursued by the hounds of Hell. Cullen lay quietly, only his chest moving up and down. It was as if he had willed his central being into a small, calm core, around which pulsated an inferno. In a way, his stillness frightened her more than if he had thrashed around and suffered more energetically.

In the next room she could hear occasional clatters, as though metal objects were being dropped. Otherwise the house was silent. Katherine and the Ives children must be asleep in the upper story of the house.

"Glynis?" Quentin Ives's voice called from the next room. "Can I see you? In here."

"Coming." She noted the familiarity created by crisis. For all the years she had lived in Seneca Falls, it had been "Miss Tryon," and "Dr. Ives."

She hesitated in the doorway of the examining room,

but the body was now covered with a sheet. *The body*, she thought. Not Bobby anymore.

"Should Cullen be so quiet?" she asked. "He's still burning hot."

"I think he's all right," Quentin said. "Could be his body's keeping him quiet to better fight the disease—after all, it's astonishing that he continued to function so long after it took hold."

She must not have looked convinced.

"He's strong, Glynis. I expect he'll come through this without much harm. You know, though, he could be sick for some weeks."

She nodded. She had been thinking of that possibility for the past hour. "Quentin, Bobby Ross didn't die in the fire, did he? I saw the body close up. And I watched you; you didn't even feel for a pulse."

"That's why I called you in here," he said. "We have to talk about this because of what you saw, and because of Cullen's condition. But first I need some information, so I can figure out what's best to do, under the circumstances. Glynis, how much do you know about the deputy, Jacques Sundown?"

"I know he's extremely loyal to Cullen. And Cullen trusts him, if that's what you mean. He puts Jacques in charge of the constable's office when he's away, unless, like this last time, he takes Jacques with him."

Quentin nodded. "I know he has Cullen's trust. The question is whether the town trusts Jacques. I think we have a bad situation on our hands."

Glynis stared at him. What had he found out?

"Because as you said, Bobby Ross was dead before the fire started."

"Do you know now how he died?" she asked. "I thought it might have something to do with his drinking."

Quentin looked at her as if considering something, then wearily took a chair and motioned for Glynis to do the same. She tried not to look at the draped figure on the table.

"When I said Ross was dead before the fire started, I

meant *long* before. And it wasn't alcohol that killed him, not directly, at least. I think Cullen guessed that, because down at the canal he asked me not to say anything; he must have seen the dried blood on Ross when he brought him out of the building."

"Dried blood?" Glynis hadn't seen that.

"Behind his right ear. And at the back of his skull. Ross died from deep, depressed skull fractures. Given that he was found in an abandoned building, there just wasn't anything he could have fallen against, not that could have produced those *two* massive injuries, either of which could have killed him. There's little doubt that the fractures were caused by violent blows to Ross's head—blows struck with something heavy. A fist couldn't have done that damage."

Glynis wasn't surprised. Shocked, but not surprised. She had begun to be uneasy when Jacques couldn't locate Bobby. But with Cullen away, she had wanted to disregard the uneasiness. Because she didn't want to think that . . .

"Another murder, isn't it, Quentin?"

And that meant Bobby probably hadn't killed Rose Walker.

She wasn't surprised at that either. While she had been in the next room with Cullen, Glynis had thought about the things that were wrong with that theory, things that had bothered her since Daisy brought her the purse. But before tonight she hadn't wanted to consider them. She'd wanted to believe it was over: that poor, feckless Bobby Ross was the answer to Rose's death.

Now she thought of something else. "Do you think the fire was deliberately set?" she asked. "To make it look as though Bobby burned to death? Remember, it was supposed to look as though Rose Walker had drowned, when really she died of strangulation."

Quentin's eyes narrowed. "I hadn't thought of that. Although it crossed my mind that the two deaths could well be connected."

Glynis thought, he doesn't know about Rose's purse—a strong connection.

"In fact," Quentin said, "if the killer did set the fire, what better time than during the Fourth of July picnic?"

"Yes, when the entire town was occupied on the other side of the canal. Or . . ." She paused, thinking. "Almost the entire town. The whole factory could have burned to the ground—it was just chance the fire was spotted early. I saw some smoke, but Cullen and Jacques had already turned in the alarm, because they happened to be riding down behind the factories. Looking for Bobby Ross."

Glynis heard a groan in the next room. "Cullen," she gasped. She dashed through the door, Ives behind her. Cullen lay in a sweat; the sheet underneath him was soaked, and his eyelids quivered as though too heavy to open.

Glynis put her hand on his forehead. It was cool. "Cullen?"

His eyelids fluttered open. His eyes were red-rimmed, the pupils large, the whites faintly yellowish. He stared at some point on the ceiling. She didn't think he even knew she was there.

"Fever's broken," Quentin said. "He should have some water," but Glynis was already on the way out with the empty pitcher.

When she returned they changed the drenched sheet under him. Cullen seemed aware of nothing and slept immediately after they made him swallow water and quinine.

Quentin stood leaning against the windowsill. It was still raining, softly now, and the air coming through the sheer curtains smelled fresh and clean.

"Why don't we talk in here," he said. "Cullen's sleeping too soundly to be disturbed."

"I've been thinking about what you asked earlier," Glynis said. "About the town trusting Jacques. He's not very . . . 'responsive' may be the word I want. There's going to be a lot of fear when people find out someone else has been murdered—one of our own. After all, Rose Walker was a stranger here. Unfortunately, everybody seems to think her death was connected with Karl Steicher and the money from Friedrich's estate, so her murder might be looked at, in a terrible kind of way, as understandable. And so it may seem that there's no threat to anyone else. It's been assumed that Cullen would find her killer, and everyone else's life would go on. Bobby's death may be viewed very differently."

They seated themselves on the bed opposite Cullen's; his breath caught for an instant, then resumed as he turned his face toward the wall and was still.

"That's exactly what I'm worried about," Quentin said. "I think Jacques Sundown is a good man, but I don't know if he can handle this situation. And there's another problem. The surrogate judge is away, which means we can't hold an inquest for several weeks. It will appear to the town that no one is investigating Ross's death, which will be true enough, with Cullen sick."

"In the meantime there's a killer walking around," Glynis said. "Do you suppose people might panic—that things could get out of hand?"

Quentin nodded. "I've seen it before. We're not that far removed from frontier justice. Lynchings still happen where there's no accepted authority with the force of law behind it."

Glynis thought of Karl. He could be the one the town would want to blame. And then she remembered the scene at the fire; Karl pulling her back from the factory door. She hadn't thought about it before—why had he been there? He hadn't been at the picnic, and the farm was too distant for him to have heard the fire bell.

"Here's what I intend to do," Quentin said. "I'll give out the opinion that it appears Bobby Ross died of smoke inhalation. I think people will accept that. You'd have to agree to it, of course. Cullen only suspected otherwise, so other than you and myself, no one knows the truth."

Glynis understood his concern and his tactic. She supposed it made sense. Still . . .

"I'm not sure I think that's right," she said slowly. "Someone in this town has committed one, probably two murders. Don't people have a right to know that and take what measures they think they should to protect themselves?"

Quentin sighed, stood up, and went to the doorway. He leaned against the jamb, arms folded across his chest.

"You sound like your editor friend, Dexter Bloomer. Do you want speculations spread all over the front page of his newspaper? It could send the town into a frenzy. Besides, why should anyone else be in danger? If you have reason to think so, you'd better tell me now."

Glynis wasn't confident the two of them had any business deciding whether there was danger or not, although perhaps Ives did have a point. But she was already fairly certain that Bobby Ross was killed because of something he had seen—or that the murderer *thought* he had seen—the night of Rose Walker's death. She hadn't had time to think it through carefully, but if she was right, then probably no one else would be in danger. Not at the moment, at least—provided the killer wasn't crazy, which she regarded as a shaky provision, since she couldn't imagine anyone *but* a crazy person committing murder.

"All right, Quentin, I'll agree to keep silent for one or two days." If what she'd begun to suspect was valid, she would need only a day or two. She would see Jacques Sundown in the morning.

She woke with a startled shiver, hearing thudding sounds above her. Probably the Ives children getting up. Glynis got up off the bed opposite Cullen's and went to feel his forehead and the sheet beneath him. The sheet was drenched again.

He didn't waken when she rolled him over and changed the sheet. He looked so peaceful; if she hadn't known better, it would seem he could just wake up recovered and go home. But she did know better: last night was only the beginning. The chills would return, and the fever, and the sweating.

Finally, after two or three weeks, the disease would likely have run its course. It was children and old people who died the most frequently; they weren't strong enough to survive it, or they couldn't tolerate quinine. But the drug extracted from bark of the cinchona tree was the only thing that worked against the disease.

At the time of her sister's illness, Glynis had read everything she could find about ague and swamp fever and western New York's Genesee fever; they all had the same symptoms. She had found that some form of ague had been killing people the world over for centuries, called by different names in different places. No one had figured out how the illness was contracted, although it seemed to have something to do with the miasmic air of wetland swamps and bogs. But how her sister had gotten it remained a mystery; she died, the doctors had said, because the quinine had produced the fatal side effect of blackwater fever.

Katherine Ives appeared in the doorway. By that time, Glynis had satisfied herself that Cullen was still cool. His breathing was steady. He would probably sleep for hours.

"Katherine, I need to go home and get cleaned up. And I've got to figure out what to do about the library for a week or two."

"You look exhausted," Katherine said. "What a night for you! Why don't we have Mrs. Dobbins next door come and stay with Cullen. Quentin has trained her for this kind of thing; she's a widow, and she can always use the money."

"That's good news," Glynis said. "When I get back I'll talk to her. Maybe I won't have to close the library."

After the stuffy room, reeking of sickness, even the rain felt good. Glynis walked to her boardinghouse in the early morning quiet. Only the roosters were alert.

# THIRTY

CAREFULLY LIFTING THE pillowcase from her bureau drawer, Glynis heard the delicate chatter of beads. That day in the library, when Daisy first handed the purse to her, she had been so stunned she hadn't even read the letter it held right away. But something since had troubled her. She hadn't been able to grasp it; it kept shifting in the back of her mind like a sly shadow.

Sitting with Cullen last night, she had gone over and over what possible reason someone could have for murdering Bobby Ross.

The purse was the one thing that seemed to link Bobby and Rose Walker—if they were linked. But why would someone kill Bobby, unless he had something to do with the previous murder and the pink beaded purse?

Had Rose Walker dropped her purse on the towpath while struggling with her killer? It could have gone unnoticed in the dark, to be picked up later by Bobby, in need of money, oblivious to the body floating below the canal wall. Or maybe Bobby saw the murder, saw the purse drop, and he remained concealed until after the killer had left.

Glynis remembered the sound outside the firehouse when she had been talking to Jacques; anyone could have overheard their conversation. Rumors spread fast in a small town. When the killer discovered Bobby was being sought, he might have feared that Bobby had witnessed the killing and could identify him. And maybe Bobby could have. They would never know that now.

Glynis thought of the murderer as "him." It was less

conceivable that a woman would have had the strength to overcome Rose, a tall woman, then heave her body into the canal, much less hit Bobby Ross hard enough to kill him. It must have been a man.

Another possibility was that Rose's killer had been worried about the purse itself, or rather, what was *in* the purse, and thought that Bobby still had it. Initially, the killer could have assumed it had gone into the canal with Rose, as Glynis herself had. Last night she had gone over the purse's contents in her mind. What had she overlooked? Then, seemingly out of nowhere, it had come to her.

She sat now on the edge of her bed, with Rose Walker's copy of the list of jewelry in her hand.

When she had glanced at it that afternoon with Daisy, it appeared to be identical to the one she had seen in the hotel safe. But last night her memory finally released the image of that hotel list, and now she could recall it fairly well in her mind's eye.

She realized something was different about the two supposedly duplicate lists. The one she held in her hand was done in small, precise handwriting, with Rose Walker's and Simon Sheridan's signatures at the bottom. Glynis remembered the one in the hotel safe as having larger, sprawling handwriting, with a single signature. If she recalled correctly, the two lists were the same length; she wouldn't know for sure until she saw the other again. But they *shouldn't* be the same length—not if the two notes were in such different hands, one so much smaller than the other.

She sat on her bed, for some reason reluctant to do the obvious. It was so simple—too simple to be so damning.

Aware that she was stalling, she went to her bookcase beside the window and stared up at the slim volumes standing between brass bookends on the top shelf. They were the collection of Edgar Allan Poe's stories and poems that Friedrich had given her the previous Christmas. How much had they had to do with somehow jogging her memory?

She reached up and pulled out *The Purloined Letter*,

flipping through it. Appropriate title, but not the story with the passage for which she was looking. *The Murders in the Rue Morgue*; that was the one. She found the passage: detective C. Auguste Dupin explaining, "There is such a thing as being too profound. Truth is not always in a well. In fact, as regards the more important knowledge, I do believe that she is invariably superficial."

She placed the book back beside its companions. The passage had reassured her. The answer to the puzzle of the two lists, and the two murders, could indeed be as simple as she thought.

Glynis stood at the window and ran her finger down the list of jewelry, item by item, looking for things that she had not seen on the list from the hotel safe, or in the jewel cases.

She found the first item about halfway down the page, entered between *Jet and silver bead necklace* and *Filigree silver brooch*. In the small, precise handwriting was written *Gold ring with moss agate surrounded by amethysts*. No—that piece had not been on the list in the hotel safe. She would have noted it particularly: amethysts were her own favorite gem. And she certainly would have looked for it in the jewel cases.

She *was* on the right track. She felt a rush of fear, then relief, like riding a toboggan down Cayuga Street onto the winter-frozen canal, and finding the ice as thick as she had prayed it would be. Karl Steicher couldn't be implicated in this.

Entered between the less valuable pieces, she found other missing items: *Necklace and earrings of Brazilian diamonds*, and *Gold ring with cabochon emerald, seed pearls in bezel*. None of those had been in the jewel boxes. She was positive. And she had been told that the pieces in the cases were paste—just costume jewelry!

If the list from Rose Walker's purse was placed next to the one in the hotel safe, the discrepancies would be immediately evident. Of course, the purse had never been expected to reappear, being safely at the bottom of the canal. Or so it was thought, by the person who had access to

Rose's room, the person who would know that the purse wasn't among her belongings at the hotel. Who, after committing murder, could then commit larceny without danger of being exposed.

Jacques Sundown had just stared at her. At first, she wasn't even certain he would go with her, although she surely wasn't going alone. Finally he stood up, fastened his holster over his hip, and said, "Better get this over with."

Now she tried not to think ahead, concentrating instead on keeping pace with Jacques's long strides. The rain had stopped and the sky was clearing. The day following a holiday, people were slow getting started; not many were yet up and about. Still, she and Jacques drew some stares on Fall Street. She glanced at him and thought what an odd pair they must have made: the tall, copper-skinned French Indian and the town's spinster librarian, gathering the skirts of her white lawn frock so she could keep up with him. She slowed her pace. After a few more seven-league strides, so did he.

When they reached the three front steps of the Hotel Bristol, Jacques took them in one lazy leap, then stood barring her way though the entrance. "Don't know what we'll meet with in there," he said. "You stay beside me. Cullen'll flay me alive, feed me to buzzards, anything happens to you."

She sincerely hoped so.

The lobby was quiet, a little less grand in the daylight. Jacques and Glynis quickly walked past the front desk and the clerk who slumped behind it; he first nodded, then sat up and gaped at Jacques with a startled expression. Before he could say anything, Glynis went to Sheridan's office. The door was ajar. She rapped on it, then pushed it open. Jacques was directly behind her.

At his desk, Simon Sheridan glanced up. He smiled, running a hand over his hair, and straightening his neck-cloth in one smooth gesture. He started to rise, then saw Jacques. A frown crossed his face, and he sat back down.

"Good day, Mr. Sheridan," Glynis said. "I don't know if you've met Jacques Sundown, Constable Stuart's deputy."

Sheridan sat forward, staring at Jacques. Jacques stared back. Sheridan's eyes shifted to Glynis.

"I'm rather busy, Miss Tryon. I don't wish to be rude, but is there some urgent reason why you're here? Otherwise, I'm afraid I must ask you to come back another day."

"We're here to collect Rose Walker's belongings," Glynis said. "Constable Stuart is indisposed, so Deputy Sundown is to bring them to the lockup. I've accompanied him, since I can identify Mrs. Walker's things."

"Good! I'll be glad to have that room free." Sheridan pulled a handkerchief from his pocket and patted his forehead before standing and moving around his desk. "I'll call for someone to bring the trunk downstairs."

Jacques stood back from the door, then followed Sheridan out into the lobby. Glynis went to the safe and stood waiting in front of it. When Sheridan returned, with Jacques right behind him, he said to her, "I trust you will give me a voucher for her things, to relieve me of further dealings with her husband. He's already been here, you know, and I told him that Stuart had impounded the property. Mr. Walker wasn't happy about that. So I'll need a receipt."

He had been speaking to Glynis. He glanced indifferently at Jacques, then said to her, "I suppose you can sign a receipt for the constable, Miss Tryon?"

"I'll sign it," Jacques said, his voice as expressionless as usual. If he had caught Sheridan's intimation that he was illiterate, Glynis thought, Jacques didn't sound the least bit resentful.

Gesturing at the safe, Glynis said, "Mr. Sheridan, would you get the jewel boxes, please."

The safe opened, Sheridan handed them to her, then pulled the handkerchief from his pocket again. She took the jewel boxes over to his desk, set them down, and lifted the lids. After finding the itemized jewelry list in the inside pocket of one, she removed Rose Walker's list from her own purse.

Spreading the two lists out on the desk side by side, she bent over them, trying at the same time to watch Sheridan from the corner of her eye. But he had moved and was standing directly behind her. She couldn't see Jacques.

"Is there some problem, Miss Tryon?" Sheridan said.

Glynis didn't respond as she ran her fingers down the lists on the desk. Finally she looked up at Sheridan. He met her eyes for a brief moment, then whirled and started for the door.

Jacques was leaning against the jamb, arms crossed over his chest. "You going somewhere, Sheridan?"

"I need to check something at the front desk. Step aside and let me pass."

Jacques didn't move.

Glynis raised her eyebrows and nodded to Jacques.

"Let me pass," Sheridan demanded again. "You have no right."

Jacques uncrossed his arms. His right hand casually brushed his hip and the butt of his Colt revolver. "Miss Tryon's got a couple things to ask you. Maybe you should answer her."

"Mr. Sheridan," Glynis said, hoping her voice wasn't shaking, "is all Rose Walker's jewelry here—everything she left with you?"

"Yes. Yes, of course it is."

"Then where are the missing items? The valuable jewelry that isn't in those boxes? The pieces appearing on her list, which you both signed. They're not on the list you had in your safe, the one with your signature—*only* your signature. Where are they?"

"I don't know what you're talking about!" Sweat dripped onto Sheridan's immaculate shirt collar. His eyes shifted back and forth between Glynis and Jacques.

"You know, Sheridan," Jacques said, "you're in one hell of a mess here. It'd be smart for you to come up with some explanation. The lady asked you where the stuff is—you going to tell her?"

"I have no explanation. And I don't have to answer to either of you." Sheridan's voice rose; his fingers tugged at his collar. "You think I'm accountable to some half-breed and an old-maid busybody? Think again!"

Remembering Rose Walker's body floating in the canal, Glynis glanced at the door, wondering if she could get past the two men—the room seemed to be shrinking. She took a deep breath and looked across the room at Jacques. His eyes, watching Sheridan, were as level and unreadable as ever.

Suddenly Sheridan lunged forward. Before Glynis could even shift her position, he was up against the wall of the office, his feet barely grazing the floor, while Jacques held him aloft by his neckcloth. Sheridan choked as the neckcloth twisted in Jacques's fingers. Jacques let go abruptly, and Sheridan slid toward the floor, his face purple. Jacques hauled him to his feet with one hand, yanking a piece of rope from his pocket with the other. He whipped it around Sheridan's hands, then shoved him back against the wall.

Glynis thought the whole thing must have taken place in the space of a single second. She had never seen anyone move as fast as Jacques. He didn't look as though he'd even exerted himself.

"You did have to go and make it hard on yourself, didn't you, Sheridan?" he said. "And it's not going to get easier. I'm charging you with the theft of that jewelry, and I'm putting you in the lockup until we get a circuit judge here. Expect you're going to get charged with murder too."

It was the longest speech Glynis had ever heard Jacques Sundown utter—and he sounded just like Cullen! She could feel bubbles of laughter boiling up in her throat. It must be hysteria; certainly nothing about this was laughable. She swallowed hard. And followed Sheridan and Jacques out of the office into the hotel lobby.

The desk clerk's eyes widened and his mouth went slack. Glynis wondered what he thought when his employer spat, "You dumb half-breed bastard! I never touched that bitch—*I* didn't kill her. The jewels are one thing, but you can't pin murder on me. I didn't kill her!"

Glynis didn't know if Cullen understood what they had just told him. He nodded a little and closed his eyes. Jacques looked at her; then he turned and walked out of the room.

When she left Cullen, Quentin Ives was waiting for her in the hall. "He had another attack, Glynis, after you left this morning, but it wasn't as severe as the first one. He looks weak now, but that's pretty much the sequence of this disease."

"I know," she said. "But I hope he heard us, about Simon Sheridan. That should make him rest easier. Cullen never liked the man, and in Ithaca he uncovered some history that makes Sheridan a possible killer."

"Well," Quentin said, "we'll *all* rest easier with the man incarcerated. How did you figure it out?"

"It was right there. I should have seen it sooner. I don't know if it would have saved Bobby Ross or not. I suppose now you'll disclose that he was murdered too?"

"Don't see any reason I shouldn't," Ives replied.

Jacques Sundown was standing on the porch steps. Glynis was glad he was still there; she wanted to tell him how much she respected the way he handled the situation at the hotel. She had been surprised, but perhaps he always rose to the occasion. Which must be why Cullen trusted him.

Jacques seemed to be watching a cat draped over the Iveses' porch railing. He hadn't said much in Cullen's room, and as they reached the road he turned to Glynis. "You think Sheridan did it? Murder?" he said, staring at her.

"Yes. Don't you?"

He shrugged, and started to walk away.

She followed him. "Jacques, why did you ask me that?"

He kept walking. Glynis ran after him, gripping his upper arm to stop him. His muscle tightened under her hand; he looked down at her, his eyes narrowed.

She felt herself blushing, looked around, and quickly let go of him. "Excuse me, Jacques—I just want to know why you asked me what you did. We went over it all before we left for the hotel."

He looked away and didn't answer. Why did she feel that she needed to convince him?

But he hadn't moved, so she said, "Jacques, it all fits! Simon Sheridan had a motive to kill Rose Walker, and he had the opportunity: she was staying in his hotel. He must have left the note for the waiter to find, to get her to come to his room. He was overheard arguing with her there by the von Lentzes. Maybe Rose had already discovered her jewels were gone. And I told you why he felt he had to kill Bobby. All of that, plus his past history. So why the question?" She stood waiting for him to say something.

He just shrugged again, turned, and walked down the road away from her.

What was the matter with him? Simon Sheridan was in the lockup. All right, so she wanted Sheridan to be the killer. And all right, so there was very little hard evidence. But there would be. There had to be. Glynis tried to ignore the alarm bell clanging in the back of her mind as she started for home.

# THIRTY-ONE

⤜∽⤛

THE LAWYER'S SHARP eyes probed the face of the man seated opposite his desk. Did Walker have the tenacity to see this through? Or would he now just pick up and go back to Boston?

Orrin Polk leaned forward. "A few days ago, I heard a hotelier named Sheridan was arrested for your wife's murder. Don't suppose that makes it any easier."

"No. No, it doesn't really," Gordon Walker said. "I'd been sure Karl Steicher did it. As it turns out, that hotel manager had stolen Rose's jewelry; things her mother had given her. To think he killed her just for a couple of old gems."

He stared past Polk out the window.

Polk cleared his throat. "Yes, well ... It was a tragic event. Nonetheless, at this time we should discuss your claim to Friedrich Steicher's estate. I have received a communication from Jeremiah Merrycoyf. Karl Steicher is prepared to offer you ten thousand dollars for a release of your inheritance claim." Polk sat back to watch the effect.

Gordon Walker frowned. He crossed one leg over the other and swung his foot back and forth. "Have you some idea of the estate's worth?"

Polk hunched forward. He jabbed the desktop with his finger as he spoke. "The Steicher farm is over eight hundred acres, all tillable. Karl Steicher owns the Phoenix Mills near the canal in Seneca Falls. I understand there was a fire close by recently, but the Phoenix building wasn't damaged."

Walker nodded. "I was there. The hotel manager's other victim was found inside the burned factory."

Polk scowled. He supposed Walker had every right to be preoccupied with his wife's killer, but they must get on with the important matter at hand.

"Ah, to continue," Polk said. "I've done some checking on Karl Steicher's farm property—barns, machinery, livestock, and so on. That doesn't include what cash he has on hand, plus this year's wheat crop. I'd say we are talking about a sizable amount of property."

"You know," Walker said, "if Sheridan hadn't been arrested, I'd have thought any offer from Karl Steicher was suspicious. I'd hoped he was the killer. It would make this claim a lot easier to collect, wouldn't it?"

Polk stared at him. "Why do you think it's going to be difficult, Mr. Walker?"

"Oh, I don't necessarily think it is. And before we go on, there's something you should know. Karl Steicher has his family Bible back—the one that was supposed to have disappeared."

Orrin Polk sat forward in his chair. He folded his hands carefully on the desk. "Just how do you know that, Mr. Walker?"

Walker grinned. "That's not important. I know, that's all. Word travels fast in a small town. And you told me to do some investigating."

Polk slowly rubbed the palms of his hands against each other. "Do you know if that Bible records your wife's birth?"

"I haven't seen it, if that's what you mean. But it must! Rose was his daughter, Friedrich Steicher's. So, Mr. Polk, with that Bible accessible—and I assume you can make Steicher produce it in court—what are our chances of getting half the estate?"

Polk didn't hesitate; he didn't want Walker to hesitate. "I'd say our chances are good. Of course, as your attorney I can't influence you to proceed. But I think the chances are very good. The only trouble we—you—might encounter has to do with local loyalty. You are an outsider; you pointed that out to me yourself. Considering that, I think we should waive our right to a jury hearing. I want to exclude the possibility of a jury predisposed to decide the outcome in favor of their hometown boy."

"So what does that mean, if there's no jury?"

"It means the Seneca County surrogate, J. K. Richardson, will decide the case. Richardson lives here in Waterloo; I've known him a good many years."

Walker uncrossed his legs. "Where do we start?"

"Right here," Polk aid. "We reject Karl Steicher's offer of ten thousand. Ten piddling thousand! So. Shall I ask for a hearing date? Do we go to trial?"

"Yes," said Gordon Walker. "We go to trial. The sooner the better."

Orrin Polk waited until the office door had closed behind his client before he pounced on Merrycoyf's letter. Snatching it up, he held it in the air, shaking it as a weasel worries a rabbit.

"Insult me with your paltry offer! Do you think me a fool, Merrycoyf? You think I would bother to fight unless I had the means to win?"

# THIRTY-TWO

❦

Seneca County Courier—July 14, 1848

WOMAN'S RIGHTS CONVENTION. A Convention to discuss the
social, civil, and religious condition and rights of woman,
will be held in the Wesleyan Chapel, at Seneca Falls, N.Y.,
on Wednesday and Thursday, the 19th and 20th of July,
current; commencing at 10 o'clock A.M. During the first
day the meeting will be exclusively for women, who are
earnestly invited to attend. The public generally are invited
to be present on the second day, when Lucretia Mott, of
Philadelphia, and other ladies and gentlemen, will address
the convention.

It was Friday they had just five days to prepare. Glynis
handed the newspaper across the supper table to an impa-
tient Harriet.

She and Elizabeth Stanton had hand-delivered the notice
about the meeting to Dexter Bloomer at the *Courier* office.
It had been written while Elizabeth was visiting Quaker
Friends in Waterloo.

On the way back to the library from the newspaper office, Elizabeth told Glynis, "I had worked myself up to
such a fever pitch that all my accumulated discontent just
poured out. I persuaded myself, as well as the others, to do
and dare anything. And we decided, right then and there,
to call a Woman's Rights Convention. Fortunately we were
able to get the chapel in the Methodist Church."

Glynis smiled. She could imagine the four other women
seated around a tea table in the Waterloo mansion of ab-

olitionist Quakers, listening to Elizabeth's "discontent." But this, then, had been the hasty initiative step of what Elizabeth called "the first organized protest against the injustice which has brooded for ages over the character and destiny of one half the race."

"You know, Glynis, Lucretia Mott is the only one of us who has had any experience in public speaking. We are all amateurs at this. We're meeting Sunday to set the convention agenda—I'm to prepare our document of resolutions."

"That's why you need the library materials?" Glynis asked.

"Yes. We're thinking of using the Declaration of Independence as our model. Of course, we shall have to make some changes."

Glynis laughed. "Starting, I assume with, 'We hold these truths to be self-evident; that all men *and women* are created equal.' And I think, Elizabeth, that you'd better be prepared to do some creative editing—to put together *only* the eighteen grievances of the Declaration signers."

"Well," Elizabeth sighed, "it will be difficult. Women surely have more to complain about than men under any circumstances. And I think I should tell you, Glynis, that the others have already expressed concern about including a suffrage plank. They are afraid it will make the meeting and its sponsors look ridiculous."

Glynis said only, "You know my feelings on that." There was no point in going over it again.

"I heard that Simon Sheridan has been moved to the county jail in Waterloo," Elizabeth said. "Do you know if that's true?"

It was true. Jacques Sundown had taken Sheridan there several days before. The mood of the town toward the hotel manager was ugly—more for setting the fire than committing murder, Glynis suspected—and the Seneca Falls lockup was not as secure as Waterloo's facility. It seemed prudent, a recovering Cullen had said, to act before things got out of hand. Besides, Sheridan's case would be tried in the Waterloo Court House.

The other reason Cullen had directed their prisoner be

moved was his chagrin at being sick—useless to anyone, he
said; if there was trouble, he wouldn't be able to help. But
he was recovering more rapidly than anyone expected, and
Quentin Ives thought he soon would be on his feet.

"It is such a relief to have that Sheridan man in jail,"
Elizabeth said. "Especially with people coming into town
for the convention. At least, we hope there will be a few.
But they might not have come at all if there had been serious crimes still unsolved here. You did a splendid job of
detection, Glynis."

Glynis stopped walking and stared at her. "Who told
you that?" she said.

"Why, Quentin Ives. He said Jacques Sundown told him
you figured out the whole thing—he just went along with
you to pass the time, so to speak."

"That's not true, Elizabeth. Jacques was the one to bring
Simon Sheridan in. And he did it most effectively. I hope
the town realizes that!"

She sounded more vehement than she meant to. She
hadn't seen Jacques since that day, at least not to talk to,
but she was certain he didn't approve of her, so Elizabeth's
comments surprised her.

"Well, they know what you did, too, Glynis."

Embarrassed, Glynis cast about for a different topic.
"Elizabeth, please let me know if I can help you in the
next few days."

"Oh, the research you've done has been invaluable. You
will attend the meeting, won't you, Glynis, no matter
what's decided on the suffrage issue?"

"I'll come, of course," Glynis said.

But she was concerned. She hoped the women wouldn't
get involved in debate among themselves; they needed to
pull together. She wished they would concentrate on a single issue—when they had, to get the Married Women's
Property Act through, they had been successful.

Wednesday, July 19th, dawned with church bells ringing
in crystal clear air; rain showers the night before had
rinsed the sky to the blue of Wedgwood china. Despite the

convention planners' anxiety that no one would come. Glynis heard the noisy rattle of wagons and carriages before she even turned onto Fall Street.

She planned to stop and see Cullen, as she did most mornings; he had not suffered an attack of the fever for five days and seemed to be on the mend. But when she neared the Methodist Church, she saw that Fall Street was jammed with horse carts. Clouds of dust were churned up as more arrived each minute.

Astride his black and white horse, Jacques Sundown watched the crowd. Glynis thought he was looking her way; she smiled, but his head turned in the other direction.

She saw a girl she knew who did piecework at home for the Seneca Falls glove industry: long, hard hours of work that earned women a pittance, which was then collected and kept by the women's husbands or fathers. Glynis went toward the girl.

"Morning, Miss Tryon." Charlotte Woodword stood beside a cart, holding the reins of a rail-thin mare with a pink ribbon wound in its mane. "Will you just look at this crowd? When my sister and I first left home this morning, we traveled alone. But before we had gone many miles we came upon other wagonloads of women, bound toward town. As we reached different crossroads we saw wagons coming from every part of the county. Long before we got here we had become a procession."

And they were worried that few Would Attend. Their survey of a month ago hadn't been accurate: there must be close to three hundred people gathering, and forty or fifty of them were men. Fall Street was beginning to take on the appearance of the autumn country fair. But no, Glynis thought; no one could mistake this for a fair. All one had to do was view the women. They didn't look completely exhausted from days and nights of plucking birds, smoking hams, grinding sausage meat, baking pies, preserving, and pickling, in addition to their endless routine chores. Their faces this day were different; some faces were haggard and faded, but there was also a look of expectancy, resolution, hope.

Her eyes suddenly filled. She reached into her sleeve for her handkerchief and as she dabbed her eyes she looked around again. Could they actually do this? Send out a call for women's rights from this little town in the middle of western New York? Would anyone, anywhere, hear them?

Elizabeth Stanton, an agitated expression on her face, stood near the church entrance. The front door of the building was closed.

"It's locked," said Aurora Usher, appearing at Glynis's side.

"Surely not," Glynis said. "I know permission was given by the pastor to use the chapel."

"Well, he's either forgotten or changed his mind," Aurora said. "Don't you think it odd that no one seems to be home at the pastor's house, that they didn't leave a key with someone so we could open the church?"

"Perhaps the good pastor left town with Henry Stanton," sighed Vanessa.

Glynis looked at Aurora. "Is that true? About Henry?"

Aurora nodded. "Elizabeth said that although Henry helped draft some of the resolutions she'll present, he hit the roof when he saw the suffrage section. Said it would turn the proceedings into a farce."

"And that if she persisted, he would leave town," Vanessa said.

"Well, apparently Elizabeth persisted." Aurora smiled. "Because he has left! And did you know, Glynis, that Elizabeth's father, Judge Cady, rushed into town yesterday? Elizabeth said he was attempting to determine her sanity, in regard to the suffrage plank."

Glynis glanced up at the small, lively figure standing in front of the church door. She didn't look imposing or particularly heroic. But her husband and her father were the most powerful people in Elizabeth's life; what had it taken to defy them both?

She saw Elizabeth motion to a young man in the crowd. The four women with her looked troubled, but Elizabeth now was smiling. She leaned over to say something to the man—her nephew, Glynis recognized—and he disappeared around a corner of the church.

People at the front of the crowd began to laugh. Glynis heard someone say, "He's being hoisted in through a window."

Moments later, to the cheers of those waiting, the young man flung open the door, and the crowd, women and men, streamed in quickly, filling the pews.

Gathered in hasty council around the altar, the women organizers decided to let the men stay—but then, bold as they thought themselves, the women didn't dare preside over the meeting. It was simply unthinkable with men present.

Lucretia Mott's husband "will take over the oars," as Elizabeth put it. A tall, dignified Quaker who believed in what the women were doing, James Mott would give the proceedings an air of respectability and authority, Elizabeth said, that no woman could have commanded.

Elizabeth began her speech: "We have met here today to discuss our rights and wrongs, civil and political."

The paraphrased Declaration of Independence had become Elizabeth's own Declaration of Sentiments: "The history of mankind is a history of repeated injuries and usurpations on the part of man toward woman, having in direct object the establishment of an absolute tyranny over her."

Glynis glanced around the chapel. Some women were wincing, most were nodding. Never let it be said, she thought, that Elizabeth Cady Stanton minced words. But Elizabeth had confessed to spending the previous week terror-stricken—the speech would be her first in public. Her voice was initially soft, difficult to hear from where Glynis sat, halfway back from the altar. However, the woman's delivery gained volume and confidence as she continued.

Glynis thought about what she knew of Elizabeth's background and what had brought her to this day. Judge Daniel Cady had exposed his daughter from early childhood to legal principles, reasoning, and language. And

Elizabeth Stanton read theorists and philosophers extensively, particularly John Locke. Thus her own philosophy was based on the eighteenth-century theory of natural rights, and she presumed women were endowed with the same natural rights claimed by American men. She granted the physical differences between men and women but argued equal mental ability. Glynis heard this reflected in her first three resolutions.

"*Resolved*, That such laws as conflict, in any way, with the true and substantial happiness of woman, are contrary to the great precept of nature and of no validity. . . .

"*Resolved*, That all laws which prevent woman from occupying such a station in society as her conscience shall dictate, or which place her in a position inferior to that of man, are contrary to the precept of nature, and therefore of no force or authority.

"*Resolved*, That woman is man's equal—was intended to be so by the Creator, and the highest good of the race demands that she should be recognized as such."

Elizabeth's fourth resolution made Glynis reflectively eye the crowd for Lydia Abernathy:

"*Resolved*, that the women of this country ought to be enlightened in regard to the laws under which they live, that they may no longer publish their degradation by declaring themselves satisfied with their present position, nor their ignorance, by asserting that they have all the rights they want."

Nell Steicher had said she couldn't attend. Glynis wondered what Nell would have made of Elizabeth's next section, though Nell was by no means alone in her convictions. Glynis knew, in fact, that many God-fearing women would agree with Nell and Corinthians: females should be silent, and subordinate. But surely that would change with education, and time.

"*Resolved*, that woman has too long rested satisfied in the circumscribed limits which corrupt customs and a perverted application of the Scriptures have marked out for her, and that it is time she should move in the enlarged sphere which her great Creator has assigned her."

Previous resolutions had been received with rapt silence, but when Elizabeth read the ninth, Glynis heard sharp intakes of breath; tongues clicked, petticoats rustled:

"*Resolved*, That it is the duty of the women of this country to secure themselves their sacred right to the elective franchise."

Elizabeth had done it—and with her voice clear as a church bell. But looking at the aghast faces of those around her, Glynis saw it would easily be the most controversial aspect of the entire two days.

At the completion of the afternoon session, when Glynis joined the line leaving the church, she heard her name being called. Through the crowd she spotted Lydia Abernathy frantically gesturing to her.

Lydia's face looked drawn; Glynis again had the impression that she was frightened. But by the time she got through the throng at the door and reached the spot where Lydia had been standing, the woman was gone.

Later that day, when Glynis returned to the boardinghouse after the convention's evening session and a brief visit with Cullen, Harriet met her at the door.

"Lydia Abernathy was just here to see you. When I told her I didn't know when you would be back tonight, she dashed off. Glynis, do you know what's wrong with her?"

"No—why?"

"Because she acted . . . well, overwrought, I would say. Almost desperate to talk to you. She practically wept when I said you weren't here."

Glynis debated with herself. Should she go to the Abernathys' house? What if Lydia wanted to talk to her privately, and Ambrose was at home?

It was almost dusk. She had been uneasy about walking after dark since the night she'd been followed. Which was nonsense, of course; Simon Sheridan was in the Seneca County Jail in Waterloo.

"I told Lydia you would be at the convention tomorrow," said Harriet.

"Good. I hope whatever it is can wait until then."

\* \* \*

On Thursday morning, the convention again heard Elizabeth Stanton's eleven resolutions. All were unanimously
accepted but the ninth, the one regarding suffrage; it was
considered so extreme a demand that even the other women
who had planned the meetings argued against it. Those who
took part in its debate feared a demand for the right to vote
would defeat other sections they felt more reasonable and
make the whole movement ridiculous.

Elizabeth delivered an impassioned speech in defense of
her suffrage plank. It was met with uneasy stirring in the
chapel. Glynis's heart sank. But suddenly an impressive-
looking black man, with erect bearing and a massive head,
rose from one of the pews and quietly made his way to the
lectern. He stood for a moment, looking out into the congregation: the noise in the church instantly diminished, as
if hushed by the motion of a giant hand. Glynis recognized
the man as Frederick Douglass, former slave and editor of
the *North Star* newspaper in Rochester. He had passed
through Seneca Falls several times, lecturing on abolition.
She remembered him as an outstanding speaker; his eyes
would grip every member of his audience as he spoke, daring each to look away from his cause.

Glynis thought later that the controversial resolution never
would have passed, as it did but barely, without Douglass's
eloquent, masculine defense, repeating Elizabeth Stanton's
claim "that the power to choose rulers and make laws was
the right by which all others could be secured."

At the noon break, Glynis wanted to congratulate Elizabeth, but first she looked around the chapel for Lydia Ambrose. As she left the church, a young girl ran up to her,
waving a small folded piece of paper. "Miss Tryon? Are
you Miss Tryon?"

Glynis nodded, and reached for the paper. The girl ran
off and disappeared into the crowd before Glynis could
question her.

Unfolding the note, Glynis read: *Must see you. Meet me
behind the library at noon. Please come.*

It was signed L.

Glynis sat on the library slope waiting for Lydia from

twelve until she heard church bells ring the half hour. She didn't know whether to be angry or worried. What game was Lydia playing?

She walked to the boardinghouse, thinking Lydia might have forgotten where she had said to meet. No one was there. Harriet was at the convention, but she had apparently picked up the mail at the general store sometime during the morning.

On the hall table was an envelope, addressed to Miss Glynis Tryon, from New Haven, Connecticut.

# THIRTY-THREE

〜〰〜

AT THURSDAY'S AFTERNOON session in the Wesleyan chapel, Lucretia Mott offered and spoke to an additional resolution:

"*Resolved*, That the speedy success of our cause depends upon the zealous and untiring efforts of both men and women, for the overthrow of the monopoly of the pulpit, and for the securing to woman an equal participation with men in the various trades, professions, and commerce."

The Woman's Rights Convention closed with the signing of Elizabeth Stanton's Declaration of Sentiments, to which all the resolutions had been added. Sixty-eight women and thirty-two of the men present went to the front of the chapel and affixed their signatures to the document.

Glynis wondered again if the meeting would ever be heard of outside Seneca Falls. Would it make any difference in women's lives, or would its resolutions pass into oblivion? Would the convention alter women's perceptions of themselves and allow them to believe they were entitled to the same rights as men, or, would women like Lydia Abernathy, living in material comfort, continue to protest that they had all the rights they wanted—in other words, Glynis thought, those rights men were willing to give them.

Outside the church, Glynis joined a group of townspeople who had gathered to mingle with those now streaming from the meeting. Elizabeth, when she finally emerged, looked jubilant.

"A grand success," Glynis heard her say. The convention planners believed that the eighteen hours of the past two days' sessions hadn't been enough, she said. They had decided to continue, reconvening two weeks later in Rochester.

While Glynis looked over the crowd, hoping to see Lydia Abernathy, Elizabeth hurried toward her. Her face was more somber than it had been a few minutes before.

"Glynis, look what your friend Jacques Sundown just handed me." She waved a piece of paper at Glynis. "It's a subpoena," she said, "from an Orrin Polk. I'm to appear at a hearing on behalf of Gordon Walker, in the Waterloo Surrogate's Court this coming Monday. Can you imagine?"

She handed the paper to Glynis, who read, *Elizabeth Stanton is Summoned: To give testimony in regard to the relationship of Mary Clarke, Friedrich Steicher and Rose Walker.*

"I didn't realize a hearing had been scheduled," Glynis said.

"I must say, I'm glad Deputy Sundown had the consideration to wait until now to give me this," Elizabeth told her. "I certainly don't look forward to Monday. But until then," she added, smiling, "I plan to enjoy the accomplishments of the past two days."

Turning to watch Elizabeth's small shoulders disappear in the crowd, Glynis saw Jeremiah Merrycoyf stepping into his office from the street. She had just started after him when she heard her name whispered from behind. A woman whose wide-brimmed hat almost covered her face clasped her wrist.

"Lydia? Is that you?" Glynis asked, startled.

"Meet me back inside the church—in the cloakroom," Lydia whispered. "Please, Glynis!" She disappeared into the crowd.

Glynis told herself to avoid Lydia's games, but her curiosity was too strong. She returned to the church and, feeling like a reluctant spy for Santa Anna's army, she pushed open the door of the cloakroom. At first it appeared to be empty. The small room smelled musty; it

must not have been used in months. She looked around for
Lydia—and jumped when Lydia slipped out from between
the opened door and the wall.

"Lydia! For heaven's sake, what is all this cloak-and-
dagger business? And where were you this noon?"

"Glynis, listen to me. You have to listen, please."
Lydia's face was chalk white. Her round doll's eyes looked
like blue agates, and Glynis could see a sheen of perspiration on her upper lip.

"Of course I'll listen," Glynis said. "Is this about your
husband? Is he the one who's terrified you?"

Lydia *was* terrified; there was no mistaking that. She
pulled Glynis away from the door and shut it.

"You don't know how violent Ambrose can be when
he's angry," she whispered. "I don't know what he'll do
when he finds out."

"Finds out what, Lydia?"

"I'm afraid he'll divorce me. And leave me with nothing. What should I do?"

The woman was now weeping hysterically, and Glynis
wondered if she knew what she was saying. She wanted to
shake her. Against the wall opposite the door was a low
bench. Taking hold of Lydia's shoulders, Glynis pressed
her down onto it and sat beside her.

"Lydia, you've got to contain yourself. Why should
Ambrose want to hurt you?"

"Because of . . . oh, Glynis, you have to promise you
won't say anything to anyone about what I tell you. Will
you promise?"

"I think you had better just tell me, Lydia."

Lydia stared at Glynis, as if trying to make up her mind.
"I just don't know if I should, if I can trust you."

Glynis started to rise from the bench, but then, in the
midst of her irritation with Lydia, she began to imagine a
dreadful possibility. She sat back down.

"Lydia, does this have anything to do with the murders?"

Lydia began to sob again. Glynis put an arm around the
woman's shoulders and concentrated on keeping her voice

steady. "I think you *have* to trust me—and tell me right now what is wrong."

Still sobbing, Lydia squirmed on the bench, twisted her skirt, and plunged one hand deep into her pocket. She pulled out a handkerchief and shook its contents into her other hand.

On her open palm lay two sparkling earrings.

Glynis looked up from the jewels into Lydia's face. "Are those diamonds?" *Brazilian diamonds*, her memory quoted to her from the list.

Lydia nodded.

"Rose Walker's earrings." Glynis whispered. "Where did you get these?"

"Simon," Lydia said. She flushed and looked at the floor.

"Simon Sheridan? Oh, dear God, Lydia. What have you gotten yourself into?"

She immediately realized that was not the thing to say. Lydia's face contorted, and Glynis said quickly, "All right, Lydia; it's all right. If you were involved with him it's certainly not my place to pass judgment. But why are you so frightened? Ambrose doesn't know, does he?"

Lydia choked, shaking her head. "Not yet, he doesn't know. But don't you see, Glynis? Simon couldn't have killed that woman, that Rose Walker."

Glynis held her breath.

"Simon *couldn't* have killed her," Lydia moaned, "because he was with me that night."

Glynis slumped against the cloakroom wall. She wondered if she might be hallucinating—or if Lydia was.

Lydia had stopped sobbing, had replaced the earrings in her pocket, and was staring at Glynis with huge eyes. "Glynis, please say something."

"I don't know what to say. Are you sure?"

That was idiotic. How could Lydia *not* be sure? It wasn't the kind of thing one could be unsure of. "I didn't quite mean that, Lydia. What I think I meant was, were you with him the *whole* night?"

Tears rolling down her cheeks again, Lydia nodded.

"Well, how could you have been?" Glynis demanded. "That doesn't make sense. Where was Ambrose? Didn't he realize you weren't home? And *where* were you, with Simon Sheridan?"

"At the hotel. In his suite. I thought Ambrose was out of town on bank business. He leaves town a lot, but as it turns out, he wasn't gone that night."

"What do you mean, he wasn't gone?" Glynis felt as though she were floundering through a dense maze.

"I got back home early in the morning," Lydia explained. "The kitchen help wasn't even up yet. Ambrose was there, asleep in his bedroom. I was terrified that he'd come home late and looked in my room, but later he never said a word about it. So I guess he just went straight to bed after he came in. That's not so unusual," she added quietly.

"Lydia, why on earth haven't you said anything about this until now?"

"Why do you think? How could I?"

How indeed could she? Glynis's first thought had been that Lydia was lying: that she was so insanely in love with Simon Sheridan that she would say anything to protect him. But no; some women perhaps might do that, but not Lydia. Glynis knew the woman's background. Raised in near poverty in Albany, she had been swept off her very young feet by a worldly, imposing Ambrose Abernathy and brought to live the life of an upper-class lady in Seneca Falls. That Lydia loved being a lady was obvious each and every moment of her life, even if she didn't exclusively love her husband.

No. Lydia would not jeopardize her money, her position, the luxuries that went with them to save Simon Sheridan unless she knew for a fact that he was innocent. And unless her conscience was unbearable.

"Lydia, surely you know what this means—how serious this is. Because if Simon Sheridan didn't kill Rose Walker, then someone else—"

"I know," Lydia interrupted. "I know, and I don't care about that! I just couldn't let Simon hang for something he didn't do."

"But I don't see how we can keep this quiet! At the very least, you've got to tell Cullen Stuart."

"I can't," Lydia began to cry again. "I just can't. He'll tell Ambrose, and I'll lose everything."

Glynis again saw herself trapped in a labyrinth of impossibilities with no escape in sight. And she was there, she recognized, partly through her own doing, her own eagerness to believe that the killer of Rose Walker was anyone other than Karl Steicher. Granted, she told herself, Sheridan deserved to be in jail; he was a thief. But if what Lydia said was true, he was not a murderer.

She realized Lydia was staring at her with a hopeful expression. Glynis put her arm around the woman and said, "Lydia, we have a terrible situation here. You can't insist on tying my hands by making me promise not to tell Cullen. Do you really think Ambrose is capable of injuring you?"

Lydia dabbed her eyes with her handkerchief. "I think he could be. The reason I didn't meet you this noon was because Ambrose saw me on Fall Street from his office window in the bank. He came charging out to tell me that Jacques Sundown had just brought him a subpoena for the hearing Monday in Waterloo. Ambrose was beside himself. Said it was my fault."

"How was it your fault?" Glynis said.

"Because I repeated what he'd said about that money being sent to Boston. Glynis, you remember how we thought it must be going to Friedrich's brother? Well, when I told Ambrose that, he said I was a fool, that Friedrich's brother had been dead for years."

Every time Lydia opened her mouth, matters seemed to become more baffling ... or perhaps not. "Has Ambrose been subpoenaed by Gordon Walker's lawyer, then?" Glynis asked her.

Lydia nodded. "But how did you know that?"

Glynis got up from the bench. She felt they had been sitting there for hours. Her head and back ached; she was almost grateful for the diversion of physical pain. She had no idea what she was going to do with what Lydia had told her. But what if ...

"Lydia, I've just remembered something. The day of the fire—the Fourth of July—were you with Simon Sheridan then?"

Lydia looked down at the floor.

"It's important, Lydia. Could he have started the fire?"

"No," Lydia said faintly. "Simon was with me. We were at the hotel. I'd told Ambrose I was going home from the picnic, but I didn't."

Glynis felt her mind slowly beginning to track again. She didn't feel quite so disoriented, but knew she had a long way to go to figure this out.

"And the night of Mrs. Walker's murder," she said. "Did you and Simon Sheridan have an argument in his room?"

Lydia looked puzzled for a moment. Then she nodded. "Oh, yes. We had a fight about money. He wanted me to persuade Ambrose to loan him bank money to buy the hotel. The owners had agreed to sell it to Simon if he could give them cash. I said I couldn't do that without Ambrose getting suspicious of me."

Well, there was another piece of the puzzle in place, Glynis thought. Not that it helped find the real killer. It just eliminated one more possibility.

"Glynis, you won't tell Cullen Stuart, will you?" Lydia whimpered. She looked like a doll with all its stuffing gone, limp and unlovely.

Glynis wanted to throw up her hands. What could she do? "All I can say right now, Lydia, is that I'll try to keep your involvement with Simon Sheridan quiet. I don't know if I can, but I'll do my best. You can stay here if you want and pull yourself together. I have to leave."

She went quickly, before she had to look at Lydia again. She heard sobbing behind her as she closed the cloakroom door.

Outside on the road a few groups of people stood talking while the last wagons rumbled off with convention participants. Glynis walked toward Jeremiah Merrycoyf's office. She didn't know if he would answer her questions, but she couldn't think where else to start. Cullen was still too sick to involve.

She had almost reached the front stoop of the law office when Karl Steicher came through the door above her, his head turned to say something to Merrycoyf in back of him. Glynis heard a deep growl behind her, then sudden harsh barking.

She swung around to see Duncan planted in the road, legs braced, tail and ears erect. His upper lip was pulled back over his teeth as he snarled between barks.

"Duncan! Duncan, come here."

The terrier ignored her. She walked forward to pick him up. His body was rigid.

"Glynis, whatever is the matter with him?" Aurora Usher called. She was standing with a group, all of them staring at Duncan, that included her sister and Harriet, Abraham Levy, Gordon Walker, and Ambrose Abernathy. Glynis stopped herself from glancing toward the church, where she'd left the weeping Lydia. She scooped Duncan, still barking, off the road. He wriggled frantically, snapping at the air. She clutched him to her and tried to hold his jaws closed. It was like wrestling with a greased pig.

"I'm sorry," she called, to whoever might be feeling offended. "I can't think what's got into him."

Glynis imagined the entire street laughing at her. Her and her wretched little beast! When she turned back to the law office, Karl Steicher had disappeared. Gripping the finally silent Duncan, she carried him up the stoop and inside, holding him against her while she knocked on the inner door.

When he opened it, Merrycoyf didn't seem surprised. "I don't usually defend dogs," he said. "But these days, hardly anything would seem unusual."

Glynis didn't smile. Nor would Merrycoyf, she assumed, when he heard what she had to tell him.

"Mr. Merrycoyf," she began. "Didn't you study law at Yale College?"

At that he seemed surprised; he nodded.

"And," she said, "isn't Yale in New Haven, Connecticut?"

# THIRTY-FOUR

❧

DUNCAN JUMPED OFF the law office stoop and trotted toward home. Glynis looked up and down the road; there was no one else on Fall Street. She hadn't realized it was so late. Then she heard hoofbeats, and a piebald horse and its rider appeared. The horse was reined within a few feet of her.

She smiled at the hands on the taut reins. "It's good you're here; I need to talk to you."

Jacques looked down at her. "Getting late. You shouldn't be alone," he said.

"You don't think someone's going to follow me again, do you, Jacques?" Glynis walked toward Cayuga Street; the horse paced beside her. "Isn't the man who followed me last time in jail? In Waterloo?" She looked up at Jacques. He said nothing.

"Well, isn't he?" she demanded.

Jacques stared straight ahead, his body moving with the horse's slow rhythmic gait. Glynis was relieved that she no longer felt quite as compelled to talk, to fill up his silence with sound, any sound, even that of her own voice answering her own questions.

She waited until they had turned onto Cayuga. She didn't want to be overheard again. "Simon Sheridan didn't kill Rose Walker," she said quietly. "But then, you knew that, didn't you?"

He reined in the horse. "I didn't know. Just guessed."

"Why? Why did you guess that?"

Jacques looked around. He dismounted and walked,

holding the slack reins in his hands. The animal's head bobbed between them.

"He's a runt, Sheridan. Padding in his jackets makes him look bigger than he is. Took somebody strong to hit Ross hard enough to kill him. But it was a hunch; Sheridan might have done it."

"You've been the only one around him in the lockup," Glynis said. "Did Sheridan continue to deny doing it as he did the afternoon you took him in?"

"Yeah, he denied it. Said we'd find out he had alibis for both killings. He thought it was funny. I didn't pay much attention to him. Man's not likable."

"Well," Glynis said, "like him or not, he does have alibis."

Jacques nodded. "It figures. Woman, most likely."

Glynis almost stumbled.

Jacques went on, "But I wasn't the only one to see him in the lockup. Abernathy did. After he was there, Sheridan quit being so cocky."

So Ambrose must know about Sheridan and Lydia. Glynis wondered how long he had known. Apparently he wasn't going to be blackmailed into protecting Sheridan, as Cullen said husbands of Sheridan's past mistresses had been. But why? Did Ambrose want Sheridan convicted of theft? Or murder?

What if Lydia hadn't confessed to her about that night? Ambrose Abernathy had been Friedrich's banker; he'd told Lydia he had been sending money to Boston. But had he really been sending it? If Rose Walker hadn't died, and if she had been entitled to half Friedrich's estate, would there have had to be an accounting, an examination of the bank's records?

"So what now?" Jacques said. "We back where we started?"

"No, not quite. There's a lot we don't know, but I have an idea."

He stopped walking. "Who do I have to watch?"

Glynis peered over the horse's muzzle. Of course he was making fun of her. Well, she'd fix him.

"Curious you should ask, Jacques; I was just about to tell you that. But I want you to do something else, too. Can you arrange a meeting for me . . . with Serenity Hathaway?"

Jacques seemed to lurch forward. He recovered, taking two quick strides ahead of the horse and turning to stand stock-still in the center of the road, staring at her. When he finally spoke, his voice had an undertone that in anyone but Jacques would have sounded like strain.

"Serenity Hathaway? No—I don't think you mean her. I don't guess you know who she is."

"I know she owns a tavern," Glynis said.

Jacques let out his breath; she could smell tobacco all the way across the horse's nose. "Yes," he said slowly. "She owns a tavern. She's . . . she's a tavern owner."

"She's a madam, Jacques. Everyone in town knows that. The tavern part just covers up the other things that go on inside, the gambling and the . . . well, the other."

Jacques jiggled the reins in his hands and looked away. "Does the constable know you want to meet her?"

"No," Glynis said. "Cullen shouldn't be bothered with this; he's still not well."

Cullen would never allow it; he would insist on doing it himself. And she was certain Serenity Hathaway would never confide in a law officer. But another woman? Maybe.

"I'm sure you can do what's necessary, Jacques. Just tell me when you've arranged something . . . discreet. I must talk to her, and I can't very well go into her place."

"No. You can't do that."

They had reached her boardinghouse, and Glynis stepped to the flagstone walk. "Would you please arrange this meeting for tomorrow? I know that's soon, but—" She looked closely at him. "Jacques, if I didn't know you better, I would swear you look distressed. Why? I don't think this Serenity Hathaway is the killer. But," she added evenly, "I do think you'd better watch Ambrose Abernathy."

Harriet was in the kitchen fixing supper. Duncan barked once at Glynis, then continued prancing around Harriet's feet; Harriet put his bowl on the floor, then went to the window to cut herbs from the clay pots lining the sill.

"Were you satisfied with the convention, Glynis?" Harriet asked. "Imagine you liked seeing the suffrage plank go through."

Glynis barely heard her. She was staring at Duncan.

"Glynis?"

"What . . .? I'm sorry, Harriet. I'm trying to remember something. It's been there on the edge of my mind all afternoon, but it keeps slipping off."

"Devilish, when that happens. But what was the matter with Duncan earlier? Such a fuss—in the middle of Fall Street!"

"I know. It was strange."

"Do you want supper? Mr. Fyfe isn't back yet."

"No, I'm going upstairs. Let me know when he gets here, will you?"

In her room, Glynis sat down in her chair in front of the window. Something in the kitchen had started to nudge whatever it was her memory was hiding. She settled back against the chair and closed her eyes, trying to clear her mind.

Outside the window the katydids and crickets had begun their night choruses. The end of July, it was dark a little earlier each evening. She hated to think of December, when it would be dark by five o'clock and you couldn't see your hand in front of your face without the moon. . . .

Her eyes flashed open, and she leaned quickly over the windowsill to look out. The back garden was in full flower. Her gaze swept over the pines to hollyhocks and snapdragons, mock-orange bushes, roses, petunias, and nasturtiums—and stopped. She sat for a moment, chin resting on her fisted hand, hardly daring to move, even to breathe.

All this time, time wasted because she had refused to consider any likelihood of Karl Steicher's guilt. It now became apparent to her that during the short time Rose Walker was in Seneca Falls, all manner of persons had been guilty of something. But only one of them had committed murder: once, twice, and quite possibly three times.

She got up to stand in front of her bookcase; her eyes went to the top shelf. She reached for Friedrich's present, opened *The Murders in the Rue Morgue*, and leafed through it slowly. And recognized, when she found the passage, that this had been the crux of it all along.

Poe's detective Dupin said, "Now, brought to this conclusion . . . it is not our part, as reasoners, to reject it on account of apparent impossibilities. It is only left for us to prove that these 'impossibilities' are, in reality, not such."

Yes. But how to do it? And with so little time?

Downstairs, she heard the front door open and close, then Harriet calling her: Mr. Fyfe was back.

She needed Mr. Fyfe. Hugging the book, she hurried out of the room.

# THIRTY-FIVE

❧

"OYEZ! OYEZ! LET all who have business before the court come forward and you shall be heard!"

The bailiff bellowed the ancient call. Heads in the court-room lifted. Handkerchiefs paused in midwipe and palm leaf fans ceased fluttering.

"All rise!"

Chairs scraped against the wooden floor amidst shuffling boots and the swoosh of cotton petticoats as people got to their feet. The courtroom was filled, overflowing through heavy double doors into a wide corridor: the Steicher farm had been a country landmark and employer for as long as many in the Waterloo Court House could remember.

Through the tall windows, occasional thrusts of outside air carried the buzz of locusts and a rich hay smell of sum-mer farmland. Glynis glanced at Cullen standing beside her. Two days of sun had brought his color back, but his face was gaunt. Still, he looked better than he had yesterday, when he'd arrived at the Peartree house.

He had tethered the Morgan to the porch rail and started up the steps. "Glynis, what in the name of the Almighty have you been doing?"

He had sounded so angry that she simply stared at him, the useful response she had learned from his young deputy.

"Don't look so innocent," he said. "I already know some of it from Jacques. He's been fretting, and I finally pried out of him why."

That couldn't have been easy, she thought.

"Glynis, there's somebody damn dangerous loose in this town. I'm concerned as hell about you—so is Jacques!"

"Jacques? Why should he be concerned? What could possibly happen to me, when he trails me like a shadow? The man doesn't even like me, but every time I turn around, there he is!"

Cullen sat down on the porch step. "What do you mean, he doesn't like you? Where did you get that idea? You're wrong; I've never seen Sundown so troubled. Now what is it you've been doing—that *I* should have done?"

Then she understood. She sat beside him and told him. Everything. Everything, that is, that she knew. The rest would come at the hearing.

Cullen had looked at her for a long time. "This isn't like you. Why did you do it?" he said finally.

"Why shouldn't I have done it?" she asked. "I'm not just a temporary lodger in this town, not anymore. Seneca Falls is my home. And I don't see why you're looking so surprised; you've been trying to convince me of that for quite a while now."

She was not sure, when he reached over to brush her cheek with his fingers, what the expression on his face meant. It might have been any number of things.

Now the bailiff bawled again. "The surrogate's court in and for the county of Seneca is now in session: Surrogate J. K. Richardson presiding."

Richardson entered from a rear door and walked to a triple-tiered, enclosed bench on the front dais. The court clerk followed him. Richardson's curved nose gave his narrow, patrician face a faintly predatory look. He seated himself, preened his black robe, and looked down at the lawyers and their clients.

Jeremiah Merrycoyf and Karl Steicher sat behind a table to the right and in front of the surrogate; Orrin Polk and Gordon Walker were to the left. The two parties faced Richardson.

The surrogate sat forward. "You may proceed with your case, Mr. Polk. Do you have an opening statement?"

Orrin Polk rose. "The petitioner, Gordon Walker, intends to prove that his wife, Rose Walker, was the daughter of Friedrich Steicher and so was entitled to inherit half the Steicher estate. With her untimely death, her share then passed to her husband and should be awarded to him.''

''Call your first witness, Mr. Polk.''

''We call Elizabeth Cady Stanton to the stand.''

Polk remained on his feet as Elizabeth Stanton stepped forward. Glynis guessed Elizabeth's flush was not so much from the heat as from irritation at being forced to appear. Her sausage curls quivered under a small lace cap while she placed her hand on the court clerk's Bible, swore the oath of truth, and seated herself on the wooden chair beside the surrogate's bench.

Polk said, ''Mrs. Stanton, you are here pursuant to the subpoena served on you?''

''Yes. I certainly wouldn't have volunteered to be here!''

Richardson looked down at her. ''Mrs. Stanton, it will be helpful if you just answer the questions, without comment.''

Elizabeth gave him a look so swift that Glynis couldn't read it from where she sat, a third of the way back in the room. But Richardson smiled.

Polk continued. ''Mrs. Stanton, did you know the late Rose Walker?''

''Yes.''

''Where did you first meet her?''

''Boston.''

''Specifically, where in Boston?''

''Her mother's home, Boylston Street.''

''Did you accompany the body of Rose Walker back to Boston, to her mother and her husband there, because of your close relationship with the family?''

''Yes.''

''And attended her funeral service in Boston with her mother and husband?''

''Yes.''

''Do you know Rose Walker's birth date?''

''She was thirty-two.''

Orrin Polk turned toward the court clerk. ''Let the record show,'' he said, ''that the witness has confirmed that the year of Rose Walker's birth was 1816.''

Surrogate Richardson nodded to the court clerk.

Polk's questions established Mary Clarke as Rose Walker's mother; then he asked, "And Mary Clarke told you that she was at one time Friedrich Steicher's wife?"

Jeremiah Merrycoyf half rose to his feet. "Objection. That is hearsay, and not admissible."

"I have no further questions of this witness," said Polk, returning to his chair beside Gordon Walker.

"Mr. Merrycoyf," the surrogate said. "Do you wish to cross-examine the witness?"

"No, no cross-examination."

"Very well. Mr. Polk, call your next witness."

When Elizabeth walked by, she gave Glynis a tight smile. Turning to watch the woman seat herself beside her husband, Glynis saw Jacques Sundown leaning in the doorway at the back of the courtroom. His arms were folded over his chest. He met her eyes for an instant, then stared straight ahead.

"Your next witness, Mr. Polk?"

Orrin Polk had been shuffling through some papers on the table in front of him. He looked up and said, "We call Ambrose Abernathy."

Ambrose Abernathy did not come forward.

Glynis leaned over and whispered to Cullen, "I haven't seen him this morning—and Lydia isn't here, not that I expected her to be. But Jacques must know where Ambrose is."

She had told Cullen about Lydia and Simon Sheridan, pleading his assurance that he wouldn't use the knowledge unless there was no other recourse. Cullen had looked disgusted.

They turned around and searched the crowd as the bailiff said loudly, "Ambrose Abernathy is called forward!"

When he still did not appear, the crowd began to fidget. Their muttering grew louder.

Richardson said, "Will Constable Stuart try to locate the witness?"

Cullen got up and went to the back of the room. He and Jacques disappeared into the corridor.

Aurora Usher, seated between Vanessa and Harriet, twisted around to say to Glynis behind her, "What do you suppose has happened to Ambrose? He has to answer a subpoena, doesn't he?"

"Yes, of course. Have you seen him today?"

Vanessa turned. "He tied his carriage next to ours. He drove alone; Lydia's been feeling so poorly she stayed back in town. I can't imagine where he is now."

Cullen and Jacques reappeared with Ambrose Abernathy walking none too steadily between them. The banker's fleshy face was red and perspiring.

"Found him across the street in a tavern. And not anxious to leave," Cullen said to Glynis under his breath as he returned to his seat. Jacques went back to his position at the door while Abernathy was being sworn in.

Polk established that Abernathy was appearing unwillingly, pursuant to subpoena, then asked, "Mr. Abernathy, how long were you Friedrich Steicher's banker?"

"Fifteen years," Abernathy said.

"And during that time, did Friedrich Steicher ask you to send money to Boston from a special account he had set up for that purpose?"

"My predecessor at the bank had been doing that for some years; I just continued the practice when I began handling Steicher's account."

"Please describe what this practice entailed, Mr. Abernathy."

"Each month I transmitted a sum of money to an account in care of the Boston Trust Bank."

"Was there a name and address for this account?"

"Yes: Mary Clarke, Boylston Street."

"Did anyone else at your bank know of this procedure?"

"No. I was solely responsible. It was to be done in total secrecy. That was Steicher's directive."

"But I presume Friedrich Steicher told you he was making these contributions to support his daughter."

"Objection, Your Honor," said Merrycoyf. "The statement calls for a conclusion."

"No," Abernathy said. "He didn't tell me any—"

"You don't have to answer, Mr. Abernathy," interrupted the surrogate. "I'm sustaining Mr. Merrycoyf's objection."

"No further questions," Polk said.

The surrogate looked at Merrycoyf. "Cross-examine?"

"Yes," said Merrycoyf. He rose heavily from his chair and trudged across to stand in front of the witness. Perspiration shone on Abernathy's forehead.

"To your knowledge, Mr. Abernathy, *no one* else knew of this peculiar transaction?"

"No. No one else knew."

"So it was entirely confidential?"

"Friedrich Steicher swore me to absolute secrecy."

Ambrose Abernathy pulled a handkerchief out of his pocket and patted his forehead.

Cullen whispered to Glynis, "Merrycoyf must want to emphasize that neither he nor Karl knew about the money."

She nodded.

"Mr. Abernathy," Merrycoyf continued, "in light of the secrecy involved, did you maintain any record of these payments of Friedrich Steicher's money to Mary Clarke's account with the Boston Trust Bank that you say you made over the past, let's see, fifteen years, I believe you said?"

"Yes. Yes, of course I did."

"And do you have this record with you?"

"Here? No. I wasn't asked to bring it. And I don't understand what these questions have to do—"

"That's all for now, Mr. Abernathy. Thank you."

As Abernathy applied his handkerchief again, Merrycoyf turned to the surrogate. "Will the court please direct the witness to produce documented proof of the payments Mr. Abernathy says he secretly made to Mary Clarke's account?"

The surrogate's eyes narrowed slightly and he nodded. "The witness is so directed."

Merrycoyf said, "I reserve the right to further question this witness when he has complied with the court's request." He returned to his seat.

"So noted," said the surrogate. "Mr. Polk, are you ready to proceed with your next witness?"

"Yes, Your Honor. I call Karl Steicher."

Karl Steicher's face held no discernible expression when he sat down in the witness chair, and Glynis could not see any sign of nervousness. His shoulders were squared, the white-blond hair and beard trimmed, blue eyes as cool as a winter sky. His tanned face seemed leaner, more seasoned—more like his father's. Had he changed so much in the past weeks?

Polk said, "Mr. Steicher, do you appear today pursuant to the subpoena directing you to produce the Steicher family Bible?"

"Yes."

"And have you brought the Bible with you?"

Karl gestured toward the table. Merrycoyf leaned forward and handed the leather-bound volume to Polk. Polk stood facing the room, holding the large book open against his chest, flipping through a few pages. He stopped, spread his hand on an inside page, rocked back on his heels, and smiled broadly.

Watching him, Glynis realized that before this moment, the lawyer never had seen the evidence on which his case rested.

"Mr. Steicher," said Polk, keeping his finger on the page, "how long has this Bible been in the possession and control of the Steicher family?"

"My grandfather Steicher got the Bible from his father—at least, that's what I was told."

"During your lifetime, was it available to each member of your family? To look at, when they chose?"

Karl said, "Yes."

"How long have you been aware of the entries on the page entitled 'Family History'?"

Karl frowned. "I don't know exactly."

"Mr. Steicher, on this page is there an entry which reads, 'Female child. Born of Mary Clarke Steicher and Friedrich Steicher. December thirtieth, 1816?"

Polk moved to stand beside Karl, lowered the Bible, and pointed at the page.

Karl looked straight ahead and answered, "Yes."

Polk paused, as though needing time to savor the moment. Then he said, again pointing to the page, "Is that your father's, Friedrich Steicher's, handwriting?"

"Yes."

Slapping the Bible shut, Polk rested it on the arm of the witness chair. "Was the birth of your sister ever discussed by you with any member of your family, or—?"

"Objection!" Merrycoyf was on his feet. "Objection to the use of the term 'sister.' The issue of relationship, if any exists, has yet to be decided by this court."

Richardson, his tone perfunctory, said, "Yes, Mr. Merrycoyf. Your objection is sustained."

"I'll rephrase the question," said Polk. "Was the birth of the female child ever discussed by members of your family?"

"No. There was never any discussion. It was understood that . . . it was a forbidden topic, never to be mentioned. Most families have at least one of those, Mr. Polk."

The people listening in the courtroom stirred, a restless sound like November wind rattling forgotten corn stalks.

Polk cleared his throat. "Very well, Mr. Steicher. Now let me ask you this: was there a time recently when this Bible was not in your possession?"

"Objection," said Merrycoyf. "Immaterial."

Richardson said, "Do you have a reason to pursue this line of questioning, Mr. Polk?"

"Yes, Your Honor. I intend to demonstrate the intent of this witness."

"Then I will allow you some leeway. Proceed."

"Did you understand the question, Mr. Steicher?" said Polk.

"Yes."

"And your answer? Was there a time when the Bible was not—"

"Yes." said Karl.

"And when was it out of your possession?"

"It was mistakenly crated up with other books that were delivered to the Seneca Falls library."

"Yes, Mr. Steicher. And the date when it came back into your hands?"

"I don't remember the exact date."

"Then can you recall the circumstances under which the Bible came back into your possession?"

Karl Steicher stared implacably at Polk.

"Isn't it a fact, Mr. Steicher, that you went to the library to retrieve the Bible?"

Merrycoyf put up his hand. "Objection. Leading the witness."

"This is a *hostile* witness, Your Honor," Polk said to the surrogate.

Richardson nodded. "Yes, I'll accept that. He's clearly a hostile witness, Mr. Merrycoyf. Proceed, Mr. Polk."

"Did you understand the question?"

Karl scowled. "Yes."

"Your answer? Did you retrieve the Bible?"

"Yes."

"How did you gain entry to the library?"

"I went in through a basement window."

"In the dark of night?"

"It was after sundown."

"Mr. Steicher, wasn't it the night following the afternoon when Rose Walker came to your farm?"

"Yes."

"And didn't you that afternoon have a discussion with Rose Walker regarding the distribution of your father's estate?"

"Yes."

"Wasn't it your intent to retrieve the Bible to prevent Rose Walker from finding that illuminating entry? And furthermore, wasn't the night you broke into the library the very same night your sister met her untimely death? Below the library?"

"Objection!"

"No further questions of this witness, Your Honor."

Still objecting, Merrycoyf struggled to his feet. His

voice was lost in the crowd's babbling and the surrogate's gavel pounding.

Glynis leaned forward to watch Merrycoyf. He had sunk back in his chair and was staring at Karl. Then he turned around; his eyes, over the spectacles, searched the room. He found her and gave her a long look. She pressed her lips together. She had told him about the broken window. What had he expected?

Polk placed the Bible on the evidence table and sat down next to Gordon Walker.

The surrogate said, "Have you questions of the witness, Mr. Merrycoyf?"

Merrycoyf got to his feet slowly. "Just a few, Your Honor. Mr. Steicher, when Rose Walker came to you and discussed your father's estate, what did she demand of you?"

"She told me she'd leave town if I gave her ten thousand dollars cash."

"She wanted it that day?"

"No, she said she'd give me two days to raise the money."

"And what was your response?"

"I laughed—called her an imposter! Told her to get off my property."

Merrycoyf said, "And did you ever see her again?"

"No. I did not."

"That is all, Your Honor."

"You may step down, Mr. Steicher," the surrogate said.

Glynis felt Cullen next to her relax slightly. When she turned to look at him, he just shrugged. The room was quiet.

Surrogate Richardson glanced at the tall clock standing against a side wall. "Have you another witness, Mr. Polk?"

"Yes, I do. Call Mr. Gordon Walker to the stand."

Gordon Walker stood up. Glynis realized that, for many, this was their first look at the man. Their necks craned.

He walked to the witness chair nonchalantly, but Glynis noticed he had made some concessions to the occasion: the gold curls were shorter, the apparel less cosmopolitan. The

soft gray suit, although beautifully tailored, almost camou-
flaged his dramatic looks. Nonetheless, in the row ahead
Glynis noticed Vanessa and Aurora straightening in their
seats. Vanessa's hand patted the black chignon at the back
of her head, and Glynis recalled the jet wings of hair
above Rose Walker's neck.

Orrin Polk stood beside the seated Walker, his arm resting companionably on the back of the witness chair. He
appeared to be hovering over his client like a fond father.

"Mr. Walker," he began, "prior to her tragic death, did
you reside with Rose Walker in a house owned by her
mother, Mary Clarke, on Boylston Street in Boston?"

"Yes, I did."

"For how long, sir?"

"Ten years."

"Where were you and Rose married?"

"In Boston Third Presbyterian Church."

"Did the officiating minister issue a certificate of marriage?"

"Yes."

"Do you have it with you?"

"I do."

"May I have it, please?"

Polk unfolded the paper Gordon Walker handed him
with a flourish, then passed it up to the surrogate. Polk
looked at Merrycoyf. "I offer this certificate. Do you have
any objection?"

Merrycoyf got up, was handed the paper, and scanned it
briefly. "No objection."

"That is all," said Polk. "Your witness, Mr. Merrycoyf."

When Merrycoyf approached the witness chair, Glynis
thought he looked somewhat recovered from Karl
Steicher's testimony.

"Mr. Walker," he began, "did you reside at your mother-
in-law's Boylston Street house from the date of your marriage?"

"Yes."

"And how were you employed?"

Walker smiled at Merrycoyf. "I haven't had to work for some time."

"How fortunate you are, sir. Tell me then, how did you sustain yourself and your wife?"

Mr. Polk rose. "Objection. Immaterial."

"I'll overrule the objection," said the surrogate. "I'm going to allow some latitude here."

"Thank you," said Merrycoyf. "Shall I repeat the question, Mr. Walker? If not, please answer."

Gordon Walker said pleasantly, "We were financially comfortable with my inheritance and Rose's mother's savings."

Merrycoyf nodded. "That's all the questions I have at this time. Your Honor, I reserve the right to further question this witness."

"So noted," said the surrogate. "Mr. Polk?"

Polk stood up. "Your Honor, I move for a directed verdict on the grounds that a conclusive case of heirship has been established."

"Mr. Merrycoyf," the surrogate said, "will you address Mr. Polk's motion?"

"With the court's permission," Merrycoyf said, "I request that argument of Mr. Polk's motion be deferred, and the respondent, Karl Steicher, be given opportunity to establish ground for denying inheritance."

Polk reared back, then thrust himself like a snake toward Merrycoyf. "That's irregular! Totally irregular!" He turned back to the surrogate and snapped, "Your Honor, there are no grounds for denying our petition. We have addressed all the issues raised. We have firmly established our case!"

Surrogate Richardson replied, "That may be so, Mr. Polk. However, I am going to grant Mr. Merrycoyf reasonable opportunity to proceed with his defense."

Polk's hands were clenched fists at his sides.

The surrogate glanced at the clock. "I think," Richardson said, "due to the lateness of the morning hour, we will recess now. This court stands adjourned until two o'clock."

"All rise," shouted the bailiff.

# THIRTY-SIX

❧

IN FRONT OF the courthouse, wicker picnic baskets and carriage rugs dappled the Waterloo town green. Gray squirrels foraged under the elms, advancing in slow rippling motions like ribbons waving across the grass.

Glynis saw Gordon Walker and Orrin Polk emerge from Polk's office and make their way back toward the courthouse. It must be close to two o'clock. Vanessa and Aurora lounged on the blanket beside her, and Harriet began rearranging the picnic basket. She was frowning.

"Harriet, are you all right?" Glynis asked quietly.

"Oh, I suppose so. This whole business is foul, if you ask me. Wrangling over money when two people are dead these past weeks!"

"If you're nervous," Glynis said, "Mr. Merrycoyf is sure you won't be on the stand long."

Harriet just nodded her head.

Vanessa yawned, sat up, and stretched languorously. "This was not what I would call a festive picnic. I don't see why everyone insists on being so grim. How often do we have something this interesting going on?"

Harriet scowled. Glynis looked around for Cullen and Jacques, who had disappeared when the tower clock struck the half hour. She hadn't seen Karl Steicher and Jeremiah Merrycoyf at any time during the recess.

All she'd had to eat was a muffin and tea; they had settled in a sour lump at the pit of her stomach. She picked at the slubbed silk of her white frock and glanced down at the picnickers on the green. The woman wasn't there yet; at least Glynis hadn't seen her arrive. But Jacques had said he delivered the subpoena yesterday. Would she refuse to come?

Cullen came striding across the grass, wearing his holster and gun, which had been absent that morning. "Let's go," he said. "I need to have a word with the bailiff before the court reconvenes, and it's almost two o'clock."

"Cullen have you seen—her?"

"No. But even if she's here, she's not going to join the town crowd for a picnic lunch. Didn't she tell you she'd come?"

Glynis nodded. She could change her mind, though.

Cullen picked up the picnic basket and they started across the green toward the Courthouse.


"How long will it take to wind this up?" Gordon Walker asked.

Orrin Polk said, "Do you mean, how long before you get your money?"

Walker smiled. "Your money too." They were standing at the top of the courthouse steps.

"It would have been over by now," Polk snapped, "except for the surrogate's last ruling. Damn Merrycoyf! He's obviously stalling. He doesn't have any case. How can he?"

"That Karl Steicher; I thought you said he was insignificant," Walker said, his smile fading. "He didn't seem so insignificant to me."

"He's changed since the last time I saw him. But he's just testified that he's guilty of criminal trespass. And he may well be a murderer—sorry. But don't worry about Karl Steicher."

"I'm not worried about him. I just want to leave for Boston as soon as this thing is over. No offense, Mr. Polk, but I've had enough of your neck of the woods."

Polk smiled. "I think you'll probably be on your way by tomorrow, my boy. Right after Merrycoyf makes a fool of himself."

\*        \*        \*

"All rise! This court is now in session." The bailiff sat down.

Surrogate Richardson leaned forward. "Do you have an opening statement, Mr. Merrycoyf?"

"I will waive an opening statement, Your Honor, and recall Elizabeth Cady Stanton."

When Elizabeth reached the witness chair, the surrogate said to her, "I didn't make the connection earlier today, but you're Judge Cady's daughter, aren't you? How is the judge?"

"Fine, so far as I know. I'm afraid he's a bit put out with me at the moment."

"Ah, yes, I heard about your women's convention—my wife attended, in fact. The newspapers have not been kind in their comments, have they?"

Glynis frowned. She knew she was anxious, but somehow she felt this parlor talk wasn't proper, not with so much at stake.

"Cullen, is this common practice—chitchatting with a witness during a trial?" she whispered.

Cullen grinned. "Once in a while. Richardson'll get down to business in a minute. He probably doesn't think there's much testimony left to be heard: Polk's case looked pretty solid."

The surrogate straightened. "Remember that you are still under oath, Mrs. Stanton. You may proceed with your witness, Mr. Merrycoyf."

"Mrs. Stanton," Merrycoyf said, "when you were residing in Boston, did you know a gentleman named Edwin Vail?"

"Why . . . yes!" Elizabeth's startled eyes met Glynis's across the room.

"How did you come to be acquaintanced with Mr. Vail?" Merrycoyf went on.

"Well . . ." Elizabeth hesitated, still looking surprised. "I think I recall that Mr. Vail was once a suitor of Rose Clarke's—yes; in fact, I understood they were to be betrothed. Then Rose met Gordon Walker, who, as they say, just swept Rose off her feet. At the time, Edwin Vail was a young professor at Harvard College, but after Rose's marriage to Gordon Walker, I lost track of Mr. Vail."

Orrin Polk stood up. "Your Honor, I must object to this line of questioning as irrelevant. I can't imagine where Mr. Merrycoyf is going—"

"No further questions," said Merrycoyf. "Thank you, Mrs. Stanton, that's all."

Polk stared at Merrycoyf. Then he muttered, "No questions."

"You may step down, Mrs. Stanton," said the surrogate.

As Glynis watched Elizabeth walk down the center aisle toward her, she heard her own name called. Her stomach heaved as though trying to leap into her throat.

Cullen reached for her hand and pressed it hard before Vanessa and Aurora had time to whirl around. She felt rather than saw the eyes of the courtroom follow her as she walked to the witness chair.

She scarcely heard the oath being administered, but said, "Yes," when she saw the court clerk's lips stop moving. She told herself to be calm; this was just like the inquest, no different from performing with her flute. But it was.

She took a deep breath and sat down.

Merrycoyf smiled, an attempt to reassure her. He reminded her suddenly of a large brown bear, purposefully shuffling toward a concealed cache of honey. She nodded to him.

"Miss Tryon, did there come a time when you had the opportunity to examine a trunk and other possessions of Rose Walker at the Hotel Bristol?"

"Yes."

"Would you describe what you found?"

"Dresses, shoes, hats, gloves—various items of clothing. There was a daguerrotype of a woman who so closely resembled Rose Walker I assumed it must be her mother. There was also a considerable amount of jewelry."

"Miss Tryon, in your opinion, did the contents of the trunk you examined indicate that Rose Walker was taking an extended trip?"

Polk shot to his feet. "Objection! This witness has not been established as a qualified expert."

Glynis felt herself flushing under the surrogate's gaze. Her neckline was fashionable, but was it too low?

"Perhaps not an expert," Richardson said, "but I am going to accept a response from Miss Tryon."

Glynis nodded. "There were a great many outfits in her trunk—a fur-trimmed muff and cape, for instance— certainly far more things than a woman would pack for a few days' stay in Seneca Falls. And she would hardly need a fur-trimmed cape and muff in the summer. I thought it was odd that I also found . . ."

She hesitated, looking at the surrogate as Polk shouted an objection; Richardson motioned for her to continue.

"Well, I thought it was curious to find a folder which contained railroad ticket stubs for the Boston to Seneca Falls trip, but no return tickets to Boston."

"Miss Tryon," Merrycoyf continued, "did there come a time when a Daisy Ross delivered to you a purse that you had previously seen in the possession of Rose Walker?"

"Yes."

"Did you examine the contents of the purse?"

"Yes, I did."

"Please tell the court what you found."

"There were a few personal items, like a comb and handkerchief. There was no money in the purse. There were two other items: a receipt for jewelry from the Hotel Bristol and a letter addressed to Rose Walker from New Haven, Connecticut, from a person whose signature I couldn't make out."

"Have you subsequently learned the sender's name, Miss Tryon?"

"Yes. I communicated with the return address given and received a response. The sender's name was Edwin Vail."

"Would you read the letter you received from Mr. Vail to the Court."

Polk jumped up. "Hearsay! Irrelevant, Your Honor."

"Mr. Polk," Richardson said, "I'm most interested in learning Rose Walker's intention in coming to Seneca

Falls, especially given the previous testimony of Karl
Steicher. So I will allow the letter to be read. Proceed,
Miss Tryon."

Glynis reached into her purse, extracted the letter, and
began to read:

57 Court Street
New Haven, Connecticut
July 10, 1848

Dear Miss Tryon,

When I received your letter this past week, I already
had been informed of Rose's death by friends in Boston.
My grief has been almost too great to bear.

It pains me to review our relationship, Miss Tryon,
but since you were kind enough to write, and to explain
your purpose in doing so, I will attempt to answer your
questions.

Within a year of Rose's wedding to Gordon Walker,
she realized she had made a tragic error. Although
charming and generous during their courtship, after the
marriage Walker revealed his true character. His behav-
ior was that of callous disregard for his wife's happiness
and well-being. He gambled recklessly, eventually losing all his inheritance from his father's considerable estate. His affairs with other women were not discreet and
caused Rose constant anguish.

I repeatedly begged Rose to end this unhappy alli-
ance. But she felt she must be in some way to blame for
the faults of her husband, and the marriage vows were
to her sacred.

It was nine years before Rose understood that Gordon
Walker's nature had been twisted long before their marriage vows were made, and to accept that she could not
redeem him. She finally made the decision to leave him,
and to marry me as soon as she was free.

To avoid what would surely be widespread scandal,
and a source of embarrassment to her mother and my
family, I took leave of my post at Harvard, and acquired

a teaching position at Yale. Rose was to file for divorce, and then join me here in New Haven.

Before she could do that, and shortly after I left Boston in the early spring of this year, she learned of her true family history and her father's death in Seneca Falls. She was determined to go to western New York and claim her rightful inheritance.

I urged her not to go. I felt it might be dangerous for her. How appallingly correct I was proved to be. I also tried to explain to her that any property she might inherit would immediately become her husband's. She felt passage of a recent New York law would prevent that from happening. And also, she wanted to see where her father had lived, and have the opportunity to meet her brother.

I trust this information will be useful to you, Miss Tryon.

Yours very truly,
Edwin Vail

Glynis finished reading and lowered the letter to her lap. The silence in the courtroom was absolute. Orrin Polk was staring at Gordon Walker, whose expression was enigmatic. Or was he just barely smiling? Karl Steicher had been gazing at the ceiling, but when he lowered his eyes and looked at her, Glynis had no doubt that his face held remorse.

Finally Merrycoyf cleared his throat. "Thank you, Miss Tryon. That will be all." He took the letter from her and placed it on the exhibit table.

Polk rose slowly to his feet. "Your Honor, I have no cross-examination for this witness, but I renew my previous objection to the letter being read and now ask that it be stricken from the record."

Surrogate Richardson rubbed the back of his neck. "Mr. Polk," he said, "surely you don't object to a letter that establishes the very point you have been trying to make in this hearing: that Rose Walker was Friedrich Steicher's daughter, and Karl Steicher's sister? Although I must confess that I am mystified as to why Mr. Merrycoyf is assisting you in proving your case. Thank you, Miss Tryon," he said to Glynis. "You may step down."

Cullen was standing in the aisle; as she slid past him into her chair, he whispered, "Good. I'm moving up front now."

Glynis watched him join the bailiff in chairs directly behind the lawyers' tables. She turned and saw Jacques Sundown position himself directly in front of the double doors at the back of the courtroom.

Harriet stood up as her name was called. She looked around at Glynis and rolled her eyes heavenward before she started to the witness chair.

"Mrs. Peartree," said Merrycoyf when she'd been sworn in, "where do you reside?"

"In my house—on Cayuga Street in Seneca Falls."

"Mrs. Peartree, who else resides with you?"

"I have two boarders, Glynis Tryon and Dictras Fyfe. And there's Glynis's dog, Duncan."

"Is the dog Duncan allowed in the house?"

"Certainly."

"On the night of June thirteenth of this year, do you recall being concerned about Duncan's whereabouts?"

The surrogate said, "Mr. Merrycoyf, does the date June thirteenth have some significance in this hearing?"

"Yes, Your Honor. The night of June thirteenth was when Rose Walker met her death."

"Proceed, Mrs. Peartree."

"Glynis was concerned about Duncan that night," Harriet said. "It had gotten late and he wasn't home."

"What time was that?"

"I imagine it was somewhere around ten o'clock; it had been dark for a while."

"Mrs. Peartree, was it unusual for the dog to be out at that late hour?"

"Depends on the time of year. Come spring, Duncan generally goes courting."

"Did Duncan ever return that night, Mrs. Peartree?"

"Yes. I woke up some time during the night, I can't say

when. The moon must have come out from behind the clouds, because it was streaming into my room. I got up to draw the shade and saw Duncan out the window. He was going to his favorite burial place, a lilac bush. He had something that looked like a fair-size piece of cloth hanging out of his mouth."

"What happened then?"

"Nothing happened then. I went back to bed. Next morning though, I mentioned it to Glynis because she was worried about Duncan's thievery. We were glad he'd graduated from silver teaspoons to cloth. And Mr. Fyfe put a fence around the lilac bush that day, so Duncan would have to go elsewhere with his ill-gotten gains."

Mr. Polk's voice was shrill. "This is absolutely, totally irrelevant—totally! It's so far afield that . . . a dog? Really, Your Honor!"

"Frankly, Mr. Polk, I'm intrigued to see where Mr. Merrycoyf can possibly be going with this. Aren't you? Proceed, Mr. Merrycoyf."

"Mrs. Peartree, did you recently have occasion to examine Duncan's 'ill-gotten gain' of June thirteenth, which he'd buried under the lilac?"

"Yes. This past Thursday night—"

"Excuse me, Mrs. Peartree, but how do you know it was Thursday?"

"It was the night the Woman's Right's Convention ended." Merrycoyf nodded, and she went on. "Anyway, Glynis came running downstairs saying she'd just remembered my telling her about Duncan and the cloth, and would Mr. Fyfe help her uncover Duncan's hole. And they did."

"And what did they find there?"

"Well, I cleaned it some after they dug it up, but here it is." Harriet reached into her purse and lifted out an envelope. She opened it and pulled out a piece of ragged-edged wool fabric.

"Thank you, Mrs. Peartree. That will be all," said Merrycoyf.

The surrogate frowned. "Mr. Polk?"

Polk was talking to Walker. He looked up at the sound of Richardson's voice and got to his feet.

"Your Honor," he said, "the testimony of the two previous witnesses has gone beyond the scope of this hearing, and far beyond the bounds of reasonable latitude directed to the issues of this case. I ask that this burlesque be terminated."

Richardson shifted to look down at Merrycoyf. "Mr. Merrycoyf, I'm inclined to agree with Mr. Polk's request. My tolerance in allowing you to develop your case is being stretched to the limit. Have you any grounds that would convince me to let you continue?"

"Your Honor, I thank you for your patience and request your permission to call one last witness. I assure Your Honor that all will become clear."

"Very well, Mr. Merrycoyf. I will cautiously accept your assurance. Call your witness."

"I call Serenity Hathaway."

As Glynis had anticipated, the crowd's response was confined mostly to gasps, although several outraged voices shot through the room like rifle reports. A few people sprang to their feet, almost preventing her from seeing Serenity Hathaway sweep through the doors past Jacques and up the aisle.

Glynis took a quick glance around, confident others were as stunned by Serenity Hathaway's looks as she had been a few days before. She wasn't sure what she had expected, but by any honest measure the woman was ravishing.

Her tall figure was barely constrained by a tight-bodiced, low-cut gown of yellow and green striped taffeta. Lace-edged petticoats seemed to fill the aisle. A green satin bow set just below the back of her waist completed the breathtaking span from bust to bustle. Coal-colored hair tipped with red henna licked Serenity's face and shoulders like flames.

Glynis watched a dozen or more women stand and leave the courtroom. A few were led by their husbands, most were followed by them. The Reverend Magnus Justine hauled his wife Verity through the door with remarkable speed—and even more remarkable silence. Henry Stanton, on his feet, leaned over Elizabeth, who stared straight ahead. Finally, his expression savage, Henry sat down.

"Miss Hathaway," said Merrycoyf when Serenity had taken the oath, "would you give the court clerk your name and address?"

"Serenity Hathaway." The voice was crisp. "I own a tavern on the canal in Seneca Falls and I live there."

"Were you served with a subpoena, ordering you to appear in this court?"

"My dear Mr. Merrycoyf, do you think I would be here otherwise?"

"And do you live at the tavern with others?"

"With the girls who run the bar, wait on the gaming tables, and so on."

"Do you have accommodations for guests?"

"We have some rooms."

"Has one of your recent guests been Mr. Gordon Walker, seated over there next to his attorney?"

Serenity nodded. "He's been with us for some time."

"Miss Hathaway, do you operate, shall we say, games of chance at your establishment?"

"If you mean do we have poker, of course we do."

Polk rose from his chair. "Your Honor, I object to this testimony as immaterial to this case. What entertainments Seneca Falls has to offer are not germane—"

"I will allow this questioning to continue for the moment, Mr. Polk," said J. K. Richardson, who with the rest of the room had not taken his eyes off Serenity since she sat down. "But please come to the point, Mr. Merrycoyf."

Serenity shifted in the witness chair, her eyes flashing up at the surrogate.

"Thank you, Your Honor," said Merrycoyf. "Miss Hathaway, has Mr. Walker participated in games of chance at your tavern?"

"He certainly has!"

"And when he's lost, has he paid off his debts?"

"Only with IOUs."

"Has he paid you for his room?"

"Not lately, he hasn't. I've been waiting—along with a lot of others—for him to get this inheritance money so he can pay me off."

"I see. Tell me, Miss Hathaway, did you know a local man by the name of Bobby Ross?"

"I don't think I ever saw him before this summer. But he was around the place in the past weeks."

"And did he spend money?"

"That's what you do at my place, darlin'. Ross dropped a bundle at the bar and poker tables."

"Do you remember when you last saw Bobby Ross?"

"He was in my place the day before the factory fire. Day before the Fourth of July, it was."

"Under what circumstances?"

"It looked like Ross and this Walker had all of a sudden got to be fast friends. They left together that afternoon."

"How did you happen to notice that?"

"I don't miss much. And I thought it was kind of queer, them being so different and all."

"Miss Hathaway, did one of your girls meet an untimely death about six weeks ago?"

"She sure did."

"Where did this happen?"

"In one of my upstairs rooms. Like I told the constable over there, she was stuffed in a wardrobe closet. Dead a couple of days before we found her, and a bad lot *that* was, what with the hot weather and all."

"Did Constable Stuart investigate and find the cause of her death?"

"Well, he asked a lot of questions. But like I told him, it happens. That girl was looking for trouble anyway—not that she should've found *that* kind. She'd already robbed a couple customers. Bad for business. I was going to let her go. Anyway, the constable there asked around some, which was neighborly, since in most towns the law acts like our lives don't amount to dog dung. But I didn't think he'd find much."

"Why didn't you think so?"

"Oh, our customers, they come and go. We get a lot of canal men and drifters just passing through. And me, I don't ask questions—that's bad for business too."

"So you thought your girl was murdered by a customer?"

"Who else?"

"Miss Hathaway, when the body was discovered in your upstairs room, was there anything else in the room?"

"We found a jacket on the floor. It was real fancy, a costly piece, good fabric, good tailoring, so I held on to it."

"You didn't mention finding the jacket to Constable Stuart when he was investigating?"

"No, it's not my practice to turn over customer's clothing to the police."

Merrycoyf said, "Do you have the jacket with you, today?"

Serenity looked at Cullen, who got up and came forward with Harriet's picnic basket. He lifted the jacket from the basket, handed it to Merrycoyf, and returned to his chair.

Merrycoyf hooked his finger under the jacket collar and held it out in front of Serenity. "Is this the jacket you found in the room with the dead girl?"

"That's it."

"How can you be sure?"

"Well, just you look at that wool: checkered, green and white. You don't see a dandy's dud like that around here only once in a blue moon. And it matches that!" She gestured toward the exhibit table.

Merrycoyf picked up the ragged piece of green-and-white checked wool cloth and held it next to the jacket.

"And the label," said Serenity, taking the jacket from Merrycoyf and turning back the collar. "See what it says? Right under the tailor's name, it says, 'Boston, Mass.' "

"Yes, Miss Hathaway. Now let me return to the date of the girl's death six weeks ago. Can you remember when exactly her body was discovered?"

"When I first got asked that, I wasn't sure. But I asked

some of the other girls, and we figured it was a couple of days after that other woman was found dead in the canal, up there on your side of town."

"And was Gordon Walker staying at your tavern then?"

Orrin Polk half rose from his chair, then sat back down.

Serenity Hathaway gave Walker a long look. Then she turned to Merrycoyf and said, "Let me ask *you* something. If I answer that, is there a chance I won't get the money this fancy deadbeat owes me?"

The surrogate rapped his gavel for silence. "Miss Hathaway, I direct you to answer the question. Was Gordon Walker at your tavern when your employee's body was found?"

"No," Serenity said. "Not when her body was actually *found*. That first time he was in town, he only stayed the early part of one night—the night before that woman's body was found in the canal."

Gordon Walker leapt out of his chair, shoving the table over. Jacques was already halfway down the aisle with his gun drawn as Walker smashed the bailiff to the floor. Cullen grabbed Walker from behind, and they crashed forward into the surrogate's bench.

People in the front rows scrambled out of their chairs. Glynis couldn't see over them. Those around her were either in a ready stance or were dashing toward the doors at the rear.

The surrogate's gavel banged like a smithy's hammer; gradually the noise in the room began to subside. Vanessa and Aurora crept cautiously back into the room from the corridor.

Harriet was still standing beside Glynis. "Can you see?" she whispered.

Glynis shook her head. The gavel banged again. "Will the room be seated!" the surrogate's voice called over the heads of those in front.

Glynis could see the bailiff on his feet again, holding his jaw with one hand, and with the other gesturing at people to sit down. Finally Glynis could see Cullen and Karl Steicher standing on either side of Gordon Walker. Jacques was tying Walker's hands behind him. Cullen's gun was in his hand at his side. Silence slowly settled over the room.

"Mr. Polk," said the surrogate, still standing, still gripping the gavel like a club. "Do you have questions for Miss Hathaway?"

"No," said Polk from the far side of the overturned table. "No questions."

It was just as well, Glynis thought, her eyes searching the room. Serenity Hathaway had disappeared.

Merrycoyf came forward from under a far window. Orrin Polk remained standing.

"Mr. Merrycoyf?" said Richardson, straightening his robe and sitting down.

"I call Gordon Walker to the stand."

Cullen pushed Walker back into the witness chair, and stood beside him. Jacques moved into one of the front-row chairs, and Karl Steicher returned to his seat at Merrycoyf's table. The surrogate reminded Walker that he was still under oath.

"Mr. Walker, is this your jacket?" Merrycoyf began.

Walker stared at Merrycoyf. "I'm not saying anything," he muttered.

The surrogate sat forward. "Yes, Mr. Walker, although this is a civil case, you may refuse to answer or implicate yourself. I myself have seen and heard enough to direct Constable Stuart to confine you forthwith, but first we are going to finish the matter before us."

Walker stared straight ahead. Glynis thought it was a measure of the man that he didn't look in the least chastened. He did look annoyed.

Merrycoyf repeated the question.

"I refuse to answer," said Walker. He scowled at Polk, who looked away.

Merrycoyf held out the checked jacket. "Mr. Walker, if this is not yours, then surely you'd have no objection to slipping it on? Because a jacket so carefully tailored as this one either would fit perfectly or not very well at all, would you say?"

Walker didn't move. He gave Merrycoyf a very slight smile.

Merrycoyf carefully laid the jacket on the exhibit table next to the scrap of cloth.

"Mr. Walker," he said, "isn't it a fact that you realized your wife was going to leave you for Edwin Vail, taking with her whatever inheritance she earned from her dead father's estate?"

Walker was silent.

"And didn't you learn," Merrycoyf said, "that enactment of New York's Married Women's Property Act would prevent you from getting your hands on that inheritance money, no matter how long you contested a divorce proceeding?"

At this, Walker gave Merrycoyf a truculent look and crossed one knee over the other. The courtroom spectators listened; all as still, Glynis thought, as though in a trance. The surrogate showed no inclination to interrupt Merrycoyf, and on Orrin Polk's face, as he stared at his client, was an expression that made Glynis look away.

Merrycoyf waited, then went on. "And isn't it fact that you planned to murder your wife when you discovered that she had left Boston, and that you started for Seneca Falls just hours behind her, traveling first by train to Albany, then by stagecoach, and lastly by packet boat on the canal, so that your arrival in Seneca Falls would be undetected and, you mistakenly thought, untraceable?

"Isn't it a fact that you killed the girl at Serenity Hathaway's tavern because she could identify you—did you catch her going through the pockets of that jacket?" Merrycoyf pointed to the exhibit table. "The last thing you wanted, Mr. Walker, was to be placed in town at that particular time. Then that night, the night of June thirteenth, you lured your wife from the Hotel Bristol with a note and strangled her, leaving her body in the canal.

"Miss Tryon's dog must have attacked you, possibly in the act of murder—or attempting to break into his mistress's library for the Bible? Had your wife told you of its existence before you killed her? The dog ripped your trousers. And with them torn, you didn't dare bring more attention to your attire by going back to inquire about the jacket you had overlooked earlier at the tavern.

"And, Mr. Walker, isn't it a fact that you then returned to Boston the same way you had come, arriving there in plenty of time to meet your wife's body and play the role of the grieving husband at her funeral? It has been confirmed that you bought a train ticket from Albany to Boston two days after the murder."

Gordon Walker slouched in the witness chair. He didn't move, said nothing, and looked only mildly surprised.

Merrycoyf went back to his table, picked up a sheet of paper, and said, "Your Honor, I move that the petition filed by Gordon Walker be dismissed, on the ground that the law does not allow a person to profit from his crime. This maxim has its foundation in universal law administered in all civilized countries."

Merrycoyf read from the paper in his hand: " 'No one shall be permitted to take advantage of his own wrong, or to found any claim upon his own iniquity, or to acquire property by his own crime.' "

"Do you have any statement, Mr. Polk?" asked the surrogate.

"No."

"Very well, Mr. Merrycoyf. I will dismiss the petition, subject to its being renewed, without prejudice, in the event Mr. Walker is acquitted of his wife's slaying. And I now direct Constable Stuart to take Gordon Walker to the Seneca County jail to await trial for murder. That is all. This court is adjourned."

# THIRTY-SEVEN

A BLACK-SIDED BUGGY was there already. Jeremiah Merrycoyf tethered their horse and carriage beside it, while Glynis climbed the porch steps of the Steicher farmhouse. The front door opened and Quentin Ives came out.

"Karl got back here just a while ago," he said. "He told me what happened at the hearing. I'd come out to check on Nell."

"How is Nell?" Glynis asked.

"She'll be all right—physically. She's still in bed. Karl's with her now. I don't imagine she'll be coming downstairs."

No. Nor had Nell come to the cemetery last Saturday, when the stillborn baby girl had been buried next to the graves of Friedrich and Caroline.

Karl Steicher appeared in the doorway behind Quentin, fine lines like downward brushstrokes around his eyes and mouth. He took a few steps toward Glynis, hesitated, then extended his hand. They both turned at the sound of hoofbeats and waited while Cullen rode up to the porch and dismounted.

"Walker's in the Seneca County jail," he told them. "Claims he'll never be convicted. Arrogant bastard. What do you think, Jeremiah?"

Merrycoyf lowered himself into a wicker chair, which creaked painfully. "I think he'll probably be convicted. Granted, so far most of the evidence we—I should say, Miss Tryon—uncovered against him is circumstantial. But the county prosecutor is having a sketch of him distributed, and I expect Walker will be identified by the stage drivers and canal men. His route to and from here can be traced, the time established, and so on. Yes, I think he's got a likelihood of being hung."

Cullen said, "I wonder if Mary Clarke ever suspected him."

"I imagine she did," Glynis said. "She must have known what kind of man he was. But even so, what could she do? A woman. An old woman."

Karl turned to take a tray of glasses and a pitcher of ice from the housekeeper, who had appeared at the door. "Jeremiah, about Mary Clarke . . ."

The housekeeper returned with a pitcher of iced tea and a clay jug of whiskey. Karl waited until she went back inside. "Is Mary Clarke entitled to anything from my father's estate?" he said. "If her daughter was, wouldn't she be? What's the law say?"

Merrycoyf studied Karl over his spectacles. "As a matter of fact, she may be," he said neutrally. "You and Mary Clarke would be Rose Walker's sole survivors—excluding the husband, of course. So the dead woman's mother is probably entitled to half her daughter's share. You're entitled to the other half."

"All right," Karl said.

"All right?" said Merrycoyf.

"Yes. You write Mary Clarke a letter to that effect, tell her we'll send the money to her."

"Yes, I'll do that."

Glynis went to the edge of the porch, looked at the sunset's gold-edged clouds, and remembered the threatening day she and Cullen had first talked to Karl about Rose Walker. It seemed almost to have been in another lifetime. And Karl Steicher had been a different man.

"Where's Jacques Sundown?" she asked Cullen.

"Rode back to town—takes his job seriously." He smiled, his worried look of that morning gone, Glynis saw. Cullen liked disorder even less than she.

"He could've joined us," Karl said.

"Jacques's not happy being surrounded by white folks."

Merrycoyf nodded. "Can't say as I blame him. I don't

think any Seneca would murder three people out of greed."

"Jeremiah," Cullen said. "What about Ambrose Abernathy? You think he was pocketing the money he was supposed to be sending to Boston?"

Merrycoyf smiled. "Looked guilty as sin, didn't he? But I don't know about the money. In fact, if Miss Tryon hadn't suggested the possibility, I never would have thought of it." He turned to Glynis. "What do you think, now?"

She leaned back against a porch column. "I think if he was taking the money, it was a recent enterprise— probably only since Friedrich died. I don't think he would have dared do it when Friedrich might demand an accounting. And it was unlikely that anyone else would contact Mary Clarke asking if she had received the money recently. Remember, no one else knew about it. But now we know why Ambrose was so furious at Lydia the night of the Ushers' party; the last thing Ambrose Abernathy wanted was for anyone to find out about the money in that special account of Friedrich's. It was Ambrose's own fault, of course. He never should have been so foolish as to say anything at all about the money to a wife who liked to gossip."

Merrycoyf smiled again. "Old Ambrose is a fox, though. A worried fox! I shouldn't be surprised if there is soon a sizable check deposited in Mary Clarke's Boston bank account. Mysteriously, of course."

"I never knew about that money, Jeremiah," Karl said. "But before I fire Abernathy, I'll get an accounting."

He looked at each of them in turn, his eyes stopping on Glynis. "I really didn't think Rose Walker was my sister," he said. "You can believe that or not, but it's the truth. Yes, I had seen the entry in the Bible, years ago. But I didn't think she was still alive, or someone would have said something about her. Something! It ... she—was never discussed, as I said today at the hearing."

For a few minutes, the crickets under the porch were the only sound in the night air. The darkness had a melancholy texture, Glynis thought, as though it sheltered all the grief of the past months.

Karl got up and lit the oil lamps, then eased himself up to sit on the porch rail beside Cullen. "Do you think Bobby Ross saw Walker kill his wife?"

"I doubt if we'll ever know," Glynis said. "The fatal circumstance was that Gordon Walker *thought* Bobby saw something and figured that's why we were looking for him. He may have overheard a conversation Jacques and I had. Or Bobby might have bragged to him at Serenity's about finding the money. Walker just couldn't take a chance on anyone suspecting he was in Seneca Falls the night Rose was murdered. He must have discovered I was asking about the murder, may even have thought I'd talked to Bobby. He followed me the night I spoke to Jacques Sundown about it, and who knows what would've happened but for Jacques sticking so close by."

"Then Walker started the fire during the Fourth of July picnic," said Ives.

"Who would have suspected him?" Karl said. "He was working in the bucket brigade. I saw him when I got there to check on the Phoenix Mills; one of my farmhands who was at the picnic rode out here to tell me he thought my building was burning."

"Walker probably wanted to be right there on the scene," Cullen said, "to make sure Bobby Ross went up in flames with the factory. I just hope the county jail can hold that scoundrel."

They were silent for a while, all of them.

"I'm curious about something, Glynis," Karl said at last. "Would you tell me—"

"How much you owe her for the broken library window?" asked Cullen.

Karl finally smiled, thinly, with the others. "Yes, that too. But I was going to ask what made you suspect Gordon Walker. I never thought of him, not once, because I assumed he was in Boston at the time of his wife's murder."

"You and everybody else," Cullen said.

Glynis jiggled the iced tea glass in her hand and watched the melting ice chips circle. "It was the convention," she said.

They all stared at her. Quentin Ives finally said, "The Woman's Rights Convention made you suspect Gordon Walker?"

Glynis nodded. "It was a tangled skein of connections, really." She sat down at one end of a wicker sofa, curling her feet beneath her. "I sat in the Wesleyan Chapel wondering just what we women had started," she explained. "What we would be leaving the next generations: my nieces, and grandnieces to come, and Elizabeth Stanton's daughters and granddaughters not even born yet. Would what they inherited be a benefit to them as we hoped—or a loss for some that we couldn't foresee? And that, in one of those twists the mind sometimes takes, made me think of the Steicher inheritance, and Rose Walker. Who, besides Karl, would lose if she lived?

"Later, when we discovered Simon Sheridan couldn't be the guilty one, and I still had inheritance on my mind, I remembered the Married Women's Property Act. You know, it was the passage of that law just a few months ago that encouraged Elizabeth Stanton to call a convention about women's rights. I suddenly thought what a terrible irony it would be if that law, designed to protect women, had caused a woman's murder!

"I had seen all those clothes in Rose Walker's trunk, the absence of any train tickets back to Boston, and I wondered who would lose the most if Rose Walker actually *got* her inheritance and then ran? Not Karl. Her husband.

"Then the letter from Edwin Vail arrived, saying Rose was going to do exactly that. But it was impossible for Gordon Walker to be his wife's murderer, because he'd been in Boston, hundreds of miles away, when Rose was killed. Somehow, as Edgar Allan Poe's detective said, we had to find a way to prove the impossible was possible: that Gordon Walker had been in Seneca Falls on June thirteenth.

"We all assumed, as Karl just said, that he couldn't have

been, mostly because we aren't used to the idea of fast travel; the railroad hasn't been with us all that long. Of course, now we know he used various means of transportation: the railroad had the speed he needed; the stagecoach and canal boats had the bustle and confusion he could get lost in."

"Well, go on," Cullen said when she'd been silent some moments. "That doesn't explain all of it. How in hell did you get mixed up with Serenity Hathaway? What made you even think of her?"

Glynis sat back against the sofa cushions. Merrycoyf had lit his pipe and was watching her through a white coil of smoke.

"I thought that after Gordon Walker got to Seneca Falls," she said, "unless it was nighttime, he would have had to stay somewhere out of sight for a while, until he could get to Rose after dark. Edwin Vail's letter had emphasized Walker's gambling. And I remembered Cullen mentioning the dead girl at Serenity's tavern, which is also the most notorious gambling place in town—even I knew that!

"The tavern is notorious for things other than gambling. So it seemed to me that the owner was not likely to have contact with the law about another murder on the other side of town, one that didn't directly concern her. But Serenity Hathaway might know something, even though she hadn't come forward with it and wouldn't have seen a connection between the two women anyway.

"Gordon Walker arrogantly assumed that no one would see a connection. He also trusted the renowned discretion of madames, of whom he obviously has a great deal of knowledge."

Karl frowned and Quentin Ives's eyebrows went up. Merrycoyf smiled. Cullen, his eyes narrowed, said, "How would you know about that? And Glynis, you didn't go to that tavern, did you? Jacques wouldn't say much about the whole episode. I can't believe he would let you go—"

"No, Cullen. Of course I didn't go to the tavern, and

Jacques . . . Jacques didn't approve of the meeting, and that's all you really need to know about that.

"I'd taken Duncan's scrap of cloth with me, not expecting much, except that I thought if he'd been there, Serenity might recall Walker wearing that green-and-white check. She did, and she'd found the jacket. Dictras Fyfe," Glynis added, looking straight at Cullen, "went to the tavern and got it for me. Mr. Fyfe spent all of Friday at the canal and the railroad station. He talked to a train engineer who, by yesterday, had found out for us that a man of Walker's description—he's not difficult to describe!— bought a ticket in Albany for Boston on Thursday, June fifteenth. That was the day Rose's body left from *here*, for Boston—plenty of time for Walker to get there first. I imagine he'd left Seneca Falls by night stage immediately after he murdered his wife." Glynis looked from one to another of them. "That's about it."

Merrycoyf shook his head. "I want to know how you convinced Serenity Hathaway to testify. The subpoena wouldn't mean much to her."

"She's a businesswoman," Glynis said. "No, don't smile, Jeremiah; I'm not being coy. She wanted to get what money Walker owed her. I told her she had a better chance of doing that with him here rather than back in Boston. And I told her if she couldn't get her money, she might as well get revenge."

For a moment they all stared at her again. Cullen finally began to laugh.

Glynis stood up. "I'm really very tired, but Karl, I'd like to see Nell before I go."

Karl nodded. "She wants to see you. I'll take you up."

Glynis followed him to the bottom of the stairs. "Karl, it was Gordon Walker who broke in here the night of the Ushers' party, wasn't it?"

"I assumed so," he said, "when I got the subpoena— how else would he and Polk know I had the Bible back? How did you know?"

"I remembered him asking me at the party to point you out to him. He naturally would have thought your wife was there with you; he didn't know what either of you looked like. When he left the Ushers' he thought he could come out here and break into the house safely, to find out if you had the Bible and see if Rose's birth was recorded in it."

"If Nell hadn't heard him and come downstairs . . ." Karl's voice was hard.

"We should be grateful," Glynis said, "that he didn't have time to really harm Nell." Of course Nell had to lie that night—she couldn't have betrayed Karl and the fact that the Bible was back in his study.

"But he did harm Nell. Our baby . . ." Karl looked away.

Perhaps, Glynis thought.

"Karl, I want to ask you something else. It has nothing to do with Gordon Walker."

He nodded. "Of course."

"I'd like to know why you're opposed to my library contract being renewed."

Karl looked at her with what seemed genuine surprise. "Opposed to your contract being renewed? Where did you hear that? Never mind, I can guess. Anyway, it's not true. I was never against your continuing with the library. For one thing, it's what my father wanted. For another . . . well, I may have had my own reasons for disliking you, and you know what they were, but I never thought you weren't good at what you do."

Curse Aurora Usher, Glynis thought. All this time she had me terrified for nothing.

"Then is Justine the only one opposed to me?"

Karl smiled. "Only the Reverend Justine. He thinks you're a libertine, dangerous to his congregation. Seabury Gould told him he was alone in that. Gould can be very persuasive: he said he'd pull his contributions to the church if Justine created trouble over your contract. Justine resigned from the library board a few days ago."

"Thank you for telling me, Karl. It's been a concern."

"I'm sorry," Karl said. "You might want to know that Justine's position has been filled by Quentin Ives."

But she hadn't worried recently about Justine. Her meeting with Serenity Hathaway had been enlightening in more ways than one—she doubted she'd have any more problems at all with the good reverend. She smiled, recalling his unceremonious flight from the courtroom that afternoon.

"I can find my way upstairs, Karl. Thank you."

He nodded, then offered his hand as he had when she'd arrived. A brief firm grasp, then he turned and went through the door to the porch.

Glynis climbed the stairs and lifted her lantern in the doorway of the boys' room. They were sprawled over their beds, sleeping soundly. Down the hall, Nell was lying on her back, staring at the ceiling, her face the same bleached white as the sheet beneath her. When she saw Glynis, she struggled to a sitting position. Glynis tried to not look at the flatness under the quilt.

"Nell, I'm so sorry about your baby girl."

Nell looked away. "My mother told me that if I wanted to raise four children, I'd have to bear eight," she said.

Glynis didn't answer. From what she knew, it was true.

Nell gave her a tired smile. "There will be others," she said. "There *will* be others. If the Lord has forgiven."

Glynis sighed. She knew what Nell was saying. And if she had believed in a wrathful God, as Nell did, she too would probably believe that He had wreaked a terrible vengeance on Karl Steicher: the death of a daughter for a sister denied, for greed, for the sins of the father . . .

And Nell? The innocent must suffer with the guilty? So it would seem. She sat silently until she knew the woman slept.

Glynis went down the stairs. Cullen was waiting on the bottom step.

# EPILOGUE

֍

GOLDENROD AND ASTERS had replaced the drifts of Queen Anne's lace beside the steps of the Waterloo Court House. The wildflowers nodded under the weight of bees, their sharp dry smell a reminder that the remaining days of summer were few.

Glynis sat on the top step, her eyes half closed against the brilliant morning sunshine. Cullen had taken his carriage to transport Gordon Walker from the jail. She listened to the harsh voices of the crowd on the green below; most of the people were strangers to her. It was the first day of the murder trial, and many of her town had stayed back in Seneca Falls to await the fireworks of the later days.

A train whistled from the busy Waterloo rail station, and hooves clopping, horses drew a large open carriage around the green. It had to skirt other carriages before the Waterloo deputy who was driving could pull up in front of the courthouse. He reined in the team while Cullen jumped down from the rear seat.

Jacques Sundown rode his piebald horse behind the carriage; he tethered the animal and went to stand at the edge of the green holding his rifle under his arm. The Waterloo deputy stood a short distance away, and together they waved the crowd back. Glynis heard some grumbling, but most seemed cooperative. They had come to see justice served, not to make trouble.

Cullen reached up to assist Gordon Walker as he climbed down from the carriage, his hands tied behind him. When Glynis stood up she could see his face clearly.

She was not surprised to see him smiling. He still looked like an arrogant golden boy, certain he would not be convicted.

From where she was standing, Glynis had an unobstructed view of what was occurring below. It appeared as though Walker hesitated at the bottom of the courthouse steps, to get his balance before climbing them. He turned abruptly toward the green at the sound of a voice; Glynis could hear the word "Stop!" several times, while someone from the crowd stepped forward.

The figure wore a black robe and a large, flat-brimmed hat concealing the face from Glynis's view. Why is a priest here now? she wondered. Cullen had stopped a few feet behind Walker, saying something that to Glynis sounded like "Keep going."

What next occurred seemed to happen as if time itself was slowed: as if all movement below Glynis was taking place at the bottom of the canal. The priest hobbled toward Cullen and Gordon Walker. Glynis saw Cullen take a step backward and frown. While he stood slightly off balance—it could not have been more than a second or two—the priest lurched between Cullen and his prisoner.

Glynis heard only the words ". . . to give you a blessing, my son."

Grinning, Gordon Walker took a step forward. From under the priest's black robe a hand emerged holding a silver cross. Glynis could see the end of it glinting in the sun.

There was a sharp popping sound, and smoke curled from the end of the cross.

Gordon Walker's expression changed from the grin to a look of surprise. Scarlet spread across the front of his white shirt like spilled wine. He coughed, then crumpled slowly to the ground.

Instantly, time resumed its normal tempo. Glynis saw Cullen lunge forward and grab the small muff pistol, knocking the person holding it to the ground. He leaned over and yanked the hat away.

Glynis ran down the steps to where an old woman lay;

she knelt and lifted the frail wrist, pressing for a pulse. Its beat was feeble. The old woman blinked against the sunlight, her eyes streaming tears that ran down the wrinkles of her face like drops of rain in ploughed furrows. Her lips moved briefly.

Glynis leaned down, but even with her ear next to the woman's mouth, she couldn't make out the indistinct sounds. The old woman suddenly stiffened, and her head rolled to one side. Taking the hat from Cullen's head, Glynis lifted the woman's head to bunch the hat under her gray hair.

Jacques Sundown and the deputy somehow managed to hold the stunned crowd back on the green. Cullen dropped to one knee and looked over the small, still body at Glynis.

"Do you know who she is?"

Glynis nodded. She recognized the face. She had seen it in a daguerrotype.

"Mary Clarke," she said. "Rose Walker's mother."

Glynis brushed the fine hair away from the old woman's forehead. And traced with her fingers the last tears.

# Historical Notes

〜

**ANTHONY, SUSAN B. (1820-1906)**

On the first morning of the Woman's Rights Convention, Glynis wondered if anyone anywhere other than Seneca Falls would hear them. In 1848, Susan Brownell Anthony was a teacher in Canajoharie, New York. She read the newspaper accounts of the convention and was amused, she wrote later, by the "novelty and presumption" of the Declaration of Sentiments. At the time, Anthony was a member of the temperance reform movement; it was another three years before she met Elizabeth Stanton and became involved in the women's rights movement.

**BLACKWELL, ELIZABETH (1821-1910)**

Graduated from Geneva Medical College in January 1849, to become the first qualified woman physician in the United States. Initially ostracized by other students and townspeople, she was befriended by an anatomy professor, who obtained for her the entrance to labs and classrooms. She eventually won over her fellow students and was ranked first in her class at graduation. Thereafter, the college changed its requirements and admitted only male students.

**BLOOMER, AMELIA (1818-1894)**

Began publishing *The Lily* in 1849. She did not design, but was among the first to wear, the Bloomer costume, a loose-waisted, knee-length dress worn over long pantaloons, which ballooned and then were gathered closely at the ankles to end with a short ruffle. In 1851, she introduced Elizabeth Stanton to Susan B. Anthony on a street corner in Seneca Falls. Her husband was *Dexter Bloomer*, editor of the *Seneca County Courier*. His was one of the few newspapers in the country that did not vilify the Seneca Falls convention, although Dexter himself was said to be shocked at the call for suffrage.

## COLT

Samuel Colt filed a patent on his Colt revolver in 1836. There was little interest in the gun, except by Texans, until the outbreak of the Mexican War (1846–1848). The government then ordered a thousand of the revolving pistols.

## CULT OF SINGLE BLESSEDNESS

Recent research by women historians has uncovered the fact that a substantial number of mid-nineteenth-century American women *chose* to remain single, in order to pursue education and careers. As developed from 1810 through 1860, the main principles of the single blessedness philosophy were to encourage the single life as a socially and personally valuable state, and to inspire the search for eternal happiness through the acceptance of a higher calling than marriage. I have included it here to indicate not that Glynis Tryon would necessarily have subscribed to its tenets, but that mid-nineteenth-century American thought was somewhat more humane in its view of unmarried women than our own twentieth century has often been.

## DECLARATION OF SENTIMENTS AND RESOLUTIONS

Written by Elizabeth Stanton and presented at the 1848 Woman's Rights Convention in Seneca Falls. In her autobiography, *Eighty Years or More: Reminiscences 1815–1897*, Stanton wrote: "All the journals [newspapers] from Maine to Texas seemed to strive with each other to see which could make our movement appear the most ridiculous. . . . So pronounced was the popular voice against us, in the parlor, press, and pulpit, that most of the ladies who had attended the convention and signed the declaration, one by one, withdrew their names and influence and joined our persecutors. Our friends gave us the cold shoulder and felt themselves disgraced by the whole proceeding."

### DOUGLASS, FREDERICK (1817-1895)

Reporting on the convention, the July 28th, 1848, issue of his Rochester *North Star* newspaper closed its editorial thus: "There can be no reason in the world for denying to women the exercise of the elective franchise, or a hand in making and administering the laws of the land. Our doctrine is that 'right is of no sex.' We therefore bid the women engaged in this movement our humble Godspeed."

### GENESEE FEVER

Genesee fever was malaria, one of the most ancient diseases known to humans. Although Glynis's research of 1848 indicated medical recognition of its association with swampy areas, the exact role of the mosquito in transmission of the infection was not known until the beginning of the twentieth century. In western New York the disease was called Genesee fever because of its association with swamps bordering the Genesee River; this river flows north from Pennsylvania through the state of New York to Rochester, where it empties into Lake Ontario.

### GOULD, SEABURY S. (1812-1886)

Founder of Gould's Manufacturing Company, known today as Gould Pumps, Inc. The company started in 1848 as Downs & Company. Gould served as its president until 1872.

### LIBRARIES

Early libraries in the United States were not the public

institutions that we know today. They were at first small private collections, usually in the homes of government officials, lawyers, and ministers. The seventeenth century saw the beginning of college libraries. As conditions in early America became more stable, and the demand for books increased, the social library became a popular means by which local communities could support their reading needs. Social libraries took various forms, but primarily the difference from today's institutions was that they were not supported by public taxes. Glynis's was a social library, financed by private individuals such as Friedrich Steicher.

## THE LILY

Amelia Bloomer began its publication in 1849 as a temperance journal but gradually increased the articles on women's rights and dress reform. *The Lily* was probably the first American newspaper to be edited entirely by a woman.

## MOTT, LUCRETIA (1793-1880)

Quaker minister, abolitionist, and pioneer in the movement for women's rights. She was one of the organizers of the Anti-Slavery Convention of American Women. Mrs. Mott and Elizabeth Stanton met in the Waterloo, New York, home of Mott's younger sister, *Martha Coffin Wright*, to plan the first Seneca Falls convention. *James Mott*, Lucretia's husband, presided over the meeting; Lucretia delivered the convention's closing address.

## POE, EDGAR ALLAN (1809-1849)

Mystery readers will be interested to know that Arthur Conan Doyle called Poe the inventor of the detective story. This claim has been questioned, but so far as fiction is concerned, it is probable that Poe *did* invent the detective, and much has been speculated about the influence of C. Auguste Dupin upon subsequent literary sleuths.

**RICHARDSON, J. K. (1806-1875)**

The surrogate judge of Seneca County. His portrait hangs today in the second-floor courtroom of the Waterloo Court House. He was elected judge at the first election under the new state law of 1846 and served until 1852.

**SUFFRAGE**

In August 1920, seventy-two years after the convention in Seneca Falls, the Nineteenth Amendment was ratified, securing for female citizens of the United States the right to vote.

**STANTON, ELIZABETH CADY (1815-1902)**

Years later, she said of the 1848 convention, "If I had had the slightest premonition of all that was to follow that convention, I fear I should not have had the courage to risk it."

**WATERLOO COURT HOUSE**

Also known as the Seneca County Court House at Waterloo, it was built in 1804 at a cost of fifteen hundred dollars. It stands today with the green in front, but the elms are gone.

**WESLEYAN CHAPEL, METHODIST CHURCH**

The site of the first Woman's Rights Convention in 1848, this former Seneca Falls church still partially stands on Fall Street. Its front and back have been demolished and the roof raised to accommodate apartments on the second floor. It has been variously used as a roller skating rink, theater, car dealership, and most recently as a laundromat. An effort has begun to restore the church under the auspices of the National Park Service as a Women's Rights National Historical Park. Actual restoration work has not commenced as funding for the project is still incomplete.

### WINCHESTER, OLIVER (1810-1880)

Moved to New Haven, Connecticut, in 1848 and operated a shirt factory next door to his house at 57 Court Street. He later became a gun and ammunition manufacturer and developed the Winchester rifle.

### WOODWARD, CHARLOTTE (DATES NOT AVAILABLE)

The young glovemaker who greeted Glynis the first morning of the convention, quoted in chapter 32. She and *Rhoda Palmer* were the only women attending the 1848 Convention in Seneca Falls who would still be alive to cast their votes in 1920.

---

Since the first edition of *Seneca Falls Inheritance* was published in 1992, the U.S. National Park Service, joined by The Stein Partnership, has reclaimed the ruins of the chapel where the 1848 first Woman's Rights Convention was held. Two women architects, Ann Wills Marshall and Ray Kinoshita, were the winners of the Wesleyan Chapel Design Competition co-sponsored by the Park Service and the National Endowment for the Arts. A preservation district has also been established in Seneca Falls, which includes the chapel on Fall Street, the restored home of Elizabeth Cady Stanton on Washington Street, as well as other extant structures from the period. (And one of those still standing is a particular house on Cayuga Street.) The Women's Rights National Historical Park has opened under the auspices of the Park Service. Seneca Falls is a ten-minute drive from New York State Thruway exit 41. Include in your pilgrimage a visit to the National Women's Hall of Fame, the Seneca Falls Historical Society, and the Seneca Falls Heritage Park.

Miriam Grace Monfredo
Rochester, New York
August 21, 2000